DANCE OF DESIRE

Mesmerized by the music and the strong arms that held her, Heller barely noticed that her unknown partner had danced her off the floor of the masquerade ball. Only when he bent his head and fastened his mouth to hers did she realize where she was, and she moaned in surprise when his tongue forced its way between her lips. She felt his arms tighten, bending her into the curve of his body, and unable to stop herself, she wound her arms around his neck and kissed him back.

He broke the kiss to nuzzle her ear. His low, intimate whispers sent shivers down her spine. She didn't understand the Spanish words, but she understood the way they made her feel. Oh, God, she thought weakly. I have to make him stop. I have to. . . . She was losing herself to him. Giving herself to a man whose face she didn't know, couldn't even see. . . .

"Joaquin Murieta is the kind of hero I love to read about."

—Bestselling author
Fern Michaels

Touch the Dawn

by

Chelley Kitzmiller

A TOPAZ BOOK

TOPAZ
Published by the Penguin Group
Penguin Books USA Inc., 375 Hudson Street,
New York, New York 10014, U.S.A.
Penguin Books Ltd, 27 Wrights Lane,
London W8 5TZ, England
Penguin Books Australia Ltd, Ringwood,
Victoria, Australia
Penguin Books Canada Ltd, 10 Alcorn Avenue,
Toronto, Ontario, Canada M4V 3B2
Penguin Books (N.Z.) Ltd, 182–190 Wairau Road,
Auckland 10, New Zealand

Penguin Books Ltd, Registered Offices:
Harmondsworth, Middlesex, England

First published by Topaz, an imprint of New American Library,
a division of Penguin Books USA Inc.

First Printing, June, 1993
10 9 8 7 6 5 4 3 2 1

 Topaz is a trademark of New American Library,
a division of Penguin Books USA Inc.

Printed in the United States of America

This book is dedicated to all those wonderful people who encouraged me to tell Joaquin's story and . . .

To my husband, Ted, who endured and tolerated throughout the years.

To Rosemary Rogers, whose classic historical romance *Sweet Savage Love* gave my life new meaning.

To Mary Kuczkir for her valuable input.

To the Orange County Chapter of the Romance Writers of America, who have cheered everything I've ever done.

To my OCC/RWA mentors Jill Marie Landis, and Dorsey Adams, aka Dorsey Kelly, who gave unselfishly of their time, advice, and expertise that went far beyond the chapter's mentor program.

To Mom, who left the legacy of writing.

And last, to Joaquin Murieta, who wouldn't let me quit until I satisfied his ego. *Viva* Joaquin!

Introduction

Man, myth, devil, or angel: who—what was Joaquin Murieta?

Every book begins with an idea—a spark of imagination that excites the writer and makes him or her anxious to pursue the subject, and then to write about it.

In preparation for a vacation, I was reading a thumbnail sketch about Joaquin Murieta (pronounced: Wah-keen) in the Automobile Club of Southern California booklet entitled *The Mother Lode*. It described Joaquin as a bandit with "Robin Hood-like qualities."

Perhaps it was the Robin Hood aspect that sparked my interest, but whatever it was, it ignited a fire in me that began over a decade ago and continues to burn.

According to the most popular legend, Joaquin was born in Sonora, Mexico. After the war with Mexico, he, like many others, headed for the California gold fields to seek his fortune. He staked his claim and built a small cabin on the banks of the Stanislaus River, where he and his beloved wife, Rosita, lived and worked in peace and harmony.

Tragedy struck when some drunken Anglos visited their home, raped and killed Rosita, whipped Joaquin, then stole his claim. And so, penniless and grief-stricken, Joaquin made an oath to get revenge.

Joaquin was reported to have robbed his fellow miners, held up stagecoaches, stolen horses, and shot down everyone connected with his wife's murder and other innocent people as well. On the other hand, he was revered by the Mexican people for his kindness and generosity—a love that exemplifies itself even today in a small California town called Three Rocks, which sponsors an annual pilgrimage for their folk hero, Joaquin Murieta.

In 1853, California's governor offered a $5000 reward and sent Captain Harry Love, a former Texas Ranger, and a group of the California Rangers to find the elusive bandit, called only by the name Joaquin.

West of Three Rocks, across Interstate 5, is the site where Love's rangers killed Joaquin. Or did they? There seems to be a question about whether it was Joaquin *Murieta* and not someone else, perhaps another Joaquin, who was beheaded that summer day, July 25, 1853, on the Tulare Plain at Arroyo Cantua in central California.

And if Joaquin Murieta did not die—if he lived— what became of him? That question was the birth of *Touch the Dawn.*

My search for the real Joaquin Murieta, California's celebrated Robin Hood bandit, and the answers to that question, have taken me all over California: to little towns where he camped with his band of men, to obscure bookstores and museums where the most unusual stories were found, and to a cattle ranch which documents his visit as having been *after* his purported death. And, much to my surprise, to my own backyard—the Tehachapi Mountains—where he is said to have buried a million dollars worth of gold.

Still, it is impossible to separate fact from fiction due to the absence of documentation regarding his birth, his life, his deeds, and his death.

While some believe Joaquin was nothing more than

a mythical folk hero created by San Francisco newspaper reporter John Rollin Ridge, aka Yellow Bird, a Cherokee Indian, in his 1854 book, *The Life and Adventures of Joaquin Murieta,* many others contend Joaquin did indeed exist.

Stories of Joaquin and his adventures have been dramatized in books, plays, and poems. Episodes of *Bonanza* and *Big Valley* brought the Murieta legend to TV. In 1936, a motion picture film, *The Robin Hood of El Dorado,* starring Warner Baxter as Joaquin, told yet another version of the bandit's life as did subsequent films, *The Avenger* and *Vengeance of the West.*

Because I am a romantic, and because of my wonderful but somewhat strange relationship with Joaquin, I have drawn my own conclusions about his life before . . . and *after* his death.

Come with me now and decide for yourself. Man, myth, devil, or angel: who—what was Joaquin Murieta?

Chapter 1

BOSTON BOARD OF TRADE

FROM OCEAN TO OCEAN

SPECIAL PULLMAN TRAIN
FROM BOSTON TO SAN FRANCISCO

A DELEGATION FROM
THE SAN FRANCISCO CHAMBER OF COMMERCE

At twenty minutes to one o'clock this morning the special Pullman train, with the Boston Board of Trade on board, arrived in this city, and the guests alighted in front of the Grand Hotel, on Market Street. From the moment they entered the outer edge of the city until the train was brought to a stand-still in front of the hotel, they were greeted with the liveliest enthusiasm by our citizens. Market Street was thronged with people, who broke forth in loud huzzahs as the locomotive light came in view. The train came down the street at a very fair pace, the engine screeching a response to the welcome cheers of the crowd. Several buildings along the route were brilliantly illuminated. The train of nine cars presented a fine appearance, and the inmates crowded the platforms and windows, waving handkerchiefs as they passed. The crowd around and in the Grand Hotel was a perfect jam. By the aid of ropes stretched from the the train, and an efficient squad of police, a passage-way was kept clear for the guests to move toward the dais where the speech makers addressed the crowd for more than an hour.

Alta California
Wednesday Morning
June 1, 1870

Miss Heller Peyton braced her legs against the pitch and sway of the train as it raced the last few miles toward San Francisco. Despite the discomfort of the steam-damp wind slashing through the severely proper jacket of her traveling costume, and the deafening clack of iron wheels rolling over track, she preferred to await their arrival outside on the observation platform, away from the odor of macassar oil and the nasty cigar smoke that permeated the hotel car.

Her nerves had been on edge for days, and she desperately needed these last moments to herself to gather her courage.

Would the people of San Francisco see through her thin ladylike veneer? It was a question she had asked herself over and over for weeks. A question that only the next two weeks in San Francisco would answer. She shivered to think what that answer would be.

Most young women of good family spent their entire adolescent lives learning and practicing the fine art of being a lady. How, she wondered fretfully, could she, the daughter of an Irish whore, presume to think that she could achieve that same revered status with her ignoble background and a few years' education? "Women are not born ladies," Abigail had told her. "They are made by strict mamas and finishing schools."

Heller had never told Abigail of her ambition to become a lady, the kind of lady that Abigail herself was. Abigail would never have understood; she had *always* been a lady. And the Peytons had *always* commanded respect and position. They were bluebloods through and through, while Heller's blood was of an entirely different shade.

Heller had no illusions about how her Bostonian companions regarded her. They knew who she was and where she came from and had graciously accepted her, though she felt they would always think of her as the little Irish urchin Abigail Peyton had rescued from the gutters of Manhattan and miraculously transformed into a respectable young woman. But there had never been any question about her place in Boston society. None would dare eschew a relative of Abigail Peyton's. The Peyton name carried a great deal of weight, as the Boston banks held a great deal of Peyton money.

But in San Francisco, where the Peyton name was unknown, Heller was on her own. This would be her first opportunity to prove to herself that in spite of everything she had indeed become a lady.

She heaved a long sigh as she realized the enormity of the situation she had made for herself by agreeing to accompany her aunt on the excursion. Not only would she have to maintain a flawless ladylike demeanor, but she had a duty to perform—a position that would require all her concentration. She had accepted the position of the Boston Board of Trade's cultural secretary. As such, she would be required to document all the board's social and business activities and speeches. Besides being involved in the sight-seeing tours, speeches, and soirees, the excursion group would exchange ideas on the possibilities of profitable commerce and culture with San Francisco's Chamber of Commerce—an exchange only now possible because of the completion of the transcontinental railroad. Of particular interest to Heller was the opportunity to share her love of art with a city she had heard had been deprived of even the meanest intellectual taste and aesthetic delights.

So many opportunities, she thought, excitement fluttering in her heart. And challenges, too: social and

personal. Just thinking about them made her stomach
jump with nerves.

Heller fixed her gaze on the moonlit California land-
scape. She had come a long way in the twelve years
since she had been with Abigail Peyton. Against her
will, Heller remembered the narrow, crooked streets
and dismal courts of that quarter of Manhattan called
Five Points. Roaches and rats infested the tenements—
all of which were in advanced stages of decay. She and
Mam lived in a cellar room, ten feet below the street
called Cow Bay. There were no windows and the walls
were damp and cold. Even now, after all these years,
Heller sometimes awoke thinking she had heard the
dismal wails of the children, the hoarse screams of
anger and violence, and the thumping of feet in dark
alleys.

The years had not dimmed Heller's memory of that
snowy night when Abigail, dressed in warm furs, had
knocked on their cellar door and announced herself to
the priest who had come to pray over Mam's
comsumption-ravaged body. Then it was over and
Mam was dead, and Heller found herself warm for the
first time that winter, wrapped in woolen blankets, in
a fairy-tale coach, on her way to Boston, to live with
her father's sister, a spinster who promised to atone
for her brother's abandonment and to love Heller as
her own.

Heller shook her head against the intrusion of any
more memories. That part of her life was over. Heller
O'Shay, child of the street, was gone; Heller Peyton,
cultural secretary for the Boston Board of Trade, was
alive and well. She would have to erect a guard and
keep her thoughts in the present, she told herself
sternly. Never again did she want to go back in thought
or otherwise to the squalor and despair of her former
life. Never, never again.

* * *

The shrill whistle of the eastern excursion train alerted the waiting crowd. The Bostonians were coming.

Inside San Francisco's Grand Hotel, moonlight spilled through an open window, cutting across a dressing table laden with porcelain jars and cosmetic paint pots to bathe the woman's body in its silver light. The hotel room smelled of gardenias, her favorite perfume.

Elena Valdez turned away from the window and sashayed toward the bed, humming an old Spanish ballad. Running long, graceful fingers across her shoulder, she slipped out of her red silk wrapper and let it drift down her arm like a matador's cape. Then she raised her arms and began working loose her long braid of hair.

She lifted her head and looked at Joaquin as she had not looked at him in years. He had always been a devilishly handsome man, but for the first time she saw that his features bore the indelible imprint of his father's Yankee blood. He had shaved off his magnificent mustache and beard—his one concession to a disguise, he had told her within moments of their greeting.

In spite of his Virginia-born father, Elena had never thought of Joaquin as a Yankee, though for a time, he had lived and studied in the East. Looking at him more closely, she wondered where his sympathies were: with the Americanos or the Mexicans? He often dressed as an Americano, but then he also dressed as a *vaquero*. Tonight, he had worn a short, fawn-colored *chaqueta* and close-fitting *calzònes,* split to the knees and studded with silver buttons—the clothes of a Californio.

Joaquin lowered his chin to look at her. Dark brows cut a cynical swath over devil-black eyes. It was Joaquin's eyes that had haunted her days and her nights.

Fathomless. Intense. Defiant. Mesmerizing. With only a look he could turn her to stone or make her melt like a candle.

Her appreciative perusal of him was rudely interrupted when the crowd outside the hotel riotously hailed the high-pitched squeal of the locomotive's whistle. Elena flinched as if she'd been shot.

"Bah! Fools!" Elena spat at the San Franciscans' noisy exuberance over the arrival of the eastern excursion train. Resolved to ignore the disturbance, she snuggled into the crook of Joaquin's arm and softly sang the words to the ballad she had hummed earlier.

Again the whistle screeched and the people shouted.

"Caramba!" Elena flounced away from him. With a vicious oath, she ran to the window and threw back the heavy damask draperies. *"Basta,* enough! Do you hear me? Enough!"

"Careful, *mi amor,* you will show more than your anger," Joaquin teased, his black eyes flashing with amusement.

Elena glared at him, her mouth a tight circle. "There is no justice, *querido.* This is our first night together in three years—ruined by a train full of bluenoses! I hope I do not come face-to-face with one of those paper-skinned, oh-so-proper Boston *ladies* or—as you say—I might show more than just my anger. I might show her the blade of my stiletto!"

Joaquin quirked a brow. "There will be other nights, Elena, since I plan on being here awhile. Be patient."

"You say the same thing when I come to Rancho Murieta and before that when we meet in Mexico City," she whined, hoping just this once for a show of sympathy.

"This time will be different." He checked his timepiece, then stretched.

At thirty-six, Joaquin had lost the rangy look of his

youth. Now, and far more exciting, he had a man's body. The intriguing play of solid muscle beneath sunbrowned flesh made Elena groan with renewed longing. How many other women had seen him as she saw him now? How many had tasted his kisses, trembled at his caresses, and loved him as she loved him? She would never know. In fact, there was much about Joaquin that she would never know or understand. By nature he was a private man, and because his name and deeds were renowned throughout California, he had become a secretive one.

When he turned to retrieve his shirt from the chair, she flinched at the sight of the white scars crisscrossing his broad back: the marks of a bullwhacker's whip, Luther Mauger's whip. She remembered the nights she had lain beside Joaquin, tending his wounds, warming him when the fever chilled his body, comforting him when delirium tortured his mind. The whip scars had faded over the years, but her memories of those first months after Mauger and his gringo *compadres* whipped Joaquin and killed his wife—those memories would never fade.

"Now, maybe you tell me why you come to San Francisco, eh? I was planning on coming to Rancho Murieta in a few weeks, but here you are!"

"To see you dance, *cara mia.* You have become a great performer, have you not? They say you dance the Spider Dance even better than your teacher, Lola Montez."

Elena made a noise of utter disgust. "Bah! *That woman?* She was nothing! *Nada!*" She stopped short when she realized he was trying to change the subject. "But of course you know that, *querido.* Many times you watch me dance, on stage and . . . in the bedroom, yes, no?" She moved around to stand in front of him. "You think me a fool? You think I do not know why you come? It is that *hombre,* no? The one who whipped you and murdered Rosita? He is here, in San Francisco?'' The narrowing of his eyes and the set of his chin gave her the answer she sought. ''Oh, Joaquin!'' His name was an impassioned sigh.

He stood in front of the bureau's wash basin slapping water over his face. Somehow, seeing him half-dressed, performing his ablutions, made him appear almost vulnerable. ''Do you think no one will recognize you just because you shave your face? You are Joaquin Murieta, *El Bandido Notorio*! *Los gringos,* they will hunt you as before, only this time they will make no mistake. It will be *you* they kill. You, Joaquin!''

Seeming to ignore her fevered speech, Joaquin fastened the buttons of his shirt and reached for his jacket. With a groan of exasperation, Elena pressed her fingertips against her temples. ''Even the cat, he has only nine lives, and you, my foolish *vaquero,* used yours up long ago at Arroyo Cantua.''

''No mas!'' His voice exploded like a clap of thunder, followed by a gust of wind that sent her hair flying about her face.

Alarm bristled the fine hairs on Elena's neck. She started to take back her words—knowing she had gone too far.

Joaquin glared at her. ''You speak out of turn, Elena. You think I do not remember what happened at Arroyo Cantua? Not a day goes by that I do not relive that day. My *compadres* were killed, Elena, because of me.''

''No, Joaquin. They did not die because of you. They believed in a cause just as you did. Justice. They fought for justice. Died for justice.''

Furiously, he said, ''For all the good it did them. Do not speak to me of the Cantua ever again. Besides, it has nothing to do with me finding Luther Mauger and avenging Rosita.''

"You're wrong, Joaquin. It has everything to do with it. There are many who know the Rangers killed the wrong Joaquin. Many who believe you are still alive."

"I know the risk and I'm willing to take it." He walked over to the window and drew it shut. When he turned around, his demeanor had changed, the savage fury replaced by the barest hint of a smile. "You are like an old woman. You worry too much." He slipped his bowie knife into the leather sheath attached to his belt.

Tonelessly, Elena said what was in her heart. "It is a woman's privilege to worry about the man she loves." She expected him to look surprised by her declaration, but instead he gathered her into his arms and kissed her lightly on the forehead. Her sorrowful expression changed, and she flashed him a sultry look. "Stay with me tonight. I need you." He would never know how much. Over the years, she had tried to rid herself of her desire for him by roaming the world like a gypsy, dancing and acting before the kings and queens of Europe. But she would always return to the province of Sonora, to Rancho Murieta and to Joaquin. It grated on her that with this man alone she had no pride. To be Joaquin's woman—to bear his name, to have his love—was all she had ever wanted.

She wondered now, as she often did, why he had married Rosita Feliz and not her.

"I must go. Lino waits for me," he announced.

She murmured a protest against his cheek, and her hands moved knowledgeably over his body. "He can wait a little longer. What harm?" she whispered, rubbing her palm against his manhood.

"Do not do this, Elena." His hand closed over hers

with a firmness that brooked no argument. He turned and reached for his hat.

Elena tossed her head and reared back like a bit-shy filly. "Lino Toral! Always it's Lino." Her eyes shone like polished onyx. "I do not know why you—"

Before she could say more, he gripped her bare upper arms. "We will talk no more of *El Bandido Notorio*, or of the Cantua, or Luther Mauger, or Lino Toral. *Comprendes?*"

Elena whirled out of his arms. "*Sí*, but I will always fear for you and I will always *hate* Lino Toral!" She turned her back on him and folded her arms across her breasts. Since childhood, Lino had always stood between them. Lino the brigand lieutenant. Lino the scholar, a man of law and letters. Lino the monk. And always, Lino the trusted confidant.

"Joa—" His name died on her lips as she turned and faced an empty room. Elena stared dumbly at the empty space where he had stood.

The urgent need for fresh air assailed her. She grabbed her wrapper from the chair and threw it around her shoulders as she hurried to the window.

Suddenly, the slowing locomotive sent a beacon of light into her window, blinding her. Elena yanked the draperies together and dashed to her bed.

The Bostonians had arrived.

The train slowed as it came into the city. On tracks laid specifically for the occasion, the smoke-spewing engine ground to a screeching stop within a hundred feet of the ribbon-festooned entrance of the Grand Hotel.

Heller reached up to tuck in the wisps of hair that had escaped her tight chignon. The upward movement caused the whalebone stays of her corset to press deeply into her side. She winced and lowered her arms.

Another hour, two at the most, and she would be free of its confinement. Beneath the brim of her fashionable hat, dipped low over her forehead, she gazed at the cheering, flag-waving throng held back from the locomotive by a squad of smartly uniformed police.

A small, white-haired woman, dressed completely in black, opened the Pullman's door and stepped out onto the platform. "There now," said Abigail Peyton, surveying the scene before her. "What did I tell you? They don't look at all like savages, do they?"

Heller sighed at her aunt's smug expression. "Please, Aunty. You misunderstood. Miss Pennyworth and I didn't say the San Franciscans were savages. We said many of the *Westerners*—the ones who carried side arms—were still uncivil—"

"I *know* what was said, Heller. I overheard your dear mentor talking to you about the various ways we could help 'save the savages of San Francisco.' Savages, indeed! Leave it to Elizabeth Pennyworth to reduce Boston's most respected social, political and commercial luminaries to soul-saving missionaries!"

Heller started to protest, then thought better of it. Arguing was unladylike. Besides, nothing she could say would change the dislike Abigail felt for Elizabeth Pennyworth.

Aware of her aunt's scrutiny, Heller fussed with the foot-long peacock feather decorating her hat. She wished now she had chosen a different hat. This one was an exact copy of Elizabeth Pennyworth's favorite, and Abigail well knew it.

"Do try to smile, dear," Abigail coaxed. "And for heaven's sake, drop that mantle of Olympian reserve. It is no wonder you have not found a husband yet. You scare men away with your uppity airs."

Before Heller could protest for the thousandth time that she did not want a husband, now or ever, the

group leader, Alexander Rice, waved them off the platform and herded them toward the other excursionists.

Velvet ropes, flanked by stern-faced police, pro-
tected the Bostonians from over-enthusiastic welcom-
ers as they headed for the area where San Francisco's
Chamber of Commerce waited.

Taking Heller's hand, Abigail rushed to catch up
with Mr. Rice, who was at the head of the group.
"Oh, do let us hurry, dear. I promised Alex I would
stand in front of the podium in case he needed me to
prompt lines of his speech."

The crowd pressed forward, stretching the ropes to
the limit. And then they were down, and a thousand
jubilant citizens shot toward the dais, cutting in front
of Abigail and Heller.

"Oh, horsefeathers!" Abigail cried. She quickly
stepped back, out of the path of the stampeding crowd,
which had separated her and Heller from the group.

Seeing her aunt's distress, Heller offered, "Perhaps
we could go around behind them and work our way to
the front. Then we could—"

"No! No!" Abigail cut her short. "That will take
far too long. By then the speeches will be over. We
will have to go right through them!" Before Heller
could protest, Abigail grabbed her hand and charged
forward. Wielding her black silk parasol like a broad-
sword, the old woman shouldered her way into the
multitude with an authority that made those in her path
move aside.

The crowd silenced when Robert Swain, the president of the San Francisco Chamber of Commerce, held
up his hand. ". . . so let it be recorded that on this
first day of June in the glorious year 1870, the people
of two great cities have joined efforts toward creating
a cultural understanding and a greater commercial en-

terprise.'' Excited cheers and applause erupted from the audience.

Heller felt Abigail double her efforts, nudging and poking, then offering curt apologies to a chorus of grumbling San Franciscans. Heller was acutely embarrassed by her aunt's rudeness, but no one told Abigail Peyton—Boston's most respected matriarch—what to do, or not to do. Holding onto her hat with one hand and her aunt with the other, she kept pace, humbly seconding her aunt's abrupt apologies.

Moments later, Heller caught a glimpse of the hotel's canopied entrance over the top of a woman's head. ''Thank goodness,'' she mumbled. Only a few yards more, and they would be in front of the dais and at the edge of the crowd. She felt her aunt tug on her arm and quickened her step.

A small boy dressed in baggy clothing darted out from between two men and ran headlong into Abigail, knocking her off balance. Heller was jerked forward as her aunt's hand pulled apart from hers. Then, in a blur of motion, she saw Abigail pitch forward and reach out her arm to try to catch herself, her parasol thrust out in front of her like a jousting lance.

It had not occurred to Joaquin that the crowd outside the hotel would be so large it could delay him for his appointment with Lino. He had read about the excursion train in the *Daily Alta California:* nine cars built by George Pullman, cars for sleeping, for dining, and one for smoking. It even had a classical library and a printing office for a daily newspaper. Special tracks had been laid for the train to come directly up Market Street to the entrance of the Grand Hotel.

Leave it to a bunch of bluebloods to make cross-country travel into a fashionable adventure, he thought, faintly amused. He supposed if he had thought about it earlier, he would have known the Bostonian arrival would bring out half the city, but his mind had been on Lino and the purpose of their meeting.

Now, he had one of two choices: wait out the speech-making or go back up to Elena's room. He hated crowds, but he hated Elena using her sexual charms to coerce him even more. She used her body with the same skill a *vaquero* used his horse. Later, when he was alone, he would think about his relationship with Elena. She had made it clear what she wanted, but he still wasn't sure what *he* wanted. One thing was certain: he would have to make a decision.

He moved away from the canopied entrance into the anonymity of the throng. An old familiar feeling of unease settled upon his shoulders, but he shrugged it off as an overreaction to the multitude of people.

". . . and now with the final tracks laid, the dark days of travel are behind us. We can travel in comfort, luxury, and safety."

The speaker's words drew a round of applause. Then, without warning, a gun barrel jammed into Joaquin's back. Instinctively, he pulled his knife, turned, and grabbed his attacker.

Heller saw the glint of tempered steel flash toward her aunt. Her face blanched. A knife! The years rolled backward and Cow Bay loomed in front of her. The fights, the awful words, the knives, blood, and death. It was always outside the door.

"No . . . please!" The words tore from Heller's throat. She had to stop him, had to save her aunt. Like a cat, she sprang forward, pushed her aunt aside, and flung herself against the attacker.

A sharp, burning pain tore through her flesh, stealing her breath. Her wail was little more than a whisper of surprise among a deafening burst of whoops and hollers. Slowly, she drew back and pressed her gloved hand against her side. Hardly daring to breathe, she turned her palm upward.

Blood.

She raised her hand and stared at it in horror.

The man lifted her chin and forced her to look at him. Cruel lips formed words she couldn't hear. He glared at her from beneath the brim of his black hat. His eyes, devil-black, searched her face with an intensity that both terrified and mesmerized her.

"Y—you s—stabbed me!"

She began to sway. She tried to fight the dizziness that had seized her but found it beyond her efforts. A warm breeze caressed her face. Gardenias. She smelled gardenias. She thought of her aunt's garden: a small, walled square bordered with flowers. Their fragrant blooms scented the air and blew in her window, lulling her to sleep. She leaned forward, seeking the rock-solid support of the man's chest, and fainted.

Chapter 2

Elena Valdez mumbled another curse as she plumped her pillow and rolled onto her side. She doubted she would be able to sleep, now while her head was filled with thoughts of Joaquin. *Dios.* How could she love and hate a man at the same time? She had loved Joaquin since girlhood and hated him when he had wed the neighboring *hacendado's* daughter, Rosita Felix. Never would she forgive him for that! After Rosita's death, she had happily comforted him and cared for him. Once he had recuperated from both his mental and physical pain, she followed him like a *soldadera,* spied for him, cooked his meals, and warmed his bed at night. No man had ever aroused her the way he did. When he made love to her, he made love to all of her— her mind and her body. It was always that way when she was with him. She would never understand why he alone had such an effect on her.

In all ways she had been a wife to him—the kind of wife a man such as he needed. But, in spite of her devotion, he refused to marry her. So she had left.

If France had not been on the brink of war with Prussia, she would have stayed in Paris and encouraged a certain rich marquis' affections. It was a weak excuse for leaving, as she was in no danger, but the prospect of a war, of fighting, allowed her to mentally justify her return to Joaquin. On the voyage home, she had contemplated how to seduce Joaquin into marrying her. She told herself now it didn't matter that he could never return her love, that he would always love Rosita. He cared for her—that would have to be enough. Her first task was to make him realize how good she was for him, then how much he needed her. She would prove to him that he could depend on her now, just as he had before, and remind him that his secrets were safe with her. After all, only she knew what devils drove him and what dreams plagued his sleep. Only she understood.

Elena turned the direction of her thoughts and settled down to sleep. The years away from Joaquin had been lonely but not entirely without reward. Her dancing and acting talents had given her worldwide fame, fortune, and the respect of polite society. Men adored her, vied for her favor by laying flowers, jewels, and their hearts at her feet. Elena had learned much about life and men during her years in Europe—enough, she hoped, to win the only man she had ever loved.

"Tomorrow night," she whispered against her pillow, "I will dance for you—for you alone, my brave and foolish *vaquero*. I will make you want me as you have wanted no other woman!"

Closing her eyes, she nuzzled her cheek against the linen pillow cover and contemplated the blissful years ahead as Doña Murieta, mistress of Rancho Murieta, the largest *rancho* in the province of Sonora, Mexico. It was her right! She couldn't—wouldn't—let herself dream of anything less. At long last, her dreams were about to become a reality.

The smile slipped from Elena's lips as the door burst open. She sprang from her bed. "*Que?* W—who is there?" she demanded. Fumbling in the darkness, she grabbed for her wrapper.

"Light the lamp, Elena. I need your help." She could never mistake Joaquin's richly timbred voice.

"Help?" Burning fear constricted Elena's chest. Was he hurt? Had someone recognized him? She had begged him to be more careful, begged him to disguise himself better, but he had laughed at her fears. He tempted fate so often that sometimes it seemed he really wanted to be found and caught.

Joaquin kicked the door shut behind him. "I need smelling salts."

"Smelling salts?" A match flared and the room filled with buttery-yellow light. "What do you want with—" Elena shrieked at the sight of the red-haired woman Joaquin held in his arms. "Who is the woman? Why have you brought her here?"

"Smelling salts, Elena. *Arriba!*" he demanded with sharp impatience.

Elena stomped around the room, grumbling and cursing as she opened and closed drawers. At length, she found the silver vial on her dressing table amid the tangle of jewelry. She hesitated, then picked up the vial and started across the room.

"She is sick? Yes? No?" Elena froze as she reached the side of the bed and saw the growing bloodstain that seeped through the *gringa*'s jacket. "She is hurt! What happened?"

Joaquin shook his head, concern marking his features. "Damned if I know. I thought I had accidentally stabbed her, but my knife is clean—" At a loss for words, he set about unbuttoning her jacket, only to discover a stiffly pleated blouse beneath it. Not long on patience, he raised the young woman's arm, and with the tip of his knife sliced through the hole in the garment, then rent it down to where it met her waist. Beneath the blouse was yet another obstacle, her corset. But it, at least, gave him the answer to his question. She had been stabbed all right. One of her corset stays had broken and a large splinter had pierced the skin just beneath her right breast.

"Damn women and their foolish vanity!" He carefully withdrew the splinter, stashed it in his pocket, then opened the corset and the chemise beneath it. "I need brandy and something for a bandage," he told Elena, who hovered over him like a red-tailed hawk, watching his every move. Gently, he pressed his fingertips against the wound to staunch the flow of blood. His thumb nudged under the warm swell of the young woman's breast. Beautiful breasts, he thought, small like the rest of her. A shadow of some memory softened his expression and took him back many years before. His wife had been small like this young woman; her breasts had fit perfectly in his hand. The desire to touch the Bostonian more intimately overwhelmed him. Instead, he jerked his hand away and damned himself and the circumstances that had brought him here.

The tender look on Joaquin's face had not been lost on Elena. It was the look she longed for—lived for—and now he was giving it to a paper-skinned Yankee!

Elena reached for her best brandy, presented to her by an ardent admirer, then thought better of it. Quickly, she set it back and snatched up another bottle of a more common variety. She spat a curse as she handed Joaquin the bottle and a length of new muslin that she had been going to take to the dressmaker. "She is dead, no? She looks dead; her skin, it is so white."

"It's only a flesh wound, Elena." He heard Elena make a soft hissing sound when he pressed his palm against the young woman's breast to clean the wound. Then, he fashioned a bandage and wrapped a torn strip of muslin around her middle to hold the bandage in place. "I suppose I should try to put her back together before she wakes her up."

Elena shooed him away, overlapped the cut edges of the Bostonian's blouse, and rebuttoned her jacket.

The sharp odor of ammonia stung Heller's nose. Her eyes flew open. Through a hazy blur she saw a dark-haired woman glaring down at her. "Mam, is it really you I'm seein'?" Her voice was a hoarse whisper, hardly recognizable as her own. Was it day or night? She couldn't tell; her eyelids were heavy and her pupils refused to focus. A smell—a cloying flower scent—made her nose twitch. She wanted to wave the foul odor away but did not have the strength.

Elena stood up and huffed away.

Heller felt the mattress lift and turned her face against the pillow. She blinked moisture into her eyes and tried again to focus.

A dark shape and obsidian eyes gradually coalesced into a terrifying vision—the man who had stabbed her! A surge of adrenalin pumped through her veins. Without thinking what she was doing, she shot up off the bed and lunged at her attacker.

With a growl of anger, the man grabbed her hands and pulled her tightly against him, putting a stop to her attack. The physical contact was utterly and frighteningly sobering. She wrenched herself out of his hold and reared back. A strangled cry forced its way past her lips as pain ripped through her body. In its wake, she lifted her tearful gaze to meet his. "Please, don't kill me." She stepped back even further and felt the edge of the mattress against the back of her legs. The adrenalin surge of a moment ago suddenly deserted her, and her legs began to wobble like a newborn colt's.

"Damn fool woman!" The man's words echoed in

the swirling fog inside her brain. She felt her knees
give way and fancied herself melting into a puddle at
his feet. "On, no you don't. You're not going to faint
on me again." Strong arms pulled her up, then he
jostled her this way and that like a rag doll. "Come
on, Boston, keep your eyes open and stay awake."

The jostling stopped, and he pulled her into the circle of his arms. He cradled her head against his shoulder and whispered soft encouragements into her ear.
At length he said, "I know I scared you, but I assure
you I never intended to hurt you." Gradually, his softly
spoken words penetrated the loud beating of her own
heart. Moments later, when she felt stronger, she
raised a gloved hand between them and pushed herself
back. She gulped down a sob as he bent his handsome
head and looked deep into her eyes.

"And now I'll accept *your* apology," he said, taking her off guard.

She arched a brow. Surely she hadn't heard him
right. "Y—you what?"

He loosened his hold. "I said I'll accept your apology.
Once you give it, that is."

So, she had heard him right after all. Righteous indignation flared within her and wiped away the gentleness of a moment ago. "Apology? And why would I
be apologizin' to the likes of you? You're the devil
incarnate, you are. You stabbed me!" She put her hand
to the wound and winced.

"I did not stab you."

She looked down, grabbed the hem of her jacket,
and stretched it taut. She paled at the sight of the still-
wet bloodstain. "What then, do you call this?"

"I call it stupid female vanity."

"Vanity? What does vanity have to do with you
stabbing me?"

"In the interest of accuracy, Boston, it was your

corset that stabbed you.'' He reached into his jacket pocket, pulled out the bloodied whalebone, and held it up for her to see.

Holding onto a lamppost outside the hotel entrance, Abigail tried to shake herself free of the dizziness that had overcome her. At sixty-two, she was not as resilient as she used to be. Truth was, she considered herself lucky to be alive after the events of the last few minutes. "Oh, Lord," she groaned, leaning her aching head against the post. If only that Chinese boy—a pickpocket—had chosen another route of escape. If only she had dropped her parasol instead of pushing it out in front of her. Heller had saved her from being knifed, but then she had been unable to help Heller because of being hurtled back into the crowd by a policeman in pursuit of the pickpocket. Putting it all together, it seemed like a comedy of errors, one on top of another. At least she knew which direction the kidnapper had taken Heller.

A young man stopped next to her. "Are you all right, ma'am?" he inquired solicitously.

Abigail turned, blinking. Help at last. "Why—Why, yes—I need some— The police." She made an effort to stand without the aid of the post but found she still needed its support.

"A bit too much Jersey Lightning, wouldn't you say, ma'am?"

"Jersey what?"

"Lightning. You know . . ."

"Lightning?" Abigail's eyes came into sharp focus. "You think I am inebriated?" She grabbed the sleeve of his coat and twisted the material into a tight knot. "Why, you young whippersnapper. I will have you know that I do not partake of spirits, not even for medicinal purposes! My niece has been kidnapped by

a man with a knife. He has taken her into the hotel."
She pointed a bony finger toward the open doors.

The young man's eyes rounded. "Kidnapped, huh?
You're absolutely right, you do need the police." He
pried her fingers from his coat. "I'll go see if I can
find a policeman to help you."

Abigail put her hand over her heart. "Oh, yes.
Please do. I will be ever so grateful. And . . . please
. . . hurry!"

She was not sure how long she waited before she
realized the young man was not coming back, and neither would a policeman be coming. Taking a deep,
steadying breath, she pulled herself up to her full five-
foot-two-inch height and moved away from the lamppost. When she was certain she was not going to topple
over, she started for the doors leading into the lobby.
The lobby was empty; not a soul in sight. She contemplated the stairs, then slowly began her ascent.

It seemed an eternity before she gained the first-
floor landing. Once there, however, a new problem
presented itself: a long hallway with door after door,
all closed.

"Heller! Heller Peyton. Where are you?" Abigail
pounded on first one door, then another. She turned
doorknobs and peeked through keyholes. By the time
she reached the last door at the far end of the hall, she
was hoarse and out of breath. She leaned her forehead
against the door and prayed. She did not know if she
had the strength to make it up to the second floor, and
she could not bear thinking about the third floor.

"Heller? Are you in there?" She turned the knob
and found the door open. Inside was Heller.

"Aunty!"

Abigail Peyton barged into the room, a tornado of
stiffened black crepe, spouting rage and shaking her

parasol. The man—the kidnapper—was threatening Heller with some sort of bloodied weapon.

"You touch her with that, and I will bash your skull in!" she railed, her already hoarse voice cracking under the strain of fear.

The man adroitly sidestepped her charge, then grabbed her parasol.

"Be warned, old woman. You have attacked me with that thing for the last time." Holding the tipped end tightly in his hand, he raised the parasol and swung it down over the back of a chair, breaking it in two.

Abigail grabbed Heller's arm and pulled them both out of harm's way.

A black-haired woman stepped out of the shadows, her red silk wrapper tightly sashed around her waist. "*Perdon*, señora," she said, addressing herself directly to Abigail. "Perhaps you have heard of me. I am Elena Valdez. There is nothing to fear. *Mi amigo*, he had no choice but to bring your *sobrina* here to my room after she fainted in the crowd. But as you can see, she is well. She has suffered no harm."

Abigail seemed not to hear her. "Heller. Child. Are you all right?" She clucked like a broody hen as she examined Heller. When she saw her bloodied jacket, she shrieked in horror. "Dear God! They're lying. These people *are* savages! I am going for the police."

Joaquin's fingers twined around her arm and stopped her headlong flight. "No, you will not go for the police."

Elena Valdez hurried across the room, closed the door and leaned against it.

Abigail wrenched her arm away. "How dare you keep us here against our will!"

Still disoriented, Heller was slow to find her voice. "Please, Aunty, you don't understand. It was all a mistake." The explanation stuck in her throat. "It—it

was my corset. A piece of whalebone broke and it—''
Unable to finish, she grabbed the bone sliver away
from the Spaniard and handed it to Abigail.

Abigail's white brows knitted together in a confused
frown. ''Merciful heavens! I have never heard of such
a thing. We need to get you to your room and see to
it. I'm sure it is just a small wound, but still . . .''
She shook her head.

There was nothing Heller would like better than to
get to her own room and let Abigail tend her. With
something like dismay, she asked Abigail to put the
piece of whalebone in her reticule.

''I suppose I owe you an apology, Mister—?'' Humiliation rose in Heller's throat like bitter bile, and
the taste of it made her angry, yet she had no one to
blame but herself. And to make things worse, the
Spaniard was right. It had been vanity that made her
buy a corset one size too small. The beastly thing had
tormented her since the first time she'd worn it.

''Montaños, señorita, Don Ricardo Montaños,''
Joaquin supplied, the alias rolling off his tongue with
ease along with an Americanized accent that he had
adopted as part of his disguise. He bowed formally
from the waist.

''Yes, indeed,'' Abigail added. ''I also owe you an
apology. If I had not been so determined to get through
the crowd to the podium, the accident would not have
happened.'' While Abigail related the series of events
that would take her to the point where she had stabbed
Don Ricardo in the back with her parasol, Heller examined her clothing. Her blouse and jacket, of course,
were ruined. Looking down, she saw her hat lying on
the floor partway under the bed, a triangular black
smudge stamped into the crown. Her eyes glanced over
to Don Ricardo's pointed-toe boots. She bent over and
plucked the feather from the crown and held it protec-

tively against her breast. She lifted her chin and met his dark smoldering gaze.

Staring back at him, she momentarily forgot her anger. Something in the way he looked at her mesmerized her. His eyes kindled with diabolical gleam over a blade-straight nose that bespoke his Spanish ancestry. Her gaze traveled down to the snow-white shirt beneath his short fawn-colored jacket. She didn't have to touch it to know it was fine linen. Light-colored, close-fitting trousers tucked into hand-tooled leather boots defined muscular thighs and strong legs. He stood with his feet apart, braced in the position of a proud, haughty Spanish grandee. He was overwhelmingly and dangerously male.

"Do you find me to your liking, señorita, or shall I turn around so you can finish your inspection?" His mouth lifted at the corners in amusement.

His question made her realize she had been staring. High color mounted Heller's cheeks. Acutely embarrassed, she looked away and caught Señorita Valdez looking at her with undisguised hostility. Jealousy.

A quick glance around the room—at the rumpled bed and the brightly colored clothes, which no lady would wear, strewn over chairs—verified her thoughts. Elena Valdez was his mistress. And they had been— She sucked in her breath and winced at the pain in her side. Memories, dozens of childhood memories, kaleidoscoped within her head: cheap flashy clothes, painted faces, whispered voices in the dark, masculine sounds—low moans, the clinking of coins, her mother's soft words. . . .

It took every ounce of her will to regain a ladylike demeanor. Straightening to her full height, she scoffed, "You're insufferable. No gentleman would behave as you have."

"No, I suppose not. But then I've never claimed to

be a gentleman, and you, my fine Irish lass, are no lady!'' he said, imitating her brogue.

Heller made a noise that sounded like the wind had been knocked out of her. Señor Montaños, a perfect stranger, had in one sentence stripped away her carefully cultivated polish, shattered her genteel veneer, and reduced her to her baseborn self. She felt her chin begin to quiver. Her eyes began to sting with unshed tears, but she held them in check. She would not let this man see the damage his insult had done. She would not give him that pleasure.

"Heller. Dear," Abigail said, taking Heller's hand and pulling her toward the door. "Since you seem to be somewhat recuperated, I think we should thank Señor Montaños and Señorita Valdez for their hospitality and be on our way. We have imposed long enough."

Heller pulled together the remnants of her pride. "Yes, thank you," she intoned stiffly. "I'm sorry to have inconvenienced you."

With a queenly air, Elena inclined her head and escorted the two women to the door.

Deliberately ignoring Señor Montaños' amused grin, Heller trailed behind her aunt, closing the door behind her.

Outside in the hall, Heller stopped and drew a shuddering breath as she heard high peals of feminine laughter.

At the stairs, Abigail suggested she leave Heller a moment and see about their rooms. "Do you think you will be all right waiting here while I try to find a desk clerk? You look deathly pale."

"I'll be fine," Heller said with conviction, when in fact she was not at all fine. She had never felt so awful in all her life. Not only was she in physical pain, but she was suffering from the indignity of his insult. He had seen right through her.

She wished now she had listened to Elizabeth Pennyworth and stayed home where she belonged.

This time when Joaquin left the Grand Hotel, no
crowd detained him. Pulling the brim of his hat down
low over his forehead, he headed north on Montgomery Street toward his own hotel, the What Cheer
House.

Even at his pre-dawn hour, the city bustled with
activity. Fruit vendors and fishmongers hurried to
display their wares for early-morning shoppers.
Closed-curtained carriages passed through the streets,
discreetly returning late-night revelers to their homes
and hotels. Joaquin adapted easily to city living, but
still he did not like it. He loathed the customs of so-
called polite society, the feigned friendliness and the
back-stabbing gossip that the Anglos thought such
sport. But most of all, he hated the confinement of
the city itself; it suffocated him. He did not belong
here or in any populated area. In less than twenty-
four hours, he already longed to hear the midnight
bay of a coyote, the sound of the wind whistling
through the trees, and El Tigre's soft nickering.

His booted feet made a hollow tapping sound on the
cobblestone street. The sound echoed inside his head,
punctuating his already disturbing thoughts. How could
he have mistaken the tip of a woman's parasol for the
barrel of a gun? Had the years of living at the *hacienda*
and playing the *hacendado* robbed him of his senses?
His black brows drew together in a forbidding frown,
discouraging a passing drunk from asking for a coin.

As he crossed Bush Street, his thoughts also took a
different route: Miss Heller Peyton. He'd never met
anyone quite like her; both fire and ice. From her stylish kid walking shoes to the ridiculous little feathered
hat that had been pinned to her high-piled copper curls,

she represented the epitome of puritanical primness, yet her Irish brogue contradicted the prudish blueblood she portrayed.

Turning left into an alley off California Street, Joaquin arrived at the What Cheer House. Lino, he knew, would still be waiting.

The scraping of a key in the lock woke Lino Toral from his catnap. He turned his ear to the door, his mind and body instantly alert. Instinctively, he reached down and drew the bowie from its fine leather sheath. The carved ivory handle felt cool against his fingers, the grip comfortable, like an old friend. In Lino's capable hands, the blade—the twin of El Jefe's—was as effective a weapon as a gun, sometimes more so since it spoke in silence.

The knob turned. On dry hinges, the door squeaked open.

Lino peered into the darkness of the hallway. Nothing. His ears strained for a sound—any sound, the click of a trigger, the rustle of clothing, breathing. . . . His nostrils flared at a flowery scent. Gardenias. He knew that scent. But from where? Who? His mind raced to make the connection.

An object sailed into the room and landed at his feet. He smiled and reached down to pick the hat up off the floor, and when he looked up again, a man's dark form leaned against the doorjamb.

"You become careless, *amigo*." The flare of a match illuminated the speaker's swarthy face. He touched the flame to the end of his cigar and inhaled deeply.

"Not careless, *mi jefe*, only confused by your . . . ah . . . lovely fragrance." Lino rose from the chair and walked toward his friend.

"*Que?*" Joaquin reached out his hand to clasp Lino's in a warm *abrazo*.

"Your scent, *mi jefe*. The gardenia flower, no? Elena's favorite."

Joaquin's jaw hardened. The match burned down to his fingers before he waved it out. "Forgive me, my friend, it is I who have grown careless." He closed the door behind him, turning the latch.

Lino returned the bowie to his belt. "I, too, could become careless after an evening with Elena Valdez." He slapped Joaquin on the back and laughed heartily, but when Joaquin did not join him, he stopped. "You are not amused?"

"*Sí*, but there is much on my mind." Joaquin removed his jacket and knife and set them on the chair. With as few words as possible, he related the events of the last few hours, leaving out his lingering thoughts about Heller Peyton.

"So? You make a mistake. You are only a man, no? Not the legend people have made of you."

"Is that what I am, Lino, a legend?"

"*Sí*. You are Joaquin Murieta, *El Bandido Magnifico*. But you are also El Jefe."

"No, Lino. El Jefe died seventeen years ago at Arroyo Cantua."

"*Sí. Yo comprendo.*" Lino shrugged. "Eh, but I did not come here to discuss your death, *mi amigo*. I came to tell you that Luther Mauger is no longer in prison. He is here in San Francisco."

The unexpectedness of Lino's statement caught Joaquin unprepared. His face froze in shock. The wired message that had brought him to San Francisco had indicated only that Lino had information about Mauger, nothing about the man being out of prison—his sentence wasn't up for another two years. "He escaped?" It was the only logical explanation he could think of.

"I don't know. I only know that I saw him. I was

having a drink, when I looked up and there he was. I wasn't sure at first that it was really Mauger; he was clean-shaven and dressed in fancy-tailored clothes. I got as close as I dared, thinking if I recognized him, he might recognize me.''

"And did he . . . recognize you?''

"No. He didn't even look my way." Lino bent over and took a light off of Joaquin's forgotten cigar. "He is not the Luther Mauger we knew, *amigo*. He's become a man of business, and from the looks of him, he appears to have acquired a bit of wealth and sophistication. I followed him to Little China in the midst of some kind of funeral parade. He went into a joss house—but never came out. I finally knocked on the door and asked to be let in, but was barred from entering. I couldn't make any sense out of what the Chinaman was saying, so I left, but I'll be damned if I can remember which joss house it was. Since then, I've asked around and learned that some of the joss houses have exclusive membership lists for wealthy, white, opium-smokers, but nobody seems to know which ones."

Joaquin sat down on the edge of the bed and dropped his head between his knees. Mauger, out of prison, after all these years. Why hadn't his informant wired him? That's what he'd paid him for—to keep him apprised of Mauger's activities. The moment of silence stretched to a dozen before he looked up. "First, I want to send a wire and find out if he escaped, then we'll go to Little China—and find that joss house."

Lino nodded. "I figured that. But first I have something to show you." From the bedside table, he took two pieces of paper and handed them to Joaquin. "This is how Mauger looked seventeen years ago, and this is how he looked two weeks ago."

Joaquin's eyes narrowed with hatred as he looked at

the penciled sketches of Luther Mauger. ''Where did you get these?''

''I learned many useful things in that Eastern law school you sent me to, but I learned only one thing in that damn monastery I put myself into, and that was how to sketch faces—because that's all there was to do!''

Joaquin laughed and Lino joined him. ''This afternoon, we go to Little China.''

Chapter 3

Lino Toral was a patient man. This was not the first time he had waited for Joaquin, and he doubted it would be the last. The missive the desk clerk had given him had been brief and to the point, *Have gone to recruit a knowledgeable guide. Return at noon.*

Lino pulled his gold timepiece out of his pocket. It was quarter past noon. Odd, he thought, Joaquin had said nothing about getting a guide last night. No, not at all odd, he corrected himself. El Jefe was a private man; he kept his own counsel and rarely shared his thoughts. Lino shook his head; he should have remembered that.

He sat down and made himself comfortable in a fat leather chair near the hotel entrance, where he could watch the comings and goings of the guests who seemed to be predominately Englishmen.

Lino reminded himself to ask Joaquin why he chose the What Cheer House, a men's hotel, for their accommodations whenever they met in San Francisco. It wasn't that Lino didn't appreciate the solid though less than luxurious comforts and amenities the hotel offered; he always made good use of the library lounge, and he enjoyed the homey restaurant that served à la carte dishes. Even the hotel's museum with its display of stuffed birds, pickled reptiles, and Indian curios proved a constant fascination to him—but damn! There wasn't anyplace where he could get a drink. And, at thirty-four, two years younger than Joaquin, he wasn't so old that he didn't like looking at a pretty face or encouraging the company of a young woman—and neither was Joaquin—so why the hell the monk's cloister?

Cloister? *Madre de Dios!* Of course! His thoughts raced as the answer became clear. Why hadn't he realized it before? he wondered, feeling foolish. But of course Joaquin would choose such a hotel! Joaquin still regarded him as the pious monk he'd been six years ago. With a short laugh, Lino rolled his eyes toward the ceiling.

One thought led to another as the minutes slipped by. Morosely, Lino remembered the fiesta celebrating his cousin, Rosita Felix's, wedding to Joaquin. A week after the wedding, Joaquin and Rosita left for the California gold fields to make their fortune, and less than six months later Rosita was dead—raped and murdered by Luther Mauger and his three cutthroat friends.

Lino took a pained breath. He seldom allowed himself to dwell on his memories, but telling Joaquin about Mauger—seeing and feeling his friend's hate—brought back all the old anger and pain. Like Joaquin, he wanted revenge—wanted to make Mauger pay for his deeds. It was for that reason that he had left the monastery; hate not being in the doctrine of the brotherhood. But the satisfaction of avenging Rosita did not belong to him. It belonged to Joaquin—to El Jefe.

The hansom cab pulled up to the entrance of the What Cheer House. Five uniformed policemen stood near the entrance; their voices loud, their gestures expressive.

"Wait here," Joaquin instructed the driver, stepping down from the cab directly in front of them.

Joaquin felt their eyes watch him as he headed toward the door, but sensed their watchfulness was from curiosity rather than suspicion. Aside from the policemen, no one in San Francisco had given him a second glance. Not even during the early morning scuffle outside the Grand Hotel, when Heller Peyton had fainted and he had carried her through the crowd into the empty hotel lobby. Everyone, it seemed, had been too wrapped up in the speech-making to notice.

Glancing over his shoulder, he saw the policemen walking down the street. Their Irish brogue reminded him of Heller's.

Heller.

It had been a long time since he'd given a woman more than a passing thought, and never had one aroused his interest the way Heller Peyton did. Everything about her intrigued and fascinated him; her innocent beauty, her feminine curves that his hands still burned to touch and caress, and her contradictory personality.

Thinking about their confrontation in the hotel room, he had to laugh. She'd been furious when he'd mocked her Irish brogue and thereafter had taken pains not to let it slip out again. Obviously, she wasn't proud of her heritage, and he wondered why.

It suddenly occurred to him that there had hardly been a minute since he'd met her that she hadn't been in his thoughts. He silently cursed himself and willed himself to think of the day ahead.

Just inside the entrance he saw Lino, looking for all the world like an American lawyer, dressed in a stiff linen shirt with a turned-down collar, black frock coat, and sharply creased trousers. Across his brocade vest he wore a stylish Dickens watch chain. On the table next to him sat his high hat. Joaquin was momentarily taken aback; he couldn't remember Lino ever wearing anything but the traditional clothes of the *vaquero*, and for a few years, a monk's robes. This, he decided, was a new Lino Toral, a man of wealth, education, and power. No longer the fast-shooting, hard-riding brigand lieutenant.

Joaquin strode over to where Lino sat with a faraway look in his eyes. "Mr. Toral." Lino's head jerked up. He stood and took Joaquin's hand in greeting. The two men were nearly equal in size, Lino only slightly shorter than Joaquin's six foot three. "Where did you get these clothes? You look like a gringo and" he— paused, leaning close— "what is that I smell?" Joaquin sniffed the macassar oil Lino had used to slick his dark, unruly hair into place. "Whew!" He arched his eyebrows and stepped back.

Lino pulled a face; he looked to be insulted. "It is better to smell of hair oil than of the gardenia flower. Yes? No?" he whispered. "Speaking of gringos—you sound like one."

"Good." Joaquin inclined his head and gave a nod. He had always enjoyed their special camaraderie, which made them more like brothers than friends.

"Did you send the wire?" Lino asked, his tone now serious.

Joaquin was careful to keep his voice low so he wouldn't draw attention to himself. "Yes. They have no record of Mauger having ever been in San Quentin."

"But of course he was there."

"I know it and you know it, but somehow the records have gotten lost . . . or been stolen . . . maybe even erased."

Lino's dark eyes squinted as he considered the possibilities. "Interesting."

"Very."

"Sounds like it might be worth a few inquiries."

Lino looked past Joaquin. "By the way, where's your guide?"

"Outside in the cab. Come, let me introduce you."

A cold, wet fog hung low over the city, muffling the sharp sounds of the early morning traffic.

The hansom cab was parked to the left of the hotel entrance. A Chinese boy of no more than ten sat lengthwise across the leather cushion, his small bare feet crossed at the ankles. He jumped up when he heard the two men approach and bowed in greeting.

Lino's perplexed expression amused Joaquin. "This is our guide, Hop Fong. He tells me he knows every inch of Little China."

"Every inch, huh? What about the joss houses? There's one in particular that I'm looking for. They cater to wealthy, white, opium-smokers. Do you know the one?" Lino eyed the boy with skepticism.

Hop Fong was quick to reply. "Me takee you lookee see joss house. You lookee inside, outside, under."

Lino tilted his head and gave Joaquin a sideways look. "What do you mean . . . *under*?"

"Big hole under menny joss house. Much busy. Bad mans run and hide. Police no go after bad mans in hole. Big trouble. No come out."

Lino's eyebrows drew together in a frown. He shrugged and turned to Joaquin with a look that asked if he understood the boy's pidgin English.

Joaquin's mouth hinted at a smile. "I suspect he's talking about the rumored underground tunnels. I've heard about them but have never seen them. They're supposed to be an escape route for thieves, and a place to hide shanghai victims and slaves."

"Opium dens, too," Hop Fong added.

After giving his directions to the driver, Joaquin climbed into the cab, Lino after him.

"Just one question, *amigo*." Lino switched to Spanish. "If we do find Mauger? What will you do with him? Things are not as they once were, *mi jefe*. There are many laws now and many lawmen to enforce them."

A light flickered in Joaquin's eyes as he considered Lino's question. "All these years, I have thought only of killing Mauger," he answered in the same language. "But now, *killing* him is not enough, Lino." Joaquin looked past Lino with a blank gaze. Speaking slowly, he voiced his thoughts. "I want to destroy him inch by inch. Take away everything he has, his money, his property, his respect—everything that means anything to him. Then, I'll kill him."

Walking excursions into Little China had become a popular pastime among San Francisco's elite—except when the Tongs were at war. Then, the Chinese hatchet men stationed themselves in obscure doorways and alleys with their sharp-edged weapons and waited to chop down members of rival Tongs.

The trio headed toward Grant Street. Their progress was slowed by throngs of fruit peddlers, pastrymen, and fish sellers hawking and thrusting their wares at timorous Chinese houseboys, who wore long white blouses and padded slippers. From every direction came the tinkling sounds of the money changers' coins and the beckoning calls of fortune-tellers.

They walked on, deeper and deeper into Little China, and finally stopped in front of a joss house decorated with red paper strips. The boy started up the steps, but Lino stopped him mid-stride.

"No," he told him, touching the child's thin shoulder. "This isn't the one. I remember there were two stone dragons by the steps."

The boy's eyes widened and his mouth dropped open. His copper-tinctured skin turned pale. "You not say you want dragon joss. That bad house. Muchee trouble. Tong mans all over. Tong mans no likee Hop Fong. Say too muchee talkee—talkee all time.''

Joaquin reached into his pocket and pulled out a handful of greenbacks. He rubbed them against each other as he watched the boy's face. "Tong mans right. Hop Fong too muchee talkee. But if you want to get paid, you'll take us where we want to go.''

The boy made a wry face. "Me no likee, but me takee. It cost you menny greenbacks.''

Joaquin shrugged.

Hop Fong led them down Dupont Street, past the area called the Queen's Room, where lewd Cantonese slave girls cried out obscenities and insults while being examined and bid upon by rich Chinese merchants.

For an area that was only six blocks long and a little more than one block wide, it seemed to Joaquin there were far too many people. His eyes passed over each face. He was relying entirely on Lino's sketch, knowing that his own memory of Mauger had dulled, and that the man had obviously taken pains to change not only his looks but his manners.

Shops of every kind—tinners, spectacle-makers, cobblers—were crowded into nooks and crannies a cockroach would have considered uninhabitable.

The sights, sounds, and smells of Little China reminded Joaquin of those first months he and Rosita had spent in the gold camps: Hornitos, Murphy's, Chinese Camp, Volcano, and others. Steam billowed out of the doors and windows of laundries to mingle with smoke from the tobacco stores. He tried to conjure up a long-ago picture of Rosita and nothing came; the only woman he could visualize was red-haired and brown-eyed. He shook himself to clear his head of her image.

Finally, they reached the dragon joss. It was an unimposing building, except for the two stone dragons that flanked the steps leading to a red-doored entry. A Chinaman with a heavily oiled queue answered Joaquin's knock and questioned his purpose in Chinese.

Hop Fong stepped between Joaquin and the doorkeeper. Haltingly, he spoke a few words to the man, who eyed him dubiously. After a moment, the door opened. Once inside, they were escorted through a wide hallway and then through another door that revealed a sloping wooden ramp that led into a dark passageway.

The door banged shut behind them. Instinctively, Joaquin and Lino reached for their weapons, concealed beneath their coats. In his pidgin English, Hop Fong assured them that there was no danger.

"What did you say to the doorkeeper to let us in?" Joaquin pulled the bottom edge of his coat back over the bowie sheathed at his waist.

"Me say you and other mista want buy muchee poppy. That okay?"

Joaquin nodded.

The dark passageway narrowed and led them into a labyrinth of connecting basements and tunnels. Their coat sleeves grazed against muddied walls. Both men pulled up short when they heard the sound of squealing, hungry rats. The air, sultry and oppressive, was thick and heavy with stupefying smoke and the sickly sweet smell of opium.

"This must be Hell," Lino said in a choked voice.

"No, I've been to Hell. It's worse than this." There was no mistaking the cold cynicism in Joaquin's voice.

The boy took a quick right and stopped. Resisting the urge to rub his burning eyes, Joaquin peered through the vapor at a wide opening that led into an opium den. He moved in closer, straining to see beyond the feeble yellow light of the opium lamps. The room, raggedly carved out of the earth, was little more than a rabbit warren with bunks laid with straw. The only sound came from the sputtering of the smoking pipes. Then a man laughed. Joaquin abruptly turned. A pig-tailed Chinaman smiled back at him with a toothless grin.

At last, satisfied that Mauger was not among the smokers, they moved on. Finally, they came to the end of a tunnel. With an expression of tired disappointment, Joaquin said, "We'll try again tomorrow." Hop Fong led them up a flight of steep steps that exited into a Chinese laundry. Outside, Joaquin thanked the boy and handed him three crisp greenbacks. "Meet us at the dragon joss tomorrow at ten o'clock."

A delighted grin split the boy's small face. He bowed and left.

Lino hailed a passing cab. "I don't know about you, but I could use a drink. Join me?"

Joaquin pulled himself from his thoughts to answer. "No, thanks. I seem to recall the last time we went drinking together, and you ordered a sarsaparilla. We ended up shooting our way out of the cantina."

"That was a very long time ago, *mi amigo*. And it was a joke, if you recall."

Just as the cab driver was reining his horse to a stop, another cab pulled up and a man stepped out.

Something in the way the man moved alerted Joaquin. Then he heard him laugh. From beneath the brim of his hat, Joaquin scrutinized the man's face.

Luther Mauger.

Mauger was giving his driver instructions. "I'll need you to pick me up here at midnight. And don't be late."

Joaquin's chest filled with a hot rage. It was everything he could do to stop himself from reaching for his knife—everything and more. He had waited seventeen long years to kill Mauger, but common sense

stopped him. Now that he had found him, there would
be time—time to destroy Mauger in all the ways he
had imagined. It would be worth the wait, he told himself.

Fearful that his demeanor would give him away, Joaquin moved behind Lino. He couldn't ever remember
feeling such consuming hate and anger. His head ached
with it. His stomach roiled with it. His body felt as
taut as a hanging rope.

The breeze off the ocean turned cold and began
whipping up gusts. Luther Mauger pulled a greenback
out of his coat pocket and handed it to the driver. He
leaned against the wheel while waiting for his change.
The wind ripped the bill out of the driver's hand and
shot it over the horse's head. The animal lunged forward, panicked by the flying money.

"You stupid son of a bitch. Can't you control that
goddamn animal?"

"I'm sorry, sir. The wind . . ."

Mauger threw the driver a savage look and stormed
off into Little China.

"We've changed our minds," Lino said to the cab
driver he'd hailed. He flipped the man a coin and
caught up with Joaquin, who was walking a discreet
distance behind Luther Mauger.

"Welcome to Hell, *amigo,*" said Joaquin when Lino
came up beside him.

Lino gave a weak smile. *"Muchas gracias, mi jefe."*

Chapter 4

A loud banging in the next room forced Heller awake. She mumbled in aggravation. She didn't want to get up—not just yet, anyway. Soon enough she would have to face herself, Abigail, and the new day and whatever it held. But for the moment, she was still alone.

She rolled over and groaned. The slight pain that accompanied the movement brought on an even more painful memory. She groaned again—this time from despair. Dear God, how had an attempt to rescue Abigail turned into the most humiliating experience of her life? Fragmented images of Abigail falling, the gleam of a steel blade, and devil-black eyes flashed beneath her closed eyelids. Inside her head, Don Ricardo's words echoed, "stupid female vanity," and "you, me fine Irish lass, are no lady."

She flung the coverlet aside, sat up and hugged her knees to her chest. She leaned her head back and stared at the ceiling, visualizing the moments prior to the locomotive's arrival. She'd had such idealistic thoughts—how she would be the best cultural secretary the Board of Trade ever had—how she would regale Elizabeth Pennyworth with anecdotes about the important people she met and the sights she had seen—how she would prove to herself once and for all that she had indeed become a "lady."

She proved herself all right—proved what a vainglorious goose she was. At the first crisis, everything she had learned about propriety and circumspection had been forgotten. Worse yet was the way she had reverted back to her Irish brogue! That was the one thing she thought she had sure conquered!

Disgusted, she lowered her head and sank her chin into the valley between her knees. How could she face today or Abigail? God forbid she should ever run into Don Ricardo again, or that waspish Señorita Valdez. How many days, months, years would it take to erase the memory from her mind? What a joke! The answer was never. She wasn't the kind of person who could easily dismiss such things. Abigail called it a character flaw, but some things could not be overcome, no matter how one tried.

With those uneasy thoughts, she grabbed her pillow, squeezed it into a ball, and pitched it across the room.

"Oooh!" Abigail cried out, the pillow hitting her directly in the face as she peered around the adjoining door.

Heller sprang from the bed and ran barefoot across the room to assist Abigail, who was swatting at the storm of feathers which had sprung from a hole in the pillow. "Why, Heller Peyton!" Abigail sputtered, spitting fluffs of goose down. "Of all the childish things to do." Peevishly, she resisted Heller's awkward attempts to help her and found her own way to a nearby chair.

"Oh, Aunty, I can't tell you how sorry I am. I didn't see you. I was just so angry . . . and . . . and I . . . I was thinking about this morning . . . and what a fool I made of myself. Did I hurt you?" She started plucking feathers from Abigail's bodice and tightly-coiled chignon.

"Do not prattle, child," Abigail scolded, waving Heller away like a pesky fly. "I am perfectly fine. A little startled at such an unexpected welcome, but physically unharmed.'' Even discomfited, Abigail retained her stiffly correct demeanor.

Heller retrieved the pillow from the floor. Instinct warned that Abigail would not let the incident go without discussion, and within seconds, Abigail proved to be her predictable self.

''I wanted to have another look at your injury and thought I would catch you before you started dressing.'' Abigail motioned for Heller to come stand in front of her, then lift her shift. ''Does it hurt much, dear?'' she asked as she snipped the bandage away with her ornate silver embroidery scissors.

Heller leaned over to look and winced. ''It's a little tender. I hope you're not mad at me for falling asleep while you were dressing it. I couldn't seem to stay awake.''

''Not at all, dear. It seems on the mend, but do not wear a corset until it is completely healed. The pressure might prevent it from healing properly.''

Heller was appalled. ''Not wear a corset? Surely, with the bandage covering it . . .'' She moved to stand in front of the bureau mirror to have a better look. A moist scab now covered a hole the size of her thumbnail. ''I suppose you're right.'' She turned back to Abigail, who was waiting with salve and a fresh bandage.

Abigail nodded approval and secured the bandage. ''Now, do you care to tell me why I received a pillow in my face as a welcome?''

''I already told you. I was a little angry, that's all.'' She hoped her offhanded answer would suffice.

''A *little* angry? You almost knocked me over. I would say you were *very* angry, Heller Peyton. I thought your *dear* Miss Pennyworth taught you to keep a better rein on that Irish temper of yours.''

Disheartened, Heller confided, "She did. It was my failing, not hers. I completely forgot myself—everything I've learned. I acted like . . . like the little heathen I was before you took me in. After all you've done to help me, I feel I've let you down."

Abigail stood up and snorted in disdain. "Oh, for heaven's sake, Heller. You were distraught. You had just been stabbed, or so you thought. You woke up in a strange room, with strange people muddling about you. You were frightened and confused. Who would not have acted a bit out of sorts? The fact is, young lady, I am proud of you. I very much doubt I would have been so brave had the situation been reversed." Lowering her voice, she added lovingly, "You risked your life, Heller, risked it to save mine." She reached out and squeezed Heller's hand.

Heller smiled tremulously and shook her head. "Oh, Aunty. I have such high hopes. Such ambitions. I do so want to make you proud of me. I want Alexander Rice to feel he made the right choice—that I'm worthy of his faith and trust. He was so kind to go to such lengths to get me appointed as cultural secretary." She smoothed her shift down over her breasts and hips. "That man—that Señor Montaños— He said things to me that— He belittled me, humiliated me. And he enjoyed it!"

She shot away, flounced down on the edge of the bed, and stared at the wall. Seconds later, with a glassy-eyed look, she added, "There's something very strange about him. He's not like anyone I've ever met. He made me feel defenseless and vulnerable. I don't like that. It makes me uncomfortable, and yet . . . Oh, I don't know." Thinking, she ran her fingertip over her lower lip, then bit down on the nail. She looked up at Abigail and realized she had been rambling. She pulled a smile and waved a hand as if to erase her

words. "It was horrid. *He* was horrid. I hope to God
I never run into him again!"

Eyeing Heller with a look of curious surprise, Abigail gave her own analysis of Don Ricardo Montaños.
"I know dear, but once he explained himself, it was
quite easy to see why he acted as he did." She smiled
and gave a little laugh. "You know, he reminds me of
your father in many ways. The same arrogance. That
infuriatingly bold confidence. That air of indomitable
strength. Quite an interesting man, if I do say so, and
so compelling. And handsome. Very handsome. All
very dangerous qualities in a man—from a woman's
point of view, of course." With a twinkle in her eye,
she looked directly at Heller.

A much too vivid picture of Don Ricardo came to
mind, and Heller swallowed against the knot constrict-
ing her throat. Yes, she thought, he was all the things
Abigail said, only *handsome* didn't come close to an
adequate description of his unique brand of good
looks. It was doubtful there was one adequate word.
He was indeed very handsome, darkly handsome, rug-
gedly handsome, roguishly handsome. One adjective
alone simply couldn't suffice. And the way he moved—
with such assurance. She remembered him striding
toward her, grasping her, holding her. A prickly sensation spread across the back of her neck. Power. He
exuded power. Not just the physical kind, but a vitality
of body and spirit.

Never having known her father, she couldn't see the
similarities Abigail pointed out—but she could relate
them to her own personal hero, El Cid, the coura-
geous, eleventh-century Spanish warrior whose heroic
deeds had become legendary. A portrait of the Cid
hung in one of the Boston museums that she had visited with Elizabeth Pennyworth three years ago and
had dreamed about him ever since.

Heller shook her head, clearing her thoughts. She jumped off the bed and padded over to the mirror and began brushing her hair with a vengeance. "I admit that he does have a *certain* masculine appeal that many women would find somewhat irresistible." Her voice was cold, flat. "But not me. He's much too arrogant and extremely crude . . . obviously not a gentleman!" she said, enunciating the last with pronounced emphasis, hoping to convince Abigail.

Abigail peered at Heller's reflection in the mirror above the bureau. On her niece's face was that damnable Elizabeth Pennyworth expression Heller had adopted as her own. But this time it did not anger her as it usually did. It was, thank goodness, only a facade after all. She had suspected it all along and now she had proof. The real Heller—the vivacious, passionate Heller—had survived Elizabeth Pennyworth's prudish teachings and was still very much intact. She had glimpsed her during her analysis of Don Ricardo. Holding back a smug rejoinder, she checked her timepiece and suggested Heller hurry with her toilette. "We have an eventful day of sight-seeing ahead of us. So you had best hurry. It would not do to be late."

"Ladies and gentlemen, please, may I have your attention?"

The chattering group gathered in the flower-bedecked hotel lobby and quieted at Alexander Rice's projected voice. "I want to remind everyone that we will be meeting here in the lobby at this same time tomorrow morning. Now, everyone bound for the inspection of the China steamer, *Japan*, please follow Mr. Eldridge outside. Those of you taking the city tours, I've enlisted the aid of members of the San Francisco Chamber of Commerce to provide transportation and to act as your personal guides."

Heller glanced at Abigail, who was frowning. Before leaving their rooms, Abigail had expressed her desire to undertake their own self-guided tour—at their own pace.

"Ladies." A man's voice drew Heller's attention away from Alexander Rice. "If I may introduce myself," he said, doffing his hat with the exaggerated flair of a dandy, "I'm Gordon Pierce. The chamber has appointed me your guide and escort." With his hat removed, his perfectly groomed blond hair gleamed in the sunlight streaming through the tall windows that flanked the hotel entrance.

Heller saw Abigail acknowledge Mr. Pierce's presence with a regal nod. Then her expression turned to astonishment when he reached for and shook her hand. "Oh— Oh, yes. How do you do?" She pulled her hand back and held it close to her body. "I am Abigail Peyton, and this is my niece, Miss Heller Peyton. You will have to excuse my surprise; we were not aware until just a second ago that we would be assigned an escort." She gave him a thorough all-over glance. "However . . . you may prove useful after all. I assume you have knowledge of the city's most popular entertainments." Her cultured voice was leaden with intimidation, a ploy she often affected with strangers.

Gordon Pierce's smile vanished. Stiffly, he bowed from the waist. "I am here to serve you, madam." His voice seemed noticeably strained, his air of confidence having gone the same way as his smile. "I— or rather, we—the members of the chamber, want to do everything we can to make your visit here a memorable one."

Heller checked her amusement. Abigail had clearly abashed the man. His ego seemed to have crumbled before her eyes but to his credit, he quickly recuperated.

"Today must be my lucky day. It isn't often I have the honor to escort two such lovely ladies about town." His hazel eyes, shadowed by heavy, hooded lids, lingered on Heller, scrutinizing her too closely to be considered good manners.

Resentful of his close study, which seemed to take in everything from the tip of her plumed hat to the tips of her shoes, Heller forced a smile of flattered thanks, then straightened her posture and half-turned to watch the queue of Bostonians leaving the hotel.

"What will it be first, ladies?" Gordon Pierce asked with enthusiasm. "Little China? The business district? Or what about Woodward's Gardens? I haven't been there since they brought in the black swans or the seals."

This, Heller decided, was her aunt's decision. With total indifference to the suggestions and to the man standing across from her, she worked starched white gloves over her hands, smoothing away imaginary wrinkles from her fingers.

Abigail appeared to be considering her options, but before she could reply, Gordon Pierce boldly sidled up next to her and offered her his elbow. He did the same to Heller, who reluctantly accepted and followed his lead out of the hotel to a shiny new park phaeton, drawn by a pair of perfectly matched bays.

By mid-morning, the sun had burned off the fog. Throughout the day, a stiff breeze played havoc with the feather in Heller's hat. Once they returned to the hotel, she vowed to hang up her hat and leave it there for the duration of their stay. Her bad mood, she admitted to herself—for she knew she was irritably sullen and churlish—was probably a carryover from her early morning misadventure. She had been eager to dislike Mr. Pierce, or any other man that crossed her path. But after an hour of surprisingly enjoyable sight-seeing, she found herself tempering her resentfulness and trying to make an effort to be pleasant.

Gordon Pierce was a personable and well-favored man—though not actually handsome—with light blond hair, deep-set hazel eyes, and a dark mustache that gave him a mark of distinctiveness. She guessed him to be in his early forties. He was a native Californian, Heller learned, who was in the business of importing goods from all around the world, and he owned a home on Rincon Hill.

After a delightful tour of Woodward's Gardens, Heller decided that, in spite of a few oddities, Mr. Pierce was not only a good guide but a charming escort. Maybe all wasn't lost after all.

Stopping for tea before returning to the hotel, Heller recorded her first journal entry, which she would eventually submit to Alexander Rice as a permanent record of their excursion. She wrote: *For such a young settlement—only twenty-four years old—San Francisco is architecturally and economically advanced. Her citizens can justify more than a modicum of civic pride. One very noticeable example of the city's architectural advancement is her newly built Grand Hotel, where the Board of Trade has accommodations. Aside from the tasteful decor, the hotel has been designed with all the latest conveniences, including an astonishing new telegraphic system that allows room-to-room and room-to-hotel office communication!*

Abagail smiled at Heller's concentration. She could hardly wait to read Heller's writings and compare their observations. Though as equally enamored with the city as she knew her niece was, Abagail found herself more than a little curious about their escort. For some reason—she couldn't quite put her finger on it—Mr. Gordon Pierce raised her suspicions. He was definitely a charmer, she thought; perhaps a little too charming, she thought again, eyeing him from beneath her bonnet. His social protocol was peculiar—as when he shook her hand, and his too bold physical assessment of Heller. If she had not personally seen to Heller's training in the art of social graces, she might not have been mindful of his actions. Even though the rules and codes governing Boston society might differ from San Francisco's, there were some universal basics that Mr. Pierce performed most peculiarly.

Still and all, Abigail thought, it wouldn't be fair to render judgment until she knew more about the man. Even if he wasn't of good family and breeding, he could still be a gentleman, albeit a self-made one. She was not so *Boston* that she judged a man's worth by his family name, or the size of his bank account.

On the way back to the hotel, Gordon drove them along Montgomery Street, with its crowded two- and three-story buildings. He displayed a rare pride, thought Abigail, in the city itself, and commented enthusiastically on everything from the cobblestone streets to the gaslamps. Despite her suspicions, it delighted Abigail to see Heller let down her guard and enjoy herself. Such moments had become rare since Heller's graduation from the Pennyworth Academy For Young Ladies.

The Foxhall Theater, San Francisco's newest and finest entertainment establishment, had been built at the beginning of the year. Tonight, the mirrored lobby was filled to capacity with San Francisco and Boston's *bon ton*, dressed in all their feathered, furred, and jeweled finery. Heller wore an exquisite Worth evening gown of pink-coral gros grain and overskirt of point lace, draped behind *en panier*. A wreath of pink blossoms nestled in her hair, and a pearl necklace, accented by a coral medallion, dipped low into her bodice and nestled at the top of her breasts.

Gordon Pierce, elegant in his black swallow-tailed coat, stiffened white shirt, and ascot tie studded with a large brilliant diamond, introduced Heller and Abigail to several of his fellow chamber members and their wives.

For the purpose of her journal, Heller carefully made mental notes of the peoples' names, the fashions, and the various topics of conversation—items that would be important to those board members who hadn't made the journey.

The most popular topic of conversation was the Franco-Prussian conflict. Heller overheard Gordon tell Abigail that the San Francisco's *Alta* had reported that the King of Prussia and Bismarck had gone to Enis, where the czar was. Robert Swain added that speculation was running high on whether or not Napoleon and his forces could hold him off if a confrontation occurred.

Fighting off an itchy nose, Heller glanced around her for the source of her distress. Conservatory-sized baskets of hot-house roses, suspended from the lobby's domed ceiling, brought to mind what she had read about the legendary hanging gardens of Babylon. Roses, because of the allergic effect they had on her, were not her favorite flower. She could only hope they didn't have too much longer to wait before the performance began.

Abigail stepped back from the circle of conversation and touched Heller's arm. "Why, look, dear. Is that not Señor Montaños?"

Heller looked up from hunting her handkerchief in her bag. Indeed it was Señor Montaños. An unexpected tremor of anticipation bubbled at the base of her spine, radiated up her back, and across her shoulders. The handkerchief was forgotten when she saw him glance around and meet her gaze. He walked toward her, his black evening cape, lined with red satin, flared open to reveal a magnificently tailored swallow-tailed coat, white silk shirt, and close-fitting black trousers. His stride was long and sure—like a cat stalking an unwary bird. His eyes glinted with a mischievous sparkle as if he were reading her thoughts—thoughts no lady would dare to think.

He was within a yard of reaching her when she sneezed. Her follow-me-lad curls bounced like coach springs against her naked shoulders. Again she dug into her bag to search for her handkerchief.

Just as a second sneeze threatened, a large white handkerchief was waved before her. Heller accepted it without hesitation and just in time.

"At your service, Señorita Peyton."

It was a moment before Heller felt safe enough to answer. "Thank you," she said, trying to regain her composure. "What an unexpected surprise to see you again." She extended a gloved hand, fully expecting him to take it in greeting, but instead, it was Abigail's hand that he reached for and touched to his lips.

"Señora Peyton, it is a pleasure to see you again. Are you enjoying your stay here in San Francisco?"

With a nonchalance she was far from feeling, Heller discreetly lowered her hand and hid it within the folds of her gown.

Seeming not to notice her niece's embarrassment, Abigail answered with aplomb. "Indeed I am, señor. San Francisco is quite different from what I expected—though what I expected, I am not actually certain, if you understand what I mean."

"Yes. I understand. It's been many years since I last visited San Francisco. Much has changed. I remember it as being little more than a pueblo."

When he laughed at something Abigail said, Heller saw him flash her a look of undisguised amusement, and she stiffened with anger.

Gordon Pierce excused himself to Robert Swain and turned to the newcomer. "Miss Peyton, will you be so kind as to introduce me to your friend?"

"Friend?" Her voice rose. Why would Gordon assume Don Ricardo was her friend? "No, you misunderstand. We aren't friends. No indeed. We met by accident in the crowd when—" Beneath the hem of her gown, Heller felt Abigail's foot bear down on hers. She made an abrupt gesture of apology. "I'm sorry. I quite forgot myself. Señor Montaños, may I present Mr. Gordon Pierce, of the San Francisco Chamber of Commerce. Mr. Pierce has been assigned to escort us to our activities throughout our stay."

Blood pounded against Joaquin's temples as his gaze met that of his enemy, Luther Mauger. Joaquin nodded formally to Heller's escort. Then, lowering his head, he whispered to Heller, "I'm pleased to see that you recuperated from your ordeal."

Heller's lips formed a sharp retort, but just as she was about to speak, the pressure of Abigail's censure increased. Thinking better of her reply, she contented herself with a searing look, which he acknowledged with an expression of surprise.

Pierce moved closer. "What ordeal?"

Heller bit down on her lip. Damn the Spaniard for causing her to have to explain. And damn Gordon Pierce for being so rude to ask what was obviously not meant for his ears. Men! "Señor Montaños exaggerates, I'm afraid. After leaving the train, we ran into the throng heading for the podium and were jostled about. Señor Montaños helped us out of the crowd into the hotel." Her raised eyebrow and tight mouth sent a warning to the Spaniard to keep silent—a warning which he visibly shrugged off but didn't breech.

"I'm sorry to hear that," said Pierce. "We—meaning the chamber—had no idea how many people would participate. We needed more police, I suppose." He waved his hand. "On the other hand, the very fact that so many did turn out is a tribute to you, Heller, and your group, and testimony that the people of San Francisco are anxious to receive what the Board of Trade has offered."

Lino was right, Joaquin thought, staring at Mauger, willing himself to appear as if nothing was out of the ordinary. Luther Mauger was not the man he used to be, at least not in front of San Francisco society. He was Gordon Pierce now, a member of the San Francisco Chamber of Commerce. Gordon Pierce, a well-to-do businessman. Gordon Pierce, a respected member of the community. Gordon Pierce, Heller and Abigail Peyton's escort.

Joaquin could have almost believed Luther's transformation was real if he hadn't followed him into Little China and seen him purchase a box of opium and haggle over a Cantonese slave girl.

Leaving Little China, they had followed him to his fancy Rincon Hill house and sat for hours watching and making plans.

Joaquin clenched his fists at his sides, hating Mauger as he had hated no other. His jaw and neck muscles bunched and knotted and his mouth went dry as the Cantua creek bed. Soon, he promised himself, the day, the hour, the moment would come when the waiting would be over and he would have his revenge. Not today, or tomorrow, but soon, when he had done everything he'd set out to do and Mauger's destruction was complete. Relaxing his hands, Joaquin turned his gaze on Mauger. "Have we met before, Señor Pierce?

You seem somehow familiar to me.'' He felt an icy chill seep into his chest. He had to know if Mauger recognized him. Only then could he decide how to proceed.

Eyes narrowed and hooded, Gordon Pierce met Joaquin's gaze. He seemed to consider the question carefully before answering. "Yes. I do remember . . .'' he started, then stopped abruptly. "Weren't you at the Fernandez fiesta last winter?''

Joaquin expelled the breath he had been holding. "No.'' He shook his head. "I spend most of my time in San Diego working our ranch and attending to family affairs. I come to San Francisco only occasionally on business. But I seem to remember you from somewhere other than San Francisco. Angels Camp, perhaps. Or Murphy's Diggings?'' The breeze from a group of people walking past brought Joaquin the spicy scent of Mauger's hair oil. No wonder Heller was sneezing. It was awful.

Quickly, too quickly, Mauger answered, chuckling. "This is beginning to feel like an inquisition, but the answer is really very simple. I've never been to any of those places you mentioned.''

Joaquin crossed his arms and leaned back on his heels. He was pushing Mauger, and he could feel his unease. "At a cattle auction, perhaps? My family is in the business of breeding longhorns. That's why I'm here, for the auction, to sell a few of my prize bulls.''

Before Gordon Pierce could comment further, Heller interrupted. "I'm sure your señorita will buy anything you have to sell, Señor Montaños. Oooh—ouch!''

Camouflaging Heller's small, pained cry, Abigail dropped her string bag. "Oh, my goodness. How clumsy of me.''

Gordon Pierce had no sooner retrieved it and handed it back, than another chamber member greeted him with a hardy handshake, which led to a second round of introductions and a new topic of conversation.

Joaquin listened to Mauger's every word—watched his every move. The bastard was an accomplished actor. No one, not even Abigail Peyton, whom he guessed to be more astute than her niece, would guess that Gordon Pierce was anything other than the perfect gentleman he pretended to be. Joaquin noted the way the man looked at Heller—as if she was one of his possessions—and he was sure of one thing. Mauger wanted her.

Turning a worried frown on Heller, he studied her eyes and her expressions for telltale signs of how she felt about Mauger. He saw blatant indifference and breathed a sigh of relief. Mauger wasn't her type. He doubted she even knew what her type was. Despite her age—well past being a debutante and nearly past the respectable age of marriageability—she seemed incredibly naive about men, a factor that made her all the more interesting. Had she been engaged and left at the altar, or was her spinsterhood by choice? Any man who would leave Heller Peyton at the altar was a fool. In her pink gown, she was even more beautiful than he remembered. And her hair, despite the silly curls, looked like spun copper. Never in his life had he wanted to reach out and touch something so badly.

An unbidden thought—Mauger doing to Heller what he had done to Rosita—made Joaquin catch his breath and sent a shiver of fear through his body. He slid his hand up under his coat until he felt the carved hilt of his knife.

Don't let anybody see it. Just move up next to him and stab him while he's looking directly at you.

He couldn't help but imagine how good it would feel to plunge his knife into Mauger's heart, to know that finally, after all these years, he had kept his promise of revenge.

What are you waiting for? By the time Mauger realizes he's been stabbed, you can be long gone.

He had never given much thought about what would happen to him if and when he did find and kill Mauger. Somehow, the consequences of his act of revenge had never entered his mind. Probably because they didn't matter; there was no price he wouldn't gladly pay.

Under the cover of his coat, he slipped the knife from its sheath.

Kill him. Kill him. Kill him.

He hesitated a moment longer to allow his thoughts free rein. Once he stabbed Mauger, it would all be over: the waiting, the searching, the hate. Though logic told him a man could only die once, Joaquin knew better; he had died many times over the years. There were all kinds of deaths; the ending of a life was only one.

He thought about the plans he and Lino were making to destroy Luther Mauger. How many times would Mauger die if all their plans were fulfilled? Unerringly, he guided the tip of his knife back into its leather sheath, then dropped his hand to his side. For once he would be patient—like Lino—and wait for exactly the right moment.

Overhead, the gaslit chandelier flickered and dimmed, signaling that the time had come for everyone to begin taking their seats. Relieved that his moment of indecision was now beyond his control, Joaquin stepped back and bowed. "I hope you enjoy the performance, Señorita Peyton." His eyes locked with hers as he dipped his head.

"I'm sure I will." Her voice was as ungiving as a new saddle.

Abigail wound her arm around Gordon Pierce's elbow and pulled him into the mainstream of the people heading into the theater. "We must hurry to our seats. We would not want to miss the start."

Before Heller could turn to join them, Joaquin captured her gloved hand in his. "I had hoped you would forgive me, but I see you have not."

Heller gasped and tried to pull her hand away. "Release me this moment or I'll—"

"You'll what? Scream? Stomp your feet? I hardly think so; it wouldn't be seemly for a *lady* to be seen having a temper tantrum." Out of the corner of his eye, Joaquin saw Abigail and Luther Mauger disappear up the stairs.

"What is it you want, señor? Forgiveness? All right. I forgive you because that's the charitable thing to do, but I will never forget how you humiliated me!"

"Humiliated you? How? By getting you out of that crowd after you fainted? By tending your wound and stopping you from bleeding to death? By expressing my disgust for corsets, which at least, you had the good sense not to wear tonight." He ran his hand down her back and smiled. "Or could it be that you simply resent me for knowing you aren't who you pretend to be?"

"I—" Heller's eyes flashed with indignation, and he knew he had hit a sensitive nerve.

He released her hand and grasped her upper arm. "Listen to me, Boston." He pulled her toward him until their bodies touched. "There will always be impostors, some of them, like you, are only trying to change their image. But there are others who pretend to be someone they aren't because they have secrets they need to hide." He lifted her chin and gazed into her angry eyes—liquid brown eyes. "I know you don't understand what I'm talking about, and I pray to God you never will, but I think you should be warned. You have to stop being so trusting of people. You shouldn't believe everything people tell you." He brushed a golden wisp of hair off her cheek. "Gordon Pierce, for instance. What do you know about the man?" Her questioning look stopped him from saying more. If he told her the truth about her escort, he could very well destroy his own plans, yet if he didn't . . . Would she become a victim like Rosita? God, he could never live with himself if that happened. He felt cornered, trapped, for he knew that from this moment on Heller Peyton would stand between him and Luther Mauger, not because she wanted to, but because Luther would use her for his own gain.

Joaquin had not intended to kiss her, at least not until he saw her lips part. Then he couldn't resist. She was so damn beautiful standing here, her face as pink as her gown, and her hair shining like El Dorado gold. And she smelled good, too—like lemons. Fresh and clean. He pulled her closer and reached his other hand behind her head. She was smaller than he remembered; the top of her head fit just beneath his chin. Small. Delicate. Soft. Feminine.

And she wasn't fighting him. Resisting, but not fighting.

He looked down at her upturned face. He felt her warm breath against his neck. Damn!

He lowered his head and touched his lips to hers. He felt her body convulse, then relax—almost go limp. He steadied her with increased pressure—pressure that brought her tightly against his length—so tight he could feel the crush of her breasts. Her moist mouth invited exploration and the sweet taste of her released a long pent-up desire. *Dios,* she was everything he imagined she would be; a little bit girl, a little bit woman, a little bit whore. He felt like a randy youth experiencing his first kiss. He considered sweeping her up into his arms and carrying her off, then realized the absurdity of such a thought. This was 1870, for God's sake. Not medieval England. And he was no barbarian.

He tore his lips from Heller's and drew back.

"I'm sorry. I shouldn't have done that." He held out a hand to her, but she twisted out of his reach.

"It's a heathen you are, Don Ricardo. An uncivilized savage, with the manners of a goat!" She stomped away.

Joaquin threw his head back and laughed. Everything about her was so damn desirable, even the Irish in her.

"*Hasta luego*, Boston."

Feeling flushed and light-headed, Heller clumsily swept into the richly draped center-stage box and took her seat, careful to to avoid eye contact with Abigail, who was certain to have something to say about her unpardonable behavior. But nothing her aunt would say could equal what Heller was saying to herself. In the few minutes it had taken to flee the lobby, climb the stairs and find Gordon's box, she had called herself every name she could think of for allowing Don Ricardo to kiss her, and a few other names—names from Cow Bay—to describe the way she had kissed him back.

She felt Abigail's eyes watching her but refused to acknowledge her look. The timely arrival of Charles Crocker, whom she had met earlier, in the next box took Abigail's attention and left Heller to the agony of her thoughts . . . and her still racing heart. She wrung her hands together so hard her knuckles cracked. Men—handsome, rich men—had kissed her before, but never like that. No one would have dared! A bead of sweat ran down from her temple. She reached into the sleeve of her gown for the handkerchief. *His handkerchief!* She let it go and watched it fall to the floor, where she pushed it out of sight beneath her chair with the heel of her shoe. If only her thoughts of Don Ricardo were as easily dismissed. The truth of the matter was that had he kissed her other than in the theater lobby—someplace private—she would have encouraged him to continue. In spite of the fact that this was only their second encounter, it seemed obvious to Heller that Don Ricardo had the uncanny ability to bring out the worst in her. He also made her realize that all these years she had been lying to herself, telling herself that she didn't want a man. But what she'd meant was that she didn't want a husband governing her life, telling her what she could and couldn't do. That was entirely different from wanting a man to make love to her. She shivered at the directness of her thoughts. Somewhere along the line, she had fancied herself above those baser human instincts. The reality of her own desire was like a slap in the face.

With her emotions in a turmoil, the last thing she wanted was to spend the next two hours pretending to enjoy herself. She wanted to go back to the hotel. Wanted to go *home*. To Boston. Nothing was going as planned. Things were quickly going from bad to worse.

From the small round table between the chairs, Heller took a program and read it quickly. The name Elena Valdez was printed in bold type across the top of the page. Heller's heart sank to an even lower level, then the overhead chandeliers dimmed and the theater was plunged into darkness.

From the orchestra pit came the first notes of a Spanish guitar. Other instruments joined in, but the guitar continued to dominate. Heller focused on the stage, her eyes not yet fully accustomed to the darkness. The footlights flared, illuminating the stage. The green velvet curtain opened and Elena Valdez, dressed in the costume of a Mexican peasant, danced out to greet her audience. With her hair fashioned in two long braids, she looked years younger than her actual age, which had to be *at least* thirty-five, Heller concluded with malice. She didn't understand why she so intensely disliked the woman, but she did.

With a jaundiced eye, Heller watched the entertainer. How very unfortunate that of all entertainments Gordon Pierce could have chosen, he had picked one starring Elena Valdez. Her gaze wandered from the stage to the audience, who were applauding loudly. Leaning forward, her gloved hands on the hardwood banister that enclosed the box, Heller searched the sea of faces. There were many she knew from the Board of Trade and new faces from the chamber, but nowhere was the one she sought. She turned her attention back to the stage, and as she did, her eyes caught a glimmer of shiny red satin in the box directly across the theater.

"Aunty! Quickly—your lorgnette!" Heller snatched the glasses out of her aunt's hands and peered across the theater to the box nearest the stage.

It was him.

She watched him take off his cape, sling it over an empty chair, and take his seat. Once settled, he poured himself a drink from the bottle on the refreshment table beside him.

Lowering the lorgnette, Heller peeked at the table next to Gordon Pierce, then at the tables in the adjoining boxes. No one else had been provided with liquid refreshment—why Don Ricardo? Who was he that he commanded such special favor? From the introductions out in the lobby, it was obvious Gordon Pierce had never met Don Ricardo before, and Gordon seemed to know everyone of importance.

Raising the handle of the lorgnette once more, she ignored the little voice that reminded her it was rude to stare. Under other circumstances, yes it was, she countered her conscience. But in this instance, staring at him freely and openly, without him or anyone else stopping her, was a sort of compensation—a very meager compensation—for the humiliation he had caused her. And after all, what was the harm if the person didn't know he was being watched?

He looked much too comfortable sitting in his deep-cushioned chair. Much too relaxed and contented—like a big black cat. His booted foot was braced on a velvet-topped stool, and his forearm lay across his upper thigh. He held the brandy glass with the stem between his fingers, his thumb rubbing the rim. The action on the stage seemed to have his complete attention. In fact, he seemed totally absorbed. She saw his right cheek twitch and the corner of his mouth lift ever so slightly. When the audience laughed, he laughed, and she was startled at how different he looked—he was even more handsome when he smiled. Then, he sipped his brandy; his lips barely touching the rim of the glass. Like a kiss, she thought, and was immediately shocked and angry at the direction of her thoughts.

Snapping the lorgnette against her gloved palm, she closed it into the silver casing and returned it to Abigail with a whisper of thanks.

Chin set and teeth clenched, she stared at the stage. It was not until the end of the first set of songs and dances, when the house lights brightened and Abigail confided that Señorita Valdez reminded her of Lola Montez, that Heller realized she had not heard a single song or seen a single dance. Instead, she had once again been listening to the voice inside her head. With a pronounced brogue, it cursed her for allowing Don

Ricardo to kiss her and berated her for enjoying it. *You're a weak-willed fool of a girl, for allowin' that scoundrel to kiss you. You should've been the one to pull away, not him! And then you should've slapped him good for his impudence! It's your mother's daughter, you are for sure, Heller O'Shay. And don't be forgettin' it!*

Heller closed her eyes and demanded the voice to stop. He had taken advantage of the circumstances and her. When she felt her eyes begin to fill with tears, she straightened and took hold of herself.

Fortified by her own resolve, she decided the best remedy—even if only temporary—was to involve herself in the performance. She laid the program in her lap, settled into her chair, and prepared to endure whatever time was left.

Again the overhead chandeliers dimmed and the footlights brightened to illuminate the stage. The new backdrop curtain was painted with Spanish scenes and vignettes of California's early mining days. Elena, now dressed in a fiery red gown trimmed with black Spanish lace, danced onto the stage. The dress fit her voluptuous body so snugly from breast to thigh that Heller was sure the seams would burst.

The theater became as still as if it were empty. Slowly, seductively, Elena dipped her hand into the bodice of her gown to retrieve a pair of castanets. She smiled at the audience, flirting with them, pretending to be unfamiliar with the use of the castanets. She clicked them once, experimentally. Twice, and looked surprised. Three times, and smiled. Then she laughed aloud and shouted, *"Olé!"*

With precisely measured movements, Elena tapped her right foot against the wooden floor. Heel, toe. Heel, toe. Heel, toe, heel. The steel taps on her shoe drummed a staccato beat that jangled Heller's nerves.

Arrogantly, Elena tossed her head, shaking her hair loose until it fell in luxurious ripples around her neck and shoulders. She lifted her arms and twined and untwined her wrists and hands above her head, all the while the clack of the castanets increasing in volume and tempo.

"*Para usted, caro mio.* For you, my love," she called out over the clacking castanets, then whirled like a living flame in a circle around the stage, her shadow a dark phantom against the curtain. Returning to center stage, she stopped and faced her audience, then bent to catch the hem of her gown and draw it slowly up over her ankle, her calf, knee, and thigh.

When Elena dropped the hem back to the floor, Heller released her breath and blinked her eyes. She had never seen such a dance, nor such a passionate dancer. The sensuous staccato of the dancer's foot-tapping against the stage floor bounced off the theater walls. Elena made the stage her world and played with all its resources.

Even without her aunt's lorgnette, Heller could see the passionate expression on Elena's face. The dancer's eyes were focused on the balcony, her red-painted lips were pursed as if readying herself for a kiss. Heller followed Elena's gaze to Don Ricardo's box.

Her heart stopped when she saw the way he was gazing back at the dancer. Unable to bear it a second longer, Heller closed her eyes and prayed for the night to end.

Chapter 5

Over the years Joaquin had seen Elena dance dozens of times, in California's gold town saloons, at Mexican fiestas, and in his own camps, to keep up the morale of his men. But never had he seen her dance as she danced tonight. She had choreographed every step to tempt and tantalize. And she was magnificent, a student no longer but a gifted artist. He was proud of her.

Her dark sultry looks, that he knew were for him and him alone, made him uneasy. He realized his feelings for her had changed. But when had it happened? All he knew was that he was no longer susceptible to her erotic gestures. Lifting the brandy glass to his lips, he tossed down the remainder of its contents. While returning the glass to the table, he happened to glance down at the audience and saw . . .

Dios!

The whole damn audience was staring at him!

Showing not a trace of the rage that swelled his veins, he slowly moved his gaze back to the stage. Above the strumming guitar, Elena shouted, *"Olé!"* and threw her arms out in front of her. From the stage, she reached out to him, then rolled her hands and drew her arms back into herself, beckoning him.

Pretending to be amused by her invitation, he laughed as he raised his hand and waved her away. But he was not amused. Not in the least. He should never have come, should have known she would find a way to get even with him for what she had called his overly solicitous behavior toward Heller Peyton.

A storm gathered within him. He tilted back his head and settled his gaze on Elena. Like honey, her seductive smile slipped from her face. The guitar demanded she resume her dancing, and when she did, her foot caught on the hem of her skirt and she clumsily missed a step.

Heller hadn't been able to keep her eyes closed for long, and now like nearly everyone else in the audience, she watched the drama between the dancer and the man in the first off-stage box, Don Ricardo. Her cheeks grew warm as the seconds passed and Elena's moves became overtly suggestive. Picking up her program, she fanned her face. She sucked greedily at the cool air and filled her lungs. Her chair, despite its cushiony softness, was fast becoming uncomfortable. She blamed her three petticoats and lifted herself to readjust her position.

Her squirming earned her a sideways look from Abigail, who said, "It's almost over, dear," and patted her hand. Shock turned Heller to stone. Surely her aunt hadn't meant to imply anything. Had she? Heller swallowed so hard her ears popped. Good grief! What if Abigail thought . . . Heller stopped herself. She didn't want to think about what Abigail might be thinking. It could be her undoing.

She arched her neck and looked straight ahead. She was being foolish. If anything, Abigail would be thinking that she was tired of sitting. Impatient to leave. Bored. Abigail was too much a lady to think anything else—just as she shouldn't think it. Only how does one stop oneself from thinking?

Out of the corner of her eye, she saw Don Ricardo finish his refreshment and glance down at the audience. Was it her imagination, or did she detect a flash of anger?

Elena's *olé's* switched Heller's attention back to the stage where she was rewarded to see the dancer stumble. She turned to see Don Ricardo's reaction and was both disappointed and relieved to see that he was gone.

A short time later, outside the theater, Heller basked in the cooler temperature and the fresh air. Never in her life had she been so glad to see a performance end. She doubted she could have endured it much longer. She longed for a breeze like the one that had made her consign her hat to the hotel room, but it was a still, windless night.

Loathe to admit it, she knew very well what the trouble was—why her pulse was racing and her body felt like she had spent the evening in front of a roaring fire. It was the observance of the sexual innuendo between Elena Valdez and Don Ricardo that had been and was now the source of her physical upheaval. It was bad enough to witness such an unseemly public display, she thought, berating herself, but unforgivable to have allowed herself to feel their passion as her own. She wondered now how she could have prevented it from happening.

Gordon Pierce escorted the two women away from the noisy exodus spilling out of the theater. Then, excusing himself, he left to see about his carriage driver.

Anxious for the evening to end, to get back to her room and forget what she'd seen and felt, Heller reached into her bag for her handkerchief, then lifted a slightly shaky hand to wipe the perspiration from her forehead.

''Why, Heller dear, you look quite fevered. Are you

in pain? Has your wound opened up?'' Abigail inquired, a look of deep concern furrowing the space between her eyebrows.

"Oh—I'm fine, thank you. Just tired. It's been a long day.'' Heller stuffed the handkerchief back into her bag, then raised her hand to stifle an appropriate yawn.

Abigail merely smiled. "Yes, indeed it has, but I must say I do not think I have ever enjoyed a performance more. I lost count of the encores. Were there six or eight? And the bouquets of roses! Why, there must have been two dozen at least. I have never seen the like. It was a crusher!''

Heller had seldom seen Abigail express so much exuberance over a performance. "A crusher!'' Heller agreed, not wanting to dampen her aunt's enthusiasm. "I can hardly wait to write about it in my journal,'' she added as an afterthought, and immediately regretted it.

Abigail beamed. "Oh yes, dear, you must. And do not spare the words—if you know what I mean. Paint it as colorfully as it was.'' A second later, her expression sobered and she amended herself. "Well, perhaps not quite as colorfully . . .''

Heller nodded, but decided it best to forgo a comment.

"Oh, and by the way, dear,'' Abigail moved to the next topic of conversation without a break, "what kept you in the lobby so long after I left? I thought you were right behind me, then, when I got to the top of the stairs you were not there.''

Heller had anticipated Abigail's questions and comments in regard to her behavior toward Don Ricardo, but she had hoped Abigail would wait until they returned to their hotel.

Luckily, Gordon Pierce's return saved Heller from having to make up a tale.

"I'm sorry for the wait, ladies. I'm afraid the cab will still be a few minutes in coming. Had I anticipated such a crowd, I would have had my driver wait for us. I had no idea Señorita Valdez was so popular. Not even Lotta Crabtree's performance last month drew this many people to the theater." Cocking his head and looking off at no one in particular, Pierce mumbled his thoughts, "You know, it's strange . . ."

Seeing his look of confusion, Heller inquired, "What is strange, Mr. Pierce?"

His attention remained unfocused. "Señorita Valdez . . . she reminds me of someone," he said, obviously thinking out loud. "I heard she's performed all over Europe, has even given command performances for several kings and queens, but I could swear I've seen her here . . . in California." He shook his head.

"Perhaps you are thinking of Lola Montez," Abigail readily supplied. "I saw her perform once in New York. Their styles are very similar."

Gordon Pierce inclined his head. "Yes, there is a similarity. I'll never forget Lola's famous, or should I say infamous, Spider Dance. I saw her in Murphy's Diggings and—" He stopped short and forcefully cleared his throat. "Excuse me, I'm afraid I lost my voice for a moment." He chuckled. "And now I've forgotten what I was going to say. Oh, well. It's not important. What is important is that I get you ladies back to the hotel. Tomorrow is a full agenda. In the morning we visit the Cliff House, then in the afternoon you need to order your costumes for the masquerade ball."

Heller listened with half-hearted interest; she already knew the agenda and what it would require of her. Tomorrow at the Cliff House, Alexander Rice would mix a vial of seawater that he had brought from the Boston harbor with water from the California shore. The ceremony signified the cultural and economic merging of the Atlantic and the Pacific. Every word of his speech would have to be recorded verbatim in her journal along with a description of the Cliff House, the weather, and an account of the attendance. She breathed a soft sigh. It was all too much to think about right now. Maybe later, after she had rested and had a chance to sort out the events of the last twenty-four hours and put them in their proper perspective. Then maybe she would be able to focus on tomorrow. Indeed, what she needed was rest, but at the rate the carriages were moving, they could all end up waiting half the night.

She was on the verge of asking if they could dispense with the formalities and walk to their carriage when she had a sense of being watched. Her skin prickled and turned to gooseflesh. She swung her head left, then right, searching for the source of the discomfiting feeling. Her search revealed nothing, yet the feeling persisted. She turned, making a complete circle.

Then she saw him.

Directly behind her, not thirty feet away, Don Ricardo stood leaning negligently against a lamppost, his arms crossed loosely in front of him. Immediately, she knew *he* was the one who had been watching her. The question was: how long had he been watching her? He uncrossed his arms and reached into his inside coat pocket and took out a long, thin cigarillo. He put the tip between his lips, then bent his head to the match. Behind his hand the match flared, casting a warm golden light upon his swarthy face and accentuating its planes and hollows. Looking up, over the ridge of his curved hand, his eyes met hers with a look that made her catch her breath.

He knew! She felt a dread chill touch every nerve in her body. He knew exactly the thoughts that had been going through her head. And worse yet, if that was possible, he knew what she had been feeling. She could read it in those devil-black eyes of his, and she could see it in the impudent way he angled his head as he continued to gaze at her.

"Ah, here we are," Gordon Pierce announced. Rudely ignoring his proffered arm, Heller hurried toward the carriage, climbed in and sat down on the opposite side, as far away from Don Ricardo's disturbing gaze as possible. After adjusting her skirts and settling into position, she sneaked a look out the window to see if he was still there, still watching her.

He was.

And he was smiling, teasing.

From out of nowhere a gust of wind came upon the waiting crowd, billowing skirts and capes, stealing programs and blowing dust and papers. A wisp of red-gold hair broke loose from her coiffure and whipped across Heller's eyes, blocking her view. She swiped the hair from her face and returned her gaze to Don Ricardo.

He was gone.

The stern lecture Heller had been prepared to receive when she returned to the hotel did not come. Conversely, Abigail seemed to purposely avoid any conversation concerning Señor Montaños or Elena Valdez, and Heller, grateful for whatever the reason, kissed her aunt and hurried off to the room next to Abigail's.

With the door closed behind her, she promised herself she would relax and try to sort out her myriad emotions. It was soon obvious, however, that the more she thought about what had happened, the more upset she became. She would have to let it go. What was done was done. Finished. With luck, she wouldn't run into Don Ricardo or Elena Valdez ever again!

After working the button hook down the back of her gown, she went about her bedtime toilette like a sleep-walker. Finally, she sat down before the dressing table and started to work on her hair, pulling out the long wooden hairpins one by one. As she removed the last pin her hair tumbled down her back and over her shoulders. She set her fingers to massaging the areas where the pins had dug into her scalp. Her head hurt, and not just from the pins, she realized sorrowfully.

A fleeting image of Elena dancing made Heller abruptly stop what she was doing. Elena Valdez was the kind of woman men lusted after. One would have to have been blind not to see the longing expressions on the men in the audience. Gazing into the mirror, Heller studied her own fair-skinned complexion and bright hair. She turned her head this way and that, raising, lowering her eyebrows, posturing her mouth, lifting a shoulder. Finally, she settled on what she thought was a seductive pose and held it. What would Don Ricardo think if he saw her like this? Would he look at her the way he'd looked at Elena Valdez?

"Bastardo!" Elena shouted. *"Cuchano! Hijo de putana!"* First you make a fool of me, then you kill me with your eyes.''

"Consider yourself lucky that it was only a *killing look,* Elena,'' Joaquin returned, his voice as cold and hard as flint. "Good night." He started toward the door of her dressing room.

"Caro mio. Wait! I do not understand your anger. I wanted only for you to grow hot with desire.''

"Your little act of seduction turned every eye in the house on me. What happened to your fears that I would be recognized?"

Elena shrieked. "Forgive me, Joaquin. I did not think!"

"You're goddamn right you didn't think. If I hadn't gotten out of there before the performance ended . . ." He shook his head. "I don't know what's gotten into you, Elena."

Crying softly, she sat down on the sofa.

Reluctantly, Joaquin sat down beside her and took her into his arms. Her tears were real, her remorse somehow unsettling. Pulling her head against his shoulder, he closed his eyes and thought about the years he and Elena had known each other. Some of them good years. Some bad. If only he could have loved her the way she wanted to be loved, his life would have been less complicated.

When, he wondered, had her love turned into an obsession? Or had it always been that way? As long as he could remember, even before marrying Rosita, there had been Elena pledging her love.

She snuggled closer and murmured. "You were intrigued by my dance, no? I make you want Elena?" Her tone cajoled.

"*Sí.* I was intrigued. More than intrigued. I've never seen you dance so well. You were *magnifico*! But you know that."

Sí. I know," she admitted as she began to unbutton his shirt. "It has been many years since I danced for you. The last time—"

Joaquin caught her hand and pulled it away. "We need to talk."

Her voice pouted. "I do not wish to talk. I want to make love."

He set her back from him and stood up.

Elena sprang to her feet. "It is that *gringa,* no?" Her eyes widened and her face contorted with rage. "I knew it. I knew by the look in your eyes that you wanted her. It was the same way you looked at Rosita!" She challenged him with her eyes, then reached out a hand and ran her fingers down his cheek. "I have waited many years for you, my fine *vaquero.* I will not allow you to stray again. You belong to me now. No other!"

Joaquin grabbed her hand and crushed her fingers together. "You have become a *bruja* and a shrew. *Buenas noches,* Elena."

Back in his own hotel room, Joaquin took his smuggled whiskey bottle out of his inside pocket and smiled as he uncorked it. If he was caught drinking on the hotel premises, he would be thrown out! The thought gave him comedic relief from his disturbing confrontation with Elena. He laughed and then upended the bottle and drank greedily. The whiskey burned a fiery path all the way down his throat into his belly. His eyes watered and perspiration beaded his forehead. Righting the bottle, he studied the label: a popular California whiskey he'd enjoyed before, but tonight it tasted like pure alcohol. He carried the bottle over to the window and looked out at the view of the next building, a solid brick wall barely more than an arm's length away. Leaning against the window frame, he breathed in the night air and contemplated what kind of *look* had told Elena that he'd wanted Rosita and now Heller Peyton. He realized he must have revealed something of his thoughts when he'd discovered the location of Heller's wound.

He bent to remove his boots and toss them into the corner, then again upended the bottle, this time relishing the liquid fire. The warmth that spread through his body was almost as pleasurable as that moment when he'd touched Heller's breast. His mind shot forward to the theater, to kissing Heller, and a different kind of pleasure warmed his body. He had never known anyone like the stiff-necked Boston spinster, but her stiffness had melted like sun-warmed butter as soon as he took her in his arms. He remembered how small she was, and pale; she had the same fragility that Rosita had possessed. After Rosita, his taste had switched to women with melon-sized breasts and ample hips and thighs. It was what he had become used to, what he'd told himself he preferred.

Until now.

There was nothing ample about Miss Heller Peyton, except her obvious dislike for him and her desire to tell him so. And yet, he could not seem to forget the feel of her breasts or the softness of her lips.

Stripped naked, he stood looking at the whiskey bottle. Heller Peyton's eyes were the color of fine whiskey. The rest of her face came into focus—the delicate mouth with a full lower lip and a small pointed chin that suggested stubborn determination. Suggested? He laughed out loud, remembering one or two samplings of her stubborn determination.

It was her hair, he decided, that had initially caught his attention. And it was her hair that made her more than simply a lovely woman. It made her beautiful. He doubted he would ever forget the day he had carried her up to Elena's room and laid her down on the bed. Her hat had fallen to the floor and loose strands of her hair spread across the pillow—like tongues of flame.

He detested women's voguish hairstyles with their false hair, elaborate adornments—feathers, stuffed birds, and God only knew what else. If Heller Peyton was *his* woman, he would insist she wear her hair down all the time, the way God meant it to be. The color and texture were adornment enough.

His woman? *Por Dios,* what the hell was he thinking?

His mouth set in a grim line, he grabbed the whiskey bottle by the neck and took it to bed with him. A few more drinks would free him from the custody of his mind—so that for tonight at least he wouldn't have to think about how he was going to say good-bye to Elena, and why he couldn't seem to erase the image of a flame-haired virgin whose heart was as cold as a Boston winter and whose blood was as blue as a Sonoran sky.

He propped himself up against the iron headboard and took another long swallow, then lowered the bottle to his side. The whiskey was doing its job. He started to close his eyes and give into the lethargy when a gentle breeze touched his face. "Rosita," he whispered. "Come here to me." He reached out his hand and . . .

. . . drew her to him until he felt the warmth of her breath upon his face. Rosita. So young. So beautiful. He loved her with every fiber of his being. All day long, he had thought of little else except coming home and making slow, beautiful love to her.

"Hey, in there!"

Joaquin bolted, but before he could get to his knife hanging in its scabbard over the bedpost, the door flew open.

"Touch that pig-sticker and I'll pin you to the wall, Mex." The man's voice was slurred and he weaved unsteadily.

Slowly, Joaquin withdrew his hand, careful to keep eye contact with the drunken gringo. "Who are you?"

"My name's of no importance to you, greaser."

"What is it you want, señor?" Joaquin asked re-

spectfully, hoping a subservient tone and manner would appease the man and speed him on his way. "Do you wish food? I will have my wife prepare a meal. Gold? I have only a small poke, but I will share it with you."

"You talk real good, Mex—almost like a Yank, but you ain't no Yank, are you? You ain't nothin' but a low-down, claim-jumping Mex."

Outside, the sound of galloping hooves signaled the approach of several riders.

"Hey! Davie. Jed. Sam. In here, boys. Come meet . . . what did you say your name was greaser?"

Joaquin hesitated. "Murieta. Joaquin Murieta."

"Señor Murieta and his puta."

Joaquin bristled, but was checked by Rosita's fingers pressing into his arm, beseeching him to hold his temper. He could hold it a lot better if he had a weapon. One man alone, he could handle, but four . . . They burst into the cabin, and he knew by the looks of them they would be trouble—Anglo vultures seeking an easy prey.

Rosita pulled her rebozo off the bedpost and wrapped it around her head and shoulders. "I will get coffee, señores, and tamales." She started for the wood stove, where the coffee was heating.

The tallest of the foursome reached out his arm and pulled her into his grasp. "I'll jes make a meal off you, sweetness."

Joaquin lunged at the man holding his wife. He slammed his fist into Davie's whiskey-blotched face, and was about to hit him again when he felt something press against his back.

"Whoa there, Mex. You best behave yourself or I might get riled and decide to pull the trigger. Never shot a man in the back, leastways not that I remember. . . ."

"*I owe you, Mauger,*" *said Davie as Joaquin slowly backed off.*

"*Please, señores,*" *Rosita pleaded.* "*We have done nothing to you. Please go. Leave us in peace.*"

Davie recaptured his prize and held her close. "*Why, sure, honey, jes as soon as old Davie here has some fun. Been a long time since I had me a woman— and you—you're such a purty lit'l thing. I kinda hate to share you.*"

Rosita screamed when Davie reached his hand down into her dress and squeezed her breast. He shouted, "*Oooooeee! Plump as a pigeon and squawks like one, too.*"

Joaquin spun around, his right knee raised, leg extended, and kicked the gun out of the leader's hand. Then he lunged at the man holding his wife. The advantage of surprise was his, but only for a moment. Once the other two men joined the foray, he knew he was beaten.

They surrounded him, knocked him to the floor, and kicked him until he was bloodied and doubled in pain.

"*Mi vida! Joaquin,*" *Rosita cried.* "*Mi corazón!*"

"*That was some fancy fightin', Mex.*" *Mauger stood back as his friends held Joaquin down.* "*But not fancy enough. Let's hope your* puta *does better than you.*"

"*No!*" *The word ripped from Joaquin's throat.* "*No!* Madre de Dios. *No!*"

Mauger grabbed a length of rope hanging near the door and threw it to Davie, who bound Joaquin's wrists behind his back. When he'd finished, Mauger sidled up next to Joaquin, bent over him and said, "*Let this be a lesson to all you Mexes. You don't own this land anymore. Yanks do. And we're tired of you foreigners taking the gold out of our rivers and streams and carrying it home to Mexico. Hear me, Murieta? You tell your* compadres. *Savvy?*"

Joaquin flinched at the stench of his whiskeyed breath.

"Come on Mauger, I'm itchin' to have a piece of this little gal," said Davie. *With a gag between her teeth, Rosita now lay spread-eagle on the bed, her hands and feet bound to the bedposts.*

"Well, then stop jawin' and go to it. We ain't got all day."

Davie shucked his pants and dropped them on the floor. His laugh, as he tore away Rosita's clothes, echoed in Joaquin's ears.

Joaquin lay on the floor, fighting and kicking against his bindings in spite of his wounds, but unable to get up. He could do nothing—nothing to save his beloved wife. He could do nothing but lay there and listen to her screams rend the air as first Davie, then Sam, Jed, and finally the man called Mauger raped her.

When they were through, Mauger and Jed hauled Joaquin outside to the hitching post. Mauger stood next to Joaquin while Jed tied his hands to the hitching post. "You got a real nice little wife there, Murieta. Tight as a new-wound clock. Can't think of a time I enjoyed myself more, even if I did have to share her." Joaquin jerked his head sideways and spat. The spittle hit Mauger right below the belt. "Bring me my bullwhip, Davie. I want to make sure Señor Murieta here gets the message." Counting steps, Mauger moved back. Davie handed him the bullwhip. At twenty steps he uncoiled the whip, then raised it up and let it fly. . . .

". . . Joaquin? Joaquin? Wake up." Joaquin opened his eyes and saw Lino's anxious expression. "You were making strange noises, *mi amigo*. Are you all right?" Still Joaquin did not speak; the past was still too entangled with the present. He was covered in sweat.

Lino picked the empty whiskey bottle off the floor. "I think you had a little too much to drink."

Shakily, Joaquin pushed himself to an upright position. "Apparently not enough."

Chapter 6

The early morning hours just after sunrise had always been Heller's favorite time of the day. But not this morning. Today she awoke thinking about last night—about the conversation between herself and Don Ricardo in the theater lobby. What was it he'd said? That *he* had stopped her bleeding?

Suddenly, she sat up. "*He* did it, not Abigail!" she blurted in horror. "*He* tended and bandaged me!" Which meant . . . She crossed her arms over her head and threw herself back into the pillows. Why had it taken her so long to realize—by the time Abigail had found her, the wound had already been dressed!

Her cheeks burned with embarrassment. Against her will, she envisioned the tall Spaniard pulling and ripping at her clothes, struggling with her corset. *He* had destroyed her traveling suit, her blouse and . . . her corset. "Oh, God," she groaned. Had he touched her? Of course he had. It would have been impossible not to. Had he taken liberties all in the name of doctoring? She would never know. Why hadn't Elena tended her? Women were usually better at such matters. Heller couldn't imagine Elena standing by and watching Don Ricardo administer to her without protest.

"Stop!" She covered her face with her hands. She was driving herself crazy with questions that she would never know the answers to. Difficult as it would be, she needed to put the incident on the shelf and forget it.

As if she could ever forget Don Ricardo Montaños!

If she lived to be a hundred, she would remember everything that had happened between them, every word, every gesture, every touch. His darkly handsome face and derisively mocking expression would haunt her dreams. And though she despised him for embarrassing and humiliating her, she would remember the satisfying warmth and comforting strength of his embrace . . . and the incredible moment when his mouth had kissed hers. His breath had tasted of the wind and his lips of fine brandy.

Finally, desperate to put a halt to her runaway thoughts, she grabbed her journal off the bedside table and set her mind to writing a description of her night at the Foxhall Theater. It was an exercise in futility. Muttering in aggravation, she flung aside the covers and hopped out of bed to begin her toilette.

An hour later, outside the hotel, Heller looked around in wonder as Gordon Pierce escorted her and Abigail to his phaeton. Everything on wheels had been brought into use to transport the Bostonians and their escorts the seven miles from the city to the Cliff House at the end of Point Lobos Road.

After helping Abigail up to the rear seat, Gordon made a point of handing Heller up to the front seat, the driver's seat. He then promptly climbed up beside her, took up the reins and guided the bays away from the hotel. Glancing over her shoulder, Heller was warned of her aunt's indignation over their seating arrangement by her peaked eyebrow and raised chin.

Having spent a difficult morning dealing with her own thoughts, Heller wanted more than anything for the Cliff House ceremonies to go well. This was the day for which she had come to San Francisco. Today, finally she would be able to test her skills as the Board of Trade's cultural secretary, recording the speech, leading the group in song, and acting as Alexander Rice's social hostess. Though nervous about the responsibilities entrusted to her, she was also excited and actually looking forward to the challenge. She acknowledged Abigail's meaningful look with one of her own that asked for continued indulgence.

A cool breeze off the ocean carried the scent of the sea as the horses drew near the shore and then began their ascent up Cliff House Road to the renowned restaurant resort that stood at the northwest tip of San Francisco on a bluff above the blue Pacific. Far beyond the low-roofed structure, Heller saw two tall-masted clipper ships, white sails full of wind, gliding gracefully across the sunlit sea toward the steep-sided channel known as the Golden Gate.

After handing the horses over to the attendants at the hitch racks, the trio joined the large group making their way down the steep wooden steps to the shore. Adding to the noisy chatter of over two hundred people was the uproarious bellowing of the sea lions clustered on Seal Rock, a hundred feet beyond the shore.

Stepping onto the sandy beach, Heller shaded her eyes and looked out at Seal Rock. Dozens of curious sea lions were propped on their front flippers, bobbing and weaving their sleek heads as they inspected the group gathering on the beach.

"Do you think anyone will be able to *hear* the speech above all that commotion?" Heller asked, leaning close to Abigail so she would not have to yell.

Abigail clamped her hands over her ears. "I don't know." She started to laugh. "My goodness, they *are* vocal, aren't they?"

Heller bubbled with laughter. At a sudden thought,

she opened her journal and dashed off a note to herself to remember to include the sea lions and their antics in her writings. A little humor would be welcome, especially after her dry and uninspiring theater critique.

No sooner had she made the note than Alexander motioned for her to follow him. She carefully picked her way down to the water's edge and stopped. Alexander continued on, stepping along a trail of large, flat-topped rocks. At length, he positioned himself and signaled the crowd to attention. Heller opened her journal and waited. She felt an overwhelming surge of civic pride when he ceremoniously displayed a bottle containing water taken from the Massachusetts Bay. Holding the bottle high, he poured half its contents into the sea, then refilled it with Pacific water.

"Today is indeed a momentous and solemn occasion." His voice boomed above of the cacophony of barking sea lions. "The union of these two waters seems typical of the commingling . . ."

The moment he finished, she closed her journal, tucked it under her arm, and clapped. When the applause died down, she raised her hand to gain the group's attention. "Ladies and gentlemen, members of the Boston Board of Trade and the San Francisco Chamber of Commerce," she called out over the pounding waves and barking sea lions. "Please move closely together and join hands. I will lead us in a song that seems particularly appropriate to our purpose here today." Heller took a deep breath and started to sing a rousing rendition of "America," after which, to her great relief, the ceremonies concluded.

Alexander then escorted her back toward the wooden steps. With a throaty laugh, he looked over his shoulder at the sea lions. "They must be Republicans." Heller's face lit up, and she gave way to gales of laughter. Suddenly a hand clamped her elbow, and she stopped short and swung around.

"Oh, Gordon!" she said in breathless surprise. He had appeared at her side from out of nowhere.

"Please forgive me, I didn't mean to startle you, but I was anxious to introduce myself to your esteemed leader."

Taken aback by his boldness, Heller said woodenly, "Well, yes, of course." She turned to Alexander with a look of apology and made the introductions.

The party was then shown to a large table next to the bank of windows overlooking the ocean and Seal Rock. Seconds after taking their seats, Heller and Alexander found themselves surrounded by a group of enthusiastic men and women offering congratulations on the eloquence of the ceremony. Until this moment, Heller had not considered her role important to anyone other than herself, but the warm thanks and myriad compliments made her feel that she had indeed accomplished what she had set out to do.

At length, when the well-wishers went off to their own tables, Heller smiled as she spread her napkin on her lap. She was suddenly and inexplicably ravenous, and her mouth watered at the extraordinary aromas coming from the kitchen.

Finally, their tray came laden with plates of sauce-covered meats and beautifully garnished vegetables, reminiscent of the culinary excellence of the finest Eastern hotel. Heller repressed a devilish smile as she thought about Elizabeth Pennyworth reading her descriptions of a *very* civilized and sophisticated San Francisco—a description far removed from the wild, dirty pueblo her former teacher had described.

Throughout dinner, the conversation was directed at Gordon. Abigail, Heller noticed, aggressively questioned Gordon about his business interests and how he expected to benefit by the merging of East with West. His answers, although full of observation and speculation, were never specific to his actual business operation. Heller could only assume that he preferred to keep his business affairs to himself.

"You surprise me, Mr. Pierce—" Abigail said suddenly, only to have him interrupt.

"Please, you may call me Gordon, if I may call you Abigail."

Abigail cleared her throat. "As I was saying *Mr. Pierce,* you surprise me. Most *gentlemen* don't concern themselves with the development of intellectual and moral education. That, of course, is why Heller and I are here. We think it is important that everyone have the opportunity to acquaint themselves with taste in fine arts, the humanities, and the broader aspects of science as distinguished from vocational skills. You do, of course, agree?"

Heller shrank in her chair. Abigail was being positively rude. Her dislike for Gordon was as plain as the nose on her face, and it appeared she didn't care who knew it.

Stiffly, he answered, "I— Well, y—yes, of course." The smile fled from his face, but after a moment it returned and he announced, "As a matter of fact, I've just begun an art collection of my own."

Heller brightened and sat forward. "Oh? Perhaps I might see it sometime. Private collections are so interesting." She had to say something to stop Abigail before the situation got any more uncomfortable.

"Maybe we can visit one of the local museums. I'm especially fond of paintings of people."

Alexander Rice leaned over his plate and looked down the table. "People?" he queried, his silver-white brows furrowing where they met the wide bridge of his nose.

"My favorite is of Napoleon."

Rice nodded. "Ah! You mean portraits, of course."

Gordon raised a brow. "Yes, that's what I meant."

The scraping of Alexander's chair against the hardwood floor ended the conversation. "I'm afraid I'll have to beg your pardon, Abigail, Gordon," Alexander said as he stood, "but Miss Peyton and I have a few duties we must attend to before we return to the city. I enjoyed meeting you, Gordon," he said extending his hand to the younger man. Then to Abigail, "I promise to have your charge back in time for our appointed departure."

Left to themselves, Abigail and Gordon looked at each other across the table.

Abigail was feeling more than a little suspicious about Gordon Pierce, and she very much resented his earlier attempt at familiarity. She hoped she had put him in his place. Sipping her tea, she watched Gordon watch Heller make her way around the room with Alexander.

"She's a lovely young woman," Gordon observed. "You must be very proud of her." He picked his napkin off his lap, opened it up, and let the crumbs sprinkle onto the floor.

Over her teacup Abigail eyed the maneuver with open-mouthed surprise. Her suspicions were confirmed: Gordon Pierce was no gentleman! "Indeed, I am proud of her," she managed with a calm that belied her shock at his atrocious manners. Lowering the cup and setting it silently upon its saucer, she added, "She has been like a daughter to me."

"You have no children of your own?"

"No. I never chose to marry. And, I might add, in that regard Heller and I are alike."

Gordon looked blank. "I beg your pardon? I don't know what you mean."

Abigail lifted her chin and raised one eyebrow. "Heller is not interested in marriage, Mr. Pierce."

Gordon studied her intently. "Do I detect a reason for your telling me that?"

"You may detect anything you want, Mr. Pierce. I am simply stating a fact. Heller does not want a husband." Glaring at him, she added, "She has turned down dozens of young men."

He leaned forward, elbows on the table. "You don't like me, do you?"

"Whether I *like* you or not makes no difference."

"I think it does. I think you have a great deal of influence over Heller. Perhaps you would like me better if I told you that Heller is exactly what I've been looking for in a wife."

"Indeed." Abigail stood up and placed her napkin on the table beside her plate. "As I said before, she has no intention of marrying."

Gordon seemed not at all intimidated. "Need I ask your permission to pay court to her?"

"Heller is twenty-six years old, Mr. Pierce. She makes her own decisions."

"I'll keep that in mind."

Joaquin was pacing the floor when Lino opened the door. Without preamble, he told Lino about running into Mauger at the theater. "He goes by the name Gordon Pierce," Joaquin said, his voice as ominous as his black scowl. "He's been appointed by the San Francisco Chamber of Commerce to escort two of the Bostonians around the city, namely Heller and Abigail Peyton." He stopped pacing and stood by the window overlooking Leidesdorff Street.

"Heller—the redhead you told me about?"

"The same." His voice was flat. "You were right about Mauger. If I didn't know better, I'd swear he had mended his ways and become a gentleman. He's fooled everyone else with his fine home, his tailor-made clothes, and gentlemanly manners. I didn't know he had it in him." He lit a cigarillo and propped his booted foot up on the edge of a nearby chair. "What a shame to have worked so hard to make a new life only to lose it." He inhaled deeply, then tossed the cigarillo out the window. Smoking no longer gave him the satisfaction it used to.

"A shame," Lino repeated, with the same remorseless tone.

"I need you to go over to the chamber office and ask for the itinerary for the Boston Board of Trade. The itinerary will make it easy for us to know where Mr. Pierce is and isn't for the next few days. If they ask questions, tell them . . . Never mind. You'll think of something."

Lino was gone almost an hour. By the time he returned, Joaquin's black mood had subsided. "Did they ask why you wanted it?"

Lino took a piece of paper out of his coat pocket, unfolded it and handed it to Joaquin. "I told them I was from the newspaper. They were glad to give it to me, even insisted that *they* write it out for me."

Joaquin seated himself at the table in front of the window and studied the itinerary. When his eyes reached the bottom of the page, his right cheek twitched and his mouth quirked with amusement. He looked up at Lino, who was leaning against the bureau. "So *amigo,* it seems that we'll be going to a masquerade ball Saturday night." He leaned back, balancing the straight-backed chair on its rear legs.

Lino gave a low laugh. "I suppose that means we'll be needing costumes." He turned around and examined his face in the mirror above the bureau. "I think I might look convincing as a Franciscan monk. What do you think?" He turned back. At Joaquin's nod of approval, Lino went on with his joking. "And you, *mi jefe* . . . you could go as a knight of the Round Table. Maybe as King Arthur himself! No, no—" he shook his head "—Roman. Caesar!" he said, squinting with close study. "You would look *interesting* in a toga, yes?" Joaquin's murderous look made Lino move out of reach. "Or maybe . . ." With his back to Joaquin, he slowly pulled his knife out of its sheath. "Maybe you should go as Joaquin Murieta, *El Bandido Notorio!* You could make a grand entrance, something they will remember." He drew his arm back, swiveled around, and tossed the knife at the itinerary.

Joaquin lunged forward and deflected the bowie with the back of his hand. He looked up at Lino, who was grinning.

"I'm glad to see your life as a *hacendado* hasn't slowed your hand, *mi jefe*."

"Neither has it impaired my aim with a gun, my skill with a rope, or my performance in bed. I have not exactly been idle these last years, you know."

They broke into laughter and the years fell away. They were boys again, laughing over the smallest incidents, sharing secrets. Finally Joaquin said, "It is good to have you by my side again, *mi amigo*. Together we will make Luther Mauger pay for his crimes." The past and present collided, and their expressions turned serious. They sat down and discussed the rest of the itinerary, after which it was decided Lino would spend the day investigating Luther Mauger's business affairs, everything from his club and political affiliations to his bank accounts.

Joaquin, on the other hand, would find out all he could about Mauger's personal life. A great deal could be learned about a man by seeing the inside of his home, and since Mauger was spending the day with Heller and Abigail, it seemed the perfect time to get to know and understand him.

He hired a hansom cab outside the What Cheer House. After delivering Lino to the business district, Joaquin instructed the driver to go to Little China, where he would pick up Hop Fong.

One the way to Rincon Hill, Hop Fong listened carefully to Joaquin as he explained his plan. Then the boy set his price. The amount settled upon was more than Joaquin had intended to pay, but the boy was a shrewd negotiator and promised to prove his worth.

"You can let us off at the top of the hill," Joaquin told the driver. He paid the man, then headed down the street toward Mauger's Doric-style home. To Hop Fong he said, "I want you to knock on the door and tell whomever answers that you're looking for a job as a stable hand. If they say they don't need one, tell them you're hungry and ask for something to eat. The point is, I want you to get inside the house and count the servants. Do you think you can do that?"

"You askee, me do."

Joaquin looked doubtful, but sent the boy ahead and watched from the cover of a shade tree in the neighboring yard. The same Chinese manservant Joaquin had seen yesterday when he and Lino followed Mauger home opened the door. He could hear them speaking to each other in Chinese, then the man motioned Hop Fong into the house. Joaquin settled his back against the tree trunk and waited. Nearly a half hour went by before the boy came back. He had a bag full of bread.

"What took you so long?"

"You say tell servant me hungry, so I eat."

Exasperated, Joaquin ran his fingers through his hair and down the back of his neck. "Well, now that you've got your belly full, how many servants did you count?''

"One."

"One? Are you sure? What about a cook? A butler?''

"Chum Soon say he cook, clean. Chum Soon say boss man very cheap. No pay more Chinee to do what Chum Soon can do. He say boss—''

Joaquin clasped his hand across the boy's mouth as Mauger's front door opened and Chum Soon stepped out. Hop Fong pried Joaquin's fingers away, silently assuring him he would not speak. Together they watched the servant lock the door and leave the house. He headed down the hill toward the shopping district carrying a carpet bag.

Joaquin looked down at Hop Fong. "You're sure he was the only one in the house?'' The boy answered with an insistent nod. "Come on. You're going to start earning that money I agreed to pay you.''

A tall, thick hedge along the east side of the house provided a screen behind which Joaquin boosted Hop Fong up to the window ledge. The window opened easily and the boy slid inside. Seconds later, he opened the back door and Joaquin stepped into the kitchen, his bowie secure in its leather sheath beneath his jacket.

They made a quick search of the upstairs. All the rooms opened out into the main hall, which was lighted by the opalescent ceiling light above. The moment Joaquin opened the door at the top of the stairs, he knew it was Mauger's bedroom. It smelled of burnt opium. Sickly sweet. The air was thick with it. An ornately carved mahogany bed dominated a windowless wall hung with red brocade. The window and closet draperies were of the same heavy, blood-red material. Chinese furniture and wine-red rugs reminded Joaquin of a fancy brothel he'd visited once in Los Angeles.

Joaquin stepped inside and looked around. All Mauger's personal belongings were neatly arranged. Too neatly, he decided a moment later when he examined the placement of Mauger's personal grooming articles. They were lined up on top of the bureau, evenly spaced and precisely positioned. *Precisely*. His mouth curled spitefully. One by one, he opened the bureau drawers and searched their contents. Here too, all was in perfect order, precisely positioned. Everything looked and felt new and expensive.

Hop Fong called him over to the table beside the bed, pointing to a wadded piece of paper.

The writing was thick and heavy, the pen nib apparently damaged or blunted. The e's and o's were difficult to tell apart, and the l's and t's were the same height. Still, the message was clear. *Heller Peyton*.

Joaquin angrily crumbled the note and returned it to the table. That's when he saw the smoking paraphernalia, an expensive gold-mounted smoking pistol with an ivory ring around its mouthpiece, and a buffalo horn box containing several ounces of the best opium money could buy.

Luther Mauger had developed some expensive habits. Some deadly habits, too, if those walking skeletons in underground Little China were an example of too much of a good thing.

The downstairs was also furnished in Chinese, but without the dramatic impact of Mauger's bedroom. The parlor was royally decorated with rare wood pieces, crystal and gold accessories, and the floors were covered with rich white carpets. After a quick but thorough search of the main rooms, Joaquin found the door to the library.

Technically, it wasn't much of a library—at least not

compared to his own at Rancho Murieta, which he had catalogued at over two thousand books on a wide array of subjects.

Fewer than one hundred books occupied the oak shelves in Mauger's library. Their topics were limited to Chinese customs, American politics, gold mining, accounting, and etiquette. The latter, Joaquin gazed at with inordinate curiosity. Etiquette. Again he scanned the titles and smiled as he began to gain a better understanding of his enemy and what he was trying to do. Turning away from the shelves, Joaquin sat down in front of a large rolltop desk. Here too, everything was neatly organized. Precisely placed. Joaquin reminded himself to be careful to put things back exactly as he had found them.

The first drawer revealed thick ledger books, the top one labeled "San Francisco." Under the income heading there were listings for firecrackers, folding fans, snuff bottles, rice bowls, water pipes, and silk. All Chinese goods. The total combined income from the first of the year totaled less than five thousand dollars. Not exactly a fortune, Joaquin concluded, and certainly not enough to offset the expense column, which came to more than twenty thousand dollars. Under the expense heading, following the cost of goods purchased, were the usual household expenses, the mortgage, and the Chinese manservant. It was the numerous listings for Canton Charlie at four hundred dollars each, Drakes disposal, Opium and T. Henderson that gave Joaquin pause. With a pencil from Mauger's desk, Joaquin copied down the entries, then continued his search through the drawers. The second drawer revealed a stack of unpaid bills—for a pair of carriage horses, a park phaeton, a diamond stickpin, and clothing from several haberdasheries. Other drawers contained files full of receipts for purchases going back five years, stationery, and notes of correspondence. But it was what was in the last drawer that made Joaquin's hand freeze midway to reaching in.

A bullwhip. He knew the second he saw it that the hammered gold handle would bear the initials "L.M."

It lay curled like a snake on the bottom of the drawer.

Joaquin stared at it, unable to move, unable to breathe . . .

. . . *The pain was worse than anything he had ever known. Bolts of white lightning cut across his shoulders and back, tearing cloth and flesh at the same time. He closed his eyes and took a deep breath, preparing himself for the next blow.*

Again the tail of the whip sang through the air, this time lashing the back of his neck. Blood spurted out of him like ocean spray. He screamed inside himself as his head fell helplessly forward. For a second, he thought his neck had been severed. Later, he would wish it had.

"I sure do wish your little puta *could've lived to see this." Mauger picked up the count. "Eight. Nine. Ten."*

Joaquin rallied at Mauger's words. He raised his head, clenched his teeth. He had to survive this, to avenge Rosita, he told himself over and over, the thought and his purpose dimming each time Mauger cracked the whip over his body.

"Fifteen. Had enough, Mex? Learned your lesson yet?"

His knees buckled, and he fell heavily over the hitching post. His shirt hung in bloodied strips off his body. He struggled for breath, but still Mauger continued, his raucous laughs echoing in Joaquin's ears.

When it actually ended Joaquin was not sure. Through a river of sweat flowing into his eyes, he saw a pair of boots standing in front of him, saw the hammered gold whip handle glinting in the sunlight.

"I'd stay a little longer, but me and the boys here gotta be goin'. Big poker game tonight. Lots of pretty girls."

Joaquin stared at the whip. "You should have killed me, gringo."

"Why would I want to kill you? I'm thinkin' you'll go around tellin' all your *amigos* what happens to Mexes who lay claims on good American soil. If you're smart, you'll tell 'em to go back where they came from."

"Mauger!" Joaquin called out as the man walked away to join his friends. "I am Joaquin. Remember my name!"

From atop his horse Mauger called back. "Sure thing, Mex. Adios, amigo."

"Whas a matter, boss? You sick?"

Hop Fong's clipped words brought Joaquin's head up. "No. I— I was studying these entries. Drake's Disposal. Canton Charlie."

"Hop Fong very glad he boy not girl. Canton Charlie no good scoundrel to sell mother, sister."

Joaquin took the whip out of the drawer, then spun the chair around. "What did you say?"

"Bad man, Canton Charlie. He buy sister, mother, forty dollar, sell four hundred. Make muchee money. Sell many slaves. Bad man."

By the time Joaquin dropped Hop Fong off at the entrance of Little China, he understood the meaning behind all but one of Mauger's expense listings. Canton Charlie was a whoremonger whose business was selling Chinese children, young girls and women into sexual servitude. The slavery market, Joaquin learned from the boy, who had firsthand knowledge because of his mother and sister, had become big business in San Francisco and throughout California. Most of those sold were twelve to fourteen years old. Most died before they reached twenty. The high mortality rate required hundreds of replacements, which meant continuing importation. Drake's Disposal, Hop Fong said, specialized in the discreet disposal of bodies.

Grimly, Joaquin entered his hotel, whereupon the clerk signaled him over to the desk and handed him a message. Joaquin recognized the flowery script as Elena's and slipped it into his pocket. Once inside his room, he tossed the stolen whip onto the floor, then proceeded to loosen his clothing and make himself comfortable. Hop Fong's description of the Chinatown slave trade had left him feeling sick with anger. He grabbed the back of a chair, swung it around, and sat facing its back.

Heller.

He should warn her about the true nature of her escort. But would she believe him? Why should she? As far as she was concerned, Mauger was the gentleman and he was the villain.

A knock on the adjoining door sounded and Joaquin bid Lino to enter.

Lino stood inside the doorjamb. "You look like hell. What happened?"

Slowly, almost reluctantly, Joaquin talked about his visit to Mauger's house, describing in detail what he'd seen. The ledger entries he saved for last. "If Hop Fong is to be believed, and I think he is, the buying and selling of Chinese women and young girls into sexual servitude is common practice." He cracked his knuckles. "And even though the authorities know all about it, they don't do anything to stop it."

Lino sat down and leaned on the table. "How many entries were there for this Canton Charlie?"

"I counted at least a dozen since the beginning of the year and just as many for Drake's disposal."

Lino sat back and made the sign of the cross.

"There's something else, but this I brought with me. A little memento of my visit." He reached behind him and grabbed the whip.

Lino jumped out of his chair. "Is this what I think it is?" He took it from Joaquin's hand and examined the gold handle. "It must have been as memorable an experience for him as it was for you." He handed the whip back to Joaquin and returned to his seat, shaking his head.

Joaquin slid it under the bed. "Now, tell me what you found out."

Lino was slow to answer. "He's not rich, but he has established himself financially, politically, and socially. The society matrons consider him to be an eligible candidate for their daughters, so he's invited to all the soirees, but he hasn't shown particular interest in any one woman. My banker friends tell me that he's seldom seen in the local men's clubs, nor does he have a reputation for excessive drinking or gambling. He seems to be well-liked and respected." Lino paused as he reached into his pocket for his note. Finding it, he continued, "I located the bank, the biggest one in San Francisco, as you might expect. There's a big mortgage on the Rincon Hill house, which isn't so unusual, except that he's behind in payments and has applied for a sizable loan. Under the circumstances, I can't imagine that the bank would give it to him, but they haven't turned him down yet."

"Maybe he has other assets to secure the loan."

Lino shrugged. "I didn't uncover anything, at least not yet. I have some other sources that I still have to investigate. But you're right. He has to have more than just the income from his import business. That alone sure as hell isn't enough to support his current way of living.''

"What about the San Quentin records?''

"I'm working on it.''

At a sudden thought, Joaquin retrieved his jacket and dug into the pocket. He pulled out the piece of paper that he'd written the ledger entries on. "This may not be anything at all, but Mauger made a number of thousand-dollar payments to a T. Henderson.'' He handed Lino the paper. "Let's go downstairs to supper. We can finish talking there.''

Lino excused himself a moment to change his coat and wipe the dust off his boots.

Meantime, Joaquin took out the chamber itinerary and noted that the Board of Trade's departure date was a week from Saturday.

A week and a day. Not much time, Joaquin calculated, for Mauger to court Heller and get her to agree to marry him, if, in fact, that was what he intended. And if it was, Heller would be comparatively safe. Mauger wasn't likely to risk hurting his future wife, not when he stood to gain so much by their union—a union that would never take place, if he knew anything at all about Heller Peyton.

Still, Joaquin would keep his eye on her. And on Mauger.

Chapter 7

Joaquin spent Friday morning at the wharf, talking to the captains and crews of the merchant ships to get a basic understanding of San Francisco's import/export trade.

Chinese goods, he learned, were much in demand, not only among the Celestials who had come to San Francisco with little more than the clothes on their backs, but by the Anglos as well. The goods Mauger purchased for resale were among the most popular and had the highest profit margin.

It didn't take nearly as long as he had thought to learn the name of the broker who sold the goods to Mauger. His inquiries took him to a warehouse in Little China, to Kim Lee, who looked like a medieval wizard with his silver-white beard, long mustache, and waist-length queue of hair. Treading noiselessly on embroidered silk slippers, Kim Lee came from the back of the building to the front where Joaquin waited.

"You have come to do business?" His high-pitched voice grated on Joaquin's ears.

"Yes, I have a business proposition for you."

The wily old Chinaman squinted. "I am a businessman. I will hear your proposition."

"I have it on good authority that you deal with a man by the name of Gordon Pierce, that you sell him firecrackers, fans, and such." When the old man didn't deny the information, Joaquin continued. "I'll pay five thousand dollars if you agree that the next time you do business with him you'll tell him that you've had to increase your wholesale prices by thirty percent and that he must pay for his purchases upon ordering."

The Chinaman thought before answering. "If I do as you ask, he will be unable to make profit and will stop buying from me and go find other broker. Then I lose good customer. Much money."

"You'll lose him anyway because he's soon to be a dead man." Joaquin said matter-of-factly.

The old man's countenance registered no surprise. "I see. Then I think it would be wise to accept your generous offer."

"I thought you would see it that way." Joaquin pulled a roll of greenbacks out of his pocket and handed them to the old man. "It would also be wise to say nothing about me or our bargain."

"You would kill me, too?" The Chinaman's copper skin paled.

Joaquin felt the old man's sudden fear but said nothing.

"Revenge makes very bad hate. Very strong weapon."

"Is that one of Confucius' sayings?"

"No. Kim Lee's saying!"

Later that afternoon, Joaquin and Lino met at the What Cheer House and took a hansom cab to the business district. Lino introduced Joaquin to Frank Miller, the vice president of the San Francisco Bank.

The banker, a tall spare man with thick spectacles that made his eyes look over-large, seemed eager to do business. "Señor Montaños, it's an honor to make your acquaintance." He extended his hand. "Mr. Toral here has told me that you're interested in making a rather sizable deposit in our bank," he said, gesturing to the chairs in front of his desk.

Lino took one of the chairs and made himself comfortable.

Joaquin pretended to ignore the man's offer and began moving about the room. With feigned interest he studied the bust of William Ralston, the bank's founder and president. Then he saw the collection of snuff bottles displayed in a velvet-lined box.

"That depends on how safe your bank is, Mr. Miller," Joaquin said, as he carefully examined a snuff bottle carved with a Chinese dragon. Why anyone would want to collect these things he could not fathom.

Miller looked inquiringly at his prospective client. "Well, I can assure you, it's very safe. Our assets are greater than they've ever been."

Joaquin set the bottle back in its nest and turned around. Smiling wryly he said, "I know *exactly* what your assets are, Mr. Miller. I already had that looked into, of course."

With a high, mirthless laugh, Miller took his own seat. "Of course. Then you know—"

Joaquin walked the short distance across the room and stood in front of Miller's desk. He looked down his nose at the banker. "I *know* you deal with a competitor of mine, Gordon Pierce. I would not be mentioning his name except that he owes me a great deal of money. I understand he's planning on repaying me with money he borrows from *this* bank." Joaquin hoped God would forgive him this one lie. He paused, straightened, and stepped back to sit in the empty chair. "You see," he continued, almost matter-of-factly, "it's my belief that a bank's security lies primarily in its lending policies. Correct me if I'm wrong, but if that *is* the case, then it would seem to me only reasonable that the bank would *thoroughly* investigate your loan applicants.'' The banker nodded and was about to speak when Joaquin added, ''I would have to question not only a bank's policies but its wisdom if a loan was approved to an applicant whose liabilities were far in excess of his assets and income.'' He leaned forward. ''I'm a business man—as you are, Mr. Miller. Before I do any business with your bank, I want to feel confident about the bank's lending policies.''

Miller studied his folded hands, and when he spoke a second later, his voice had a new, strained edge. ''If what you're implying is true, Señor Montaños, then of course, we will not be able to grant Mr. Pierce a loan.'' He ran a finger under his collar as if to loosen it. ''If you'll allow me until the end of next week, I will personally investigate Mr. Pierce's financial position and consult with Mr. Ralston—''

Joaquin stood up. ''I'm afraid I don't have the luxury of time, Mr. Miller. I'm returning to San Diego Monday afternoon, and I intend to have *all* my business matters finalized.''

''Monday morning, then,'' returned the banker in a coldly resigned voice. ''I'll see what I can do between now and then.''

''*Adiós*, señor.'' Joaquin inclined his head and started out of the room, Lino closed behind. With the door shut behind them, they exchanged a warm handshake.

''This is too easy, *mi jefe*. I'm getting anxious for a real challenge.''

''Be patient, Lino. I have a feeling there will be plenty of challenges coming our way.''

Elena's note had requested that Joaquin come for her at her dressmaker's at five o'clock. He told Lino he would meet with him later and hired a cab to take him to the address Elena had given him.

The moment he saw her standing on a pedestal, irritably turning this way and that while the dressmaker stuck pins into the red satin of her new flamenco gown, he knew she was in another of her churlish moods and that this was not going to be a pleasant meeting.

"So, did you find Mauger?" she asked over the dressmaker's gray head.

At the mention of Mauger's name, Joaquin flashed her a warning look that she ignored. He ground his teeth in anger. For all that she professed concern about someone discovering him, she seemed to be doing her best to expose him. He sat down and stretched his long legs out in front of him. "I don't think this is exactly the place to discuss it, but since you're so eager to know, yes, I found him."

Elena obviously had not been expecting an affirmative answer. Her face blanched and she started to sway but was immediately brought about when a pin stuck her in the side. "Ouch!" She glared down at the hapless dressmaker as if the woman had stuck her intentionally. When Elena found her voice again, her tone was changed. "Oh, Joaquin. *Querido,* I did not know. I did not think . . . After all these years . . . did he recognize you?"

Despite the fearful concern he saw in her eyes, he was not anxious to continue this conversation in public. "No," he said sharply.

Elena shot him a look of vexation. Then to the dressmaker she said, "Can we continue this another day, Maria?"

"Yes, of course, madam," came the immediate reply. "If you will excuse us, sir, while I remove the pins . . ." She turned to Joaquin.

Elena waved her hand. "It's all right, Maria, he can stay. He is my *novio*."

The woman's face turned an unflattering red. With clumsy fingers, she set about removing the pins that held the gown's long back seam together. As soon as Elena stepped out of the skirt, the dressmaker excused herself to the back room to put the gown away.

Once outside the dressmaker's shop, Elena badgered him with question after question, all of which he refused to answer. They had walked nearly a block when Joaquin abruptly stopped and turned toward her. "I don't know you anymore, Elena. I don't understand what you are doing. You beg me to forsake my search for Mauger because you fear I will be recognized and caught. Then you focus an entire theater audience's attention on me, and now you call me by name and name my enemy in front of a dressmaker who's probably the biggest gossip in town!" He threw up his hands. "What am I to think? Do you want me alive or dead?"

Tears gathered in her eyes. "*Caro mio,* I am sorry." Again, she seemed genuinely shaken by the realization of what she had done. "I was so shocked I did not realize what I was saying. Forgive Elena." She had stopped mid-stride to plead, but Joaquin kept walking. "Joaquin, *por favor,*" she called after him. When he would not stop, she lifted her voluminous skirts and ran to catch up.

He halted just as she reached him, and he leveled grave black eyes upon her classically beautiful features. "We can't continue like this, fighting every time we are together. I care for you. I have *always* cared for you, but I will *never* love you." He grabbed her shoulders. "You know that, Elena. You've always known that. I can't help how I feel any more than you can help how you feel. So, why do you persist?"

She slipped her arms around his neck and pressed herself against him. *"Querido,"* she cried. "I can make you happy. You know I can if only you give me a chance." She ran her hands down his arm, driving home her message with the pressure of her fingers. "I have always been there for you—I always will be. You do not have to love me. I have enough love for us both. *Por favor,* I am tired of this life—tired of waiting for you to come to your senses. Tired of waiting for you to put away your memories of Rosita. Enough is enough, Joaquin. I want to marry—to have children, your children. Sons, Joaquin. I will give you strong sons to carry on the Murieta name. Take me home with you to Mexico—to Rancho Murieta."

Her plea was desperate, sad. He had never known Elena to beg. He pulled her into the privacy of a doorway. "No, Elena. Dammit! You never seem to understand. I have made a vow. I will not break it. Not for you. Not for anybody." He loosened his grip and looked down at her. Softening his tone, he added in a tired voice, "You would make a fine wife and a wonderful mother. . . . I have taken advantage of you, used you. I can never repay you for your loyalty."

"Repay me? Oh, Joaquin. I do not wish for you to repay me. Please, *querido,* I *need* you." Her voice broke and she leaned into him. Then, she reared back, suddenly angry. Her fingers clutched the lapels of his coat. "That *gringa!*" she spat, making an ugly face. "She has seduced you with her paper-white skin and her oh-so-proper manners. She is the reason you would not make love to me the other night. She is the reason you say these things now!"

"Come on, I'm going to see you back to your hotel, madam." He stepped around her and hailed a hansom cab. "Grand Hotel." They rode the distance in silence, alighted the cab in silence, climbed the stairs to the first floor in silence. At the landing Elena ran ahead, unlocked her door, and slammed it in his face.

Heller awakened several times during the night thinking she heard Abigail up and about, but when she listened there was only silence, not even a footfall. Finally, she sat up, wrapped her arms around her knees, and stared out the window. It was not even dawn yet, and here she was wide awake. Would she never get a full night's sleep?

A quarter of an hour later, she gave up trying to convince herself that she should make an effort to go back to sleep and lit the lamp next to her bed. Since it was still too early to begin her toilette, the only thing left was to work in her journal, a chore she had actually begun to enjoy. She read over the last page, then recorded in detail the trip to the Cliff House. As she started to describe the sea lions, she started to chuckle. What wonderful funny creatures! She had never seen sea lions so close to shore. A great deal of discipline was required to limit her description of their antics to only one page.

Near the end of the entry, Heller remembered that Gordon Pierce had promised to show her his art collection. Tonight, when the two groups converged over supper, she would have an opportunity to remind him and set a date. But first she would have to inform Abigail of her intentions and try to convince her aunt that her interest in Gordon Pierce was only as an art enthusiast. Hopefully, there wouldn't be a fuss.

It was obvious to Heller that Abigail did not like Gordon. Yesterday afternoon on their way back from the Cliff House, when Gordon announced the time he would pick them up to escort them to the ball, Abigail had rudely said, "I beg your pardon, Mr. Pierce, but I have decided that Heller and I no longer require you to act as our personal escort." Heller had stood there with her mouth agape, too shocked to speak. Abigail was often outspoken, always imperious, but never had Heller known her to be blatantly rude!

As if expecting his dismissal, Gordon had immediately made an appeal, which Abigail promptly and emphatically denied. Abigail then explained her decision by saying she was tired of time schedules and preferred to go back to their original plan of seeing the city on their own at their own pace. There was more to it, of course, but Heller thought better of publicly interrogating her aunt.

The two women spent the whole of Friday in the company of Alexander Rice, Robert Swain, and other members of the Boston Board of Trade and the San Francisco Chamber of Commerce. By early afternoon, the group had compiled an extensive list of performers, artists, and lecturers from the East and West coasts. Heller drafted an invitational letter, stating their joint purpose and proposing terms and conditions of appearance.

By the time the meeting was over, she was exhausted from trying to keep up with the note-taking, but exhilarated by her success and the praise from her peers for her *valuable* suggestions.

Value.

Another goal reached.

That evening, before supper, Heller was in her room, standing in front of the mirror. At last, things were going as she had hoped and she was accomplishing what she had set out to do. For the first time, she thought about Mam without anger. The one thing in the world Mam had wanted most was for her only child to become a lady. She could almost see her mother's face in the mirror beside her own, almost hear her voice: *"It's a fine and proper lady ye've become, Heller, me love. For sure it is that I'm proud of ye."*

Chapter 8

The crystal prisms hanging from the gaslit wall sconces tinkled as the guests entered the ballroom of the Cosmopolitan Hotel. Holding onto her aunt's arm, Heller presented their invitation and walked into the already crowded room under a canopy of silver-twined evergreens suspended from white Italian pillars.

Catching the all too familiar scent of roses, Heller looked up at the ceiling and saw dozens of spring flower baskets hanging from the ballroom's domed center. She had seen more flowers, both in variety and quantity, in San Francisco these the last few days than she'd seen in her entire life.

Feeling her nose begin to itch, she reached for her handkerchief. "Aunty, we need to move over by the open doors. I'm afraid if I stand under all these flowers, I'll start sneezing the way I did in the theater."

"Of course, dear." Arm in arm, they moved slowly toward the doors which led out onto the veranda. "Did you bring something to write down your observances with, dear? You want to be sure to describe everything for our friends at home. All the beautiful flowers, the costumes, the dances . . ."

"I'll remember," Heller assured her, pretending not to notice the pairs of watchful eyes that followed her across the room. They were friendly eyes, smiling eyes, but watchful all the same. Because she knew they would be watching—as they always did—she had spent hours at the costumers trying to decide upon something eminently appropriate to her position, comfortable, and feminine. Nothing too fancy, bold, or exotic. Finally, forced to make a selection because of the shop's closing, she had chosen a thirteenth-century French noblewoman's gown, made up of a long-sleeved undergown of light blue silk topped by a sleeveless surcoat in the most magnificent sky-blue velvet. The costume was plain in comparison to what most of the women were wearing, but its beltless loose-fitting design concealed the fact that she wasn't wearing her corset.

A shallow white hat, which looked like a scalloped crown, sat atop her head, and a white barbette framed her oval face and kept her unbound hair from falling forward.

As they neared the open doors, Heller felt the cooling wind from outside. All day long storm clouds had threatened, but nothing yet had come of them.

"Oh, look, dear. There's Alex." Abigail took Heller's arm and steered her to the right of the doors, where their leader and his female companion were standing. "I promised we would join him as soon as we arrived." Abigail had never looked more formidable than she did tonight in her seventeenth-century black Dutch court gown. A ruff of stiffened white lace circled her neck like a wheel, and ornate lace cuffs reached more than halfway to her elbows. A tall, wide-brimmed black hat covered her tightly coiled hair and shaded her eyes. The poor dear looked miserably uncomfortable, yet she said nothing.

Alexander Rice, resplendent as King Arthur, was talking to a dark-featured woman boldly costumed as a natty jockey in tops, spurs, and carrying a crop. He looked up from his conversation and waved them over.

"Ladies." He held out his arm and took Abigail's hand and pulled her up next to him. "I'm sure you remember Señorita Valdez. She can only stay a short while as she has an eleven o'clock performance."

Elena didn't wait for him to finish his introduction. "Ah, it is the Señora and Señorita Peyton." She turned her full attention on Heller. "It is *muy bueno* to see you both again. Everything is well, yes, no?"

Heller was more than a little suspicious of Elena's enthusiastic greeting. She forced a smile. "Yes, everything is quite well, thank you."

"I can't begin to tell you how much we enjoyed your performance the other night," said Abigail with pleasure. "By any chance were you a student of Lola Montez? I thought I recognized something of her style in the magnificent way you dance."

Elena preened beneath the flattery. "*Sí*. I meet Lola many years ago in the town—" She laughed. "I forget the name—" She held up her hand and looked to the ceiling. "Ah! It comes to me. Grass Valley. No! Murphy's Diggings. Such a name for a town!"

"Murphy's Diggings." Abigail glanced at Heller as she repeated the town's name. "Such an unusual name, but memorable. Indeed, very memorable. An acquaintance of ours was just talking about it." Having made her point, she changed the subject. "By the way, I wanted to tell you, my niece has written a review of your performance for our friends at home."

"Oh?" Elena lifted finely arched brows and gazed inquiringly at Heller.

All but forced to speak, Heller chose her words with care. "As the Boston Board of Trade's cultural secretary, it's my job to write about all our activities," she stated without elaboration.

"Ah! *Muy bueno!* You write good things about Elena Valdez?"

Heller couldn't believe the woman's conceit. "I write the truth, Señorita Valdez—whatever it may be."

Elena's mouth formed a pucker that made her look like she had just sucked a lemon.

Heller was saved from Elena's ill-concealed wrath when a man costumed as a Persian warrior in pointed helmet and plated armor approached their small group and asked Heller to allow him to sign her dance card. While Heller was making polite conversation with the young man, she heard Elena begging Alexander and Abigail to forgive her for leaving but that she had to get to the theater.

Gordon Pierce arrived a half hour later, handsomely garbed as a Norman knight in chain armor and a black surcoat bearing the Maltese cross. The costume's soft padding added a manly breadth to his chest and shoulders that his regular clothing did not. From his belt hung an intricately scroll-handled sword. "I hope you haven't been enjoying yourself too much without me." A pillar on one side and Abigail's wide farthingale on the other side prevented him from standing next to Heller.

"No, not *too* much," Heller said, offering him another of her forced smiles. Though she hadn't had time to give the Murphy's Diggings matter much thought, she knew it was significant to Abigail and that made her wary.

"You've saved me a place on your dance card, I hope."

"Why . . . yes." Heller noted Abigail's disapproving look, but what was she to do? To refuse to let him sign her still half-empty dance card would have been an insult.

Gordon looked the card over, then at Heller. "I'm not very good at quadrilles, polkas, or the schottische, but I do enjoy waltzes." Encouraged by her lack of comment, he wrote in his name beside two of the waltzes.

When the music began, Heller's first partner came to claim her for the promenade. The second dance, a waltz, was Gordon's. He took her hand and led her onto the dance floor. She felt his hand at her waist and was thankful she'd had the foresight to wrap her bandage around her middle so that her partners would not detect her missing corset. He skillfully steered her onto the dance floor. There seemed something different about him tonight, an impatience and tenseness that she hadn't noted before. When the music ended, he suggested they retreat to the sidelines for some refreshment.

"I've had my eye on that lemonade ever since we arrived," Heller admitted. Of course, she hadn't, but she was at a loss for other conversation. As they approached the refreshment table, decorated with a huge vase of pink-and-lavender sweet peas, Heller was intrigued by a brown-robed monk who was ladling lemonade into silver cups. He handed one to Heller and another to Gordon.

"Thank you." She smiled, then raised the cup to her lips. Peeking over the rim of her cup, she tried to see the monk's face, but the heavy cowl completely covered his head and threw a shadow onto his face.

"*De nada,* señorita." He turned away to fill more cups.

Gordon slid his free hand around her waist. "Let's take our drinks and join Alexander and your aunt."

Curious about the monk's identity, Heller was reluctant to leave, but good manners forbade her from asking who he was. This was, after all, a masquerade. Those guests who had chosen to disguise themselves were not required to reveal their identities until midnight. Halfway across the room, she looked back to see if the mysterious monk was still passing out cups. He was. It was then that she noticed the one flaw in his costume. Instead of a monk's humble leather sandals, he wore highly polished, pointed-toed boots. The incongruity of the boots made her giggle like a schoolgirl, which made Gordon glance down at her in surprise.

The fifth dance, a mazurka, Heller danced with Robert Swain, who seemed uncomfortable in his musketeer costume.

Upon her return, Gordon complained of the room's temperature and invited her to accompany him outside into the garden. Again, she suffered one of Abigail's disapproving looks, but blatantly ignored it as a silent statement to her aunt that she would make her own decisions.

A strong wind rustled the trees and bent the tall irises.

"How do you like San Francisco so far?" Gordon asked, his hand at her elbow, guiding her toward a marble bench half-hidden in the shelter of an ivy-covered trellis.

She clutched her handkerchief and prayed she wouldn't sneeze. "Very much. It's a beautiful city. Far more sophisticated than I was led to believe."

"And what was that exactly?"

Heller thought of Elizabeth Pennyworth's dire warnings about the savages who roamed the streets. "I'm a little embarrassed to say. It was all so silly."

He shook his head. "Please, tell me what you heard," he coaxed. His wheat-colored hair reflected the light from the ballroom.

"To be honest," she began, reminding herself to be careful what she said, "I expected to see dirt streets with deep wagon ruts and crater-sized holes, and faded wooden buildings strung together by a boardwalk. I

was told there were more saloons than stores, and . . .
wild Indians and gunfighters roaming the streets.'' In
spite of herself, she had to laugh. Elizabeth Pennyworth
could not have been more wrong—about everything—
which made Heller wonder about the validity of some
of her other teachings.

Gordon laughed with her. ''It used to be like that,
back in the forties, after gold was discovered in the
foothills. It's come a long way in twenty years. Three-
and four-story brick buildings. Gaslights on every corner. Cobblestone streets. Sidewalks. Fine restaurants
and hotels. As you said, it's a beautiful and sophisticated city. Are you anxious to leave and return home?''

She sat down and smoothed her wind-blown hair as
she looked up at the night sky. A dark cloud scudded
across the face of the moon, throwing the garden into
temporary darkness. ''I—'' She started to say no, but
stopped herself, for it would have been a lie.

''You don't have to leave, Heller.'' He seized her
hand and raised it to his lips. ''You could stay awhile
longer. There is still much we haven't seen or done.''

Heart pounding, she pulled her hand away and held
it against her breast. She should have known he had
an ulterior motive for bringing her out into the garden.
Gardens were notoriously renowned for stolen kisses
and romantic rendezvous. She'd fled enough of them
in Boston to know. ''Oh, yes, I'm afraid I do. Obli-
gations await.'' She pinned him with a look that she
hoped would serve as a warning not to touch her again.
Trying to sound nonchalant, she added, ''You've been
a charming escort and a wonderful guide. Abigail and
I are ever so grateful.'' Confident in the finality of her
words and actions, she was taken by surprise when
suddenly his arms went around her.

Shocked into speechlessness, she opened her mouth,
but nothing came out. Why hadn't she seen this com-

ing? She was twenty-six years old for God's sake! Old enough and experienced enough to recognize the signs and avert them before it came to—to this!

Finally, she managed a word. "Gordon!" She tried to wriggle out of his arms, but he held her fast.

"I've come to care a great deal about you, Heller. I know how sudden this may seem to you . . ." His hazel eyes seemed to be on fire as he searched her face. "I would have preferred to wait to reveal my feelings, but time is running out and your aunt has made it clear that she doesn't want me around. So you see, I had no choice but to tell you tonight. Now. There might not have been another opportunity."

"Let go of me this instant."

"Heller—" He fought to hold her still as she twisted and turned in his arms.

She wrenched herself out of his arms and stood up. She threw him a murderous look and slapped his face. "How dare you? I find your behavior utterly deplorable and entirely improper. You aren't the gentleman I thought you were." A rush of wind cooled her heated cheeks and blew her hair across her face. Abigail was right. He wasn't to be trusted. Not at all.

He rose up beside her, his demeanor so completely changed that he didn't look anything like himself. Anger narrowed his eyes, flared his nostrils, thinned his lips. For a moment, she thought he might actually strike her, for his hands were open and shaking.

Then, like magic, he turned back into himself again.

"I have offended you," he said coolly. "Of course, I apologize, but I thought—" He didn't even have the courtesy to look shamefaced. "Obviously I have misinterpreted your feelings."

His lightning-quick moods confused her. Somehow, he had turned things about and made her feel that she should be the one to apologize.

Nothing would have pleased her more than to slap his face again, but her years of training and discipline interceded and forced her to be civil. There was more at stake here than just her anger—there was the reputation of the Board of Trade, whom she represented.

"Gordon," she began with a calm she was far from feeling. "You've put me in a very awkward position. I had no idea what your intentions were. After all, we've known each other such a short time. Not even a week!" Wringing her hands together, she continued in a well-modulated voice, "I know virtually nothing about you, and even if I had the opportunity to get to know you better, my interest would only be as a friend." She shouldn't have to be explaining herself, she thought, resentment building. "I have no intentions of marrying anyone."

Looking unconvinced, he said, "All women want to marry and have children."

Placing her hand on his arm, Heller said, "Not all women. I'm sorry, Gordon. I hope we can still be friends."

He looked away from her and didn't answer. The silence between them stretched to the point of being irritating, and Heller was about to walk away when finally he spoke.

"Please, forgive me, Heller. I should never have presumed. Let's put it down to my own wishful thinking."

In an effort to hold back an unladylike retort she bit down on her lower lip, then marched back into the ballroom where they rejoined Abigail and Alexander and several other couples.

It was nearing midnight when the musicians put down their instruments for a short rest. During the intermission, a tall man with thick spectacles joined the group, introducing himself as Frank Miller, vice president of the San Francisco Bank. Dressed not in a costume but in formal black evening clothes, he stood out from all the maskers. He seemed a nervous sort, Heller noticed. He had the habit of running his finger beneath his collar and stretching his neck like a goose. After a while, he drew Gordon away from the others and spoke to him sotto voce.

Gordon's expression turned angry and his voice rose. From where Heller stood, not ten feet away, it looked as if he was going to challenge the bespectacled man to fisticuffs; his hands were balled into tight, shaking fists.

Abigail drew Heller aside, away from Alexander and Robert Swain, who were watching the heated exchange, which was growing worse by the second. "Your Mr. Pierce is making a scene, Heller," Abigail whispered. "Everyone is staring at him. Mark my words, that man is not only a liar, but he's dangerous. I beg you to have nothing more to do with him after tonight."

"We'll talk about this later, Aunty," she said, patting Abigail's arm.

Gordon grabbed Miller's shoulder and shouted. "Goddammit. You promised me!"

Looking as if he was on the verge of apoplexy, Frank Miller made a wounded animal sound and moved back a step as Gordon raised his arm. A collective gasp from some of the onlookers alerted Gordon that he was being observed. He glanced around, then inclined his head, signaling the banker to follow him out of the ballroom.

Sometime later, he returned and his composure appeared restored. "Ladies, I hope you can forgive me, but that man's stupidity just cost me a lot of money." He exhaled a ragged breath.

Heller knew the ladylike thing to do was to pretend

she was unaware of the disturbance, but since everyone was staring at him and whispering, she could hardly make such a pretense believable. "I'm so sorry, Gordon. I can understand how upset you must be."

He gave an ironic laugh and touched his hand to his temple. "It was one of those unfortunate misinterpretations. I seem to be doing a lot of that lately," he said pointedly. "Would you care to step outside with me for a breath of fresh air?"

Abigail cleared her throat meaningfully.

"Thank you, but no." So he wouldn't be offended by her refusal, she pointed outside. "I think we may be in for a storm."

As if to punctuate her statement, a blast of wind blew a shower of leaves and twigs through the veranda doors into the ballroom. The gaslights flickered and the musicians faltered as they looked around to see what the trouble was.

The threat of ruined costumes sent the men and women nearest the doors scurrying back away from the small wind storm that had invaded their midst.

In knightly fashion, Gordon hurried over to the doors and pushed them shut. But as he was making his way back to Heller, they blew open again, and the zephyr eddied into the ballroom, lifting skirts and kilts alike.

A woman screamed. "Look! There on the veranda!" Her fearful cry drew everyone's attention to the open doors. The hair raised on the back of Heller's neck. Squealing, the women ran into the arms of their escorts for protection.

Heller blinked, not sure what she was seeing. She blinked again, opening her eyes to what appeared to be a black horse with a rider seated upon his back.

"My God! It's Joaquin!"

"Joaquin Murieta!" Like wildfire, the name of the

intruder passed from mouth to mouth until the entire assemblage was in a state of heightened frenzy.

"Murieta's ghost!" shouted one man.

"Murderer!"

"Bloody Bandit!" said still another.

Deep, dark laughter from the masked devil hushed the voices, and silence hung over the assemblage like a shroud. The man swung his leg over the saddlehorn and slid easily to the ground. He wore a low-crowned flat-brimmed sombrero, held in place by a cord beneath his chin. Under his black cape he wore a short black jacket, held together with a silver frog. A red sash circled his lean waist and silver buttons ran down the outside length of his leg, stopping at his high-heeled leather boots.

Holding on to a coiled bullwhip, he stepped forward and addressed the room at large. "It has been many years, *mi amigos*." His heavily accented voice rumbled like thunder across the room. "I am honored that you still remember me." He flourished a bow, bending low and sweeping his arm out before him.

Clapping, Robert Swain advanced on the intruder. "An excellent performance, my friend. You've succeeded in scaring the devil out of everyone with your portrayal of the bandit Joaquin, but enough is enough. Everybody knows Murieta is dead—has been for many years. If I recall correctly, his head is even on display at one of our local museums. Now, please, tell these good people that you're only *en masque* as they are, and not some apparition from Hell!"

A raised hand halted Swain's approach. "I assure you, señor, that is *exactly* where I come from, but since I do not wish to ruin your party, I will do as you ask." Stepping away from Swain, he said, "*Por favor, mi amigos, mi amigas*, I am sorry to have frightened you. I wish only to amuse you. Please go on with your dancing.''

Robert Swain mumbled his thanks, then waved the musicians to resume their playing. He then hurried away to close the veranda doors, leaving Joaquin to stand alone near the doorway.

A lively quadrille drew the attention away from the caped figure and sent the maskers back to their conversations, dancing, and refreshments.

Heller didn't know whether to be amused, afraid, or intrigued. Leaning toward Gordon, she whispered out of the side of her mouth, ''Do you know him?'' When he didn't acknowledge her, she tugged on his arm and repeated her question. His continued silence made her turn her attention from the masked intruder to Gordon.

His eyes were wide and staring. His face so pale it appeared bloodless. He looked as if he'd seen a ghost. ''Gordon! What on earth? What's wrong?''

The masked man stood with feet apart, legs braced, perusing the crowd. Wicked rowelled spurs jingled as he strode into the room and across the middle of the floor through the dancing couples, who parted like the Red Sea to allow him to pass.

Heller was struck by his sure stride, the confident set of wide shoulders, and his blatant arrogance. Even with the mask covering half his face, she could see the dark intensity of his gaze.

He was searching for someone.

When she saw him head in her direction, she froze.

Suddenly, he was standing before her, gazing down at her from beneath his black sombrero.

Not a ghost, thought Heller. A man.

A magnificent man.

''Señorita.'' He removed his sombrero, threw his arm across his middle and bowed. A black piratelike scarf bound his head, covering his hair. Heart pounding like a shipbuilder's hammer, Heller could only stare at him.

There was something in his eyes, in the way he looked at her that reminded her of . . .

Don Ricardo?

Could it be? She cocked her head and studied him closely, looking at him with a critical eye, comparing him to Don Ricardo. There was definitely a likeness, but then they were both of Spanish ancestry, which would give them the same swarthy coloring.

She listened carefully to his heavily accented voice. He often substituted English words and phrases for their Spanish counterparts, whereas Don Ricardo spoke English nearly as perfectly as she, using only an occasional Spanish word, such as in address.

Slowly, Joaquin drew himself back up to his full height. Now, his gaze rested on Gordon Pierce. "*Buenos nochos.* Señor *Pierce,* is it not?" His eyes glittered. "I have something of yours." He held the bullwhip in front of him, then opened his gloved hand and let the lash fall at Gordon's feet. "You recognize it, yes, no?" Turning the handle, he said, "It bears your initials, *mi amigo.*"

Gordon's pale face became mottled with patches of color. His fists clenched and Heller saw him swallow back a hard lump. "No, I've never seen it before. And you're mistaken; my initials are G.P., not L.M."

It was Gordon's clipped words, spoken in an unvaried key, that betrayed him and made Heller realize the fear she had seen on his face a few moments ago was still with him, perhaps even stronger.

But afraid of what? The man standing before him? The whip?

She glanced back and forth between the two men, making mental comparisons. Joaquin exuded confidence and wore it like a shield. Gordon—fear and cowardice.

"Ah, of course," Joaquin continued. "You are Gordon Pierce now, a gentleman, a man of business, a member of the Chamber of Commerce. I almost did not recognize you, gringo." Inch by inch, he recoiled the whip, then pushed it against Gordon's chest. "I am deeply touched that you saved this little memento of our first meeting."

She waited for Gordon to reply, but disappointingly, he said nothing at all.

"You would do me a great honor to dance the next dance with me, señorita."

Heller started. Her concentration had been so intent upon Gordon and trying to interpret his reactions, that she hadn't realized she was now the object of the masked man's attention.

"Why, I—" Her voice caught in her throat. "I can't. The next dance is spoken for." Belatedly, she handed him her dance card.

He studied the card. "The next dance belongs to Señor Pierce, yes, no?" At her nod, he took her pencil and started to write his name over Gordon's.

"Miss Peyton is with me and the next dance is mine!" Gordon said, snatching the card out of Joaquin's hand.

Heller hissed with outrage. "I bet your pardon, *Mr.* Pierce, but I am *not* with you or anyone else for that matter. And furthermore, I'm perfectly capable of speaking for myself, thank you." Disregarding the inner voice that cautioned her to be careful, to remember her goals, she turned away from Gordon and moved a step toward Joaquin. "I would be honored to dance the waltz with you, Señor Murieta."

Gordon caught Heller's arm. "Heller!" The one word was rife with warning.

Heller flashed him a look of withering scorn. Without waiting to see his reaction, she moved away and accepted Joaquin's proffered hand.

Flipping his cape over his shoulder, Joaquin took Heller into his arms and waltzed her onto the dance floor. She felt the roughness of the bullwhip against her back, telling her in advance which direction his steps would take. He was a skilled dancer, his moves intricate but smooth and easy to follow. Effortlessly, he guided her around the dance floor to the slow, swirling rhythm of the "Blue Danube Waltz."

"You are *muy* beautiful, señorita," he said in a low, rusty voice meant for her ears alone.

His voice. It had the same rich resonance as Don Ricardo's, she thought. Was it possible he was Don Ricardo? It certainly wasn't impossible. "You flatter me, Señor Murieta. Or perhaps I should say Montaños?" She threw out the challenge and breathlessly waited for his reaction.

He threw his head back and laughed. "I assure you, señorita, I am not an imposter. Joaquin Murieta does not play games."

Heller smiled, confidence making her expression smug. "I don't believe you. You look and sound almost exactly like *him.*" She lifted her hand toward his mask.

He caught her wrist and held it. "No, señorita, you will not unmask me. If you choose to believe I am someone else—your Señor Montaños—then so be it. It matters little to me."

Unconvinced, she decided to test him further, to play with him for a moment, as a cat plays with a mouse. "You're confusing me, señor. If you're not Don Ricardo *en masque,* then am I to believe Mr. Swain? That you are an apparition from Hell? A ghost, as some here think?"

He smiled at her playful look. "Do I *feel* like a ghost?" His arms tightened around her back and his warm breath stirred her hair.

With an effort, she pretended to feel nothing at all. "I don't know," she said, hoping to bluff her way through. "I've never danced with a ghost before." She moved her hand down his muscled arm. "Come now, tell me. Who are you, really?"

"I have already told you."

"But Robert Swain—Gordon—They seemed afraid of you. Why? I want to—"

He interrupted her questions by pulling her closer— much too close for propriety. "No more questions," he commanded in a gruff voice that didn't sound at all like Don Ricardo's.

"How dare you order—"

"I dare, señorita, because I am Joaquin Murieta."

"I don't understand. What are you saying?"

"You would make a very bad *soldadera*, señorita."

"Dare I ask what a *soldadera* is?"

"In your language, a camp follower."

Heller's mouth gaped in astonishment, then snapped shut. "Why, of all the—" She stopped mid-sentence, when it suddenly dawned on her that they were no longer on the dance floor but in a large draped alcove. She had been so involved with her questions and so mesmerized by the man holding her, she hadn't noticed where he had been leading her.

A million thoughts raced through her mind, but before she could put them in order and think what to do first, he pulled her to him, bent his head, and fastened his mouth to hers.

She didn't struggle, didn't even make a halfhearted attempt at it. His mouth moved demandingly over hers and she moaned in surprise when his tongue forced its way between her lips. She felt his arms loosen then grab her again, bending her into the curve of his body. Passion and need had been just words until now. *Now* they were . . . feelings . . . feelings that his body was transmitting to hers.

In her wildest dreams, she hadn't imagined she could feel like this, or that there was actually a man like this one. . . .

He broke the kiss to nuzzle her ear. His low, intimate whispers sent shivers down her spine. She didn't understand the Spanish words, but she understood the way they made her feel. *Oh, God,* she thought weakly. *I have to make him stop. I have to* . . . She was losing herself to him. Giving herself to a man she didn't know and whose face she couldn't even see.

"I'm a whore, Heller. One man's much the same as another. Their names, their faces—they don't matter anymore."

Her mother's words sounded a warning bell that gave Heller the impetus to pull away. "Please, you have to stop. I can't—I can't do this. I don't even know you."

He stood back. "Forgive me, *querida*. I did not mean to take advantage of you." He tilted his head to the side to look at her and smiled. "But you surprised me."

It was everything Heller could do to regain some semblance of composure. She wished he would just stop talking and leave her alone. Focusing on the silver frog that held his jacket together, she willed her pulses to a slower pace. Slow. Slow. Slow. If only she could exercise that same will over the other parts of her body.

She pushed him away and immediately affected an air of prim restraint. "You have indeed taken advantage of me, and now I'll thank you to let me go and return me to the dance floor before our absence is noted."

He did as she asked, discreetly returning her to the

ballroom. When the music ended, he stood back from
her and bowed.

Heller saw Abigail across the room. A look of concern marred her aunt's features, and she hurried across
the room toward them.

"We will meet again, Señorita Peyton. I will come
for you from nowhere, like the wind that brought me
here tonight, and we will finish what we have begun."
He turned on his heel and left, crossing the ballroom
in long, sure strides. He opened the doors, letting in
the wind, and walked out on the veranda. He swung
onto his horse's back, then touched his sombrero in
salute.

Again, the music stopped. All eyes turned to the
veranda.

"*Gracias*, señores, señoritas, for allowing me to join
your entertainment." The horse danced impatiently
beneath him, then he applied his spurs to the animal's
flanks and galloped off into the night.

Heller grabbed and lifted her gown and ran across
the room to the veranda doors. Her gaze followed his
shadowy silhouette across the gardens and the wide
expanse of lawn. Then a bolt of lightning streaked
across the eastern sky, illuminating both horse and
rider. It was followed by a clap of thunder that rattled
the veranda doors and made the maskers retreat to the
back of the room. Heller stood firm, watching, until
he rode out of sight. Who was he *really*? she wondered. Joaquin Murieta, a feared bandit, or Don Ricardo Montaños, a San Diego *hacendado*?

That night before retiring, Heller wrote in her journal.

*This evening a delightful party was held at the Cos-
mopolitan Hotel, given by the San Francisco Chamber
of Commerce. All the guests appeared* en masque. *The*

effect on the floor was like a gathering of rare and exotic birds. Some of the costumes were very rich, and some of the maskers sustained their character in excellent style.

Heller reread her journal entry. There was so much she couldn't allow herself to say about one particular masker. So much she would never forget.

Joaquin slowed El Tigre to a trot when they reached the city street. Minutes later, they made the eastern edge of town, but still they kept moving in spite of the threat of rain. They were well beyond the city when Joaquin reined the stallion to a halt and turned in the saddle. "Whoa, boy. Easy now. We will rest here a while."

Behind him was San Francisco. At night, with her lights flickering, she was like a beautiful woman draped in diamonds. In front of him—a vast emptiness. Land. She, too, was beautiful. By day, a lush green goddess. By night, with the moon shining upon her face, an enchanting seductress. Though it had been many years since he had seen her, he remembered her well. He had ridden her hills and valleys, bathed in her lakes, rivers, and streams, rested beneath her piny boughs, and slept in her secret caves.

Looking at her, at this land he loved, he knew he had already been in the city too long. He rose high in the saddle and felt the strength of the land seep into his being. Like fine brandy, her power flowed through his veins, renewing him as she always did.

If only she could work her magic on his mind to release him from his memories. Then he could be whole again.

He had enjoyed seeing Mauger's look of stunned surprise and reveled in watching his fear. He could almost imagine what was going on inside his head, and he had no doubt the first place Mauger would go when he got home was to his desk drawer—to see if the bullwhip was really *his*. He wished he could be there to witness his confusion.

And then there was Heller. The taste of her still lingered on his lips. The feel of her still lingered in his senses and stirred his body.

One day he would keep his promise to her and they would finish what they had begun.

Until then . . .

Chapter 9

The whip was gone.

Luther Mauger jumped back from the empty drawer as if he'd been stung.

All the way home from the ball, he'd assured himself that *his* bullwhip would still be in the drawer where he put it two years ago, the day he moved to Rincon Hill and became Gordon Pierce, a bona fide member of San Francisco society. Since then, he'd not given the whip another thought.

"Damn!" He flung the chair aside and sent it crashing into the wall. "He stole it! That goddamn Mex broke into *my* house and stole it!"

His head jerked, mouth fell open, and words without voice tumbled out. His lungs deflated and he gasped for air.

"Murieta's dead!" he shouted. "Dead men don't break into houses and steal bullwhips!" He roared like a lion, then began pacing the room, thinking, swearing, and thinking some more. Common sense told him the man at the ball couldn't have been Murieta. But who, then? One of Murieta's *compadres*? Or maybe a relative of Murieta's wife? Either answer was logical, and either way, someone was out to get revenge.

"Jesus Christ!" He stopped pacing and clutched the edge of a table.

It didn't matter *who* the hell stole the bullwhip. What

mattered was that the thief knew he wasn't Gordon Pierce! The ramificaitons of that revelation nearly choked him.

Not for the first time, he wished he'd never heard the name of Joaquin Murieta.

Murieta was like a plague.

Of all the foreign miners Luther and his mercenary companions had robbed and whipped, the women and girls they raped, the claims they'd stolen, only Murieta and his *cholo* pack of cutthroats had pursued them, day after day, month after month. Davie, Jed, and Sam—all dead within six months after they'd visited Murieta's cabin. Chills chased themselves down Luther's spine as he recalled the day Murieta found Sam and staked him out Indian-style, then poured sugar water over his head and let the ants do the killing. That was the day Luther had known Murieta was playing a game—saving him for last.

Luther wasn't a fool. He knew when to keep out of a man's way, when to run. Murieta's hate made him an invincible foe. Luther couldn't have been more relieved than when the Wells Fargo agents caught up with him for stealing a shipment and threw him in jail. The circuit-court judge found him guilty and sentenced him to twenty years in San Quentin. He remembered thinking how funny it was that he'd cheated Murieta out of his revenge.

The Lord worked in mysterious ways, Luther thought, still clutching the table.

So did the law.

Soon after he'd been incarcerated, the California Rangers ambushed and killed Murieta near Lake Tulare. Luther had laughed again when he'd read the newspaper report. They'd cut off Murieta's head, presented it to the governor, and collected a five-thousand-dollar reward.

Another brand of California justice.

With Murieta dead, the safety of San Quentin no longer held any appeal, so he'd used the only means he could think of to buy his freedom. The Wells Fargo payload. He'd never revealed where he'd hidden it. Warden Henderson, a man long overdue for retirement, had been easily bribed. For half the payload, ten thousand dollars, paid in thousand-dollar drafts, the warden had arranged a release and erased Luther's name from all the prison records.

Once out of prison, Luther was free to go anywhere and do anything he wanted without having to look over his shoulder for Murieta. He'd spent enough time locked up behind bars to know he didn't want to go back to being a mercenary. He wanted to work for himself, make something of himself. The other half of the payload had given him the opportunity.

So now what was he to think?

He moved about the room in a daze. What did the thief want? Money? If he'd wanted him dead, he would have already killed him. Or maybe he was waiting until later. Maybe even tonight.

With that thought, he took his derringer out of its hiding place from under the table and checked to make sure it was loaded. It had been a long time since he'd carried a gun. Compared to his old Dragoon, with its seven-and-a-half-inch barrel, the little derringer seemed like a child's toy. Still, it gave him a sense of preparedness and safety.

Breathing easier, he sat down and tried to think what action he would take to find out more about the thief, but a small nagging thought kept him from concentrating.

What if the masked man really was Murieta? He knew it was ridiculous to even think such a thing, but there had been rumors that the rangers beheaded the *wrong* Joaquin. What if Murieta had survived the ambush?

And if he had, where had he been all these years? Why hadn't anyone seen him or heard about him?

They had.

He tilted his head back and damned himself for not immediately remembering. Months after the ambush, there had been a report that Murieta had been sighted in Los Angeles; a year or so later, another report saying Joaquin had robbed a stagecoach near Bakersfield. And two years ago, he recalled, with blinding clarity, right after he'd moved into the house, a woman at the Quarter Circle U Ranch in Walker Basin, east of Bakersfield in the Tehachapi Mountains, reported that Joaquin and a band of men had stopped by her ranch and asked her to give them some breakfast.

Luther scowled. Murieta—a damn *peon* who, in the name of revenge for his wife's death, had become a bandit, then a Mexican hero, and now, thanks to some Cherokee Indian who fancied himself a writer, a goddamn legend!

Luther ran his fingers through his hair and jumped out of his chair. At a sudden, almost hopeful thought, he looked back at the open desk drawer.

Maybe the bullwhip wasn't the only thing that had been stolen.

His gaze darted around the study, looking for anything missing or out of place. Frantically, he crossed the room and searched his desk. As far as he could tell, nothing else had been touched. But what about the rest of the house? The silver? His new diamond stickpin? He'd been so obsessed with the missing bullwhip and Murieta that he hadn't asked himself if something else might have been taken.

Torn between the hope that the theft had been committed by a common thief and the dread that it wasn't,

Luther raced from room to room, looking into every drawer and cupboard. An hour later, he was convinced that only the whip had been taken.

"Chum Soon!" Luther's voice bellowed. "Chum Soon, get out here you goddamn slant-eyed heathen. I want to talk to you. Now!" Luther stalked down the hall and reached Chum Soon's bedroom just as the sleepy-eyed Chinaman opened his door.

"Whassamatter, boss?" Chum Soon hastily belted his dragon-embroidered robe. "You want me get slave girl? I get dressed and go."

Before he could turn around, Luther stopped him. "No . . . I mean . . . yes, but not now. Later." He paced back and forth. "You know that bullwhip in my desk drawer? It's been stolen. Have you seen any signs of someone prowling around the house? Have you noticed anything missing or out of place?" At Chum Soon's negative headshake, he asked, "Have you invited anyone into the house? Any strangers?"

Again the Chinaman shook his head, then his eyes widened. "Small Chinee boy come beg food. I feed in kitchen, then send away."

Luther had stopped pacing and stood glaring at his servant, intent upon his answer. "He never left the kitchen?"

"No, boss. He stay in kitchen, then go away."

"What about when you went shopping? Did you close the windows and lock the house?"

"Yes, boss. Chum Soon very careful. You want me get slave girl now?" the little man timidly inquired.

Luther sighed in frustration. "Yeah. Go." Luther waved him away. "But be quick about it, and tell Charlie I'm tired of those worn-out nags he's been sending. They're half-dead before they get here. Most of them don't survive the first night. Tell him if he doesn't send me a good one this time, I'm going to stop buying from him. There are plenty of other slave traders, and I'll find one who'll give me what I want. You hear me?''

''Yes, boss. Me tell him good.''

Luther left the Chinaman to his late-night errand and went up to his room to make himself ready. Could he believe Chum Soon? What reason would the Chinaman have to lie? He was well-paid and he was given one day off a week to go visit his family in Little China. The old man never complained, never said one way or another how he felt about the slave girls. In the two years Chum Soon had been in his employ, the Celestial had proven himself a loyal and trusted servant, but loyalty and trust lasted only as long as the money, Luther ruefully reminded himself.

Unless he could bribe another banker, or talk Kim Lee into extending his credit, he had two weeks at the most before he would be out of money. Two weeks before Chum Soon would be out of loyalty and quit. And when that happened, he had a new problem: what to do with a talkative Chinese house servant who knew too much about Gordon Pierce's private affairs.

''Miller. Frank Miller. Fool,'' Luther grumbled as he climbed the stairs. He wouldn't have to think about doing away with Chum Soon or losing his business or his house and everything else he'd worked so damn hard to get if it wasn't for that weasely bastard Miller promising that the loan would be no problem. Just a matter of providing some information and getting an approval, Miller had said. But now, suddenly, the loan had been refused because of fraudulent financial information.

Fraudulent! Luther made a loud guffaw. Hell yes, it was fraudulent. Every asset he'd listed had been an out-and-out goddamn lie, but Miller knew that and was willing to risk presenting the false information to Ralston for the five thousand he'd been promised to see that it went through. It would have given Luther immense satisfaction to take his favorite whip to Miller's lily-white back, but after tonight's little public confrontation, anything that happened to Miller would instantly be blamed on him. It wasn't worth the risk.

As he saw it, there was only one thing that could save him. He had to get Heller to marry him. Even if she didn't have any money of her own, which he doubted, the Peyton name would give him the time he needed to make good on his rapidly mounting debts. El Dorado was about to pay off. Any day now, Zeke, his mining foreman, had wired him the middle of May. A bonanza, he'd said. Bigger than Sutter's Mill!

Closing the bedroom door behind him, he stripped off his surcoat, then lit the opium lamp next to the bed. A warm yellow light filled the room. A soothing light. He continued to remove his costume, tossing the pieces in all directions. Chum Soon would pick them up tomorrow and return them to the costumers.

Wearing only his knight's hose and boots, he gathered his smoking paraphernalia. Groaning, he sat down on the edge of the bed. Everything seemed to be happening at once, he thought, throwing his head back, wondering when and if it would end before he was ruined. First, old lady Peyton telling him in no uncertain terms to keep away from Heller, then Heller spurning his affections, that fool Frank Miller telling him there would be no bank loan, the Murieta masker . . . and the stolen bullwhip.

Anxious for the bliss that only the poppy could bring, he held the pipe over the lamp to warm it, then dipped a wire poker into the opium box and extracted only what adhered to the tip. The heat from the lamp caused the opium to swell until it was many times its original size. Then he rolled the opium flat to expel the steam that had built up inside it. When, at last, the process was complete, he inhaled the warm opium vapor and sat back against the mound of pillows.

An hour later, the bedroom door squeaked open and Chum Soon led a young Cantonese girl into the room. "This Ning Toy." He gestured for her to walk ahead of him, then turned and quietly closed the door and retreated back down the stairs.

Slightly dizzy, Luther moved over to the edge of the bed and watched the girl as she timidly made her way toward him. She was tiny, barely five feet tall and probably not even a hundred pounds. She wasn't pretty, at least not in the way Caucasian women were pretty, but she had the look of childlike innocence that he coveted even more than a pretty face.

"Come here." He backed up his words with a gesture she understood. "Do you speak English?"

"Little." Her voice tinkled like a bell.

Luther smiled. "Good. Then we'll understand each other." He gestured again, and she sat down beside him and started to unbelt her baggy blue blouse. "So you're not as innocent as you look," he said, pleased that she knew what was expected of her. He hated it when Canton Charlie sent him virgins. They knew nothing about how to please a man, especially a man like him, whose needs were slightly out of the ordinary and far more specialized.

Her slowness aggravated him, but he waited patiently until the last of her clothing was removed. Then he pushed her backward, to lie flat on the bed. For the moment, he wanted only to look at her while he smoked his pipe and savored the delicious feeling spreading throughout his body. But after a while, his thoughts grew fuzzy and he imagined it was Heller he was looking at.

"Miss Heller Peyton," he whispered, leaning over

Ning Toy's prone body. "Miss High and Mighty. You humiliated me," he jeered. He drew a breath and spit on the bed next to her. "And to think, you almost had me convinced that you were sincere about spinsterhood. Ha! You think everyone didn't see you throw yourself at that Mex? God, how I hate women like you. Bluebloods—you all think you're better than everybody else. But I know your kind. Whores. All whores!" He hit her then, and she screamed. His hand left a blaze of color across her snow-white breast.

Her scream cleared his head. He reared back, instantly aware of what he had done. "Fool! Stupid fool," he berated himself. He'd had too much of the poppy. It had made him lose sight of reality. He stood up and went over to the window for a breath of fresh air. In the future, he'd have to be more careful about how much he smoked. The tunnels beneath Little China were full of sick old men who had thought themselves immune to the power of the poppy.

Disgusted with himself, he paced the length of the room while Ning Toy crawled beneath the covers. He shouldn't have had Chum Soon fetch the girl. Not tonight. Not when he had so much on his mind. He needed to think—think about how he was going to get a wedding ring around Heller Peyton's finger, think about who stole the bullwhip and why. He paced back to the other end of the room and stopped suddenly.

"The head! Murieta's head!" he blurted as his thoughts came together. If he could see the head, then he would be reassured that Joaquin was dead. Swain said it was on display in a museum somewhere here in San Francisco. Tomorrow, he would have Chum Soon start making inquiries about its location, and Monday afternoon, after his appointment with Kim Lee, he would pay a visit to the museum and . . .

Another thought bolted into his mind.

Heller had said she wanted to visit a museum. He smiled with wicked delight. Inviting her to accompany him was the perfect way to get back into her good graces. And then—then he could invite her to the house to see *his* art collection. He had to laugh at that. His *collection* consisted of one painting. "A *portrait*," he choked out the word, loathing the memory of his embarrassment at the Cliff House. Well, he knew the right word now, and he'd also learned a lesson. Never again would he enter into a conversation in which he lacked a basic knowledge.

And after he brought her home . . . Luther raised a brow. What if the proper Miss Peyton suddenly found herself in a compromising position? Possibly a situation where her virtue was in question? She could hardly go back to Boston and resume her life there—even as a spinster—if her reputation was in ruins. Maybe then she would be more receptive to his affections.

Returning to Ning Toy, he patiently showed her how to please him, and when she was done, he rewarded her efforts with a hard slap across her face.

He stood back and gazed at the fearful girl, then pulled a quirt out from under the bed.

He'd always done his best thinking while enjoying himself.

Chapter 10

"After my offensive behavior at the ball, I wasn't sure you'd accept my invitation." Gordon wore a sheepish look as he walked beside Heller down the steps to the lobby, which was quickly filling with Bostonians and chamber members preparing for their afternoon excursions.

"Please, Gordon. You promised you wouldn't bring it up," Heller said lightly, pretending an easy unconcern she didn't feel. If Alexander Rice hadn't been sitting right next to her at the breakfast table when Gordon had invited her to the museum, she would have politely refused, just as she and Abigail had planned she would do, but Alexander's presence had put her in a difficult position; a refusal would have made her seem inordinately rude.

"I realize now, of course," he continued in the same humble vein, ignoring her reminder, "that it was much too soon to expose my feelings. But, as I said, I was worried there wouldn't be another opportunity."

Chiding herself for a lack of compassion and understanding where his obviously wounded ego was concerned, Heller smiled and shook her head, wishing now she'd had the gumption to decline the invitation in spite of Alexander Rice's presence. The apologies, the explanations, and the embarrassed awkwardness

were the very things she'd wanted to avoid, not to
mention the man himself.

On the other hand, she had to give Gordon credit.
First, for persistence. Second, for courage. She knew
from personal experience what it was like to want
something so badly that you wouldn't let anything or
anyone stand in your way. Though Gordon would be
fighting a losing battle, she supposed the least she
could do was treat him kindly. After all, the museum
had been her idea, not his. He was only trying to
please.

With Gordon at her elbow, they maneuvered their
way through the people. If nothing else, she hoped the
museum visit would take her mind off Don Ricardo
and Joaquin Murieta, if indeed they *were* two separate
people. She still wasn't sure in spite of her comparisons, which included everything from the way they
spoke to the way they kissed.

Since that long-ago day when she'd decided to follow in her aunt's footsteps and devote herself to charitable and philanthropic causes, she'd never once
allowed herself more than an intellectual interest in a
man. Now, to suddenly find herself consumed with
everything *but* an intellectual interest—with unadulter-
ated passion. . . . It was most disconcerting. In truth,
it worried her to no end. She'd analyzed her reactions
and physical responses until her head ached. She had
totally abandoned all propriety and cast off her own
strict codes of morality as if they'd never existed. It
was baffling.

Or maybe there was an explanation.

Maybe the truth was that she had not escaped Five
Points, that it would always be a part of her. She was,
after all, her mother's daughter.

A whore.

God, how the word grated! Somehow just thinking

it reopened the wound she'd spent half her life trying
to heal.

Thankfully no one but herself could know what was
in her heart or her head. And technically a woman
couldn't be a whore unless she sold her body. Therefore, as long as she remained chaste, she could continue her ladylike pretense. Spinsterhood offered her
that shelter.

She could hardly wait to leave San Francisco and
temptation behind. Back home in Boston, she could
forget all that had happened to her here. Eventually,
time would dim the memories of what she'd experienced, and she'd forget the two men—or one—whichever
the case may be—who had awakened the woman in her.
The whore in her. Back home in Boston, she'd be safe.

Low gray clouds hid the sun. A cool, damp breeze
filled with the tang of salt made Heller glad she'd worn
her mantle. East of the hotel entrance, a seemingly
endless line of people waited to tour the locomotive
and the Pullman cars that had been her home on wheels
for over a week and would be again next Saturday.

Gordon helped her into his phaeton. "I've never ridden a train. What's it like?" He took up the reins and
started the bays down the street.

"Jarring. Your body never stops shaking. Not even
during meals."

She hadn't forgiven him. He could tell. Getting conversation out of her was like trying to get gold out of
a Chinaman. Bitch! He supposed he'd have to make a
bigger effort to charm her if he expected her to accept
his invitation to come to his house and see his art
collection.

The need to get her there had become even more
urgent after his morning visit with Kim Lee. Last
week, the white-haired old man had been understand-

ing about his financial problems, but now, suddenly, he was raising his prices so high there was no room for profit. Not only that, but he was changing his policies and wanted to be paid for his merchandise upon ordering. "No more wait money," he'd said, then demanded the balance from the last shipment.

Gordon cursed himself for trusting Kim Lee's verbal agreement. He should have demanded a written contract stating the terms and conditions. He'd thought himself a good businessman, needing only a handshake to make a bargain. There was much he had yet to learn, he realized bitterly.

"While I'm thinking of it." He turned toward Heller, looked directly in her eyes to make sure he had her attention. "I've checked with the chamber, and there has been a change in the itinerary. They've scheduled another theater performance for this evening. Señorita Valdez was so popular, they decided to arrange for everyone to see her new performance. Frankly, one evening of all that toe tapping and foot pounding was enough for me. I couldn't help but notice that you didn't seem overly enthusiastic about the first performance, so I wondered if you'd care to forgo the theater and see my art collection instead?"

"Thank you, but no. I'm staying in the hotel this evening and having a quiet supper. I have to get up very early Tuesday morning for my trip to the woods. I'm told there will be a lot of walking, so I want to be well-rested."

"Another time, then." Gordon proffered one of his practiced smiles to hide his displeasure. "Here we are," he announced as they pulled up before a narrow, three-storied brick building.

Within seconds after Heller stepped inside Dr. Jordan and Co.'s Museum, she sneezed. She had barely recuperated from the first one when she felt a second coming on. She dug into her bag for a handkerchief and held it to her nose. A quick perusal of the gloomy interior told her it wasn't flowers making her nose itch and her eyes water, but dust, mold, and mildew.

Looking over the handkerchief, she saw that the museum wasn't a museum of art as she'd been led to believe, but a dusty, dirty collection of oddities and curiosities, the likes of which she heard was exhibited in a circus sideshow.

Gordon seemed unaware that anything was amiss. She considered directing his attention to an overhead sign that read, "Dr. Jordan's Pacific Museum of Anatomy and Science," then thought better of it. This only further substantiated Abigail's suspicions about his character: he was not a gentleman. A gentleman would have known the difference between an art museum and a museum of anatomy and science. But surely Gordon would soon realize that a stuffed two-headed goat, a four-legged chicken, and a kangaroo in spirits were not art.

After sneezing a third time, Gordon asked if she was all right. "Oh, yes. I'm fine," she replied, speaking through the tail of the handkerchief. "I always sneeze in museums. The dust, you know." To illustrate her point, she drew a circle in the thick lawyer of dust covering the nearest glass case. "They don't seem to be able to eliminate it no matter how often they clean."

A sign atop the glass case read: "Section of the cranium, ribs, pelvis, etc. This was prepared from the body of Richard Hardinge, an Englishman, who poisoned a family of eight, and afterward shot himself."

Heller wiped a larger portion of the glass and peered into the case. She drew back sharply when she realized that the object of her study was a long-dead human being. Grimacing, she stepped back and moved down the row of wood-framed glass display cases, casting a

quick glance into each, hoping to see something besides disease-ravaged or malformed bodies. At the end
of the second row, she looked up to find herself facing
an elevated life-size plaster and wax figure of a man.

She gave a gasp of surprise, then her mouth clamped
shut. The figure was naked and nothing had been left
to the imagination, except for skin tone and hair. An
embarrassed flush heated her face, but she didn't turn
her eyes away. Indeed, she had always wondered about
the male anatomy, but had no experience to draw upon,
not even from Cow Bay.

It was intriguing. It was frightening. She checked
Gordon's position in the museum to make sure he
hadn't witnessed her encounter, then hurried away to
the next row of exhibits: animals.

Joaquin had been keeping a close eye on Heller and
Mauger. Last night, during his watch on Mauger's
house, he'd overheard the servant Chum Soon tell
Mauger where the museum was that was displaying
Joaquin Murieta's head. He'd also seen a dark green
cart pull around the drive to the back of the house.
''Drake's Disposal'' was printed in discreet gold let-
tering on the side of the closed cart.

When Lino's watch came, Joaquin left to locate the
museum. He noted the hours painted on the door, then
returned to his hotel. Not only did he want to see this
head for himself, but he wanted to see Maguer's reaction to it.

Joaquin pulled a face as he closed the museum door
behind him. The place smelled musty.

He and Hop Fong had no sooner stepped inside when
a man dashed in behind them, yelling for Dr. Jordan
to come quick. Apparently there had been some kind
of accident.

''You just make yourself at home,'' said the doctor,

as he grabbed his bag off the coat tree. "I'll be back quick as I can to answer your questions."

Joaquin nodded and went about his business.

"This some place," said Hop Fong. His eyes were wide with wonder.

Joaquin smiled. He'd figured that the boy would enjoy the museum, with all its unusual exhibits and displays.

After a half hour, Joaquin had made no progress in finding the head. The inside of the museum was bigger than it looked, and it was filled to capacity. It was now half past noon, and still Mauger hadn't arrived. Joaquin was growing more impatient by the moment. He had assumed Mauger would be coming to the museum today, right after its noon opening. Obviously he had assumed wrong. Maybe he wasn't coming at all. No, he thought again. He'd come. After the incident at the ball, he would want to prove to himself that Joaquin Murieta was dead.

Moments later, the door opened again, admitting a man and woman. Joaquin couldn't have been more surprised than when he realized the woman was Heller.

It seemed to Joaquin that a museum of anatomy and science was no place to take a respectable young woman for an afternoon outing. It just went to prove that for all Mauger's fancy new manners and expensive tailor-made clothes, he hadn't changed.

An idea came to him. He bent over and whispered to Hop Fong what he had in mind. "There could be trouble. He's a dangerous man."

"No trouble. You see," the boy whispered back. Then he disappeared, silent as a shadow among the displays.

Across the room, Joaquin saw Mauger walking down an aisle, glancing back and forth between exhibits. Heller went in the opposite direction. From the back of the museum, he watched her confrontation with the male mannequin. At first, he'd thought he was going to have to rescue her from a swoon, but she recovered herself admirably, then studied the mannequin with a critical eye. It was rare entertainment.

"So we meet again," he said, as she walked his way. She stopped short and looked up.

"Indeed."

"It's a small world."

"And getting smaller, it seems, every day."

He felt the full brunt of her stare and knew she was comparing him to his alter ego. Her fingers fidgeted with her handkerchief.

"Are you alone?" he queried, careful to speak without an accent.

"No, no, Mr. Pierce is with me." She turned around and pointed to where Gordon stood inspecting a large glass jar on the other side of the museum. "And you?" She glanced around behind him.

"Yes, Miss Valdez is busy with rehearsals and performances." Her question told him more than she would have guessed. She was jealous. He wasn't sure why that should please him when he hated it so much in Elena. Not for a second would he admit that he was smitten with the redhead; Heller Peyton was far too rich for his blood, with all her academy airs and ladylike refinery.

Over Heller's head, he saw Hop Fong silently weave his way between the aisles and around the exhibits toward Luther Mauger. He had begun to respect the boy's many talents, and after today's impromptu assignment, if all went well, Hop Fong would be getting a sizable bonus.

Moments later, there was a scuffle across the room. Joaquin saw Mauger jerk around just in time to catch a large animal skeleton from falling on top of him.

"What the hell?" he shouted. Then, "Hey. Hey, you! Come back here. Thief!"

Quick as a fox, the pig-tailed Chinese boy darted away from Mauger and zigzagged between the display cases toward the exit.

Bellowing with rage, Gordon shoved the skeleton away from him, then reached beneath his coat and pulled out his derringer. "Stop or I'll shoot!"

Heller glimpsed the tiny pistol. "Gordon, no! He's just a boy! You can't shoot a child!"

A shot exploded next to Heller's right ear. She made a loud shrieking sound.

The derringer flew out of Gordon's hand, stunning him into silence. He stared dumbly at the blood trickling off his fingers.

Holding her hands over her mouth, Heller searched for the boy, terrified of what she would see when she found him. The museum door swung open and the sounds of the traffic on the street poured into the tomblike museum. She felt a movement behind her and swung around, turning her shoulder into Don Ricardo's chest.

Her gaze froze on his right arm, held out in front of him, raised and level. In his hand was a gun, black as black could be, with deeply cast scrolls and gold mountings. A curl of smoke hovered over the barrel; its acrid odor stung her nose.

"You'll regret that, Montaños," Gordon warned.

"I have many regrets, Señor Pierce, but stopping you from shooting a child is not one of them."

Heller released a relieved sigh.

Gordon bent and picked the derringer up off the floor, then tucked it back under his coat. He turned his angry look on Heller. "Come on. I'll take you back to your hotel."

She met his look and lifted her chin defiantly. "No, thank you. I'll find my own way back."

He looked dumbfounded. "Heller, I—"

She held up her hand to stop him. "There's nothing you can say that can excuse what you tried to do. Nothing!" Her eyes darkened with loathing. "Don't ever come anywhere near me or my aunt again, or I'll tell everyone on the Board of Trade and the Chamber of Commerce just exactly what you tried to do here this afternoon."

"The little bastard stole my money! I had a right to shoot him and protect my property!" When Heller turned her back on him, he started across the room toward her, only to be stopped midway by the hollow click of the Colt's hammer. With a venomous look, he glared at the two of them, then strode to the exit and slammed the door behind him.

The second he was gone, Heller turned to Don Ricardo and shouted, "We have to follow him—to make sure he doesn't go after the boy. If he finds the boy, he'll kill him."

Don Ricardo pulled back his coat and tucked the gun into a slim leather holster belted around his waist.

"The boy's long gone, Heller. He'll never find him."

"You can't be sure of that," she insisted with rising hysteria.

"Yes, I can. That boy is a notorious pickpocket. He does this sort of thing all the time. There isn't a hiding place in San Francisco that he doesn't know. He'll be fine."

Through a blur of tears, she stared at him. "What kind of man would try to kill a child?" She felt like a child herself as flung herself into his arms. Mumbling, she added, "Aunty said she thought there was something suspicious about him, but I—oh—" She gave into the tears and leaned her cheek against his coat front.

Joaquin had had little experience in calming hysterical women, but he supposed it wasn't much different than calming a frightened horse, and his *vaquero* days had given him plenty of experience with horses. It required only a gentle touch, some softly spoken words, and letting the animal sniff his scent.

At length, Heller pushed herself out of his embrace. "I'm sorry. I was overwrought. Guns terrify me."

"I'll let you in on a little secret," he said in a quiet voice. "Guns frighten me, too."

Her nose wrinkled into a frown. "Then why do you carry one?"

"A man has to protect himself."

Sniffing, she dabbed her nose with her handkerchief. "None of the gentlemen I know in Boston carry a gun."

He laughed. "I never said I was a gentleman, Heller." Her look of utter dismay goaded him to ask, "Why are you surprised? If I remember correctly, you decided I wasn't a gentleman as soon as you opened your eyes in Elena's room."

If he had doused her with iced water, she could not have looked more indignant. "Yes," she agreed. "Thank you for reminding me. I don't know how I could have forgotten, but I assure you it won't happen again." Her chin jutted forward at a mulish angle.

Even when she was angry, she was beautiful. Too beautiful for her own good, he thought, watching the agitated rise and fall of her breasts beneath her prim forest-green day dress. He ached just to look at her. It seemed that lately, since he'd met her, he'd done a lot of aching. Without a word, he walked past her and started looking in the display cases.

"What are you doing?"

He continued down the aisle. "Looking."

"Looking for what?"

"Nothing in particular. Just looking. It's why I came here."

Silence.

"There's nothing here but a lot of *dead* things."

"Well, I'll concede that it doesn't compare to any of Boston's museums, but it's still fascinating," he said offhandedly as he studied the contents of the case nearest him.

Heller's interest sharpened. "You've visited them?"

"Once or twice, when I was studying at Harvard."

"Harvard? *You* went to Harvard?"

He looked up. "Yes, Heller. I went to Harvard. Is that so difficult to believe?"

She shook her head and gave him a watery smile. "No. Of course not." But her look told him differently.

"Maybe you'd like me to recite Shakespeare. Do you have a favorite play? *Merchant of Venice? Romeo and Juliet?*"

She turned her head to the side and gave an exasperated groan. "I believe you. It's just that I didn't think a gunslinger would have been educated at Harvard."

"I am not a gunslinger."

She clicked her tongue and waved away his answer as if it meant nothing at all. "I hate to impose on you, but you see, my escort left in something of a rush. Do you think you could at least pretend to be a gentleman long enough to take me back to the hotel?"

Joaquin halted at the large jar Mauger had been examining. Floating in some kind of liquid was a human head. *"Sangre de Cristo,"* he whispered as he bent to have a closer look. The man's eyes were open and black as two pieces of coal. Straight, thick hair hung down the sides of a bloated face—a face that in spite of its distorted features seemed terribly familiar.

Curious, Joaquin read the card describing exhibit number 563. "Head of Joaquin Murieta, a celebrated bandit and murderer. Shot and killed in an early morning ambush by the California Rangers at Cantua Creek, July 25, 1853. Captain Harry Love used this head to prove capture and claim the state reward of $5,000."

His breath cut through his body like a knife as he spoke the name of his one-time *compadre*. "Joaquin Carillo." Now he knew the reason why everyone thought the head was his. Seventeen years ago, Carillo had been as close to him as Lino was now. They had even looked alike. Pain tore into his gut, making him want to vomit, but still he couldn't take his eyes off the jar and its grizzly contents.

"Carillo. *Mi amigo. Dios!* It was you!" All these years, he'd thought Carillo escaped the ambush. All these years, whenever he thought about him, he imagined him holding a pretty señorita on his knee. All these years, he had been wrong.

Had Elena known, he wondered. Lino? Somebody must have known! Somebody should have told him! He took off his hat and ran his fingers through his hair and down the back of his neck. Bending forward, he wrapped his hands around the glass. "It *should* have been me." His throat constricted, cutting off his words.

"Señor Montaños," said Heller. "Please, I—"

The museum door opened and banged shut, announcing the arrival of the tardy curator. "I hope you folks'll forgive me for not being here to answer your questions. A woman down the street was struck by a runaway horse cart. I had to see what I could do for her until she could be taken to the hospital." The curator, a short, gray-haired, portly man, headed toward

Heller. "I'm Dr. Jordan, by the way. I hope you've been enjoying yourselves." At Heller's nod, he turned his attention on Joaquin. "Ah-ha. I see you've met my star boarder. Joaquin Murieta."

"Murieta?" Heller parroted the curator in a voice that was off-key. "The bandit?" She followed the man to where Don Ricardo stood.

"Among other things," Dr. Jordan replied.

"What other *things*?" Heller protested. Then she saw what was in the jar and drew back as if she'd been struck. "Dear God."

Dr. Jordan seemed to take her revulsion in stride. "Well, I suppose that depends on who you talk to. The Mexican people revered him. The gringos hated him, called him the scourge of California. The Chinese were scared to death of him. Seems he and his friends liked to cut off their ears and make them into necklaces."

Joaquin tore himself away from the exhibit and concentrated on a point of light coming in through the grimy window near the entrance. Only once in his entire life had he let his emotions get the better of him—when he'd buried Rosita. It had taken more out of him than he cared to admit, and he'd promised himself it would never happen again.

Heller cringed. "He was a murderer, too?"

"So the story goes," the curator said with a harsh guffaw. "The worst kind of murderer—killed for the sheer pleasure of it."

Joaquin could stand it no more. "Excuse me, señor, but I believe you have been misinformed. Joaquin Murieta was not a murderer, nor did he cut off the ears of Chinamen."

Dr. Jordan shrugged. "Well, that's what I mean. Depends on who you're talking to. Everybody's heard something different. Guess the only one who knows for sure is Joaquin himself, and as you can see, he isn't saying much these days. If you're really interested, you might want to read this book."

Joaquin took the book from the curator's hand and read the title: *The Life and Adventures of Joaquin Murieta, The Celebrated California Bandit.*

He took a half-step backwards, his senses reeling. This, on top of the shock of seeing Carillo's head, was more than he had counted on. "Who wrote this?" he demanded, barely maintaining his control.

He read the author's name at the same time the curator said it, "Yellow Bird, otherwise known as John Rollin Ridge."

Thumbing quickly through the pages, he noted several names of people he knew and places he'd visited. "When was it written?"

"Seems to me it was 1854, just a few months after our star boarder here met his Maker."

Joaquin handed the book back to the curator. "You shouldn't believe everything you read."

Heller intercepted the transaction. "Is the book for sale? I'd like to have a copy."

"Yes, ma'am. Four bits."

Heller dug into her bag and extracted the required coinage.

Joaquin gritted his teeth. "I thought you wanted me to take you back to the hotel."

Heller looked up from examining the book's cover. "I do! But I thought— Oh, never mind." She tucked the book under her arm. "Ready when you are, Señor Montaños."

"I'd like to thank you for bringing me back," Heller said as they came up to her door. She reached into her bag to search for her key.

"You're welcome."

Something had come over him when they were in the museum, but she wasn't sure what it was. "I'm sorry to have inconvenienced you." At last she found the key and inserted it into the lock.

"I just hope you've learned your lesson to stay away from Gordon Pierce."

Heller rolled her eyes. "Oh, believe me. I have. I never want to see that man again!"

The door lock next to hers clicked open, but before Heller knew what was happening, Don Ricardo had his hand on the key and was opening the door and pushing her inside. She whirled about, prepared to give him a significant piece of her mind, when suddenly, he pulled her into his arms and smothered her insults with a hard angry kiss that stole her breath away.

Outside in the hall, Abigail Peyton was saying good-bye to one of her friends. Fully expecting Don Ricardo to let her go once Abigail went back into her room, she bore up to the savage assault, sustaining herself with the knowledge that as soon as he released her, she would slap his face.

It seemed forever before the other woman left and Abigail closed her door. Then, after a moment, when he still didn't let her go, she felt a shiver of apprehension—and something else, something that had nothing to do with anger but everything to do with desire. It was like a wildfire, racing through her system, igniting every nerve in her body.

Without her realizing it, her fingers splayed like blooming flowers against his chest. Beneath her palms, she felt the rapid beat of his heart. The fact that he was as excited as she, emboldened her to move her hands up to his shoulders. His muscles were rock solid beneath his jacket. She couldn't help but wonder what it would feel like to touch them with nothing covering them. Were his arms and shoulders as sunbrowned as his face and hands? Was his skin smooth and supple? Wanting, needing to touch some unclothed part of him, she moved her hands up to his neck.

His skin *was* smooth and supple. And warm. So warm. And that same rapid heartbeat she'd felt in his chest pounded the vein in his neck, faster and faster, keeping pace with her own. That *she* could excite a man had never occurred to her. That she could excite this man in particular gave her a heady sense of power. It also scared her. With trembling fingers, she explored the corded muscles of his neck, then ran her fingertips into his hair.

He, apparently, had the same thing in mind. She felt him tug at the large wooden pins that held her chignon. One, two, three, they were out and her hair spilled from its confinement into his hands. She heard him groan as he grabbed a handful and crushed it into his fist.

He mouthed her name, "Heller—I've never wanted a woman as much as I want you. If you weren't so damn prim and proper—so Boston—I'd make love to you right here and now." The last was said as his tongue penetrated her mouth, so she wasn't sure of the words. She wasn't sure of anything except that she was dizzy with her own desire. Her head was spinning and her eyelids fluttered shut.

"You what?" she asked, dragging her mouth from his.

Her release was so unexpected that she stumbled backwards and came up against the edge of the bed. Her body shuddered as she sucked in great gasps of air that sounded like hollow whooshes.

She was still trying to catch her breath when he pounded his fist against the bureau top, scattering her toilette articles in all directions.

"You'd better find a *gentleman* to escort you home

next time," he said as he heeled around and headed for the door.

Catching her breath, she called out, "No! Don't go!" It took her a second to realize what she'd said, and another to know she'd meant it. She didn't want him to go. Not now, now ever! She took a tentative step toward him. When he didn't move, she took another. "I don't want you to leave," she said again, with more conviction. Her stomach muscles clenched with the realization of what she was doing. Inviting trouble. She was throwing herself at him like a common whore. Only a few hours earlier, she had rebuked herself for such behavior which she had done unconsciously, and now here she was consciously—very consciously—offering herself to him. "I'll be leaving Saturday and I—" She hesitated, swallowing back a lump of fear. "It's just occurred to me that I might never see you again and—"

"Heller, do you know what you're doing?" He seemed to be searching her eyes.

"Yes!" she said emphatically, then, "No." She pulled a long, laborious breath. "You'll have to help me. I don't know anything about—" Her chin quivered, then her knees started to give way.

"Dammit, woman." He was across the room in three long strides, catching her beneath her arms and hauling her up against him. She leaned into him, her bright, shining head against his shoulder. The sudden tenderness he felt for her overwhelmed him as nothing ever had. More than anything, he wanted to prove to her that he was not the beast he had seemed a moment ago. He couldn't explain to her what had happened; he wasn't sure himself. Carillo, he supposed. Seeing Carillo's head had severely wounded him. Like Rosita, Carillo would be one of those wounds that never healed.

He felt her hand steal beneath his jacket, and he sucked in his breath and held it as her fingers worked the buttons of his shirt. Bending his head close to hers, he whispered, "Look at me." He drew back from her ever so slightly and cradled her face between his hands, then traced his thumbs from the corners of her eyes, down her cheeks, to the uptilted corners of her mouth. "You're beautiful." He lifted her chin and traced the outline of her mouth. "Really beautiful." He saw her lips part, felt the moist tip of her tongue against his finger, and moaned. Her eyes were open, bright with a flame he understood all too well. He couldn't think of another thing to say that his actions couldn't say better, so he kissed her cheek, the tip of her nose, then the tender corner of her mouth, and finally, her lips.

She was as naive as he was knowing, as innocent as he was experienced.

He stared down at her while she finished with the buttons. He had never anticipated a moment as much as he anticipated her hands coming in contact with his skin. But the moment it happened, it was nothing like he imagined, it was better . . . and it marked the end of his control.

He kissed her with a fervency that surprised even him, and in seconds he had her bodice unbuttoned and was caressing her chemise-covered breasts. "A gentleman wouldn't touch you like this," he told her in a husky voice.

"But you're not a gentleman," she reminded him in an equally husky voice.

"A lady would demand I stop now before this goes any further."

She smoothed her hands down the front of his chest, following the V of dark, coarse hair that disappeared into his pants. Reaching that barrier, she paused as if to consider what to do next, then turned her index

fingers downward and slipped them beneath the waist-
band. "But I'm not a lady."

"So it seems!" Abigail Peyton spouted from the
adjoining doorway. She marched into the room, brandishing her parasol. "This is the second time I have
found you fondling my niece, young man. Unless you
intend to propose marriage, I suggest you unhand her
this very instant!" She jabbed the tip of her parasol
into his ribs, pushing him away from Heller.

Joaquin released Heller and grabbed the tip of the
parasol. "That's a very nasty habit you have, old
woman." He pulled the parasol toward him and Abigail with it.

Abigail Peyton was not intimidated. With a snort of
outrage, she jerked back on the handle.

So she wanted to play tug-of-war, did she? The old
woman had nerve, he'd give her that. He fingered the
tip of the parasol, letting her wonder what he was
about, then gave it a sharp pull, and brought it and
Abigail into his grasp. Pinioning her arms to her side
like trussed turkey wings, he held her in place. "You
remind me of my *tia*—a bothersome old woman, always showing up uninvited, sticking her nose in places
it doesn't belong and giving orders. One day her husband just decided he'd had enough and shot her for the
old crow she was."

"How unfortunate for your *tia*," Abigail rejoined,
her blue eyes snapping indignantly. "Luckily for me,
I do not have a husband to concern myself with. I have
always contended that men were far more trouble than
they were worth. You, young man, are a case in
point!"

For all her haughty ways, he liked her, but he wasn't
about to let her know it. He released her but held onto
her parasol, and then snapped it over his knee. "Bad
habits should be broken."

Heller groaned in despair. "Don Ricardo! Aunty—"

"Quiet, child. I will thank you to let me handle this." To the tall Spaniard, Abigail said with controlled patience, "I am going to ignore your obvious lack of manners, Señor Montaños, and pretend that in spite of what I have seen, you are indeed a man of honor and integrity. As my niece's only living relative and her guardian, it is my duty to discover your intentions where Heller is concerned."

Fumbling with the buttons of her bodice, Heller issued a protest, but Abigail silenced her with a wave of her hand.

"What do *you* want me to say?" he respectfully asked.

"Why, I want you to declare yourself, of course. Either you offer for her now, or you abandon your pursuit and leave her alone." Hugging herself, Heller turned toward the window. She was mortified. She wished she had never heard of the Boston Board of Trade, the San Francisco Chamber of Commerce, or San Francisco, California.

Behind her, she could almost hear Don Ricardo thinking. In spite of her utter mortification, a part of her wondered what his answer would be.

Chapter 11

"You leave me no choice, Señora Peyton. Much as I would like to court your niece, I am in no position to do so."

"You already have a wife?" Abigail boldly asked, and when he shook his head, she said, "Then you are betrothed. To Señorita Valdez?"

Joaquin cocked his head consideringly. "You *do* remind me of my *tia*," he said, laughing richly. "But I will answer your question anyway, because I respect your deep concern for your niece." He took off his hat and held it against his leg. "I am widowed, for many years now. And no, Elena is not my *novia*, nor am I betrothed to anyone else. There are other reasons." At Abigail's curious look, he put up his hand to stop her before she could ask. "I have given you all the answers I can." He walked to the door. "Good-bye, señora, señorita. I apologize for my bad manners and any embarrassment I may have caused you."

Heller turned around to watch him go.

Long after he'd gone, Heller sat on her bed, staring out the window at the slowly setting sun. She was sure in her own mind that what she felt for Don Ricardo was more than passion. But was she falling in love with him? How could she tell? She had never experienced it and had doubts that it even existed. Love seemed more of a fantasy than a reality.

Elizabeth Pennyworth had taught her to evaluate a situation by detaching herself from it. Closing her eyes, Heller imagined herself back in Don Ricardo's arms and tried to recall *exactly* what she had experienced physically and emotionally. The obvious physical responses—the tingling sensations, the quickening of her pulse, the stomach butterflies, the rushes of heat to the nether regions of her body—all these she considered to be the results of passion, pure and simple.

Emotionally, she felt a need to be near him, a sadness to be separated from him, a tenderness and caring that, until now, she had felt only for Abigail.

But was it love that was making her heart ache at the thought of never seeing him again? She tried to imagine going home to Boston and continuing her life without him. Somehow she knew she would always wonder where he was, what he was doing, and who he was with.

Heller's thoughts were temporarily stayed when she heard Abigail open the adjoining door. Dressed in a white muslin nightgown, her silver-white hair fashioned into a single braid that hung over her right shoulder, her aunt could have passed for a ghost.

"There is something I want to discuss with you, Heller Peyton."

Heller stood up and began braiding her hair. "Please, Aunty, I really don't want to talk. I know what I did was wrong. I know I jeopardized my reputation, and yours." She couldn't help the tears that filled her eyes. "If you hadn't come in when you did—"

"Heller! Please, will you kindly allow me to speak? Honestly, dear, sometimes you go on like an old woman."

Heller heaved a sigh, then gave a resigned shrug, sat back down, and propped herself against the high, oak headboard. She wiped her eyes with the back of her hand.

Abigail inclined her head and sat down in the rocking chair. "First of all, let me remind you that I know you better than anyone else, maybe even better than you know yourself," she began, returning Heller's sour expression. "As a child, you saw things no child should have seen. I do not doubt that you could tell me tales that would make my hair stand on end. But I have come to the conclusion—after careful thought and long observation, mind you—that there are certain things you obviously do not know and other things you have misunderstood."

"I don't know what you're talking about. What does this have to do with what happened between Don Ricardo and me?"

"Everything, dear. Absolutely everything. It all begins with your dear mother. Mara O'Shay. I wonder if you really knew her."

The mention of her mother made her stiffen. "Of course I knew her. I lived with her for twelve years."

"And did you love her or hate her?" Abigail asked with startling frankness.

Heller gasped, then expelled a ragged breath. "I hated—I—" She broke off, choking on a sob.

Abigail sat forward in the chair. "Just as I thought. You need to forgive her, Heller, and forgive yourself for hating her. You were only a child. You could not know the truth."

Heller sighed in disgust. "I don't want to discuss this!" She resolutely set her jaw and turned her ravaged face to the wall.

"Well, we are going to discuss it, whether you like it or not. It is time to bring the matter out in the open so we can put it to rest. For instance, did you know that your mother was a well-to-do young heiress when she met my brother, Gerald?'' Abigail looked down at her folded hands. ''Gerald wrote me letters all about her and how much he loved her. My darling brother, I am ashamed to say, was something of a scoundrel and a gambler. Our father knew this, and for that reason he left his estate to me. Gerald, of course, had a tidy stipend, but he constantly complained that it was not enough. He borrowed money from your mother to pay his gambling debts, promising to pay her back. He borrowed and borrowed until she had nothing left, not even her home. In Gerald's last letter to me, he confessed his sins and asked me to bring Mara home to the Boston house and provide for her until he could leave his post. Unfortunately, by the time I received the letter and was able to take the train to New York, your mother had moved and the neighbors had no idea to where. I often wonder how things would have turned out if I had found her and been able to bring her back to live with me. She might still be alive.''

Shocked by her aunt's testimony, Heller stared bleakly out the window at the night sky. ''Why didn't she write to *you*? Obviously she knew how to contact *you,* since she did just that later, when she was dying. She could have asked for help. You would have helped her, wouldn't you?''

''Yes, of course I would have, but your mother was a very stubborn and proud woman, just as you are, Heller. You have to understand that Gerald had not proposed, so she did not know he intended to marry her. She had only his promises, and when he did not return . . . well, she probably thought he had abandoned her.''

''That was no reason to become a whore.''

''Perhaps, but I want you to ask yourself what her

choices were. She was Irish—and you know how the Irish immigrants are treated in New York. A man is very fortunate to be able to get a job, but a woman? She was destitute. Gerald had robbed her of everything she had. And she was pregnant. What kind of work could she have gotten? A maid? A washerwoman? Maybe she tried to find work and was unsuccessful. We will never know.''

"Why are you telling me this now?'' Bitterness tainted Heller's voice: the bitterness and cold despair she always experienced whenever she thought about Mam and Cow Bay.

"Because I see what you are doing to yourself. You think that loving a man will turn *you* into a whore. I should have guessed it before—'' Abigail gave her head a shake. "It explains everything—why you never wanted to go to the cotillions and balls, why you turned away every man who gave you a second notice, why you chose to follow in my footsteps, and why you took your mother's wish for you to be a lady and turned it into a crusade.''

Heller jerked her head around. "A crusade?''

"Yes, Heller, a crusade! Think about why you were so anxious to come to San Francisco. To prove to yourself and that Pennyworth woman that you *are* a lady.''

Heller vehemently protested. "That's not true!''

"It is true and you know it! You are not fooling anyone but yourself, Heller Peyton.'' Abigail groaned in exasperation. "But what you have to understand is that a woman can be a *lady* without ever achieving a superior social position.'' She rose from the chair, crossed to the bed, and sat down beside her niece. "A woman can also be a lady and love a man. Your mother was such a woman, and so was I.''

Heller's mouth opened but nothing came out.

"I am sorry to shock you—or maybe I am not! It is

time you realized that I am not the paragon of virtue
you seem to think I am. There was a time, when I was
young, when I was very much in love with a colonel
from West Point. It so happens, however, that he had
more tactical mancuvers in him than Napoleon, and
when I found out, I was devastated. Thus, my first and
last love affair.

"My point being," she continued in the same stern
voice, "that I am not so naive that I do not recognize
a strong attraction between and man and a woman
when I see it. You are very close to falling in love with
that handsome devil, Don Ricardo, whether you wish
to admit it or not.

"Do not shake your head at me, young lady. You
know very well that I am right, just as I was right
about that no account Gordon Pierce, who, by the way,
has told us nothing but lies about himself from the
moment he introduced himself. I took the time to sit
down and list all his conflicting statements. If needed,
I will show them to you, but right now you have to
decide what you are going to do about Don Ricardo."

Heller was still recovering from the shock of Abigail's admission when she asked, "You want me to
pursue him?"

"I would hate to see you lose him. I think he would
make you a very good husband."

"I don't want a husband. And besides, he isn't a
gentleman!"

"I am not blind, Heller. I know exactly what he is.
An adventurer and a rogue, but also a man of honor
and integrity."

"Even if I were to admit to having feelings for him,
which I don't, there is nothing I can do to make him
want *me*. If you remember correctly, you gave him a
choice and he made it. He left."

"Oh, horsefeathers! He did what any man does when

he is cornered by a woman. He made up an excuse, then he ran. That does not make him a coward, just a man.''

Heller sprang off the bed and paced the length of the room. ''I can't believe we're having this conversation. I'm telling you there is nothing between us—nothing but—but lustful passion—''

Abigail's mouth dropped opened and her eyes opened in astonishment. ''Where in the name of heaven did you come up with that?'' She raised her hand. ''Do not tell me, I know. Elizabeth Pennyworth!'' She snorted in disdain.

Heller put her hand on Abigail's arm. ''No Aunty. That's what Mam called what she pretended to feel with her nightly visitors. She said pretending to feel something made it all easier.''

Abigail paled visibly. ''That just goes to prove what I was saying. Your mother used her best resource—herself—to provide food and shelter for the two of you. She did not enjoy the men sh—she— Oh, for heaven's sake, Heller! Just think about what I have said, will you please? Think about it long and hard. Your mother was a good woman in spite of what she did. It is time you stopped condeming her! We will talk again later.'' Moving from the bed to the door, she muttered, ''Exasperating girl. Stubborn to a fault. Pig-headed.''

The door between the rooms slammed shut, then it opened again and Abigail peeked in. ''Don't forget to write in your journal.''

Heller nodded. She was tired. It had been a long and exhausting day. The only thing she wanted was to go to bed. She didn't want to think about any of it—about Gordon Pierce, the museum, the head in the jar, Don Ricardo . . . Mam.

But how could she stop herself from thinking about the things that were important to her?

She suddenly recalled the book about Joaquin Murieta. Reading would take her mind off things, if only she could remember where she'd put it. She searched her room, but it was nowhere to be found. She must have left it in the cab.

Abigail retired to her own room to prepare for bed. An hour later, just as she was pulling down her bedclothes, there came a knock at the door. She opened it to a richly garbed Chinese boy carrying the oddest-looking bouquet she had ever seen.

"Boss man say he sorry he break parasols. He say mabee these make better." At Abigail's invitation, the boy walked into the room and set the bouquet on the floor, then backed his way out bowing.

Abigail could only stare at the colorful bouquet. Parasols! A dozen of them, each one a different style and color, some with ruffles and lace. A fringed one and a striped one. A parasol that looked like a pagoda and another with a scalloped edge.

She started to laugh. What a clever man, that Don Ricardo. He almost made her wish she was younger. Such a dashing figure he cut with his tall, powerful frame and his dark good looks. If only she could make Heller see what she saw. They would be so good together. And their children! Abigail threw up her hands in frustration.

She went to the adjoining door to tell Heller about the bouquet and found her niece propped up against the headboard sleeping. Best to leave the girl alone, she decided, gently closing the door between their rooms.

Heller's dreams were filled with vague images and strange noises. From a distance came soft footsteps and whispery voices, then something clamped over her mouth. She awakened with a start. An evil-looking Chinaman with a long black queue leaned over her. She threw herself toward the opposite side of the bed, only to be confronted by another man who held a wicked-looking knife.

A scream rose in her throat but was cut off when a rag replaced the hand covering her mouth. A powerful odor filled her nostrils and her lips burned against the sweet-tasting rag. Then nothing.

One by one, Luther Mauger dropped the gold coins into Canton Charlie's open hand. ''Three hundred eighty. Four hundred.''

The Chinaman raised his chin sharply. ''Slave girls four hundred. Steal white girl, six hundred. We agree. You pay or I send Tong.''

''Don't you threaten me, you son of a bitch. You cheated me on the last three girls. You owe me. This is all you get. Take it or leave it.'' Luther seized the whip hanging on his hat rack and assumed a ready stance.

Charlie turned to go down the stairs, his queue swinging behind him like a rodent's tail. At the landing he grunted, mumbled a curse, then stomped away.

Luther knew that Charlie, for all his threat of the Tong, was no fool, and gold meant too much to him to take revenge on a long-time customer. Returning the whip to the hat rack, Luther crossed the room to where Heller lay sleeping in his bed.

The moment he'd seen her in the hotel lobby, he'd known she was exactly what he was looking for: rich, beautiful, sophisticated, educated. The perfect wife for an up-and-coming San Franciscan businessman. If the incident at the museum hadn't happened, he was sure Heller would have eventually accepted his invitation and come to his house to see his ''art'' collection, but he'd lost his head over that boy and had been made a fool of by that damn Spaniard.

His hand throbbed at the memory. Montaños' bullet had taken a chunk out of his index finger that would leave a large ugly scar.

The only good thing that had come out of his visit to the museum was seeing the head. There was no doubt—it was Murieta. Even bloated, he recognized his features.

Smiling, he leaned over Heller and set about carefully removing her clothes. "After I'm through with you, Miss Heller Peyton, you'll beg me to marry you!"

When all but her shift was removed, he stood back and gazed down at her. Until this moment he hadn't given much thought to enjoying her physically, only about getting her to agree to marry him. Unexpected urges and sensations that not even his slave girls had been able to induce now stirred within him as he gazed at her lush curves. Was it possible that he was close to a recovery? The prison doctor had said that the injury to his groin shouldn't affect him permanently, but that the healing process would take time.

More than anything, he wanted that time to be over now—so that he could be a man again.

Not knowing how long it would be before the ether wore off, Luther proceeded to kiss her and touch her in her sleep as he would not be able to once she awakened.

The lone horseman headed east, galloping hard across the grasslands, miles beyond the city limits. He pulled up sharply when he reached the moonlit ridge. For long moments, horse and rider stood overlooking the arroyo, breathing in the night air.

Wearily, Joaquin dismounted and untied the shovel and the oilskin bag from behind his saddle. Then he sent El Tigre off to graze on the spring grasses while he undertook the unpleasant task of burying Carillo's head. The big black stallion nickered softly, then moved away.

Time after time, Joaquin jabbed the shovel into the earth with a vengeance until at last the hole was dug. He could not undo what had already been done, nor could he right the wrong, but he could put an and to the indignity.

He picked up the bag, set it into the grave, and quickly replaced the dirt. Standing back, he made the sign of the cross and prayed for Carillo's immortal soul. There was nothing, not even prayer, that could ease the pain he felt, diminish his anger, or mollify his hate. Nor was there anything to take away the guilt.

It should have been me.

He could not ignore the voice in his head; it spoke the truth. It *should* have been him. He understood it all now, thanks to the book Heller had bought. He'd slipped it into his pocket on their ride back to her hotel and read it after returning to his own hotel. The author had combined fact with fiction. Mostly fiction. Nevertheless, it gave him some insight into what was believed to have happened to him and his band at the Cantua. The rangers made a mistake. They had been looking for a *Joaquin*, any Joaquin, and they found one—the wrong . . .

"*. . . Joaquin. You wear a troubled look, amigo.*" *Lino Toral handed El Jefe a cup of steaming black coffee, then added another piece of greasewood to the morning fire.*

Frowning, Joaquin accepted the tin cup and hunkered down beside his friend. "*You know me too well,* mi amigo," *he said in a low tone. Voices carried in the valley and he didn't want to disturb the others. They needed their rest; they'd gone for days, riding hard in the hot July sun, with little or no sleep. They'd followed his orders to the letter, leaving Placerville, then zigzagging an impossible trail down the western slopes of the Sierra Nevada, then across the valley floor to Los Tres Piedras, The Three Rocks, his one permanent hideout. "I am anxious about Carillo. He should have been back by now."*

Lino looked up at a point over Joaquin's head. "He's coming now."

Joaquin stood up and searched the lookout point at the summit of the three rocks. Jack Garcia was waving his rifle, his signal that a friendly rider was coming. Joaquin tossed the last of his coffee down his throat and set the cup aside. He had been waiting all night long for Carillo to return from Mariposa with the news of Luther Mauger's trial.

Joaquin Carillo galloped into camp and reined to a halt. Carillo and El Jefe were often mistaken for brothers; they were of the same age, height, weight, and complexion.

Joaquin grabbed on to the horse's bridle. "Well?"

Carillo threw his leg over the saddle and dismounted. He looked tired and disgruntled. "The news, it is bad, El Jefe. The judge convicted Mauger of robbery and sentenced him to many years in prison."

Joaquin heeled around and strode beyond the fire. He had vowed to avenge Rosita, and so far three of her four murderers were dead. Only Luther Mauger had eluded him, time after time. He had been so close, and now . . . He would have to wait.

Lino called out to him. "It's better this way, mi jefe. With the gringo dog in prison, you can go on with your life."

"I have no life!" Joaquin called back. "Mauger and his friends took it when they killed Rosita."

The three men, close friends since youth, turned in unison as a shot rang out.

"Riders," Lino shouted. The alarm sent the banditti *into a flurry of activity, each man hastily preparing himself and his brace of weapons for a fight.*

Joaquin withdrew his long-barreled Colt Dragoon, checked its readiness, and tucked it into the waist of his calzoneras. *He ran toward Jack Garcia as the man came down from the lookout.*

"How far?" Joaquin asked the winded sentry.

Between labored breaths, Garcia answered, "The pass."

"How many?"

"Fifteen. Twenty. I don't know. Their horses, they kick up much dust."

"It's got to be the rangers," said Joaquin knowingly. "God knows, those bastards are like bloodhounds chasing a fox."

"Sí, mi jefe, you are the zorro *eh?"*

Garcia was right. Joaquin had known it would only be a matter of time before Captain Love and his California Rangers found him. But he had led them a merry chase, sending out decoys for Love and his men to follow, feeding them bogus information, even setting false tracks so they ended up riding in circles, chasing themselves. But the captain was no fool; he'd caught on quickly and started to think the way a bandit leader would think.

"Tell the men to prepare their weapons and wait for my signal," he ordered. "The rangers can't know for certain who we are and shouldn't start a fight unless we give them reason."

The order was given, but Joaquin wondered if he shouldn't have ordered his men to abandon the camp as quickly as possible instead of counting on being able to bluff his way through a confrontation. The rangers had been searching for him for nearly three months. He prayed their patience had not come to an end. If it had, then he supposed the only thing he could do was give them what they wanted. Himself. Joaquin Murieta. Moments later, his thoughts were broken by pounding hooves. The company of rangers rode into camp, their weapons drawn at the ready.

Pretending nonchalance, Joaquin, Lino, and Joaquin Carillo approached the company of hard-bitten men.

"One of you Mexes savvy English?" the leader shouted, bringing his sorrel to a skidding halt. In the man's right hand was a cocked six-shooter.

Joaquin recognized the heavy-featured leader as Captain Harry Love, the man Governor Bigler appointed to lead the rangers and hunt him down. Thinking quickly, Joaquin realized that though he knew Love by sight, having seen a drawing of him in the newspaper, the captain would probably not know him. He hoped he was right.

Adjusting his sombrero against the sun, Joaquin moved forward. "Sí señor, I speak your language," he admitted.

From atop his sorrel, Love gazed at the Mexican. An evil smile lifted the corners of his bushy black mustache. "Bueno," he said, after a prolonged silence. "Where are you and your campañeros headed?" His tone was almost cordial.

"We go to Los Angeles to sell our horses, then home to Mexico," Joaquin answered, exaggerating his accent.

"Horse drovers, eh? How many head you takin' in?"

"Three hundred."

"Collecting your pesos, then going home, eh? You don't like California?"

Joaquin knew the game Love was playing; he'd played it himself on occasion. "We are, how you say . . . longing for home."

"Homesick? You're homesick?" He laughed.

Joaquin nodded. "Sí."

Love glanced over his shoulder. "Well, ain't that sweet? Kinda makes you wanna cry, don't it boys?" Heads nodded and voices rose in mocking laughter. Love turned back. "I'm lookin' for an hombre *named Joaquin. Think you might know 'im? Mebbe he's one of your* compañeros *here?" His question received blank looks and shrugs. "You savvy what I'm sayin', Mex?"*

"Sí, señor, I comprendo, *but what you ask is very difficult. There are many Joaquins."*

"Byrnes!" Love called over his shoulder. A man detached himself from the rest of the company and spurred his horse to the front of the column. "You said you saw this Joaquin fellow once. Do you see him here?"

Byrnes' eyes swept the Mexicans' faces. At length he focused on Joaquin. "Him. He's the one. He's Joaquin."

"No. I am Joaquin!" shouted Carillo, pushing El Jefe aside.

"He lies," Joaquin said, pulling Carillo behind him. He removed his sombrero. "I am the man you seek. I am Joaquin Murieta," he said, then gave a shrill whistle. It was his signal to Garcia and the others to draw their weapons.

The rangers spurred their horses forward, their guns spewing hot lead.

Throwing off their serapes, Lino and Joaquin Carillo pulled their pistols and fired into the company of riders. Their steady blaze of bullets provided cover for their leader.

Joaquin flung himself behind a boulder and started shooting. He and his men were at a disadvantage. They had only six-shooters, while the rangers had rifles, revolvers, and shotguns. Through a haze of gun smoke, Joaquin saw Garcia take a bullet and fall. Other members of his band were running on foot into the thickets where the horsemen couldn't follow.

Love's horse whinnied and reared when Joaquin's bullet grazed his rump. The captain fell to the ground and temporarily lost consciousness.

Joaquin dashed for the edge of the encampment where the horses were tethered to picket pins. He pulled up El Tigre's stakerope and threw a noose around his neck. Vaulting onto his back, the stallion lunged to a gallop and raced along the rocky embankment. Joaquin rode low over El Tigre's neck, holding onto his mane. He twisted back to shoot and unseated one of his pursuers, but still the bullets rained about him, singing death.

Joaquin knew he was a dead man unless he escaped. He guided El Tigre toward the arroyo, assured the animal could easily make the eight-foot jump. He felt the horse's muscles bunch, felt the front legs extend, back legs kick off the ledge and into the air.

A bullet whizzed past, followed by another, then a high-pitched scream.

"El Tigre!"

Shot in the neck, the stallion plunged into the creekbed, his front legs buckling beneath him. Joaquin threw himself off the animal's back and somersaulted over his head. He heard the splintering of his own bones as he landed on his side in the rocky creek bottom. Through a blur of pain, he opened his eyes and looked down at the angle of his right leg. It was broken.

Hearing El Tigre's groans, he used his arms and elbows to pull himself toward the dying animal. It *wasn't until he tried to catch his breath that he knew he had also been shot.*

Looking up, Joaquin saw two of the rangers standing back from the embankment. Smoke curled from the ends of their rifle barrels. They started to reload, then take aim.

"Hola! *Gringos!*" Lino jumped out from behind a cottonwood. His twin Colts spit fire as they pumped balls of lead into the rangers' bodies. The two men fell to the ground. Lino gathered their rifles and walked their horses down into the creekbed.

"El Tigre," Joaquin said, clenching his teeth. When he saw Lino, he said, "Give me your gun."

"I'll do it," said Lino, taking aim.

"No! This for me to do." Lino offered his arm and helped Joaquin move up close to the horse. The stallion's breathing was labored. Blood gushed from a hole in his neck and the bones of his legs had broken through his skin. "Adios, *old friend.*" He pointed the barrel at a spot behind El Tigre's ear. "I'll miss you." He squeezed the trigger, ending the animal's misery.

Lino bent over Joaquin. "I have to get you out of here before others come."

"No. I can't move. My right leg is broken and I've been gut shot. Leave me here, my friend. You can't save me. Leave me the gun." When Lino protested, Joaquin shouted in anger. "I am El Jefe! Do as I say! Siga! Pronto!" He reached up and took the gun.

Lino backed up, then turned and climbed out of the creekbed and ran for the protective thicket of cottonwoods.

With Lino's pistol cocked and read to fire, Joaquin laid back and pillowed his head against El Tigre's shoulder. Absently, he wondered what would come first: the rangers or death. Moments later, the gun dropped from his hand and he knew.

A gentle wind out of the east blew across the Arroyo Cantua, carrying Joaquin's dying words, "Forgive me, Rosita. I have failed you for I have . . ."

. . . died." Joaquin looked up suddenly from Carillo's grave into a pinkening sky. The world was readying itself for a new day. He wanted to reach out and touch it, but something held him back, as it always did. He slammed his fist into the palm of his other hand in frustration. Would he ever be free of the past and able to face a new day without his ghosts?

Walking away from the grave, he turned into the wind. The feel of it on his face, the moist smell of it in his nostrils, the taste of it on his lips was the only thing that gave him comfort.

Pulling himself together, he called to El Tigre, climbed into the saddle, and headed back to the city.

The sun had risen high into the sky when Joaquin returned to his hotel, smelling of sweat, horse, leather, and earth. On his way through the lobby, he told the desk clerk to send breakfast and a bath up to his room as soon as possible, then he sprinted up the stairs two at a time.

Lino was sipping a cup of coffee as Joaquin opened the door to his room. "I was beginning to wonder what happened to you," he said, looking up over the rim of his cup.

Joaquin's eyes sparked, but his response was cool. "I took El Tigre out for a ride. He was in need of exercise."

Lino set his cup aside. "Has he the spirit of his grandfather?"

"It's hard to say, but he's young yet. Time will tell."

"Do not forget you promised me his first colt."

Joaquin removed his jacket and unbuttoned his shirt.

"I have not forgotten. But what if he sires only fillies? There is that possibility, you know."

Lino's eyes narrowed suspiciously. "Have you promised my colt to someone else?"

"No. I just thought that if there were no colts, you should prepare yourself to take a filly."

Lino bristled. "Why would there be no colts? The first El Tigre sired seven colts, and the second sired five."

Joaquin threw his hands wide. "One never knows."

The arrival of the bathtub, bathwater, and breakfast halted the conversation. Joaquin flipped the small army of boys some coins and hurried them out the door. Stripped to the waist, he sat down and devoured his breakfast.

Lino dragged his chair around and sat down straddling it. "I've discovered who Henderson is. Seems he was warden of San Quentin a few years back."

Joaquin turned the fork in his hand as he leveled a look on Lino. "Warden, huh?"

"Mauger apparently bribed him to clear off the prison records."

"Sounds like something Mauger would do. Where did he get the money for the bribe?"

"According to Wells Fargo, the payroll shipment he robbed was never recovered. They were more than interested to learn that Luther Mauger had been *prematurely* released from San Quentin. They were also interested to learn that his incarceration records had vanished."

Joaquin pushed his chair back on its rear legs. "I assume they're planning an investigation?"

Lino smiled. "I believe it's already underway. Luther Mauger will have an agent calling on him any day now, if one hasn't already." His mouth curled with cynicism. "Everything seems to be coming together as we hoped."

Joaquin only nodded.

"By the way, I met Miss Peyton at the ball before you got there. You didn't bother to mention that she was beautiful."

"Didn't I?" Joaquin replied indifferently.

"No. You didn't."

"Beautiful, but cold as a Boston winter." He swallowed the lie along with a sip of strong black coffee.

Lino watched him carefully for a moment. "You also didn't bother to mention that you're in love with her."

Joaquin shoved his plate away and stood up. "You're another one who reminds me of my *tia*." He shucked his pants and stepped into the tub.

Lino started across to the door.

"Lino. What happened to Joaquin Carillo?"

Lino stopped short of the door. "He died at the Cantua along with Garcia and—"

"I thought he escaped."

"No, he didn't. Why do you ask?"

"I saw him yesterday."

"You saw him? That's impossible. Where did you see him?"

"In Dr. Jordan's Museum. He was exhibit number 563, only they had his name wrong. They said he was me." Joaquin lathered his chest with soap.

Lino closed his eyes and leaned his head back. "I didn't know, *mi jefe*. I've heard rumors about the infamous head that the rangers used to collect the reward, but I swear to you I didn't know it was Carillo." He moved over to the edge of the tub. "We have to do something. We can't leave him there. We have to—"

"I've already taken care of it, Lino. He's at peace now."

Chapter 12

"Wake up. Heller, wake up now. Open your eyes. You've slept long enough." The man's voice above her grew more persistent. Her eyelids felt weighted and her mouth was parched and sore. "Come on, Heller. You can sleep later." He shook her shoulders and turned to his Chinese servant. "Chum Soon, go down to the kitchen and get Missy Peyton some of your herbal tea."

Heller's head was in a fog; she couldn't seem to make sense of what was wanted of her or who wanted it, yet the voice did seem familiar. She forced her eyes partway open and saw a blurred figure bending over her.

"W—who are—?" Her voice cracked. She tried to draw saliva into her mouth but none would come.

"Here, I'll help you up."

Cold hands clasped her shoulders. "No, I—" she protested, barely able to make her dry lips form the words. Her head whirled as he pulled her up, grabbed her beneath the arms and moved her backwards. She squeezed her eyes shut and moaned at the nauseating dizziness. The only thing she could think of was that she was ill and the man talking to her, helping her, was a doctor. As the vertigo faded away, she dared once again to lift her eyelids. Looking through her lashes, she saw Gordon Pierce standing quietly beside her. Immediately, she sensed something peculiar about him—something about his hair and his clothes. He looked . . . disheveled, she thought, and vaguely wondered why. He had always been so impeccably groomed, never a hair out of place. She blinked several times to focus. "Gordon?"

"Yes, Heller. It's me. I was beginning to think you would sleep forever." She felt the bed sag beneath his weight.

"Am I ill?" She put her hand to her throat in an effort to control her croaking voice. "Is this a hospital?" she asked, trying to gather enough strength to see her surroundings. "I feel so weak."

"No, you aren't ill, just very tired, I imagine." He leaned toward her and lightly bussed her cheek with his lips.

Too late, Heller raised her hand to stop him. "Gordon! What do you think you're doing?"

Gordon gave an amused laugh. "Heller. You delight and amaze me. One minute the seductive enchantress begging for my kisses—the next, the prudish Boston spinster. It's very confusing but . . . interesting and amusing, I must say." He made a noise low in his throat, like a growl, then bent toward her again, his lips pursed.

This time when he started toward her, she found the strength to slap him. Gordon reared back. A murderous glint leaped in his hazel eyes, and his pursed lips flattened, then drew taut against his teeth. Abruptly, he stood up and turned his face away. With a mixture of anger and trepidation, Heller watched as a moment later he turned back with a look of patient indulgence. As before, his demeanor had magically changed.

"At the risk of offending your tender sensibilities, don't you think it's a little late to be playing the vestal virgin?"

She was suddenly filled with an awful dread.

He lifted an eyebrow. "You don't remember last night, do you?"

She shook her head.

Gordon moved to the end of the bed. "It was about eleven o'clock. I came to your door to apologize for my behavior at the museum. You invited me in and when I went to kiss you, you didn't stop me. In fact, you encouraged me. That's when I suggested we leave the hotel and come here, to my house." He lips spread into a smile. "We drank some champagne and . . . we made love, Heller." He leaned forward and pressed his palms on the foot of the bed.

Heller's mouth gaped open. She gasped as if in acute physical pain. "N—no. That's not true. None of that happened. I didn't—We didn't—You're lying!" But how had she gotten to his house? She didn't remember a thing after Abigail had left her room. No, it wasn't possible. She wouldn't have invited him in, much less offered himself to him.

Gordon straightened to his full height, hiding his disappointment beneath a smiling face. He'd thought for certain the recovery process had begun, but it hadn't. It had been a long time since he'd enjoyed a woman in the normal way; he was beginning to doubt he would ever be able to again, despite the doctor's optimism.

"I admit, it does seem a little odd that you don't remember something so important. I've heard a woman never forgets here first lover, but obviously that isn't necessarily so," he said, pretending to be hurt. "Too bad, too; it was really quite a memorable night. I can't think of a time I've enjoyed myself more. I also can't think of a woman I've enjoyed more." He leaned toward her but stopped when she raised her feet and kicked at him from beneath the covers, acting as though he was some kind of encroaching vermin. "For God's sake, Heller, it's not as if I forced you to do something you didn't want to do." He swung around, stormed across the room, and pounded his fist into a padded-backed throne chair.

Suddenly contrite, he offered, "Maybe it was my fault. I shouldn't have allowed you to drink so much champagne, but you kept asking for more. I assumed you knew what you were doing."

"You're lying," she cried, frightened by his lightning-fast mood changes and accusations. "I *never* drink champagne. I hate it. It makes me sick—"

Looking over his shoulder, Gordon cocked an eyebrow. "Yes, I know. It also makes you dizzy, weak, forgetful, and disagreeable!" The bedroom door opened and a bland-faced Chinaman stood at the threshold holding a tray. "Ah," said Gordon, "your tea, at last. Maybe you'll feel better after you've had some soothing refreshment." He stood behind the chair as Chum Soon padded his way across the room, set down the tray on the bedside table, then padded back to the door and left, all without a word or a glance at either his employer or Heller.

Heller began to shake uncontrollably. Was she supposed to actually believe that she had left the hotel with Gordon and gone with him, unchaperoned, to his house in the middle of the night? And even if she had drunk champagne, which she wouldn't have done under any circumstance, it wouldn't have caused her to forget what had happened before she drank it, only after!

It was crazy! *He* was crazy! A terrible thought suddenly occurred to her. Maybe Gordon really was insane. A madman! Desperate to get away from him, she flung back the bedclothes and moved toward the edge of the bed.

"I wouldn't if I were you," said Gordon, interrupting her flight. "You need to give yourself a little time to regain your strength. Besides, Chum Soon isn't finished with your clothes."

"My clothes?" she asked in a small voice, at the same time lowering her gaze. She wore her shift, nothing more. "What have you done with them?" she asked, pulling the covers up in front of her.

"I told you, my servant has them. He's using one of his Chinese concoctions to get out the champagne stains." He started back across the room toward the bed. "Let me pour you some tea. It'll help clear your head."

Gathering her knees beneath her on the bed, she clutched the bedclothes and sat like a cat ready to pounce. When he came close, she reached out a hand and touched his arm. "Gordon, please, you must tell me the truth. We didn't—You didn't—Please say this is some kind of trick, or joke, or even that you're lying. Please, Gordon, I vow I won't hold it against you."

Gordon poured the dark fragrant tea out of an ornate Chinese teapot into a cup. He wore his patience like a cloak and gathered it round him, hoping she wouldn't see beneath it. "I don't think anything less of you, if that's what you're worried about. As I told you at the ball, I care for you." Handing her the cup, he said, "Just to reassure you that I mean what I say, let me ask you again, right here and now—will you do me the honor of becoming my wife? I promise to take care of you and make you a good husband."

Heller looked up at him in utter disbelief. A madman, without a doubt. Accepting the proffered cup with both hands, she touched it to her lips and inhaled the tea's herbal fragrance, then slowly sipped the steamy brew, savoring its warmth.

By the time she had drained the cup, she knew he was wrong. Nothing could make her feel better—nothing except finding out that this whole thing was an awful nightmare.

All at once everything came back to her: waking up in her room with the two men hovering over her, the threat of the knife, the foul-tasting rag with its overpowering odor, the giddiness. She had been kidnapped!

Instantly, she was relieved to know she hadn't come to him on her own, but terrified at the enormity of the crime that had been committed. Kidnapped!

She wondered what other lies he had told her. Had she encouraged his seduction, or had he taken advantage of her? Maybe neither. Maybe nothing at all had happened. Other than feeling extremely weak, she didn't feel any different. But then, how was one supposed to feel after losing one's virginity? She tried to think what Abigail might tell her to do. *"Stay calm. Keep your wits about you."* Tears welled in her eyes, but she refused to give in to what she considered to be typical female hysterics. She was Heller Peyton, a grown woman, not some simpering little miss. If he had indeed taken her virginity, then so be it. She could live without it.

The important thing now was to get away from Gordon Pierce as quickly as possible, but she would have to be careful how she handled him. If he was unbalanced in any way, he could easily take offense at anything she said or did and take out his anger and frustration in any number of ways. She would have to handle him gently, reason with him as she would a child.

Gordon was still looking at her, waiting for an answer. She handed him her empty cup. "I'm sorry I yelled at you, Gordon. I was—am—upset. Whatever

happened, I don't blame you for it, really I don't.''
She watched his expressions carefully as she spoke,
trying to determine what, if any, effect her words were
having on him. "I shouldn't have doubted you. The
champagne—it must have made me forget." She noticed he seemed to be scrutinizing her as carefully as
she was him. "But please, try to understand when I
tell you I *can't* marry you. I don't doubt you would
make a good husband—a fine husband, I'm sure—but
I wouldn't make a good wife. Marriage—children—
they just don't appeal to me and besides . . . I don't
love you. Surely you don't want a woman who doesn't
love you." She paused to catch her breath and judge
his reaction, but his expression was impassive and un-
readable. "So please, ask your servant to get my
clothes, then leave me to dress and help me get back
to the hotel before my aunt finds out I'm gone."

He smiled endearingly and slipped his left hand into
the pocket of his Chinese robe. "If that's what you
want. . . .''

Heller nearly cried out with joy. "Yes, oh, thank
you, that's exactly what I want."

"All right, then. I'll go downstairs and tell Chum
Soon to hurry. Meantime, let me pour you another cup
of tea."

Heller nodded and took the cup from his hands.
"Thank you, Gordon. I'm so sorry about . . . everything. I truly wish things could have been different."
To cover her embarrassment, she greedily downed the
aromatic tea and watched him walk out of the room.

The moment the door closed behind him, she set
down her empty cup, threw back the covers, and
slipped out of bed. There was a second when she
thought her legs were going to buckle, but it passed.
Nevertheless, she decided to stand still a moment and
give her equilibrium a chance to adjust.

Her gaze settled on the throne chair with its deeply carved near-black wood, so cold yet so beautiful. In the week Gordon had acted as her and Abigail's escort, Heller had never given a thought to what his home would look like or wondered about his tastes in furnishings. Even if she had, she wouldn't have guessed it was Chinese. She thought the furnishings too few in so large a room: only a chair, a bedside lamp and table, a bedstead, and a bureau. And she disliked the blood-red brocade window coverings, the draperies behind the bed, and the bedclothes. . . . Her face drained of all color as she looked down at the indentation where she had lain.

Blood!

Her blood.

Virgin's blood.

Until this moment, she hadn't really believed it was true—that she had given herself to Gordon Pierce, but there was no denying the blood and what it represented. There was also no denying the weakness that was creeping back over her like a fog.

"Oh, no," she said, putting her hands to her head. "No . . ."

Early the next morning, as was his daily custom, Gordon sat down in his study to a cup of coffee and the *Daily Alta California*. Reports of the Bostonians' activities were still on the front page, but more to his interest was "The Very Latest" column, taken off the telegraph wire. From Washington was word of a another political scandal. Nothing new there, thought Gordon, moving his gaze to the adjoining column headed "Pacific Coast Dispatches California, Sacramento." There he read:

"Today Governor Haight and Attorney-General Hamilton, a majority of the Board of Examiners, counted the

money in the state Treasury. They found therein the total
sum of $632,455.10, of which the majority was gold and
silver coin and the rest legal tender. . . .

The Union Gold Mining Company, operating at How-
land Flat, Sierra county, today filed a certificate of increase of the number of shares of stock in the Company
from 500 shares . . .''

"Someday," said Gordon. "Someday El Dorado
will have shares." He sat back, sipping his coffee,
imagining himself sitting behind a large paper-bound
desk in the president's office of the El Dorado Mining
Company. Maybe the vein of gold his foreman wired
him about would be large enough to begin legitimate
operations and allow him to start replacing the slave
laborers who worked the mine. Only a matter of time,
he thought, exhaling a long sigh of anticipated con-
tentment.

He started to turn the page when he saw the "Local
Intelligence" column and decided to see who had died,
been assaulted, or robbed. He scanned the column,
until halfway down the page his eye stopped.

"Murieta's Head Stolen
The head of Joaquin Murieta, the bandit of Calaveras,
who was reportedly captured and killed in July of 1853
by Capt. Harry Love's Rangers, was stolen sometime last
night from Dr. Jordan's Pacific Museum of Anatomy and
Science. Messr. Jordan states that the head is in a fine
state of preservation and bears the impress of the character of the famous robber. A letter, allegedly signed by
the bandit himself, was left to explain. 'I, Joaquin Murieta, do state to all interested persons and to the State
of California, that my head is still very much on my
shoulders, although it has been proclaimed by various
unreliable sources that I was decapitated at the Cantua.
In fact, there was a decapitation—that of my lieutenant,
Joaquin Carillo, who, at that time, bore a similar likeness to me and was therefore wrongly murdered and

falsely offered to the state in exchange of the reward. To all of you who paid to view this atrocity—you have been victims of a cruel hoax.' Local authorities refuse to comment on the possibility that the letter was that of the celebrated bandit, but they do not deny that there have been several reports of Murieta once again operating in the state.''

Luther threw the paper across the room. He didn't believe it. It was some kind of joke. Having seen the head himself, he knew for certain that it belonged to Murieta. Whoever had written the letter was a liar, trying to stir things up . . . or maybe, Gordon thought suddenly, maybe it was the same person who had stolen his whip. He was giving the possibility serious thought when Chum Soon opened the study door.

''Two men at door want to see you. They say they from Well's Fargo. Say they need talk to you. I say you not home. Come back later.''

Luther sprang out of his chair. ''Wells Fargo! Jesus Christ!'' He ran his hands through his hair. ''What the hell is going on here?'' he yelled at the top of his voice. He grabbed Chum Soon by the shoulders. ''What else did they say? Anything?'' The servant shook his head. ''Did they say when they'd be back?'' Again, a negative response. ''Get out of here. Go make some soup or something. And whatever you do, don't answer the door.''

Though it was early, Luther poured himself a drink, then another. It took him nearly an hour before he was calm enough to begin considering his options. He quickly realized there was only one: get out of San Francisco as fast as he could.

At least he had a place to go: the ranch. El Dorado. He had always been careful to be vague about its location, for the very reason that confronted him now. The ranch offered a safe haven to hide himself. Later,

after things calmed down . . . He mentally backed
away from thinking about the future; it was the present
that he needed to be concerned with: the Rincon Hill
house, Chum Soon, and Heller.

The house, he decided, he would have to leave exactly as it was, packing only his few personal items so
it would appear he was still in residence. The phaeton
he would trade for a serviceable wagon and hitch it to
the bays. Wells Fargo would eventually discover the
absence, but by then he would be long gone.

As to Chum Soon, there was no question about how
to handle a deposed servant who knew too much—the
same way he handled the girls he bought from Canton
Charlie. He would have his fun, then he would use a
bullwhip on him.

He paced the length and breadth of the room, feeling as tight as a new pair of boots. As for Heller, he
didn't need her anymore. Didn't need a wife at all now
that he was leaving San Francisco. Her only value had
been in her name and how he could use it to help him
achieve his social, political, and business goals in San
Francisco.

If he was sure she had any of her own money, he
wouldn't hesitate to keep her, but undoubtedly her aunt
held all the purse strings. If he was smart, he would
get her clothes from Chum Soon and take her back to
her hotel before her aunt had half the city out looking
for her. He doubted she would report him to the authorities. Reputation meant everything to a woman like
her.

On the other hand, he thought, lingering over the
last of his drink, he had spent a great deal of money
to hire her kidnappers, and he had gone to a lot of
time and trouble to work out a plan that would convince her that she had come to him willingly. He had
to laugh at her gullibility and naivete; he had been

looking through the peephole when she'd discovered the chicken's blood on the bedclothes.

He cursed himself for thinking about keeping her. It wasn't a sensible thing to do. So why was he even considering such a thing? He wasn't stupid enough to think he loved her; he hated women—all women—for their lying, conniving, and cheating ways. Hate was the one good thing his mother had taught him when she'd left with the whiskey drummer.

Taking Heller with him wasn't a decision he had to make immediately; he had the rest of the day if he wanted, and he planned to use every minute enjoying his prize and measuring its worth.

He visualized Heller lying upstairs in his bed and reached for himself. Someday, he would heal and be a man again.

When Heller awoke for the second time, Gordon was again standing over her.

"Have a nice little catnap, my darling?"

Despite his words, Heller heard the mockery in his voice. Obviously he had put something in her tea to make her sleep. But why had he drugged her when he had only just offered to take her back to the hotel?

She glanced warily around the room.

"I'm through playing games, Heller. And I'm tired of pretending to be someone I'm not," he spat contemptuously.

Before she could anticipate his movement, he reached out, grabbed her arms and pulled her to her knees. "I've always wanted a white slave girl," he said between his teeth as he tossed aside the bed pillows and forced her to move up close to the headboard. "Chinese slave girls don't understand much English. But you, Heller, you won't have that problem, will you?"

"Slave? Gordon—please, stop! You're hurting me."
Heller pushed and pulled, but the drug had weakened
her. He forced her to move to the top of the bed.

"Ever been inside a prison, Heller? The guards have
ways of making a prisoner do anything they want—*say*
anything they want. I was in San Quentin not too long
ago, so I know what I'm talking about." Kneeling behind her, he used his body to keep her arms pinned
against the headboard while he tied her wrists to the
bedposts.

"No—Gordon—no! You mustn't do this. They'll
only put you back in prison when they find out what
you've done."

"But they won't find out, Heller, because you won't
tell them. By the time I'm through with you, you'll say
whatever I ask you to say. Don't look so worried, my
darling. I'm not going to do you any lasting harm. I've
decided I care for you far too much to hurt you." He
moved back and stood up.

A dread chill started at her toes and moved up her
body, totally consuming her. She had to fight off a
wave of nausea. "Why are you doing this?"

"Why? That's a question I asked myself only a little
while ago. Let's just say that you're what I want. You
have an air about you—an air of sophistication that
most other women don't have. I like that."

Heller gave an ironic sigh. Sophistication—that elu-
sive air that marked a real lady—was what she had
always strived to achieve, and now that she had achiev-
ed it, it would become the very thing that would destroy her.

"I'll never agree to marry you, Gordon. Never."

"Well, we'll see about that, won't we? I should warn
you though, I can be *extremely* persuasive." To punctuate his meaning, he forced her to turn her face toward him. "You're beautiful, Heller. You have such

a childlike face, so innocent, so naive. But the rest of you," he ran his hand down the side of her breast, "is very womanly." He unbelted his robe, shrugged out of it, and let it drop behind him. He was clad only in baggy black trousers. He moved up behind her and rubbed himself against her.

Heller cried out, and Gordon's laughter rang hollow.

"Such a little prude. Miss High and Mighty, that's what you are." He fingered the round neck of her shift. "You know what you need, Heller?" He placed his knuckles beneath her chin and jerked her head up. "You need a lesson in humility. I'll bet they never taught you to be humble in that fancy academy you attended, did they?"

"Please, Gordon. Whatever I did to make you hate me, I'm sorry. I'll do anything I can to make it up to you, but please let me go." Hate glittered in his eyes, making her shiver with fear.

"I didn't think so," he continued as if he hadn't heard her. He moved off the bed, reached out and grabbed the thin fabric at the back of her shift. "Well, here's lesson number one," he said, twisting it into a knot. She shrank away from him. Gathering even more of the fabric into the knot, he yanked her back. Her arms pulled and strained against the ties that held her wrists until she cried out in pain. "Did I hurt you? I'm sorry." He laughed softly, moving up close to her. She could smell his fetid breath, and it made her turn her head away. In the next instant, he pulled back sharply and rent her shift down the middle of her back, leaving her naked to his gaze.

For minutes he did nothing but stare at her. His gaze touched every inch of her body until she felt she would die of the shame. Abruptly, he strode across the room, and when he returned, she cried out at what she saw in his hand.

"Lesson number two is obedience." He caressingly stroked the wide cloth whip with his fingers. "I've found it isn't enough to simply demand a woman's obedience. She has to understand the punishment first." He looked into her fear-darkened eyes. "I can see that you're intrigued," he said, giving her a considering look. "I had it specially made." He held it out for her inspection. "You see, this is an unusual whip. It was made more for pleasure than pain. Of course, that depends on the user, too, but you needn't worry, I'm an expert."

Heller went cold with terror. He *was* a madman!

The sun had barely set when Gordon Pierce escorted his newly promised fiancée down the hall of the Grand Hotel to her room. The couple was within a few steps of reaching the door when Abigail opened her door and peeked out.

"Oh, my God. Heller!" the old woman cried, throwing the door wide and grabbing her niece in a frantic embrace. "Where on earth have you been? I've been absolutely beside myself with worry, child."

As her aunt's arms went around her back, Heller stiffened but held back her cry. "I'm sorry I worried you, Aunty."

"Indeed, you should be sorry. I thought you had gone on the Woods tour, but that group returned hours ago."

Heller had dreaded this moment, when she would tell her aunt that she and Gordon had become lovers. She dreaded seeing her aunt's disappointment and disillusionment, but more than that she feared what Gordon would do to the entire Boston Board of Trade if she didn't say and do what he wanted.

"Enough dynamite to blow that locomotive from here to kingdom come," Gordon had threatened.

"Only me and one other knows where that charge is set. Could be anywhere within a hundred miles, on the tracks, on a mountainside, under a bridge, anywhere. You say anything, Miss High and Mighty—I'll find out. And remember," he'd said, squeezing her right breast until she'd cried out in pain, "even if they do catch *me,* there's still my partner who'll carry out my orders."

His words echoed in her ears as she turned and saw his false smile of reassurance. God, how she hated him. If only there were some way to stop him. . . .

Clearing her throat, Heller stepped out of her aunt's arms. "I—I've been with G-Gordon." The words caught anyway. "At his house. We spent last night together . . . and today."

Abigail's face had turned a sickly shade of white. "Last night? You went out last night?" At Heller's nod, she said, "But I looked in on you and you were sound asleep."

"It was later," Heller choked out in frustration. "Really, Aunty. Please don't embarrass me. Let it suffice to say that we have—" She broke off, unable to say the words.

"What she's trying to say is that we're going to be married," Gordon supplied.

Abigail shrieked in horror, then rounded on Gordon Pierce with a withering look and clenched fists.

"It's what I want, Aunty," Heller interjected. "I—I love him."

"Abigail," Gordon said with quiet emphasis. "I assume I may call you Abigail now, since we're soon to be related by marriage?" It was a statement more than a question. "I hope you can forgive us our impulsiveness, but you know how things happen sometimes—when people fall in love."

"I don't believe you. I don't believe any of this."

He continued as if she hadn't spoken. "I'd invite you to the wedding, but as it happens we're leaving for my ranch early tomorrow morning. We'll be married there in a couple of weeks."

Abigail gasped. "Leaving? No, you can't leave . . ."

"I do hope you'll give us your blessing."

Heller felt a despair the likes of which she had never known, yet there was nothing she could do. Not a comforting look or word. It was imperative that Abigail believe her and even more imperative that she let her go.

Heller pretended to yawn. "I know this is a shock to you, Aunty. It's something of a shock to me, but it's what I want. You did want me to marry after all—and have children. . . ." She yawned again. "Can we talk about this in the morning? I'm awfully tired."

Gordon leaned toward her and bussed her lightly on the lips. "You'll need your rest, Heller. It's not a short trip, and it's all by wagon." He squeezed her hand, then turned and walked down the hall.

"Good night, Aunty." Before her aunt could respond, Heller fled into the privacy of her room.

Joaquin had once again given into Elena's pleas and had escorted her back from the theater. On his way out the door, Abigail Peyton accosted him.

"Oh, Señor Montaños. Thank goodness I found you. I was afraid I had forgotten which room you and the señorita were in. Please, may I come in? I desperately need to speak with you."

He opened the door and let her in.

Elena leaped out of her chair and approached Abigail with a hostile mien. "What do *you* want?"

"Please forgive me for intruding, Señorita Valdez, but I must speak to the señor." She turned to him then.

"What is it? What's wrong?"

"Heller. I do not know what has come over her. She—Oh, my. This is terrible. Just terrible!"

Joaquin put his hands on her shoulders to steady her. "Calm down and tell me what has happened."

Abigail quickly told him of her worry over Heller's absence. "They came back just a few minutes ago and—"

"They? Who's they?"

"Heller and Mr. Pierce. She said she and Mr. Pierce had spent the night together and that they were going to be married. I did not believe it, of course, but she assured me that it was what she wanted. They will be leaving at dawn for Mr. Pierce's ranch, wherever it is."

Elena Valdez threw herself into a chair, laughing.

Joaquin was not amused. Quite the contrary, he was mad as hell. "She's a grown woman. Free to marry whomever she chooses." His voice lacked conviction.

Abigail's head shook in denial; her whole body quaked with it. "But that is just it. She would not *choose* to marry Gordon Pierce, despite what she said. I know it!" The old lady's frail body seemed to droop like a fast-wilting flower. "She has locked the door between our rooms and refuses to talk with me. That's not like her, I tell you. She and I have always been able to discuss things. I can hear her in there, sniffling."

"Maybe she sick, like the first time I see her," Elena suggested as she bent to retrieve one of her earbobs off the floor.

A tear fell from Abigail's eye, but she quickly swiped it away. "Señor Montaños, I have no right to involve you in our problems, and I would never have spoken if I did not know for certain"—she glanced at Elena,

then back— "that Heller *thinks* a great deal of you."
This last she whispered as she strained toward him.

Dispiritedly he asked, "What are you implying?"

"He is *forcing* her to marry him. I do not know why
or how, but I know he is. I would stake my life on it."
She put her hand on his arm and clutched his sleeve
with shaking fingers. "I need your help." Her voice
started to give way, along with her control. "I think
she will talk to you." Again, Abigail glanced at Elena.
"You seem to have a way with her, if you know what
I mean," she said quietly. "Regardless, I am begging
you—do *whatever you have to do* to find out what has
happened and stop it!"

Joaquin wasn't exactly sure what Abigail Peyton had
in mind, but seeing the determined set of the matriarch's chin, he was hard-pressed to refuse her. Abigail Peyton was so much like his old *tia* that they
could have been sisters. God, that was a chilling
thought. If ever there was a woman who could talk
him into doing what he didn't want to, it was Tia Maria. So too could Abigail Peyton, and given the chance,
Heller.

Elena bounded across the room like a she-bear de-
fending her cub. "No, it is not his place to talk to her.
You gringos, you go too far, you ask too much! Go
back where you came from. Go back to your Boston.
Leave us alone."

Clenching Elena's upper arm, Joaquin marched her
over to the bed and sat her down. "Stay out of this."
He flashed her a warning look that he knew she would
understand and heed. Then to Abigail, "I'll see what
I can do."

Abigail breathed a sigh of relief. "Thank you. I'm
upstairs in Room 206."

The second Abigail showed herself out, Elena
sprang off the bed and flung herself against him. "Tell

me you do not care for the paper-skinned *gringa*, Joaquin,'' Elena demanded. Her long fingernails were like claws where they dug into his arms. He pulled her hands away and held them between them. "Tell me she is nothing to you. Tell me, *querido*, tell me!''

"What I feel for Heller Peyton or any other woman is none of your damn business. Her aunt thinks she is in need of help. The least I can do is talk to her.''

"Why should you care about these gringos, Joaquin? Did they care when they came to your *casa* and raped and killed Rosita? Did they care when they whipped you? You betray Rosita's memory with your concern for these gringo dogs!''

He pushed her away from him. "Damn you, Elena. Damn you for accusing me of betraying Rosita's memory when everything I've ever done—everything I do *now*—is to keep my vow to her, to avenge her! Heller has brought me all that much closer to getting that revenge. Gordon Pierce *is* Luther Mauger!''

"Madre mia!" Elena fell to her knees.

Joaquin had not intended to tell her that Gordon Pierce was Luther Mauger, but her jealousy had made her impossible to deal with. And a jealous woman—especially a woman like Elena Valdez—could be a dangerous foe. He didn't doubt she would reveal his identity if she thought he cared even two pins for Heller Peyton. And he did care, he admitted. He cared very much what happened to the little Bostonian. The admission took him off guard, but he didn't dare ask himself if Elena was right in that he was betraying Rosita's memory. He didn't want to know.

Disgusted, he didn't bother to offer her a hand up, nor a word of comfort or apology. This time she deserved whatever remorse she was feeling. If only it would last long enough to do some actual good—to bring some warmth and caring into her soul. She was a hateful woman, Elena Valdez. He had only just begun to realize how much.

Before she could recuperate from her shock and start plying him with a thousand questions, he left her room, went upstairs to Abigail's room, and rapped on the door.

"Do you have a hairpin?" he asked Abigail as he walked past her to the door that adjoined her and her niece's rooms.

"She has stopped crying," Abigail remarked.

"*Bueno*. I've had enough of weeping females in the last few minutes to last a lifetime." He took the proffered hairpin, inserted it into the keyhole, and turned it until the lock clicked.

"I should warn you," said Abigail, "sometimes she throws things."

Chapter 13

Hot tears slid down Heller's cheeks as she leaned back against the adjoining door. She had listened to Abigail's desperate pleas to let her in so they could talk, but she had refused. Talking was the last thing she wanted to do. She couldn't risk saying something that would give Abigail reason to believe she was being forced into marriage with Gordon.

Heller thought she would never forget Abigail's disbelieving, pained look when Gordon had announced their marriage plans. The poor old dear had been devastated. Perhaps someday she would get the chance to tell Abigail the truth, or at least what she could remember. . . .

Sick with revulsion, she ran, stumbling, across the room to the bureau and hung her head over the washbowl. Again and again she retched until her stomach ached from the strain. Moaning, she reached for a cloth, dipped it into the water pitcher, and wiped the perspiration from her face and neck. She considered upending the pitcher and dumping its contents over her head, but realized nothing could wash away the horror of the last hours. Gordon Pierce was a rapist, a murderer, and a demented monster who took sick pleasure in hurting women.

And tomorrow, once she left with him, she would be totally at his mercy.

"Mercy!" she scoffed. He had no mercy. She thought about the Chinese girls he'd said he bought for his pleasure then killed when they were no longer of use to him.

Her fingers shook as she struggled to undo the buttons down the front of her dress. She was half-afraid to take it off for fear of what she would see. Though the whip hadn't broken her skin, there had to be marks to evidence what he had done.

Joaquin quietly unlocked the door, opened it, and stood inside watching Heller in the mirror. She seemed intent upon unbuttoning her dress, but her hands shook so badly she was having difficulty coordinating her fingers. From across the room, he heard her frustrated sighs and felt her nervous consternation.

"Heller." When she didn't respond, he said her name again. "Heller."

With a startled cry, Heller dropped her hands to her sides and spun around.

"I didn't mean to frighten you," he said, as if reading her mind. The wild look in her eyes warned him of her panic. Cautiously, he moved into the room. She was as tense as a coiled rattler. In the mirror behind her, he saw her fingers curl around a silvered hairbrush and remembered Abigail's warning.

With an anxious cry, Heller dropped the hairbrush onto the bureau top, then turned to face the mirror. She glanced uncertainly at his mirrored image. "You startled me. I'm not used to men walking into my bedroom unannounced."

"If I had announced myself, would you have let me in?" Careful not to upset her any more than she was, he strove for a tone of congeniality.

"No." She looked away from his mirrored gaze. "What do you want?"

"Your aunt sent me in to talk to you. She's upset and worried."

Her tentative hold on her composure begin to slip. Leaning her weight on her hands atop the dresser, she stole a breath and drew it deep into her lungs. "I know. She doesn't like Mr. Pierce." She raised her head. "I also know she meant well by asking you to talk to me, but there's nothing to talk about. I've made my decision, just as you made yours yesterday when you walked out of here. Now, if you don't mind, I'm awfully tired and I'd like to go to bed. So, would you please go?" Looking away, she set about tidying the mess on the bureau top.

"Not just yet. I promised your aunt I'd talk to you, and that's what I'm going to do," he insisted, his jaw tight. Patience had never been one of his better qualities. Already he was feeling himself becoming aggravated.

She stopped her tidying and clenched her fists. "Why must you persist? I've already told you there's nothing to talk about." Her anxiety turned sharply into anger. She wheeled around and spat out contemptuously, "Be assured that I'll let Abigail know you kept your promise and fulfilled your *gentlemanly* duty."

Joaquin stiffened as though she had struck him. Bristling with anger, he retorted, "Despite what you think, I'm not here to fill any damn gentlemanly duty. I came to offer my help." He moved to where she stood and reached out to touch her arm, but she jerked back. A muscle ticked along the side of his mouth. "I don't know why I thought you had more sense than most females. Obviously I was wrong. You can't see what's right in front of your nose. You're making a big mistake, Heller. You have no idea what kind of man Pierce is."

Icy fear tore at her insides. He was mistaken. She

knew exactly what kind of man Gordon Pierce was, and that was why she was going with him. "*If* it's a mistake, then it's my mistake and I'll live with it."

"Heller, dammit. No matter what's happened between you and Pierce, no matter what he's done or what he's threatened, you don't *have* to marry him. If you'll just talk to me, tell me what hold he has over you, I promise you I'll take care of it."

She stared at him, her heart pounding. He knew . . . and yet he didn't know, not for certain. He was only guessing that something was wrong, but he was much too close to discovering the truth, which, of course, she couldn't allow him to do. Lives were at stake; Abigail's life, the lives of everyone on the train—her own life, as well. She *had* to make him believe that she was wasn't being threatened or coerced, and that she was happy with her decision.

Reaching deep down inside herself, she dredged up what was left of her tenacity. Then, looking down her nose at him, she said, "Why is it that both you and Abigail doubt me? Why can't either of you believe that I *want* to marry the man? Because of what he did yesterday? He was right. The boy stole from him and deserved to be punished. I shouldn't have chastised him so, but as I said before, guns terrify me." Defiantly, she added, "I don't have to explain myself to you or anyone! I agreed to marry the man and I spent the night with him . . . to seal the bargain."

A shadow of annoyance crossed his face. "Yes, your aunt mentioned that you had spent the night with him."

She bent to pick up a glove off the floor, the movement hiding her flushed cheeks. She supposed she should be glad he believed at least one part of her story, but she wished he hadn't chosen that part in particular.

"He's not the man for you, Heller. Believe me, I know!''

"Well, that's where you're wrong,'' she shot back, biting down on the lie. "Gordon Pierce is just right for me. He's a *gentleman,* unlike someone else I know. And he's exactly what I've been looking for but never found until now. He's a respected member of the community and a well-to-do businessman who shares my love of the arts. He even collects art and displays it in his home. He gave me the grand tour. Did you know he owns a mansion on Rincon Hill? It's almost as grand as Abigail's, and when I marry him, the house and everything in it will be mine.''

"Oh! So, that's the way it is. Now I'm beginning to understand your motives. You really don't love him; it's his position and his wealth you're seeking.'' She nodded, then shook her head. "You'd better hope your friends on the Board of Trade don't find out that their beloved cultural secretary is really a greedy little coquette. It might prove to be a bit of an embarrassment to your aunt.''

"No—You misunderstand—'' she said, faltering. He was taking her explanations out of context, turning them around and using them to confuse her. She felt a raging headache coming on, and her stomach gave a warning lurch. His badgering had worn her down and befuddled her. Her head whirled with lies and half-truths.

Beside herself with frustration, she reached around behind, grabbed the hairbrush, and flung it across the room. "Be gone with you!'' she shouted, the remembered Irish phrase popping out of her mouth before she could catch it. But what did it matter? She was beyond trying to sound like a lady. In fact, she was beyond *acting* like one!

He ducked the flying hairbrush adroitly and stood

tall, an invincible force. She paused to catch her breath and consider what to do next, as what she was doing apparently wasn't working. "Can't you get it through your head? I'm doing this because I want to do it."

Something snapped inside him. Gone was all patience. All reason. Like Abigail, he didn't want to believe that she actually wanted to marry Mauger, but she sounded so damn sincere. . . . "What you're telling me then is that you willingly gave yourself to him? You let him make love to you?" This, he realized, was going beyond what Abigail had asked him to do. Now he was asking for himself, because suddenly it mattered very much that he know.

She boldly returned his gaze. "Yes, I *gave* myself to him."

He looked away and a second later turned back to study her expression. "You're lying. You wouldn't willingly give yourself to a man you don't love. And, goddammit, you don't love Gordon Pierce!"

In the light of the oil lamp, Heller saw his face contort with rage. His dark brows drew together in a forbidding line and his eyes narrowed dangerously, sending a ripple of alarm along her spine. He was more than furious. He was incensed!

An idea came to her, took root, and blossomed. "You think you know me, don't you?" she asked sarcastically. "You see a chaste, twenty-six-year-old Boston spinster." She gave an ironic laugh, then placed her hands on her hips as she had seen Mam and the other whores of Cow Bay do. "You're as bad as Abigail. The two of you seem to think I'm some sort of . . . vestal virgin," she said, using Gordon Pierce's words, then forced out another laugh. "Well, I'm not!"

He quirked a dark brow. "Fine. So you're not a virgin. Neither am I. But what does that have to do with anything?"

She raised her arms and plucked the pins from her hair and tossed them aside. With the last of them removed, she dug her fingers into her scalp, fluffing her copper curls into a riot of motion. "Well, for one thing, it should tell you I am not as naive as you think I am." She had decided to play a role, one that would make him change his mind about her and see her in a different light. If she played it well, he would leave in disgust—which would be best for all concerned. Careful of the tone of her voice now, she said, "You see, you have *your* way of getting what you want . . . and *I* have mine." She stood in front of the bureau, picked up the silver-handled comb, and drew it slowly and repeatedly through her hair until it fell it soft waves around her shoulders. Despite twelve years of continuous observation of the whores of Cow Bay, acting like a whore didn't come easily.

Out of the corner of her eye, she espied her hat hanging on a wooden peg next to the bureau. She hadn't worn it since that first windy outing. She plucked out its foot-long feather. "You're like every other man, I suppose. You can't see what's right in front of your nose." She threw his words back at him, then touched the feather to the tip of his nose and skimmed it's tip down over his lips and finally his strong-boned chin. To his credit he didn't move, not even a muscle.

"What don't I see, Heller?"

"Heller O'Shay. Me," she answered simply. She started to unbutton her bodice, then realized it was already halfway undone and that there was nothing beneath but bare skin; her ruined shift had been left in Gordon's bedroom.

She made the mistake of looking up and immediately sobered when she saw him staring at her exposed bosom. She started to turn away, but such a movement belonged to a chaste twenty-six-year-old Boston spinster. Her heart skipped a beat, then another, but she made herself undo the rest of the buttons. Because her hands were shaking so badly, it took her a full minute, during which time she prayed that it wouldn't take too much more to offend him.

"I told you yesterday that I'm not a lady," she blurted out. "Truth is, I'm not a Boston blueblood either, but then, of course, you've already guessed that." His inquiring look gave her pause. "Abigail's *esteemed* brother never married his Irish whore, my mother, so I grew up a bastard, running in the streets of New York. When I wasn't trying to pick some fellow's pocket or steal from the fruit vendor's cart, I spent my time rooting in gutters for scraps of food." She held onto the back of the chair and leaned over to remove her shoes and stockings, fully aware of her gaping bodice. "As I got a little older and filled out some, I discovered that I could make more money doing what Mam did than picking cinders and collecting rags." She gathered up the hem of her skirt and set her fingers to work untying her petticoat strings, but all she succeeded in doing was tying them in knots. She started to look down to see what the trouble was when she saw that all too familiar blade heading for her stomach.

"So you're a whore—is that what you're trying to tell me in so many words and . . . actions?" He slipped the tip of his knife into the knot and jerked backwards. The tie snapped apart and her petticoat fell to the floor.

She tried to conceal her shock by dropping her skirt hem and turning away, but he pulled her back and forced her to look at him. "Answer me, Heller."

She lifted her chin and repeated an expression Mam had used over and over again. "I'm whatever you want

me to be." She followed his dark questing gaze to her
bosom and saw that her nipples had drawn taut. Her
breath caught in her throat when his hand stole up
between their bodies, folded back the sides of her bodice, and lightly grazed her skin.

Suddenly she knew she had taken her role too far.

"An intriguing thought, but I like you just the way
you are." He rubbed her nipple between his thumb
and forefinger. "Let me make sure I fully *understand*.
You gave yourself to Gordon Pierce to get what you
wanted, which was a mansion and marriage to a
wealthy businessman."

"Yes!" At last he was beginning to understand.
Maybe it wasn't too late after all.

"And now you're going to give yourself to me." He
opened his hand and surrounded the firm fullness of
her breast. "But what do you want in return?"

"Want? I—" She could hardly think, let alone answer his question.

"Maybe this will satisfy your greed." He reached
into his pocket with his free hand and pulled out a
twenty-dollar gold piece. "I may not have a mansion,
but I'm willing to pay well for my pleasure." He
slammed the coin down on the bureau top. "I've never
paid in advance for services rendered. I usually wait
until I've decided what they were worth. Just keep in
mind that that's a lot of money for one night with *only*
one woman."

Heller was outraged but dared not show it, nor could
she show her apprehension. She'd cast herself into the
role of a whore and now, it seemed, she would have
to *be* a whore.

Dear God. What had she done?

Was there no other way out? If she backed down, he
would know she had been lying about everything. She

couldn't back down. There was too much at stake. And what did it matter that she gave herself to him? It wasn't as if she still had her treasured virginity. Gordon had seen to that.

But there was one major problem besides fearing the sexual act which was still, for all intents and purposes, unknown to her. In all her life, she had never initiated even so much as a kiss, let alone a complete seduction. She called up a memory of Mam greeting one of her sailors, and mimicked the welcome by leaning into him and pressing her lips against his.

He pulled back. "You call that a kiss?"

She blinked up at him in surprise, then tried again, this time standing on tiptoe and twining her arms around his neck. He was as unresponsive as Dr. Jordan's wax and plaster figure, and she wondered what she was doing wrong. A little shiver of fear ran the length of her. This wasn't a game, she reminded herself. Lives depended on whether or not she succeeded in making him believe her. With new determination she kissed him again, closed her eyes, and slid her tongue between his lips. Then, at last, she felt him respond.

What started out a moment before as a planned, emotionless seduction, quickly became something else. A desperate wanting grew inside her and made her burn. A wildfire of passion spread throughout her body, touching her breasts, her stomach, then her abdomen, consuming her, until minutes later, the only role she was playing was that of a woman desiring a man.

With a soft moan, she wrenched her mouth away and dragged her lips over his jaw and down the side of his neck. Her hands followed her mouth, and she loosened his tie and the top button of his shirt to get access to the rapidly beating pulse at the base of his muscled throat.

Only when Joaquin heard her moans, only when he knew she had thrown herself into the fire of her own passion, did he draw her into his embrace. As yesterday, once released from the prison of her self-imposed propriety, she was like wild thing in his arms—warm, responsive, naturally sensuous. But not a whore.

He grabbed the opening edges of her bodice and pulled them over her shoulders and down her arms. A second, shorter effort sent the dress sliding down past her drawers into a heap at her feet.

"You don't have to do this Heller," he said without conviction. When she didn't answer, he knotted his fingers in her hair and pulled her head back. His eyes narrowed at the look on her face: a mixture of passion and desperation. It was the latter that confused and unnerved him.

"Damn you!" he said as his mouth took possession of hers. He kissed her roughly, cruelly, ravaging her tender mouth with his tongue. He ignored her little cries, never asking himself if they were from pain or pleasure. It didn't matter. She had thrown herself at him, and he would take her as she deserved to be taken, without tenderness or gentleness. He removed her underwear, then began on himself, pulling off his boots, and tossing his jacket, shirt, and trousers across the room onto the bed.

Heller was beyond all thought, all reason. Her body reacted to his with a will of its own—a will so strong, so intense, that it dragged her along in the torrent of its passion. Sensation after sensation—all new—fought for dominance within her, making her crazy with need.

She wrapped her arms around him, seeking his warmth, his power, his possession. When she felt his manhood press against her stomach, she went weak with longing. He bent her backwards and grasped her buttocks, and lifted her off her feet until their bodies were perfectly aligned, breast to breast, stomach to stomach, manhood to womanhood.

Wrapping her legs around him, she clung to him and rained feverish kisses over his mouth, his jaw, the side of his neck, then back again. A hoarse sound escaped him and he carried her across the room to the bed. He laid her down on her side in the middle of the bed, then blew out the light and laid down beside her on top of his clothes. When he touched her breast, she thrust herself into his hand. Then he lowered his head and took her nipple between his lips, nipping it lightly with his teeth. The exquisite shock of it sent a lightning bolt of pleasure throughout her body. A raspy sound escaped Heller's lips as he suckled her.

With his mouth still at her breast, he lifted himself onto his forearm and pulled her partway beneath him. His hand moved down her body, over her hip and thigh until he reached the junction between her legs.

Heller spasmed and tightened her legs. She had never imagined he would want to touch her there. She gave a small cry of alarm. She reached down and grabbed his hand, trying to halt the invasion, but he was too strong and the will to stop him died when his fingers plunged inside her.

"Please, I—I want—"

"Want what, Heller? What do you want? Tell me."

"You," she breathed against his face. "I want you."

He rolled her onto her back and rose above her like an ominous storm cloud. She had all but forgotten about her bruised back until it touched the cool bed-clothes. Somehow she would have to remember to keep herself facing him at all times. She looked down between their naked bodies, then closed her eyes.

The stage was set, the curtain about to go up and the performance begin. She doubted she could stop him now even if she tried—even if she wanted to. He bent to kiss her, then wedged one knee between her thighs, then the other. She felt him shudder as he moved into position. Then he drove deep inside her.

Her body arched and she screamed inside his mouth.

She *had* lied. She *was* a virgin! She *hadn't* given herself to Mauger. Then Mauger must have some other hold on her.

He pulled back sharply and stared down into her wide, pain-glazed eyes. Damn! He should have realized she was playing a game. He'd seen her look of desperation, but when she'd thrown herself at him, he'd selfishly put everything out of his mind—everything except wanting her. And now he'd had her and there was no turning back, no righting the wrong.

She had closed her eyes and turned her cheek into the pillow. He thought he should say or do something, but then she moved beneath him, fitting her body to his, and he lost his train of thought to the longing of fulfillment.

Telling himself that her pain would soon pass, that it would subside into pleasure, he pushed himself back into her tight sheath, groaning with the wonderful feel of her. He stayed embedded inside her as long as he could, until his body forced him into movement, slow at first, controlled, to show her she need not fear any more pain.

Little by little the hurt went away, but before she could catch her breath, he began to move inside her, filling her to near bursting with his length. She began to feel a peculiar sensation, a kind of heat, a smoldering itch that needed to be scratched. She lifted her hips to his thrusts and heard him urge her on, speaking to her in an odd combination of Spanish and English, in a voice deep and heavy with resonance. The vibrations of his voice crackled in the air above her, all around her, like thunder before a storm.

Heller cried out as the spark inside her ignited and burst. She grasped him around the neck, pulling him toward her with all her strength, pressing her fingertips deep into his muscled shoulders.

"Relax, *cara*," she heard him whisper as he soothed her fevered brow with his lips. He moved slowly within her, giving her a chance to savor the moment. She thought she had never felt anything so good, so perfect, so right.

His movements quickened then, and she felt his urgency as he drove himself into her deeper and harder, until at last he called out, "Heller. *Dios*. Heller," and gave a final powerful thrust that filled her with liquid heat.

A warm night wind, redolent with the scent of moist earth, soothed their heated bodies as they clung to each other, spent and breathless. Moments later, he rolled off of her onto his side.

"Are you all right?" he murmured, pushing the hair back from her face. He kissed her forehead.

"Yes, I'm fine. Kiss me again," she said, then traced her index finger across the strong contours of his face, willing herself to remember him always just as he was now.

After a while he got up and left the bed. She started to protest, and he ignored her and walked over to the open window. He stood in the path of a moonbeam— his tall, magnificently muscled body straight as a statue. Moonlight touched his face, emphasizing the strength and character of his patrician features, his proud Spanish ancestry. The same light gilded his powerful shoulders, his chest and stomach, and his manhood.

She'd heard the Cow Bay whores swapping tales about losing their virginity—the ones who could remember that far back. Some of them said they'd experienced pain and bleeding several times after the first time. She'd also heard them giggle over how well a man was or wasn't endowed and concluded that all men were not created equal after all. Given the time, she supposed her body would learn to accommodate Don Ricardo's, until there was no more pain.

But there was no time.

Tomorrow she was leaving, and she would never see him again.

The wind ruffled the draperies, and Heller watched, fascinated, as he took the wind into his body and held it within him as if it were a life-giving substance. He seemed unaware of her observance as he performed what might have been some ancient pagan ritual.

Then the wind whispered her name and she drifted off to sleep, safe for the night in its warm embrace.

Joaquin stepped out into the dimly lit hallway and paused with his hand on the doorknob. Turning around, he gazed back at Heller. She was sound asleep amid the rumpled bedclothes. He couldn't recall ever having been so confused.

Until tonight, his sole purpose in life had been to avenge Rosita's death by bringing down Luther Mauger once and for all. Now he found his destiny inexplicably entwined with a Boston spinster, who had somehow not only worked her way into his heart but had become Mauger's pawn as well as his own. As he watched her in her sleep, Joaquin swore to himself that he would find out what hold Mauger had over her. In the meantime, he would be her constant companion. Her invisible constant companion. It was the only way to protect her against Luther Mauger.

He closed the door and ran a hand through his hair, straightening it as best he could. As he turned to go, the door to the room beside Heller's swung open without warning. Forcing an expression of bland composure on his face, Joaquin smiled at Abigail Peyton as she stuck her head out and in a stage whisper asked, "Don Ricardo, how is she? What happened? Should I go to her now?"

The old woman's hopeful, trusting expression made him squirm like a schoolboy; a new, foreign feeling, to be sure. He cleared his throat before he assured her, "I think she's feeling better, señora, but she said she's going right to sleep and does not wish to be disturbed."

Abigail peered over her spectacles and glanced up and down the hall. Dressed in a tightly sashed wrapper that covered her from neck to ankle, she kept one hand protectively at her throat as she stepped out into the hallway. "What about this ridiculous notion of her marrying Gordon Pierce? Is she still going through with it?"

He nodded, slowly. "*Sí*. I could not change her mind." He paused as the memory of his exchange with Heller stirred his blood and his temper. "She is very stubborn, your niece, despite my persuasiveness."

Abigail's expression saddened. She sighed. "For once I find myself at a loss as to what to do."

Unwilling to tell her anything just yet, Joaquin lowered his voice to just above a whisper. "Go with her, señora. Make it impossible for Pierce to leave you behind. And don't let her out of your sight. I don't trust him, but maybe with you close by, he won't overstep his bounds."

She nodded, her face alive with purpose. He only hoped he wasn't making a bad situation worse by complicating matters.

"Now, if you'll excuse me, señora. It's late."

"It is, indeed," Abigail readily agreed. "And I have

a lot of packing to do if I am going with Heller tomorrow." She reached out for Joaquin's hand to stop him before he could walk away. Her sincerity was more than evident as she said softly, "Thank you, Don Ricardo. I knew the moment I laid eyes on you that you were an honorable man. I only wish Heller and you—" She shook her head and laughed softly. "Oh, well. I guess it was not meant to be. Thank you again, for everything."

With that, Abigail turned and disappeared behind her closed door. Joaquin stood in silence for a moment, then headed for the stairs. Abigail's parting thanks lingered in his mind and formed a knot of guilt that sank to the bottom of his stomach.

The next morning, Heller bleakly walked back and forth between the wardrobe and the trunk, carrying one item of clothing at a time, as if she could prolong the inevitable. Mercifully, Abigail had left her alone to bathe and ready herself for her journey. Now, with her hands shaking as she folded each article into the trunk, she looked at them as if they belonged to someone else. They *did* belong to someone else; they belonged to Heller Peyton, the chaste Boston spinster who was the Boston Board of Trade's cultural secretary.

The last item to be folded was the dress Don Ricardo had taken off of her. Laying it on the bed, she carefully rebuttoned the small wooden buttons and pressed out the collar with her hands.

She had expected to feel shame at what she had allowed to happen. Quite the contrary; she was glad it had happened. It was the most beautiful experience she had ever known. And even though he had never declared his feelings for her, she had interpreted them through the way he made love to her.

The thought of never being with him again was like a knife stabbing deep into her breast. The wound would never heal. Not a day would go by when she wouldn't think of him, wondering what he was doing and who he was with.

But at least she had last night. At least she could take her memory. She laid the dress into her trunk and tucked the twenty-dollar gold piece inside the bodice where it wouldn't be lost.

She had another reason to be glad, she told herself, staring into the open trunk. Making love with Don Ricardo had somehow purged the vileness of Gordon Pierce's rape. Though she had no actual memory of Gordon raping her, because of the ether, her body had felt violated all the same. In spite of the fact that Gordon had taken her virginity, she promised herself that she would always think of her night with Don Ricardo as her first time—her first love.

She heard Abigail open the door and turned around sharply.

"Finished packing, dear?"

"Almost." Heller proffered a falsely bright smile. She would miss Abigail, miss her terribly. Abigail had saved her from a life of poverty and disease, taken her into her home, clothed and fed her, educated her, loved her. The thought of never seeing her again was too painful to bear. Someday—maybe someday . . .

"I hope you aren't angry with me that I took it upon myself to ask Don Ricardo to talk to you."

Heller kept her eyes averted, afraid her aunt would see how much the very mention of his name affected her. "No. I'm not angry."

"I saw him as he was leaving—"

Heller swung around. Surely he wouldn't have said anything. "What did he say?"

"Only that despite his persuasiveness, he could not change your mind."

So that's what he called it. "No, he couldn't."

Abigail sighed in disappointment. "I would imagine he tried everything he knew—"

Heller turned away again and began carelessly dropping her toilette articles into her trunk. "Oh, yes, I'm sure he tried everything . . . but my heart is set on marrying Gordon, Aunty."

"Don Ricardo loves you, Heller."

Heller sank down on the bed. "No, Aunty, you're wrong. He doesn't love me." She hoped she wasn't wrong, because it would be best for all if he hated her. She didn't want to cause him any pain.

"Oh, yes, he does, my dear girl, and furthermore, you love him!"

A briny breeze sailed into the room, reminding Heller of Don Ricardo standing in front of the window. Her throat constricted painfully.

"What did you tell him last night, Heller?"

"Aunty, please. I don't want to talk about this. There's nothing to be gained by—"

"Good morning, ladies." Gordon Pierce blithely opened the door and walked into Heller's room as if he had every right to. After kissing Heller lightly on the cheek, he asked, "All packed and ready to go?" He turned toward the door and waved the bellboys into the room.

Heller shot him a sideways look of undisguised contempt.

Imperiously, he told the boys, "Take this trunk, the hat box, and that valise down to the lobby. We'll be along momentarily."

"You can collect my trunk and hat box, as well," Abigail directed one of the boys.

Heller looked up in surprise. "Where are you going, Aunty?"

"Why, I am going with you, dear," she announced with a Chesire Cat smile that she flashed at Gordon. "I thought about it all night and decided it was the only proper thing to do." Waving an admonishing finger at Pierce, she said, "You of all people, Mr. Pierce, would not want people thinking improper thoughts about your relationship with Heller. So to prevent wagging tongues, I thought it best for all concerned that I go with you and act as chaperone until such time as you are married."

"You can't, Aunty—"

"Oh, yes, I can, dear." She patted Heller's cold hand. "And I have thought of everything. When I went down for breakfast, I talked to Alex and told him about the whole situation—that we were leaving right away for Mr. Pierce's ranch. Alex made me promise to wire him in a day or two so he would know we arrived safely. I also told him I would wire him again when I was coming home."

Heller didn't know whether to be upset by Abigail's announcement or relieved. But in spite of what she felt, there was nothing she could do to prevent Abigail from doing exactly what she pleased. And nothing Gordon could do, either, she realized when he said nothing to stop the boys from collecting her things.

"By the way, Heller, dear. I told Alex you would give him your journal as we left."

"Oh! Why yes, of course."

"Come along now. I am sure that by now he has told everyone that Mr. Pierce won your heart and that we are leaving straightaway. They will probably all be waiting in the lobby to see us off."

Chapter 14

Joaquin and Lino stood by their horses a half block down Market Street from the hotel entrance. They'd been waiting since sunup and it was now three minutes past eight A.M., according to Lino's timepiece, which he wound faithfully at the same time each day.

"Nice day for a long ride. Looks like the weather's going to be warm and sunny," Lino remarked, stealing a sideways glance at Joaquin's stony expression. El Jefe had been in a surly mood when he'd returned to the What Cheer House and announced that they were heading out at dawn to follow Mauger to his ranch.

Up until this morning, Joaquin had said little about his relationship with Heller. But his actions these last few days had spoken for themselves. He had fallen in love with the fiery little Bostonian. Lino hoped, for Joaquin's sake, that Heller felt the same. God knew that Joaquin had mourned Rosita's death long enough.

Heller Peyton was a beautiful intelligent woman, and would be a compliment to El Jefe—that is, if they ever overcame the hurdles that kept them at odds with each other.

Lino had felt like a father confessor again when, as they were preparing to leave the hotel, Joaquin told him the sequence of events that had ended with him and Heller making love.

"It wasn't rape, Joaquin." Lino had explained. "You didn't force her."

"In a way I did. I should have realized what she was doing and seen through it. She did everything she could to try to make me believe that she *wanted* to marry Mauger. I don't know what he threatened her with, but it had to be something that frightened her so badly she felt compelled to do whatever he asked. I wish she'd trusted me enough to confide in me, but then I guess I haven't done anything to win her trust." He paced the room, kicking a chair with his boot, slapping a tabletop. He stopped and ran his fingers through his hair. "Then she started to act like a whore. At first I believed her, then I realized . . . I can only guess that she must have thought the act would disgust me enough to leave." He shook his head. "Hell, I don't know."

"Who can know what is in a woman's head, Joaquin?" Lino resisted telling Joaquin that it was his love for Heller that was causing him this agony. He would realize it soon enough, if he hadn't already.

Joaquin tilted his head at an angle to look at Lino. "You should be chastising me, not consoling me."

Lino's head jerked around. "Dammit, Joaquin. I gave up giving absolution from sins when I left the monastery, remember?"

"Did you give up *all* the holy doctrines as well?"

"No. Not *all* of them," Lino snapped indignantly. I've held onto a few archaic beliefs." He turned his gaze to the window. "I almost forgot to tell you in all the excitement," he added nonchalantly, "the Wells Fargo agents visited Mauger's house, but according to his servant he wasn't at home."

Joaquin smiled and nodded. "That explains Mauger's wanting to leave in such a hurry."

After a hearty breakfast, they had checked out of the

hotel, paid the liveryman, saddled their horses, and rode over to the Grand Hotel to wait.

Again Lino checked his timepiece. Now, it was almost quarter past eight. He started to say something to Joaquin when a wagon, pulled by a pair of bays, rounded the corner and drove up in front of the hotel. Mauger set the brake, jumped out, and disappeared inside the hotel lobby.

"It doesn't look like he's taking much with him," Joaquin said, seeing only one small crate and two medium-sized carpetbags in the wagonbed.

"And he won't be able to come back for it later, either," Lino added. "Wells Fargo will confiscate everything to satisfy their claim." Lino drew a deep breath. "Which means, *mi jefe*, we've destroyed everything he built here. His business. His home. His dreams and his ambitions."

Joaquin gave a satisfied chuckle. "Not quite everything, Lino. There's still his social creditability. But I think my letter will take care of that." He unbuckled his saddlebags and took out a letter he'd written to the editor of the *Alta*. "I don't think I've left anything out: Wells Fargo, San Quentin, Canton Charlie, Drake's Disposal, and an ex-prison warden by the name of Henderson. I wish I were going to be around to see it all put together on the society page."

Lino laughed, the mood lightened. "I doubt the Chamber of Commerce will be sending Mr. Pierce a membership renewal."

Seconds later, a bevy of red-jacketed bellboys loaded the women's two trunks, carpetbags, and hat boxes into the back of the wagon. Then, amid a chorus of good-byes, from what looked like the entire Boston contingent, the trio exited the hotel. Mauger handed the women up to their seats then took his own.

When the wagon was halfway down Market Street,

Joaquin rode up to the hotel entrance, where he captured the interest of one of the bellboys with a ten-dollar gold piece.

"I want you to take this to the newspaper, directly to the editor. Tell him Joaquin Murieta sent you."

Joaquin and Lino followed the wagon out of the city at a discreet distance. Morosely, Joaquin kept his eyes fixed on the wagon tracks. For once, Lino was silent, and Joaquin was grateful for the respite.

Joaquin was pleased that Abigail had taken his advice about going with Heller. He wondered what female trickery she'd used. Abigail's presence wouldn't keep Heller safe, but it would be an added deterrent in case Mauger decided to get too cozy with Heller. The only drawback was that now he and Lino would have two women to worry about, two women to protect.

He could have stopped this, he reminded himself. He could have easily taken care of Mauger last night or early this morning. But he wasn't finished with him. Not yet. Not since he'd found out about the ranch, which was yet another possession of Mauger's to be destroyed.

He lifted his head and stared off into the distance, berating himself for his stubborn determination to keep his vow no matter who stood in the way, no matter what the cost. Destroying Mauger little by little had become an obsession. He'd convinced himself that no single punishment, physical or mental, was severe enough to avenge Rosita's murder.

If not for this damnable obsession, he would have killed Mauger the moment he had laid eyes on him at the entrance to Little China. But seventeen years of wanting and waiting had hardened his resolve and, he supposed, his heart. Only his own death could stop him from seeing his goal to the end.

He wouldn't be trying to justify his actions at all, he thought, scowling, if he hadn't let himself get involved with Heller in the first place. She had confounded him from the moment she accused him of stabbing her and fell into his arms. During their first confrontation in Elena's room, he had thought she was both fire and ice. He should have realized then that the two didn't mix. He knew that now.

Fine thing, hindsight; it was always so damned honest and unerring.

He thought about last night and how he'd badgered Heller to gain the answers he sought. Despite his aggressive questioning, she adroitly avoided telling him what he wanted to know by inventing answers and explanations as she went. The end result, of course, was that he confused her so badly she started countering herself, and by the time she finished, practically nothing she said made any sense.

Whatever threat Mauger held over her had forced her to lie, but her virginity negated those lies. She had *not* given herself to Mauger, *nor* was she a whore. Yet, something still didn't seem quite right. Joaquin had the oddest feeling that she was unaware of the gift she had given him. He switched the reins to his left hand and scratched his head beneath his hat. She couldn't be so naive as to not know he had taken her virginity. Could she? Somehow, incredibly, he knew the answer was yes, and that raised a whole other set of questions.

A string of Spanish curses made El Tigre's ears perk and head jerk up in alarm. Lino, too, glanced his way, but quickly cast his gaze back to the trail when he saw Joaquin's disagreeable scowl.

* * *

By late afternoon of the third day, three miles east of Angels Camp, in the foothills of the Sierra Nevada, Mauger turned the wagon north and headed to higher ground.

Joaquin and Lino reined their horses to a halt when they saw the wagon tracks had turned sharply to the left and abandoned the road.

"*Dios!* Joaquin!" There was an anxiousness in Lino's voice. "He's heading toward . . ."

Sí, Lino. I know. El Dorado." Joaquin had suspected Mauger's destination since yesterday afternoon but hadn't shared his suspicions, hoping he was wrong.

"I don't suppose it could be a coincidence."

"It doesn't seem likely. The valley isn't on a route to or from anywhere. Mauger must have declared my claim to be abandoned and filed on it."

Lino rose up tall in his saddle and craned his neck as he watched the wagon disappear over the hill. "I wonder . . . Have you ever considered the possibility that maybe his coming to El Dorado in the first place was no accident, that maybe he knew you had found a bonanza?"

"It didn't seem that way at the time, but as I said, the valley isn't on the way to or from anywhere." Joaquin's jaw was set in a grim line.

"I wonder who might have told him? Who knew about El Dorado besides me?"

"Only Rosita's brother. He visited us soon after we finished the *casa*."

"You are certain you never said anything when you went into Angels Camp for supplies?"

"I am many things, Lino, but I am not a fool. And no, not Rosita, either; she never went into town without me by her side. But I think you could be right; someone may have told him and his *cholo* pack."

"You know, *mi jefe,* if he has filed on the claim, then El Dorado belongs to him now."

"*Sí*, I know, Lino."

"But that means—"

"It means I will have to destroy it."

"But don't you want to get back what belongs to you?"

"I no longer think of it as belonging to me. My life in El Dorado ended when Rosita was killed. Rancho Murieta is my home now." Joaquin tapped his spurs against El Tigre's flanks and cantered off, taking a route parallel to Mauger's, up a steep-sided ledge that went up into a mountain, high above the valley of El Dorado.

Lino rode beside him, keeping pace.

The climb was short but windy and steep. At the top, their old hideout loomed in front of them, a great yawning hole. A cave. Joaquin pulled El Tigre to a stop several hundred feet from the cave opening and drew his gun. The ground beneath him was covered with new tracks, some less than an hour old, judging from the sharp outside edges. There were two sets of prints: those of a man with badly worn boot heels, and the unshod hooves of a burro. A lone miner, perhaps. Joaquin looked up and studied his surroundings with sharp-eyed vigilance, a habit that had been with him since boyhood.

"Cover me," he told Lino, who was already backing his big chestnut into a thicket. Cocking one of his six-shooters, Joaquin dismounted, dropped El Tigre's reins to ground-tie him, and skirted a pine tree near the cave's entrance.

"Whoever you are, come out with your hands up." He leveled his Colt and looked straight down its barrel through the sight.

A voice from inside the cave echoed. "Please, se-ñor, I will come out. No shoot Pepe." Joaquin glanced around at Lino, then back into the darkened interior of the cave. Chattering like a monkey, Pepe Lopez emerged into the light of day. "Don't shoot, *por favor.*"

Joaquin's first thought was that he knew this man—or did he? "Pepe? Pepe Lopez?"

The little man pushed his sombrero to the back of his head, exposing his weathered, brown face. "*Sí.* I am Pepe Lopez and you—You are—Joaquin! El Jefe! You have come back. At last."

Releasing the hammer, then holstering his Colt, Joaquin stepped into the open and walked up to the old man. "Pepe, it is good to see you. It has been a long time, old friend. I thought you went back to Mexico." Smiling, Joaquin motioned Lino over.

Pepe flashed a gap-toothed grin. "*Sí,* I did, then I come here. I go where I am needed, Joaquin. You know that."

"Hello, Pepe." Lino greeted the old Mexican with a hearty embrace.

"Ah, I should have known," said Pepe. His rusty-brown eyes danced with excitement. "The two of you found each other and are one again. This is good. *Muy bien.*"

"Who is it that needs you, Pepe?" Joaquin inquired. He crossed his arms and took a spread-legged stance.

Insulted, the old one answered, "Why *you* do, El Jefe. Paco and me, we have waited here for you, two, three years now."

Lino gave a short laugh. "You don't still have that old blue jackass? That was the meanest nastiest animal I—"

Pepe put a big knuckled index finger to his lips. "Sh! He will hear you." Pointing that same finger at Lino, he scolded, "He has not forgotten what you do to him."

"What I did to *him*?! Why, that old biscuit-eater nearly kicked my head in—and all I did was try to saddle him and make him earn his feed like any respectable horse would do."

"Paco is not a horse and he does not take to the saddle. You know that. I warned you, but you no listen. So I leave it to him and he take care of it. Now, maybe you no forget, eh?" Pepe slapped his backside and broke into laughter.

A deep wheezy bray from the thicket beyond the cave made Lino take a step backwards. "You do have him tied up, don't you, Pepe?"

Pepe nodded. "*Sí*. For now. Maybe you make friends with him, no? Maybe you offer him a tortilla and beg him to forgive you?" he suggested with grave sincerity.

At that, Lino clamped his teeth together, mumbled a curse, and strode off to where he had picketed his chestnut.

Joaquin's expression turned from amusement to curiosity. "What made you think I would come back here, Pepe? I didn't even know myself until yesterday."

"You ask Pepe Lopez how he knows what he knows? For shame, Joaquin." Shading his eyes with a brown, wrinkled hand, the old man looked up into the sky. "I see it in the heavens and I hear it on the wind. The wind, she say, El Jefe, he will come back to El Dorado to avenge his Rosita."

Joaquin considered Pepe's answer, the same kind of answer he gave anyone who questioned how he knew what he knew. The gringos would call such a man a magician; the Indians, a shaman; and the Mexicans, a *curandero*, a healer. Joaquin wasn't sure what Pepe was; he only knew that Pepe had brought him back to life when . . .

. . . there was no life within him and no reason to fight to bring it back. In the distance, he could hear gunshots and wondered how many of his brave compañeros would die this hot July day on the Cantua— because of him, because he had insisted they wait to drive the horses south until he had news of Mauger's trial. The sun and the wind burned his face, and he heard a voice above him. He squinted his eyes and saw the wavering figures of an old man and a burro. The hot summer sun made them shimmer like a mirage.

"You will no die, El Jefe. You will live to see many mañanas. You will live to begin a new life." The old man knelt down beside him and cooled his sun-burned brow with water from his canteen, then laid hands on his head and sang a chant . . .

. . . that still haunted Joaquin. He would never forget the words.

He walked to the eastern edge of the plateau and looked down at the densely wooded valley. El Dorado. The Stanislaus River cut through the valley floor and rushed downhill over moss-covered boulders. Gray smoke curled up into the sky from the chimney he and Rosita had built out of the gold-colored stones lining the shallow river bottom. The house, fronted with the same stone, was hidden behind a stand of pines. Rosita had chosen the stones because of their color and called it her house of gold. She had named the house and valley El Dorado, which signified something of great value but ephemeral. Joaquin often thought she must have known that their time together would be short.

"There is much sadness at El Dorado, El Jefe." Pepe hunkered down and sat on his haunches, looking out over the valley. He had not aged a day since Joaquin had first seen him at the Cantua. "The gringos, they pan the river and find gold in the river sand. When the rains come, they move up where the river she widens and the current slows. There they find more gold dust than before, nuggets, too, so they bring men—many men—to build one, two, many sluice boxes. The men do not wish to work for the gringos, Joaquin. But the gringos, they no listen. They shoot their guns and force them to leave their homes, then they take them down there and chain them like dogs.''

Joaquin was incredulous. ''They use slave labor?

''*Sí*. Slaves.'' Pepe looked down at his hands. ''It is a sad thing, El Jefe. Some die of the whip, others because of no food or shelter.''

''What about the local authorities?''

''Ha! It is no good. The sheriff, he is paid to close his eyes and mouth.''

''How many slaves?''

''Many—like a small village. Mexicans. Chileans. Chinamen, too.''

''What about their families? Where are they? Do they know what's happened?''

''Ah, *sí,* some know, some don't, but what can they do?'' He threw up his hands in a gesture of helplessness. ''They are only women and children.'' Lowering his head, he said, ''You have much to do, Joaquin.''

Joaquin glanced down at Pepe. ''There are only two of us, Pepe. I would need many men to help them.''

''They will come, these men you need. They will come from here, there, everywhere. They will come because you are Joaquin, El Jefe!''

''How will they know to come? How will they know where to find me?''

Pepe rose to his feet. ''They will know, as I knew.'' Without further explanation, Pepe walked away, calling to Paco, who answered him with a mournful bray.

* * *

The cave consisted of a dozen or more chambers of varying sizes interconnected by long winding tunnels that led deep within the mountain. One of the tunnels wound its way downhill to a pool formed by an underground river, and another served as a second exit.

The cave was just as Joaquin and his men had left it almost seventeen years ago. Pepe's cook fire burned brightly at the mouth of the cave and his pine pallet lay nearby. Beyond the campfire stood the hand-hewn table and chair where Joaquin had eaten his meals, and where he and Lino had spent long hours studying crude survey maps by lantern light.

He and his men had spent many weeks holed up in the cave, planning their raids on gringo camps, then returning to the cave to hide themselves from the local posses and vigilante committees, who thought justice would be served by bringing them in. If only they had known that justice *was* being served, and it wasn't their worthless California justice. Joaquin and his band had robbed no one who hadn't stolen from someone else, or hurt anyone who hadn't caused others to suffer.

Joaquin sat down in the chair and thought about what Pepe had said. If it was true that help was coming, then he and Lino would need to prepare.

But first, he needed to pay a visit to Rosita's grave, which was deep within the mine in one of the smaller chambers at the end of a dizzying series of tunnels.

The grave appeared untouched. Joaquin held up the lantern. Rosita's gold crucifix still hung from the carved wooden cross that bore her name. "Rosita Felix de Murieta," Joaquin whispered, summoning the image of the woman-child he had married and brought north to the California gold fields.

Hat in hand, he knelt beside the earthen mound. "There is much you should know, *mi vida*," he began, closing his eyes to make it easier for her image to come to him. He saw her still as a young girl, making eyes at him when her mother and father came to visit his parents at the *rancho*. He saw her on their wedding day, her dark glossy hair covered by a white lace *rebozo*. He saw her in their *casa*, lying across the bed, bloody and broken, struggling for a breath to tell him that she would love him always.

He told her about the battle at the Cantua and the strange things—that even he couldn't explain—that had happened to him since. He told her about his work, that he had become prosperous in spite of himself and had rebuilt Rancho Murieta. He talked of his loneliness and confessed his relationship with Heller, knowing Rosita would understand.

Two hours later, he picked himself up and made the sign of the cross as he stared broodingly at the grave. He had been a fool to think he would find peace at Rosita's graveside. He had known as soon as he saw the image of her sweet, young face that she would not have wanted him to spend his life mourning her death, nor would she have sanctioned his vow of revenge in her name.

His spirits were low and his mood black when he returned to his bedroom chamber and started to unpack his saddlebags. But in spite of his graveside revelations, his plans had not changed.

Lino walked into the chamber, carrying an armful of animal skins. "Pepe has a regular storehouse of supplies set aside, including jerked beef and feed for the horses. And these skins," he said, laughing. "There's everything here from bear to deer to rabbit. We will be sleeping on what Pepe has had for dinner for the last three years." He dumped the skins into a pile and stood back as if to measure their comfort. At Joaquin's continued silence, he asked, "All is well at Rosita's grave?"

"Nothing has been touched since I left." He paused.
"I thought we might saddle up and go—"

Pepe entered Joaquin's chamber. "A big storm is
coming," he announced. "You should leave for the
valley now, do what you must do, and come back
quickly before she comes." He turned and disappeared into one of the branching tunnels.

Joaquin and Lino exchanged looks of bewilderment.

"He reads my mind, Lino, though I don't know why
that surprises me. It's eerie." A chill ran the length
of his body. "I was just about to suggest we go see if
El Dorado has changed after all these years."

The same chill that shook Joaquin's body passed into
Lino's. *"Sí, mi jefe."*

The valley floor was densely wooded with several
species of pine and juniper, and tall spring grasses
waved in the wind. Joaquin and Lino tied their horses
to a tree and cautiously made their way toward the
lights of the house, stopping every few yards to look
and listen. They spotted two guards at the front of the
house and another pair at the back; they talked and
walked, their attention more on their conversation than
their duty.

Lights shown out of almost every window, illuminating the covered wooden *corredor* that surrounded
the house. The little *casa* Joaquin had built had been
greatly enlarged so that it now resembled a Spanish
hacienda with more than a dozen rooms, all opening
onto a central patio. Most of the multipaned windows
were without curtains, allowing Joaquin and Lino to
see much of the impressive but spartan interior.

Silent as shadows, they circled the house, moving
undetected from tree to tree, looking in all the uncur-
tained windows to identify the rooms and to count the
number of servants and note their duties.

Joaquin motioned for Lino to halt when he spotted

Heller seated in a rocking chair, staring out her bedroom window into the night. Though the oil lamp behind her burned low, it gave off enough light to see her forlorn expression.

Lino crouched up next to him. "Does she look all right?" he whispered.

"She looks— I don't know, Lino." The chair rocked back and forth. Heller looked like a rag doll, her expression never changing, her hands hanging limply over the ends of the arms of the chair.

"You could let her know you're watching over her. It might make it easier for her."

Joaquin gave the idea a moment's consideration. "I wish I could, but I can't. She'd expect me to champion her and rescue her and Abigail. And I can't do that. Not yet. I don't know enough about what Mauger is doing here, or how far this operation reaches. When I know that, then I can help her, but not before."

"What if a friend of ours paid her a midnight visit?"

Joaquin knew exactly what Lino was suggesting. His dark eyes caught the light from the house and his mouth curved in a knowing smile. "*Sí*, that's a possibility."

"*Viva* Joaquin!"

A banging door brought them back to Heller, who had jumped out of her chair. Mauger stood in her doorway. By the way he was weaving, he had either had too much liquor or too much opium. He seemed to be trying to reason with Heller, but she kept shaking her head, then she turned her back to him.

When Mauger stormed across the room and grabbed her arm, Joaquin reached for his Colt and cocked the hammer.

"No, *mi jefe,* wait! Give her a chance to defend herself." Lino wrapped his fingers around the gun barrel and pushed it down.

Heller wrenched out of Mauger's grasp, then kneed him in the groin. Mauger's bellow of pain echoed across the valley, bringing the guards from every direction.

Joaquin motioned to Lino, and they hid under a heavy-needled pine bough. Mauger cursed and shouted but kept his distance. He seemed to know he was in no condition to fight an angry woman. Holding himself, he backed out of her room and slammed the door behind him. A second later, Abigail came into the room and took Heller into her arms. The guards started back for the bunkhouse.

Joaquin lingered a moment to make certain the women were all right, then he signaled Lino to follow him, and they left their hiding place and moved on past Heller's window to the next, which was curtained. Having now been around the entire house, the two men investigated the newer outbuildings: a barn, a large bunkhouse, and a storage shed. They counted a handful of Mexican and Chinese servants as well as a dozen guards.

The report of a gun brought all the guards back out of the bunkhouse and sent them running toward the front of the house.

Luther Mauger stepped outside onto the *corredor,* waving a smoking rifle. "Zeke!" he shouted. "Where the hell are you?" Again he fired into the air, then started down the worn dirt path for the river.

Once the guards realized what was happening and saw that their boss was in no danger, they again reholstered their weapons and went swearing and grumbling back to the bunkhouse or their posts.

Staying within the shelter of the trees, Joaquin and Lino followed Mauger.

"Zeke! I want to talk to you. Zeke!" he yelled, then fired four more shots into the air.

With Lino following directly behind, Joaquin zig-zagged through the trees toward the rushing river. Storm clouds moved across the moon and the stars, giving Joaquin and Lino the advantage of darkness.

"What the hell are you yellin' about?" Zeke came into a clearing. "They can hear you screamin' all the way over to Angels Camp, for God's sake." Zeke was tall as a lamppost. He walked with long, loose-legged strides, like a giraffe. He stepped into Mauger's path.

"You want to know what I'm yelling about? Well, I'll tell you. I want to know what the hell's going on here. Two weeks ago, you wired me that you were expecting to find the mother lode any day—so where is it? All I see are a half-dozen sluice boxes and more goddamn guards than I can count. I've looked at the books. You're hardly shipping enough dust out of here to keep things going, unless you're skimming a little off the top!"

Zeke was obviously insulted. "Skimming? Why, you miserly bastard. If you weren't always drunk or off in some poppy dream, you'd know what was going on around here. We got a partnership, remember? I've got too much at stake here to rob the operation," he yelled back. "Go back and take a better look at those books. I've accounted for everything. And as for the additional guards—I needed them for the new operation, the one that'll make you and me so rich it'll make the Sutter strike look small." Zeke spat a stream of tobacco juice past Mauger into the trees.

"Show me this new operation." Mauger peered past Zeke through the pines.

Lino and Joaquin crouched low and moved silently as they followed Zeke and Mauger a half mile upriver, past another pair of guards.

Zeke pointed a finger. "Right there, behind where those men are standing, the river forks. I've got two shifts of ten men working eighteen hours a day filling flour bags with river sand and rocks and building a dam to divert the water into the eastern fork. Once we stop the water flow into the western fork, we can dig a shaft down past the bedrock to where the lode is.''

"And how long is that going to take? Another month? A year?'' Mauger leaned negligently against a tree.

"I'm no soothsayer and I sure as hell ain't God. It'll take as long as it takes. I only just found the vein two weeks ago, when I wired you.''

"How many men you got working on it?''

"I told you. Twenty. I sent the boys out as soon as I found the vein to find me some more men. But it ain't like they can ride into town and hire on a crew. The boys had to ride down Mariposa way to find those new Mex slaves. Some of them was working on an old *rancho,* training horses, and they've been nothing but a peck of trouble since they got here, especially the one called Alvarado.'' Zeke shook his head. "That one's got the whole mess of them riled.''

"I don't want to know about your management problems. I just want to know when I'm going to start seeing some of this promised gold.''

"Just as soon as we can get to it. There ain't nothing more I can say.''

Mauger threw up his hands in exasperation. "All right! I'm impatient, that's all. I just lost everything I had in San Francisco, and the only thing that's kept me going is knowing that you're so close to uncovering that lode.''

Zeke spat again. "Say, what about them women you brought back with you? Everybody's askin'. That young one's a real looker. You gonna keep her all to yourself or you gonna share her?''

"I'm going to marry her, so don't even think about

getting close to her. Maybe later, when I'm tired of her, you can have her." He slapped Zeke on the back. "Now, listen. She and the old lady have no idea what's going on here, and I intend to keep it that way as long as I can. Leastways, until I can send the old lady packing. Meantime, we all have to behave ourselves and act like gentleman."

Zeke guffawed. "Gentlemen, huh? That ought to be real interestin'—for *all* of us."

Mauger raised an eyebrow, then swaggered back toward the house.

As soon as Mauger and Zeke were out of sight, Joaquin and Lino made their way back downriver, carefully passing the guards. When the moon peeked through the clouds, it provided a good view of the sluice operation on the riverbank. All was quiet now, but by day each sluice required two men to shovel river sand into the hopper at the top. The sand washed down the wooden trough and the gold caught on the riffles or wooden strips that were nailed across the trough.

Now, the men who worked the sluices were gathered around a campfire in a clearing up from the riverbank. They were a sad-looking lot; their clothes were in rags and most of them looked malnourished. In the firelight, Joaquin could see their dirty, unshaven faces—faces of boys, of young men and old men. Mexicans. Chinese. Chileans. He could also see their leg irons and the thick black chains that attached each man to the other. "I've seen enough," Joaquin said to Lino. "It's time we get back. We have much to do."

Joaquin and Lino returned to the cave before midnight to find Pepe and two strangers hunkered around the campfire inside the mouth of the cave.

"Ah, *mi jefe*," Pepe called. "What did I tell you? Did I not say the men, they would come?"

"*Sí*, you told me, Pepe," he agreed for the sake of pacifying the old man. But he was not yet ready to accept Pepe's fortune-telling.

Joaquin poured himself a cup of coffee and sat down across from the two men, studying them closely. They looked to be *vaqueros*, like himself. "Where are you from?"

"Mariposa." It was the younger of the two men who answered. "You are Joaquin Murieta?"

"*Sí*, I am Joaquin."

"They say you died many years ago near Lake Tulare after you were ambushed by the California Rangers."

"I have heard the rumor of my death, but as you can see I am very much alive."

Lino sat down next to Joaquin. "Twelve of us escaped the ambush. I am Lino Toral, Joaquin's lieutenant."

"My name is Santos and my silent friend here is Ocho. He is mute, but he is very fast with the gun. We have come for help. *Los gringos* have stolen my brother, Juan Alvarado."

Joaquin regarded the two men with interest. "You are of Las Mariposas?"

Santos nodded. "Juan Bautista Alvarado is our *abuelo*."

"I know of your grandfather." Joaquin held his cup out to Pepe for a refill. "What gringos? Why would they steal your brother?"

"I do not know their names. Many men have been taken from their homes. We do not know why. That is why we are here."

"How did you know to come here?" Joaquin asked, and met Pepe's gaze across the fire.

"How do I know?" Santos looked surprised by the question. "I go to the church, I light a candle, and I ask for help to find my brother. When I leave the church, I get Ocho and we ride north and ask friends along the way. They tell us *El Bandido Notorio* will help us, then they show us the way. It is not so hard to understand, no?''

''That pretty much explains it,'' said Lino, blithely ignoring Joaquin's sideways glance.

''You know where to find my brother? You will help us get him back?''

''I have a good idea where he may be found. And we will help each other, *mi amigo*.'' Joaquin rose to his feet and gazed into the firelight, the weight of new responsibility already heavy on his shoulders. It was as before. Men, strangers all, found him and asked him to lead them in a fight against injustice. ''You say Ocho is fast with a gun—what about you?''

''I am faster, El Jefe. You want that I should show you?''

Lino held up his hand. ''No. No shooting, not even in practice. That is the first rule of the camp. The second is that there will be no fighting among the men.''

''I have no argument with you, Señor Lieutenant,'' said Santos.

''But there will be others, and you will tell them as I have told you. *Comprende?*'' Lino also rose. ''We have much to do *mi jefe*. Tonight we will draw the map of El Dorado so that we may have it ready when the others come.''

Pepe gave Lino two more oil lanterns and a large tanned hide to make his map, then showed the two newcomers where to store their gear.

Shortly after midnight, the storm struck. Outside the cave, the lightning flashed and rain slashed down, but inside all was warm and dry, thanks to Pepe's smokeless fire. Joaquin's black eyes kindled with enthusiasm as he stood behind Lino and watched him draw first the house and then the outbuildings onto the hide. Between them, they remembered every building, fence post, and tree. Then Lino sketched the river, placing the sluices, the slaves' campfire, and the up-river operation.

They agreed on the number of slaves they had counted, and Lino made a note on the hide. The same for the house servants and guards, and their horses.

When they were finished, they tied long branches of wood together with rawhide strips and stretched the hide over its new frame and set it against the back of the chamber where all could see it. Then they brought Santos and Ocho over and talked about where they would place lookouts and guards of their own, both to protect the camp and to keep watch on El Dorado and the two women being held prisoner there along with the slaves.

The next morning the rain stopped, but the sky continued to be gray and gloomy. Joaquin spent the morning hours going through all the cave tunnels and chambers to refamiliarize himself with his old camp. When he returned from his exploration, he found Lino adding more details to the map.

"A Chinaman rode in while you were exploring. He is a big man, maybe a member of a Tong. Says his name is Wong Lo. His story about how he knew to come here makes as much sense as Alvarado's—something about his sister being sold into slavery in San Francisco and killed. He heard the man who killed her lived near here. He says he can cook, Joaquin. I don't think we should turn him away, especially after seeing those skins of Pepe's. It doesn't look like Pepe has much imagination where cooking is concerned."

"Did we ever turn anyone away?"

Lino merely smiled and shook his head.

Joaquin examined the map, which in his absence had become more of a painting than a sketch. "So it seems Pepe's fortune-telling will come true. We will be a band again, *mi amigo*. I will leave it to you, as my lieutenant, to be in charge of order."

"I would wish it no other way, *mi jefe*."

Throughout the day, as if by magic, men rode into camp, alone and in pairs. Each had a different story of injustice and each had been mysteriously guided by friends to El Jefe's hideout. By nightfall, there were more than a dozen men sitting around Pepe's campfire, drinking coffee and swapping stories.

After the Chinaman's arrival, Joaquin had stayed within his own chamber preparing himself for the work he had to do. It had been many years since he had been a leader of men. It was not an easy task to win their trust, nor was it easy to trust men he knew nothing about with duties that could mean life or death to others. But he had done it before and he would do it again.

Tonight he would once again ride as Joaquin Murieta, *El Bandido Notorio*. He would pay a late-night call on Heller and try to give her reassurance that she and her aunt would soon be free.

He dressed with care, wearing the same costume he had worn at the ball. He tucked his black shirt into equally black trousers, then wrapped his waist with a red silk sash. The silver conchos that studded the outside length of his legs gleamed, as did his high-heeled boots. His *charro* jacket ended at the top of the sash. It was adorned with silver buttons and a frog of double silver. He bound his head with a black silk scarf, then he put on his sombrero and pulled the cord tight beneath his chin. Finally, he strapped on his gunbelt, checking to make sure the Colts were loaded and that he had a spare cylinder.

He was about to leave his chamber when he remembered his cape and Yellow Bird's little book. He tossed the cape over his shoulder and tucked the book under his arm.

Even before Joaquin stepped into the large outside chamber, he heard a sound from his past, Levi Orgeta's guitar, then the man's voice singing the song of the *vaqueros*. Levi was one of the twelve who had survived the Cantua. It would be good to see him again.

The men were seated on logs around the fire, drinking coffee and talking quietly among themselves.

"Joaquin Murieta! *Carumba!*"

"Madre de Dios!"

Joaquin was just as surprised to see that so many more had arrived.

Lino stepped forward, shaking his head. "I've been trying to tell them that what they heard about you wasn't true. That you didn't die at the Cantua. . . ."

"So they think I'm a ghost?"

Lino rolled his eyes and shrugged.

Levi Orgeta jumped to his feet and reached out a hand. "You look well, *mi jefe*. My brother Carlos sends many pardons for not coming when he knew you had need of him, but his wife is expecting a baby any day now."

Joaquin smiled at his long-time friend. "That is good news, Levi. I will look forward to seeing the baby after all this is over. Do you know why you are here, Levi?"

"I heard rumors, Joaquin, but I don't know for certain."

"Amigos y paisanos." Joaquin turned and addressed the men. "It makes me proud that all of you have come. Your help is much needed. In the valley below, a gringo by the name of Luther Mauger has ordered

his guards to kidnap your friends and relatives. He has made slaves of them. He chains them like dogs and uses them to work his placers so that he may become rich.

"Tonight, while I am gone, my lieutenant will explain the details and show you the map he has drawn of the valley. It is *muy importante* that you memorize the location of each building and know how many guards and servants there are at the *casa* and down by the river."

As he gazed upon their faces, so solemn in the firelight, he thought about another band of men: Jack Garcia, Joaquin Carillo, Vasquez, and others. All brave and loyal men. All had accepted him as their leader, done his bidding, and made his vow of vengeance their own.

With an air of proud reserve, he nodded and walked out of the cave. Pepe had saddled El Tigre and was trying with little success to calm the prancing stallion.

"He is glad to go, I think," said Pepe, "as is his master."

"*Gracias,* Pepe." Joaquin tucked the book under the back of the saddle and threw his cape over El Tigre's neck, then vaulted up into the saddle. "I should be back before dawn." The horse danced beneath him with excitement. "Whoa, boy." Joaquin patted the animal's muscled neck and he calmed instantly. "Easy boy. Good, El Tigre." Pepe held onto the bridle a moment longer, as Joaquin wrapped his cape around his neck and tied it at his throat.

The men had left the campfire and were gathered at the mouth of the cave.

"*Viva* Joaquin!" one of them called out. His cry was followed by another, then another, until it was unanimous.

A storm wind caught Joaquin's cape, causing it to

billow behind him. Joaquin signaled El Tigre with a familiar command and the magnificent black stallion gave a high-pitched whinny and reared.

"*Adios, mi amigos!* Joaquin lifted his arm in salute, then he wheeled the horse around and galloped off into the night.

The men shouted after him, and their voices were carried on the wind. "*Viva* Joaquin!"

Chapter 15

Heller paced the length of her bedroom. Telling her story to Abigail was not going to be easy, but she had to do it. Abigail had to know what they were up against and what kind of man Gordon Pierce was. "I must have fallen asleep right after our talk," she began in a voice she hardly recognized as her own. "The next thing I knew was when I woke up in Gordon's bed wearing only my shift." Her eyes glazed with despair. Balling her hands into fists, she walked to the window and stared out at the tall pines that surrounded the house. Her voice shook as she spoke. "He told me I had willingly come home with him and that we made love," she paused, steadying herself, then pressed on. "And when I didn't believe him, he said the reason I didn't remember was because I drank too much champagne." She lifted the window and breathed in the woodsy scent, so different from any of the outdoor scents she had known. "You know I *never* drink champagne. It makes me sick. But I didn't know what else to think. I thought I must have done the things he said. So, I blamed myself and he tried to comfort me by asking me to marry him." She leaned her palms against the windowsill and bent her head forward. "That's when I remembered."

"Remembered what, dear?" Abigail inquired in a shaky voice.

"I didn't go with him willingly. He had me kidnapped. They came into my room sometime in the middle of the night, held an ether-soaked rag under my nose and . . . that's all I know."

Abigail's hands flew to her face. "He's a madman!"

Heller agreed, then explained her cautious response to his marriage proposal and that he'd agreed to take her back to the hotel. "But when I got out of bed to prepare to leave, there was—" envisioning the scene, she dropped into the rocker in front of the window "—blood on the bedclothes."

Abigail let out an anguished sigh. "Then he—he must have raped you. Oh, my God, Heller. I'm so very sorry."

Heller leaned her head back and gazed at the adobe ceiling.

"There's more, Aunty. I wish there wasn't, but there is." She proceeded to tell Abigail about being drugged, then about her whipping and about the Chinese slave girls Gordon whipped to death after they'd pleasured him. "Because he wants me to be his wife, he was careful not to hurt me so others could see. He used some kind of cloth whip. It stung me, but it didn't break the skin. In fact, it didn't leave any marks at all."

Sobbing, Abigail managed to ask, "When he brought you back, why in heaven's name didn't you tell the authorities, Heller? They would have—"

"Aunty!" Heller stopped her short, knowing what she was going to say. "Don't you think I wanted to? Of course I considered telling the authorities, but I knew that Gordon would know the second I did, and he'd carry out his threats. I couldn't risk it—I couldn't risk the lives of you and Alex and everyone on the board, and that's what he was threatening." She went into detail about his threats, then finished with a long shuddering sigh.

Abigail nodded in understanding. "I suppose I just made matters worse by sending Don Ricardo in to you, but I thought if anyone could persuade you that you were making a mistake, he could. He loves you and you love him. Is it not remotely possible that he could have done *something*? He is a brave and resourceful man, Heller. He may have been able to find a way to help."

"It doesn't matter. It's too late now." In spite of everything that had happened between her and Gordon, it was what had happened between her and Don Ricardo that made her heart feel as if it were breaking in two. "I know you meant well by sending him in, Aunty, but I *couldn't* risk telling him about Gordon's threats, either, although I'm certain he suspected. You mustn't fault him; he did everything he could to dissuade me, and I did everything I could to convince him that I really wanted to marry Gordon, and that I'd already given myself to him—which was true, in a way."

"Oh, Heller," Abigail moaned. "You do not have to say anything more, dear. I know how awful this is for you."

"Oh, but I do. I need to tell you everything. I *need* to tell you in case something happens. . . ."

"Heller, for heaven's sake. Nothing is going to happen."

"I hope not," Heller said, afraid to take the subject any further. "But you see, I wanted you to know that you were right—that Don Ricardo is an honorable man, and that I do care about him. I think I may even love him, for all the good it will do me now," she added. "He wasn't easy to convince. He refused to believe me and said that I wouldn't give myself to a man I didn't love, and that I didn't love Gordon.'' She paused to gather her courage for the next admission. ''So I—Oh, God, Aunty, please try to understand how very desperate I was when I tell you that I . . . I pretended to be like Mam. . . .''

Abigail's face pinched. ''Like your mother? Whatever do you mean?''

Heller bit down hard on her lip. ''I played like a whore and started to seduce Don Ricardo so he would go away in disgust, but he didn't. He stayed, and after a while I forgot what point I was trying to prove. I wanted him so much, Aunty. And afterwards, it was as if by letting him make love to me, it had taken away what Gordon had done.''

In tears, Abigail crossed the space between them and leaned over Heller. ''I understand, dear,'' she said in a choked voice. ''Truly, I do. A woman's virginity is such a precious gift. Don Ricardo would not have taken it lightly.''

Gordon Pierce's handwritten supper invitation, pushed under Heller's door, was more of a demand than a request.

Heller and Abigail had been seated nearly ten minutes before Gordon left his room, crossed the courtyard and entered the dining room. ''Good evening, ladies.'' His pleasantness belied the evil that Heller knew lurked below the surface. ''I hope you'll forgive me for being late, but I needed to finish up in my account book.'' He took his place at the head of the table. To the Chinese houseboy standing behind him, he said, ''Pour three glasses of wine, Lu, then tell Marta to serve supper.''

Heller patently ignored the wine and chose her water goblet instead; she didn't want to partake of anything that would dull her senses.

Gordon pretended not to notice her small show of rebelliousness. Tonight, as per his orders, the table had been formally set with linen, silver, glassware, and china he'd been shipping to the ranch one crate at a time for months. Light from more than a dozen candles gave the room a rich golden glow. It was a picture-perfect setting, made even more perfect by the addition of the beautiful woman at his right.

He sipped his wine and looked across at the two women. "I trust you found your rooms comfortable and to your liking."

Heller had decided to exercise caution where Gordon Pierce was concerned. His moods were too volatile to predict: one minute a gentleman, the next a madman. "Yes, we're very comfortable," she commented without inflection and without looking at him.

"If there's anything you want, you have only to ask."

Abigail picked up her napkin, snapped it open, and spread it across her lap. "Well then, in that case, Heller and I would appreciate it if you would send us back to San Francisco as soon as possible."

Gordon arched an eyebrow and stared at Abigail, then burst out laughing. "Why, Abigail, you've only just arrived! You haven't even had an opportunity to see the valley. It's really quite beautiful. I'm sure once you've had a look around, you will find it very much to your liking."

"You can stop playing games, Mr. Pierce," she boldly rejoined, not bothering to conceal her rancor. "Heller has told me *everything*." Pinning him with a look of utter contempt, she added, "I warned Heller about you at the very beginning." She scoffed. "I knew she had more sense than to *want* to marry a crude misfit like you."

"Aunty!" Horrified, Heller sent Abigail a look that

begged her to keep silent. After this morning's discussion, she had thought Abigail understood the danger and would be careful where Gordon was concerned.

Gordon smiled and chuckled. "A crude misfit, am I? I've been called a lot of things, but never that." He paused. The smile turned down into a frown. "I'm immune to your insults, Abigail, so you don't need to bother yourself on my account. If we were back in San Francisco, I might react differently. . . ."

"You are obviously immune to a lot of things," Abigail continued, in spite of Heller's anxious look, "including common sense. Alexander will be expecting me to wire him with news of our arrival. If he does not receive that wire, he will ask the authorities to come looking for me."

Gordon glanced over his shoulder and snapped his fingers at the houseboy, who immediately refilled his wine glass. "You made that perfectly clear before we left. He'll get his wire. I'll send one of the boys into Angels Camp in a day or so."

Heller sat forward on the edge of her chair. "Gordon, I beg you to tell us what you intend to do with us."

Gordon leaned toward her. "A very sensible question, Heller, but then you're always sensible, aren't you?"

She lifted her head and boldly met his gaze, unwilling to let him see her fear. "I try, but sensible isn't always smart."

"No, it isn't," he agreed. "In spite of what you might be thinking, I'm not hiding anything from you. My intentions haven't changed. Beginning next week, I'll start making arrangements for our wedding. We'll have a big outdoor fiesta with music, singing, dancing. I'll send for a priest to come from Angels Camp."

"And if I refuse to marry you?"

"But you won't," he said with an air of confidence that made Heller's face drain of all color. "You value your life and Abigail's too much to refuse me."

She inhaled sharply. "More threats, Gordon?"

He reached under the corner of the table and grabbed her hand. He seemed in earnest when he said, "I don't *want* to have to threaten you. I want you to be agreeable." He gently squeezed her hand. "*That* would be the *sensible* thing to do, Heller." Letting go of her hand, he sat back.

Heller thought a moment. "*If* I should agree to marry you, will you allow Abigail to leave?" Sensing that Abigail was about to speak, Heller found her aunt's foot beneath the table and gave it a nudge.

"After we're married, not before."

"All right. We have a bargain."

"Good. That will make things much better for both of us." After a moment of silence, he said, "Now, there are some house rules you and your aunt need to understand if all is to run smoothly. Although the valley is isolated, I have a number of armed guards patrolling the property at all times. They've been instructed not to talk to either of you or approach you in any way—unless you try to leave the boundaries. I'll show you later exactly where they are. Should either of you attempt to escape, my men have been instructed to shoot first and ask questions later."

Abigail pressed her palms against the edge of the table. "Surely you jest."

"I never make jokes, Abigail. Troublemakers are not tolerated, as you will see tomorrow morning. I want you both out on the *corredor* by the *sala* door at precisely eight o'clock. We'll consider it your first lesson." He turned his gaze on Heller. "Hopefully, you'll pay such close attention that there won't be a need for a second lesson."

The kitchen door opened, and Marta wheeled in a cart carrying platters and bowls of steaming food.

After supper, Gordon insisted the two women join him in the *sala,* where the Chinese houseboy served him a glass of port. Lifting his glass, Gordon slowly swirled the contents around the sides of the glass, then lifted it and tipped it to his lips. With a satisfied smack, he sat back, feeling better than he had in days. He'd spent the day going over the account book, talking to Zeke about his management techniques, and observing the handling of the slaves. He knew now that Zeke had been truthful about the amount of gold he was taking out of the placers and shipping to Sacramento.

Maybe losing his import business wasn't such a disaster after all. Once the new river operation was finished, he would have more gold than he needed, more money than his import business could have made him—and without all the social and political hogwash that had made him so uncomfortable. As for his Rincon Hill home—the *casa* would do for now, but as soon as he recouped his losses, he would find himself a new mansion, perhaps in Los Angeles.

Sitting back, glancing around the *sala* which had been the whole of the original structure, he thought about the first time he'd seen El Dorado almost two decades ago. He'd been hired by the representative of someone whose identity he never knew to kill Murieta's wife and run Murieta off his claim. He'd wondered about his mystery employer, but he knew better than to ask questions. Not that he cared one way or another about Murieta, his pretty little wife, or any other Mexican. They were foreigners. They'd lost their right to California gold when the United States had won the war with Mexico. If it hadn't been for Murieta's vengeance, he would have filed on the abandoned claim right away, but instead he'd been forced to run and keep running for damn near two years.

All during that time and the years he'd spent in prison, he often thought of the valley and wondered if anyone had discovered the abandoned claim. It wasn't only the gold that he coveted, but the magnificent beauty of the valley itself, nestled between two mountains, like a perfectly cut diamond between the breasts of a beautiful woman.

After bribing his way out of prison, he discovered that no new claim had been filed. For a small fee, El Dorado became his.

This, however, was the first time he'd taken up residence at El Dorado, and he found he had a real fondness for the place. From anywhere in the house he could hear the river rushing over rocks and boulders, and on the hottest summer days, the tall stately pines provided a cooling canopy from the California sun.

El Dorado's isolation made it a perfect place to hide himself from the Wells Fargo agents, and even if they did find him, they'd never get out of the valley alive. He needed only to give the word and his hired gunmen would take care of the matter.

The isolation also made it a perfect place to bring Heller, unwilling as she was. If he hadn't been so set on having a particular kind of woman, he could have had any one of a half-dozen young women of prominent San Francisco families. But none held a candle to Heller. She had everything he'd ever wanted and more. He'd never in his life had an emotional attachment to a woman—other than hate and loathing. It was almost unsettling to find himself sympathetic toward her fear and hostility.

Last night's visit to Heller's room had been a mistake, he admitted. He'd smoked too much opium and it had affected his judgment. From now on he was

going to take a different tack, but he wasn't sure yet
just what it would be. He was growing more and more
dependent on the poppy.

For nearly two hours, Heller and Abigail sat side by
side in the *sala,* across from Gordon, who was staring
at the wall in deep thought. No one had spoken a word.
Outside the wind howled through the trees, announcing the coming storm. It was Abigail's snoring that
prompted Heller to beg Gordon to allow them to be
excused and retire to their rooms.

"Yes, of course, but don't forget: eight o'clock on
the *corredor* for your first lesson."

Heller put her arm around Abigail's shoulders and
helped her aunt down the hall.

"Good night, dear," Abigail said when they reached
her door. She took a step inside her room, then
grabbed Heller's hand and pulled her back. "Wedge a
chair up under your doorknob just in case he decides
to break in on you again," she warned.

Heller sighed. "A chair wouldn't stop him, Aunty."
She kissed Abigail's cheek then entered her own room.

After changing into her bedclothes, Heller opened
the curtains and took her position in the rocking chair
before the window. She had barely sat down when she
saw two men, dressed in yellow slickers and carrying
rifles, stroll by. They glanced in her direction, then at
each other. Undoubtedly two of the number of guards
Gordon had spoken about.

After midnight, when the full fury of the storm broke
over the valley, Heller closed her curtains, extin-
guished the lamp, and crawled into bed facing the
window. Lightning flashes illuminated her room
through the dark curtains, followed by thunder rolls.
Wind-driven rain pounded against the roof, sounding
like hoofbeats.

Heller had always loved stormy weather, loved to sit

in a corner of her aunt's parlor drinking hot cocoa and pouring over the latest issue of *Godey's Ladies Book* with its color fashion plates, letters from avid readers, poetry, novelettes, and a hundred other things.

A particularly close bolt of lightning lit up Heller's room through the curtains and was immediately followed by a deafening clap of thunder that rattled her window and shook the house. She leaped out of bed when the door leading onto the *corredor* flew open, letting in the wind and the rain. Shivering with cold, she dashed across the room to close the door and set the bolt.

"I thought I locked the door," she mumbled to herself as she headed back to bed.

"Heller."

Startled, she stopped where she was. The fine hairs on the back of her neck raised in alarm. Was it her imagination or had she heard someone say her name? She looked from left to right but saw nothing; the room was black as pitch. "Is someone here?" Another flash of lightning revealed a tall dark shape. "Gordon?" she asked uneasily. She cringed as thunder broke overhead. She prayed the house could stand the punishment it was getting.

The room returned to darkness. "No, Heller. Not Gordon." Spurs jingled as the man moved.

"Then, who?" She began to shake as her anxiety grew.

"We met in San Francisco at the masquerade ball. I told you I would come for you—"

"From nowhere. Like the wind," she finished for him in a whisper.

Again, lightning streaked through the sky, providing a moment of illumination. Its thunderous accompaniment seemed to have lessened in intensity. He stood a few feet in front of her, a tall, commanding figure.

With the exception of the red sash tied around his waist, he was dressed entirely in black, exactly as he had been at the ball. He wore a low-crowned hat, a cloth mask that covered only his eyes, and a flowing black cape that gently swung behind him.

Recognizing him, her fear somewhat abated. "Joaquin Murieta, or rather you were masquerading as Joaquin Murieta."

"No, I told you, I was not masquerading. I *am* Joaquin Murieta." His deep resonant voice was heavily accented.

Heller shook her head. "I visited a museum, saw Murieta's head, and talked with the curator. . . ."

"The head you saw was my *compadre,* Joaquin Carillo. The rangers mistook him for me." Between lightning flashes, he lit her lamp. "But enough of me. I am here to help you. You are being held prisoner here, are you not?"

"Yes." Her heart beat a rapid tattoo against her chest. "You've come to help us escape?" She gave a little cry of excitement. "I'll go tell Abigail. We'll take only one change of clothes." She started for the door, only to have him reach out a hand and pull her back.

"Not tonight, Heller. I need *your* help with something first." At her questioning look, he explained, "Gordon Pierce's real name is Luther Mauger. Many years ago, he and his friends raped and killed my wife, Rosita. I made a vow to avenge Rosita's murder. I lost track of Mauger for many years, and now that I've found him I intend to fulfill my vow, which is to destroy everything he owns and loves.

"Mauger has been under the illusion that I was dead. When I showed up at the masquerade ball, I reminded him of his past, even though he was convinced he was confronting an impostor."

''Then that's why he looked so stunned,'' she interrupted, remembering the moment vividly. ''I don't know how I can help you. I'm a prisoner here.''

''You need only to be aware and watchful. Watch Mauger closely, watch the servants and the guards. Keep track of their habits and routines. Learn where every door and window is in the house. And when you're outside, learn your way around. Those are the things that will help.''

''For how long?''

''A few weeks. No more.''

''Oh, no, please. You have to get us out of here sooner than that. He's planning for us to marry. He said at supper it would be a big outdoor fiesta.''

''Try to find out the exact date.''

''But once I'm married to him—''

''Trust me to take care of things. I'll never let him marry you. Meantime, my men and I will be watching over you, every second of every day.''

''I don't think I can—''

When she started to turn away, he caught her arm and brought her back around to face him. With his hand beneath her chin he tilted her head back and looked directly into her eyes. ''You can do this, Heller.'' Before she could utter a word, he bent his head and kissed her.

Joaquin groaned low in his throat as he pulled her up tight against him. He had resolved to do nothing but talk to her, but now, with the talking out of the way, he wanted to hold her, and kiss her, wanted to release her from her anxiety and give her comfort. She had endured much in the past week, probably more than he knew. In truth, he was surprised that she and her aunt had held up as well as they had. Neither of them had struck him as being particularly hearty women; he thought of them more as hothouse flowers that wilted once they left their own environment, but they had proved him wrong so far.

He hated himself for taking away her excitement at being rescued. In fact, he could help them escape this very night. The storm would provide all the cover they needed. But again, the damnable vow stopped him. That, and the knowledge that Mauger would be hot on their trail and become the pursuer, not the pursued.

Still kissing her, he made himself another vow—that once he avenged Rosita's death, he would never make another!

The kiss took Heller by surprise, but even more surprising was her reaction. All she could think about as his mouth expertly moved over hers, was that he kissed the way Don Ricardo kissed. He even tasted like Don Ricardo! They were so much alike it was uncanny. With a whimper of bewilderment, she fastened her arms around his neck and parted her lips to allow him the access he obviously sought. He drove his tongue deep inside her mouth and her body responded without conscious consent. His one hand ran over her bottom and pressed into her flesh. Then he bent his knees so that he stood at her own height, and she felt the power of his arousal project against her abdomen.

Suddenly, she pushed herself out of his arms. With wide, searching eyes she stared at his masked face.

Thunder rolled in the distance.

"I have to go, Heller." And strangely, his voice was no longer heavily accented. It was the clear, beautiful voice of . . .

As he opened the door, the wind billowed his cape. Heller reached the door a second after he stepped outside onto the *corredor,* yet by the time she got there, he had vanished into the night.

Like a ghost.

She closed the door and set the bolt, then raced over

to the window and threw back her curtains. The storm had passed over the valley and the sky was amazingly clear. She searched for him among the trees but couldn't find him. Instead, she saw two yellow-slickered guards walking slowly around the house. Obviously they had not seen her late night visitor. One of the guards saluted her as she went by. In response, Heller tugged the curtains shut, then opened them again a moment later after peeking out to make sure the men had gone.

Through a break in the pine trees she saw the moon, full and golden like a big medallion. It lay nestled in the valley between two hills. Suddenly, a lone figure on horseback appeared in silhouette against the face of the moon.

"Joaquin!" she whispered. Then, "Don Ricardo. I should have known before," she said, smiling. Heller's heart raced as she watched his horse pick up his front hooves and rear.

"I am Joaquin!" he called out and the valley echoed his cry. "Hear me, Luther Mauger, murderer of my Rosita. I have come back to collect my revenge!"

A chill raced down Heller's back. The horse lowered his hooves, turned, and disappeared into the face of the moon.

Chapter 16

After closing the curtains, Heller saw the book that she had lost laying on her pillow. *He* had brought it. She crawled back into bed, intent now, upon reading it. Beginning with the first page, the author, Yellow Bird, made it clear that he had thought well of Joaquin and had described him as being "remarkable for a very mild and peaceable disposition." The wordy and colorful prose described the beautiful Sonorian girl Joaquin had married, their rich mining claim in the Stanislaus placers, and how everything had come to a violent end when the drunken Anglos visited Joaquin's house. The rest of the book elaborated on Joaquin's vow of revenge, his life of banditry, and finally, his death at Arroyo Cantua.

At daybreak, Heller finished the book and set it aside. Yawning and stretching, she got out of bed and walked over to the window. Bleary-eyed, she pushed back the curtains to see a bright orange sky.

Joaquin's sad story weighed heavy on her mind as she watched the sun rise and the orange fade to pink. Gordon Pierce, or rather Luther Mauger, had taken everything from Joaquin: his gold claim, his home, and the woman he loved. Indeed, she thought, sighing, Joaquin had good reason for making his vengeful vow. She wondered what circumstances had prevented him from finding Mauger earlier, as he had the other three men. She also wondered what kind of man would devote so many years—his life—to a single cause. He must have loved Rosita very much to have spent all those years trying to avenge her.

Staring between the trees at the glistening river, she tried to imagine a man loving a woman so much he would kill for her—loving her even long after she was dead.

That was the kind of love she wanted.

Her pensiveness turned to concern when another thought, this one disturbing, crossed her mind. According to the book, Joaquin had become a ruthless bandit and a brutal killer, seeking not only revenge on those who had harmed him but on all Americans. Having met him twice, and now having read the book, she could see much of him in the author's descriptions and didn't doubt that he was physically capable of the crimes attached to his name. Yet, he *had* given her the book, knowing full well what conclusions she might draw. That in itself seemed to be a statement about the kind of man he was.

Voices outside Heller's window interrupted her thoughts. Turning her head she saw two men not twenty feet from her window, leaning against a storage shed. Carefully, she drew the curtains closed, hoping they hadn't seen her. She had started back toward the bed to straighten the bedclothes when she heard a question she couldn't resist knowing the answer to.

"What did Pierce say? Did he see the ghost?" The man's voice had a pronounced Southern drawl.

The second man's broken English forced Heller to move back to the window so she could catch his every word.

"I done tol' ya before, Hank. That weren't no ghost! Ain't no such thing as ghosts. But yeah, he saw him all right. He's been up nigh on all night pacin' like a caged coon.''

Hank sounded tired and aggravated. "It had to be a ghost because Murieta's dead! Killed by the rangers back in '53. I remember it as well as I remember my own name. Besides, it was in all the newspapers.''

"Yeah, well, maybe he was kilt and maybe he weren't. Ain't nobody knows fer sure. That's the thing 'bout Murieta. Weren't nothin' he did that a body could prove. Smart fellar, that one. I done played a little Monte with him up old Hornito's way in the fall of '52. Saw him call down a gambler for cheating. Fastest damn draw I ever did see. Deadly with a knife, too. A posse came ridin' into town and, quick as lightning, Murieta lit out and escaped through a tunnel in the basement of the Fandango hall. The posse went lookin' fer him but had to turn back when them Santa Ana winds started blowin'. They came back madder than hornets. Couldn't find a trace of him. Disappeared—just like last night. It's almost as if . . . Nah, I ain't gonna say what I'm thinking, but I will say this, and you can think what you like: Joaquin Murieta ain't no ordinary man. I dunno what it is, but there's something real peculiar about him.''

There was a long silence that made Heller wonder if they had ended their conversation and left. Then the man called Hank spoke up.

"Wonder what Murieta wants with the boss.''

"To kill him, more than likely. I heard tell that Pierce ain't Pierce, that his real name is Luther Mauger, and this here house used to belong to Murieta. . . .''

Heller gasped, shocked by this latest information. El Dorado had been Joaquin's home? No wonder he could make his way around so easily without the guards seeing her. Her curiosity aroused, she continued listening to the story so similar to the one she had read. At its end, one thing was clear: Joaquin Murieta had become a California legend.

After the men left, Heller washed and dressed, then knocked on Abigail's door. A few minutes before eight o'clock, they walked out onto the *corredor* outside the *sala*. With his back to the women, Gordon Pierce stood shouting at a group of unhappy, sour-faced men.

"What do you mean, he disappeared? He's real, for Christ's sake—and so is his goddamn horse! That much flesh and blood doesn't just vanish. They had to *go* somewhere."

One of the men stepped forward. "Nick and me rode out after him as soon as we heard him yell out, but by the time we got to the rise, he was gone and so was the moonlight. It was so damn dark out there, a pack of wolves couldn't have found him."

Raking his fingers through his hair, Gordon snapped out orders. "From now on, I want six men covering the entrance to the valley. Horses are to be saddled at all times. If you see anything or anyone, you're to track it down and bring it back to me. Understand?"

The men nodded and started backing away, grumbling as they went.

"Just a goddamn minute. I'm not finished. I want four extra men riding with that gold shipment this afternoon."

"Four? But, boss, that'll leave us shorthanded for the night shift," complained Nick.

"Not if you each work an extra few hours, it won't."

Grimacing, Nick rolled his eyes and turned away.

When Abigail sneezed, Gordon jerked around sharply.

Heller noticed Gordon's mussed hair and untidy clothes—the same clothes he had worn last night at supper. He did indeed look like he had spent a sleepless night.

Staring at Heller with a look of challenge, he barked out orders to the man standing closest to him. "Tell Zeke I'm ready for Alvarado." His countenance underwent an unbelievable transformation, and a slow smile tipped the corners of his mouth. "Good morning, Heller, Abigail." He gestured toward two pine-branch chairs. "If you ladies will please have a seat, the performance can begin."

"Performance?" asked Abigail, maneuvering to her appointed chair.

Gordon seemed particularly pleased with himself as he elaborated. "Yes, performance. Admittedly, it's not up to San Francisco standards, but I think you'll find it interesting all the same. I caution you, however, that this is one performance during which you may *not* at any time leave your seats." He raised a finger to alert two of his men to take up positions on either side of Heller and Abigail. At the women's startled faces, he asked, "Do I make myself clear?"

Wordlessly, Heller readjusted her position. Knowing what little she did about Gorden Pierce, or rather, Luther Mauger, as she was now beginning to think of him, she didn't need to rely on instinct to tell her this was going to be one performance she wasn't going to enjoy.

Two men came from the direction of the river into the clearing in front of the house. The first man, a young, proud-spirited Mexican, stumbled ahead of the other man, who continuously prodded him forward with the barrel of his rifle.

"Zeke, lock him up to the post," Gordon absently ordered as he moved to the other side of the *corredor,* where he picked up two coiled whips and appeared to be examining them.

Zeke shoved his prisoner against the wooden post next to the *corredor* steps. Gordon glanced around "No, not that one. That one there," he ordered, pointing his finger and indicating the support post directly in front of Heller and Abigail.

Realizing what she and Abigail were about to witness, Heller jumped to her feet. "Gordon, if this is your idea of a joke, I don't think it's the least bit humorous."

"Sit down, Heller. I'm in no mood to put up with your female hysterics."

"But Gordon, whatever this man has done, surely he doesn't deserve anything as brutal as a whipping. Please, there must be other ways to punish an employee, something less severe."

He laughed, sobered, then laughed again. "Not an employee, Heller, a slave. The guards are employees, the workers are slaves."

"Slaves?" Appalled, Heller looked at the handsome young man. He was filthy all over: his hair, his face, and his hands. His shirt and pants were even dirtier and ripped, and he wore no shoes.

Gordon smiled. "I use slaves for everything, Heller. You know that." He uncoiled the whip and tossed its braided length on the dirt in front of him. "Sit down, Heller!"

Heller was quick to regain her seat. She took Abigail's hands within hers and whispered some words of comfort.

Zeke had finished locking Alvardo's wrists into iron manacles that hung from short chains from the top of the post. "Ready, boss," Zeke announced.

Taking his time, Gordon moved away from the *corredor* into the clearing. Dragging the tail of the whip behind him, he walked to where the trees began, then turned around. The guards spread out in a circle, well out of reach of the whip's twenty-foot length.

Assuming a spread-legged stance, Gordon asked, "You ready, Alvarado? I know you don't much care, but you're going to help me teach these ladies a lesson in discipline. So give them a good performance."

The slave Alvarado glanced over his shoulder at Gordon. "I'll help you to your grave, you gringo dog."

Without another word, Gordon raised his right arm and swung the whip into motion.

Heller heard the whip sing as it flew through the air toward its target. She cringed at the memories the sound evoked, then screamed when she heard Alvarado cry out in pain. She clung to Abigail and Abigail to her, as again and again the whip arched and lunged forward like a hungry tiger to take bites out of the young Mexican's back. With tears running down her cheeks, Heller held Alvarado's pain-glazed stare. "Be brave," she whispered, barely moving her lips. "It'll be over soon."

But it wasn't. It went on and on until Alvarado fell into unconsciousness. Finally, Zeke stepped into the circle as Gordon was readying himself for another swing.

"He can't take any more, boss. You'll kill him."

Joaquin crested the pine-covered hill at the same time the wagon and the ten outriders started through the pass which led in and out of the valley. Holding his hand up high, he waited until the wagon was at a point on the road directly beneath him, then he sliced his hand downward in a signal that told Levi Ortega to release the rocks into the pass just ahead of the wagon.

The wagon horses reared and whinnied with fright

as the avalanche of rocks tumbled down the hillside. The thunderous noise shook the ground and the horses bolted, causing the wagon to flip over and its two passengers to be tossed onto the ground. The outriders, having better control of their horses, turned to flee the danger. Heading back the way they had come, they rode headlong into a bulwark of Mexican *bandidos* brandishing an ominous collection of rifles, carbines, and six-shooters.

From atop the hill, Joaquin watched his men with pride. They were good men, eager to fight for his cause and theirs. In a matter of a few days, they had formed themselves into a band, loyal to their leader and loyal to each other.

Nudging El Tigre's flanks, the horse started down the steep-sided hill at a fast pace while Joaquin kept a tight rein and leaned back to secure his seat. Loose rock and dirt fell behind him, creating a cloud of dust. Reaching the bottom, he rode to the front of the group.

"*Buenas tardes,* señores. In case you do not know me, I am Joaquin Murieta and these are my men. We intend you no harm. We want only the gold you were carrying in that wagon, then we will be on our way."

"And what will you do if we don't want to give it to you?" asked one of the guards.

"Shut up, Hank," said one of the other men. "This gold ain't nothing to us, and I sure as hell ain't gonna fight fer it."

"A wise decision, señor." Turning his attention back to Hank, he added, "You do not want to lose your life and the life of your *compadres* over a little gold, do you?" He watched the man closely, sensing him to be the kind who would relish flaunting his bravery by starting a fight.

Lino ordered Mauger's armed guards to toss their weapons to the ground. The man called Hank drew his rifle out of the scabbard and threw it in front of his horse.

"Now your Colt, *por favor.*"

Looking straight at Joaquin, Hank drew his hand back and touched the butt of his gun. "Over my dead body, Mex," he shouted as he went for his gun. Before he could clear leather, Joaquin's bullet found its way into his hand, shattering bone and severing muscle.

Still holding his smoking gun, Joaquin rode over to where Hank was nursing his injured hand and pulled the gun out of his holster. "You should have listened to me, gringo. I told you we intended no harm. Now, get down off that horse."

"All of you get off your horses," commanded Lino, waving his gun for emphasis. "Then, move together and form a nice little group." While Lino was gathering the guards together, Levi and Santos rounded up the horses, then led them away. "What shall we do with these *muy* brave *hombres, mi jefe*?"

Joaquin rode over and appeared to give the matter deep consideration. He threw his leg over the pommel of his saddle. "String them together, wrist to wrist, then join the first and last so they form a neat circle. It will be interesting to watch them decide who should lead them back."

Lino chuckled. "*Sí, mi jefe.*" Lino signaled the others to give him a hand.

"*Uno momento, por favor.* Before you tie them up, relieve them of their clothing. All their clothing. That should make things even more interesting." Joaquin laughed and patted El Tigre's sleek neck.

"Strip," ordered Lino. "*Andala, pronto!*"

While the guards removed their clothing, Joaquin's men gathered up the discarded weapons and stowed them into their saddlebags. Joaquin tossed Lino a rope and watched as he strung the ten men together, then joined the first and last to form a circle in which they all faced out.

Spitting with chafe, Hank vented his fury. "You won't get away with this, Murieta. The boss will hunt you down and kill you, sure as I'm standing here."

Joaquin merely gazed at the man.

It was Lino who gave the final order. "Tell your boss that from now on nothing gets in or out of this valley unless Joaquin Murieta wants it to. *Comprende*?" When there was no answer, Lino drew his gun and fired off four shots within inches of Hank's bare toes.

Hank jumped like a frog in a frying pan. "Okay. Okay. I understand," he shouted. "I'll tell him."

"*Bueno! Muy bueno!* Now, head out before I decide to use you for some target practice."

The brigands laughed uproariously as the naked men yanked and pulled each other as they tried to gain position for the lead. After several riotous mishaps, they headed back toward El Dorado at a pace that would no doubt take them until evening to reach their destination.

That night, back at camp, Pepe's bonfire became the center of a celebration. Several women had joined the band, and when Levi Ortega began strumming his guitar, their voices sang loud and clear with the happy songs of Mexico. Swirling and lifting their brightly colored skirts, the women danced around the fire as the onlookers clapped and shouted, "*Ole! Ole!*"

Three men gathered inside the cave to play *Chuza,* a game similar to roulette. Another group tested their skills with their whips, flicking pinecones off rocks. Wild game roasted on a spit over the fire, and a pot of beans bubbled like molten lava.

Joaquin strolled around the perimeter of the camp,

stopping occasionally to make small talk with some of his men, many of whom had friends or relatives enslaved at El Dorado. He listened to their concerns for their loved ones' lives and patiently explained how he planned to gain their freedom. Sitting on a large boulder near the entrance to the cave, Ocho, the mute, sat braiding himself a new lead rope made from the hairs of horses' manes and tails.

Lino, walking stiffly, came up next to Joaquin. "Pepe and I just finished setting the dynamite. It should be just enough to create havoc with the river operations."

"What's the matter with your leg?" asked Joaquin.

Lino tried to change the subject, but Joaquin stopped him short. 'I was kicked," he said, with obvious reluctance, and it was just as obvious that he was unwilling to elaborate.

"Kicked? Who or what kicked you?" Joaquin prodded, suspicious of Lino's behavior.

Lino mumbled beneath his breath. "Paco."

"Pepe's little burro kicked you?" In spite of himself, he began to laugh. He might have been able to contain himself if Lino hadn't give him such a contemptuous look.

"*Little burro*? Paco isn't a little burro, Joaquin. He's a five-hundred-pound demon from Hell and he hates me with a vengeance. All I have to do is look at him, and he rolls back his lips and gnashes his teeth." Crossing his arms in front of him, he turned and pretended to ignore Joaquin's laughter. "How long do burros live, anyway?" he asked after a moment's thought. "It seems to me Paco has outlived his usefulness, if he ever had one."

Steadying his voice, Joaquin answered, "About as long as old *curanderos*, Lino. Forever," he said, then laughed and walked away.

Suddenly, a rider galloped into camp shouting for Joaquin. His horse was sweaty and winded. White foam edged his saddle blanket. The man told about

Juan Alvarado's whipping and how Heller and Abigail had been forced to watch.

Santos Alvarado stepped out of the darkness into the firelight. His face was a mask of pain and anger. "Is my brother alive?"

"*Sí*, but he is badly hurt."

"I must go to him," said Santos, starting toward the messenger.

Joaquin reached out an arm and halted his progress. "No, my friend. You cannot go. It would be foolhardy and they would kill you. We will make a plan—"

"Bah! You and your plans. It will take too long. My brother may be dying." Levi Ortega had put down his guitar and came forward, as had the other men and women. "You play a cat and mouse game with your old enemy while we—we suffer."

Joaquin held himself stiffly. "I am sorry for your brother, but you can't just ride in there. They'll shoot you down before you ever get to him. Mauger's men outnumber us three to one."

"Then why didn't you order those bastards killed this afternoon? That would have decreased their number by ten."

"You would have me order the outright slaughter of ten men? Without even giving them a chance to defend themselves? I don't do things that way, *mi amigo,* but if you do, then perhaps you should go your own way." There was a long pause, during which Joaquin clenched his hands at his side. Then, turning away from Alvarado, he confronted the others. "Listen to me, all of you. I thought we had an understanding about how things were to be done, but apparently we do not. If any one of you dislikes the way I do things, then say so now, because I will not have my orders disobeyed. We *will* free the slaves and we *will* get Mauger, but we *will not* become cold-blooded killers. Is that understood?"

There was some grumbling, but all the men eventually nodded.

"What about my brother?" Santos cried.

Turning slightly, Joaquin said, "Lino and I will discuss how best to help your brother."

Later that night, after thoroughly questioning the messenger, Joaquin and Lino rode down the mountain, through the gauntlet of unwary guards and into the pines surrounding the house. Juan Alvarado was being cared for on a staw pallet outside the kitchen door by Marta, the cook. When she took a few minutes to relieve herself, Joaquin stole up the path onto the *corredor,* lifted the unconscious Alvarado and carried him back to the cover of the trees, where Lino helped lift him across Joaquin's saddle.

"He looks very bad," Lino observed, as Joaquin mounted behind Alvarado's limp body.

"He's young. He'll heal," said Joaquin, wheeling El Tigre around in the direction they had come. Cautiously, he led them back through the guards, hoping Alvarado would not regain consciousness and make a noise until they were well on their way. Joaquin realized his answer to Lino must have sounded very cold, but in truth, seeing the young man's bloody bandages, knowing exactly what he had suffered, had had a devastating effect on him. So thinking, he shifted his hold on him so he wouldn't add to his suffering. They had a short but hard uphill ride ahead of them. Alvarado would probably be better off if he never regained consciousness. The physical pain he would suffer over the endless weeks of healing—if he healed—would make him wish he had died a thousand times over. And the hate that would fill his heart . . .

Joaquin knew all about hate.

Because of it, he had forgotten how to love . . . until Heller had fallen into his life.

Chapter 17

Two nights after his first visit, Joaquin returned to Heller's bedroom and woke her from a restless sleep. "Heller." He knelt on one knee down beside her and whispered her name.

Her eyes flew open and she became instantly wide awake. Without thinking, she threw her arms around his neck and pulled him to her.

"What's wrong? Has he hurt you? Abigail?"

She had meant to confront him with the fact that she now knew his identity, but the events of the last two days had made that particular issue seem insignificant. What did it really matter what his name was? He was the man she loved.

She clung to him, wishing some of his strength would seep into her. "No. He hasn't hurt us, but— The next morning, after you were here, he forced us to watch—" She pulled him even closer, seeking comfort. "He made us sit and watch while he nearly whipped a man to death." She squeezed her eyes shut at the memory of Alvarado's torn and bloody body.

"*Bastardo*!" Joaquin hissed, lifting his head and looking toward the window. "Did he do it because he discovered I was here?"

Heller pulled away from him and shook her head. "No, he'd already planned it, but his discovering you'd been here didn't improve his disposition." She raised up, clutching the bedclothes tight against her breasts. "He was like an enraged bull, shouting orders, snapping at everyone. He ordered six guards to watch the valley entrance, and he demanded that horses be kept saddled at all times. Then he whipped the boy. I lost count of the number of lashes. One of his own guards had to put a stop to it before the boy was killed." Forgetting herself, she dropped the covers and scrambled to the edge of the bed. "You shouldn't have come back. Not now. Not until things have settled down."

"I don't intend to let things settle down. Harassing Mauger is part of my plan. I *want* to keep him worried and wondering what's going to happen next."

She compressed her lips and frowned. "But, Joaquin. How many more will suffer or die in the meantime? He uses slave labor here. He said so, though I haven't seen them myself. What if he decides to take *his* vengeance out on them, or on me or Abigail?"

Something akin to regret flashed across his face. "You have to trust me, Heller. I know it must be difficult to understand why I need to do this. Sometimes I don't understand it myself. It must seem to you that you've become a victim of my vengeance, and maybe in a way you are, but I *have* to have more time." He hunkered down in front of her and placed his hands on her arms. "I don't think there's much likelihood that he'll hurt you. From what I've seen, he considers you to be his future. As for the others . . . If it looks like he's going to do anything, we'll stop him. My band is growing in number every day, and I have men watching El Dorado very closely. At the first sign of trouble, we'll move in and stop him."

"The boy, Alvarado," she said forlornly, "he must have died. I asked about him and they said he was gone. He was so young, such a handsome young man."

"He didn't die, Heller. We took him back to our camp and he's being well cared for."

She looked up, her face brightening. "You came and got him? Oh, Joaquin, I'm so relieved. I haven't been able to stop thinking about him. His poor back— It was . . . awful. I can imagine how it pained him. When Mauger whipped m—" She abruptly bit back her words. If she told him that Mauger had whipped her, he might feel duty-bound to try to rescue her and Abigail now, when he needed her there at the ranch to provide him with information. She placed her hands alongside her head, pretending to be so overwrought that she couldn't continue.

"I won't pretend that he wasn't badly hurt, but he'll live."

Heller exaggerated a sigh of relief. A change of subject was needed. Something less volatile. "I read the book you left me and I overheard some of the guards talking about you. Now I know how you come and go so easily. El Dorado used to be yours?"

"A long time ago." He had a faraway look in his eyes as he answered her. "Rosita and I were very young when we found the valley. We thought God had put it here just for us. We staked a claim, built a house, and dreamed about our future. But you read the book, so you know."

"*This* is the house you and she built?"

"The *sala* was the original house. Mauger's added on to it."

"Then, it was in the *sala* where—" she hesitated, almost afraid to go on for the emptiness she saw in his eyes "—Rosita was raped and killed?" Was there any nonvolatile subject, she wondered.

"*Sí.*" He expelled a ragged breath.

"The book, Joaquin—"

"*Sí*, the book. Some of it's true, some the work of

a very imaginative storyteller. Someday, perhaps, I
will tell you the story.''

"But the book said . . . you died.''

"I have to admit, it felt like I had at the time. I'm
still not exactly sure what happened. All I remember
is an old man and his burro standing over me. He told
me I wasn't going to die.'' He spread his hands in a
dismissive gesture.

"One of the guards I overheard, he remembered
meeting you a long time ago. He seemed to think there
was something *peculiar* about you.'' She looked down,
embarrassed to finish. "He said you weren't an ordinary man.''

Stroking his chin, he regarded her. "I don't have an
answer for that, Heller, except that I am only a man,
nothing more.''

Heller thought his answer evasive, but then what did
she expect him to say? That he possessed some sort
of magical power? That he was a sorcerer? As if such
things existed. To even consider the possibility was
absolutely ridiculous, and yet . . . There were a few
questions she would have liked answered. A few things
that deserved an explanation. One thing, however, was
certain: he wasn't ordinary. She wished he did have
some magic power. Then he could cast a spell and
send her and Abigail home to Boston.

"Heller.''

The sound of her name broke into her thoughts. She
came to attention.

"I don't have all night. I came to tell you to prepare
yourself. From now on, things are going to get difficult
around here. I still need to know the date of the wedding, but it can wait awhile. I know it won't be anytime soon. It isn't going to be easy for you, Heller.
Mauger's going to start losing a lot of ground, inch by

inch, and he's going to be desperate to regain it. You need to be especially cautious.''

Her pupils dilated at a question that popped into her head. "Joaquin. Were you responsible for—? Was it you who ambushed that gold shipment and sent all those men back—" She broke off, unable to say what she'd seen.

He finished for her. "Naked and linked together in a circle?"

Blood rushed to her head and she looked askance. All she could do was nod.

"I take it Luther didn't appreciate my little joke?" Amusement flickered in his eyes, and the slashing grooves on either side of his mouth deepened. Hugging herself, she tried to suppress a giggle, but when she turned and saw his broad grin, she couldn't stop the bubble of laughter that rose within her and demanded release.

Before she could utter a sound, he leaned forward and kissed her hard on the mouth, absorbing the noise. He pressed her back onto the mattress, his body partially covering hers. He broke the kiss and whispered against her lips, "Shh, you'll give me away." But he laughed, too, nuzzling his mouth against her cheek.

Heller couldn't dissolve the image of the ten naked men from her mind. Trying to keep her voice low, she half-laughed, half-choked, "It was so— It was so funny—" Her body quaked. "There's so many trees around the house. They tried to bunch together, then they tried to form a sort of double line, but they couldn't, and they tumbled into the yard, falling over each other, cursing and yelling." She tried to stifle her laughter by arching her neck back and forcing herself to stare at a point of light that shown through a gap in her curtains, but it was no good; she couldn't hold back the laughter.

"Heller, shh!" He kissed her again, thoroughly and completely, turning her laughter into soft moans. The image of the naked men vanished. The only thing on her mind now was what he was doing to her. He moved his mouth down across the sharp ridge of her jaw and kissed her beneath her chin, then her throat.

The tickle of his day-old beard sent shivers down her spine, and she put her hands on either side of his face. She shifted his head and stared deep into his eyes.

"You *are* a gentleman, are you not?"

"When I need to be."

"You need to be now," she whispered breathlessly. "Because you see, I've lost my willpower where you're concerned, and I find you and what you're doing to me very, very hard to resist." She moved her thumbs down to his mouth.

A hint of a smile touched his lips. "I don't want you to resist me. I want to make love to you."

She pushed into him, pressing her body against his. Suddenly, a warning bell rang inside her head. She couldn't let him make love to her, not here, not now. It was too dangerous. She'd never forgive herself if something happened to him because of her. She decided now was the time to tell him she knew who he was. That would cool his ardor.

"If I let you make love to me, I'll be betraying my love for Don Ricardo." She felt him tense. "You wouldn't want me to do that, would you?"

He straightened and started to stand up. "No, I wouldn't. It's late. I'd better go."

She intercepted his sudden response. "Joaquin, wait." She threw her arms around him and held him close. "You can trust me with your secret. I know who you are, and who you are not. Don't you know there are some things a man can't hide from a woman? Like the way he tastes,'' she murmured, brushing her lips against his, ''and the way he feels.'' She ran her hands across his shoulders, up his neck, then into his hair. She untied the cloth mask behind his head and drew it tight across the back of his neck.

''How long have you known?'' He stood up.

''I've suspected since the night of the masquerade ball, but I didn't know for certain until the other night when you left. Your voice gave you away.''

''You're not angry with me?''

''No. You did what you thought you had to do. I can't fault you for that, but I am angry at you for making me want you so much that it hurts inside.''

''Heller—''

She waved him away. ''You must go now.''

He hesitated, watching her expressions. As he turned to leave, his cape swung around his legs. ''*Adios, mi cara.*''

And then, like a phantom, he was gone, disappearing into the night.

It was almost a week later when she saw him again, but she heard about him practically every minute of every day from the servants, the guards, and mostly from Gordon.

As before, he came to her room in the middle of the night. She assured him she had become familiar with every detail of the house and was becoming familiar with the grounds that she was allowed to explore. She related bits and pieces of overheard conversations regarding ways Mauger planned to stop him and his men from harassing the ranch. She told him anything and everything that she thought might be useful to him, including how Mauger spent his evenings, sitting in the *sala*, staring at the far wall, smoking a foul-smelling pipe.

She was awed at the way her petty observations were put to use. Little things like habits and certain routines helped him create havoc among the guards. False footprints set outside Mauger's window at a time when Heller knew he would be down at the river, caused a tremendous uproar and sent everyone chasing their own tails.

Before long, El Dorado was all but crippled. Heller was privy to Gordon's frustration more than once. After a third gold shipment was robbed and the men sent back covered with mud, he accused two of the guards of shirking their duty and had them chained to the *corredor* and whipped.

Supplies had also been cut off, but the only effect Heller could see it was having on the ranch was at mealtime. There was a definite lack of fresh fruits and vegetables.

All communication to the outside world ceased, and Mauger was as much a prisoner of El Dorado as she and Abigail.

Late one night, an explosion caused a rock slide to fall into the river at the very point where the slaves had been working. Tons of rock and dirt filled the river bottom, taking the operation almost back to its beginnings, she overheard Gordon say.

It was nearing evening, the day after the rock slide, when Gordon knocked at Heller's bedroom door and surprised her with an invitation to stroll with him along the riverbank. With the exception of that first night when he had forced his way into her room and the day of the whipping, Gordon had been considerate and courtly, very much the gentleman she had originally thought him to be. In spite of her utter boredom, she had refused. Gordon, however, was insistent and turned his invitation into an order, which Heller had no choice but to accept. Once outside, she decided she might as well make the best of the situation and use it to her advantage—or rather, to Joaquin's advantage—by carefully noting everything she saw.

"I wanted to talk to you about our wedding," he began, as he steered her through the trees. "I've set the date for the eighth of July. After we've said our vows, there'll be a fiesta. Everything will be outside under the trees. I wondered if you have any special requests or needs."

His thoughtfulness made her suspicious. He knew she didn't want to marry him, so why did he think she would care about wedding plans? Remembering to be cautious, she held herself back from telling him just what he could do with his plans and endeavored to sound amicable. "No, I don't want or need anything special, thank you." In spite of her best efforts, she sensed he detected her animosity.

"What about a wedding dress? I could arrange for Marta's sister to help you make one out of material I have stored away. I don't want you to go without, Heller. I *never* want you to go without. As my wife, you will have every advantage, every elegance money can buy."

His speech unlocked a door she couldn't resist entering. "What about happiness and love, Gordon? To me, those things are far more important than a fiesta or a wedding dress."

"You'll have that, too," he assured her with smiling certainty.

They strolled along the sandy riverbank until they reached a fork in the river.

Heller stopped and bent to pick up a shiny river rock. "You can't *make* me love you, Gordon. Don't you understand that? You can't buy love. Love is something that is given freely."

He took the rock from her fingers and tossed it into

the river. "Love is also something that grows. You'll learn to love me, and then you'll find your happiness." Catching hold of her hands, he pulled her against him. "I've hated most of the women I've known, Heller, but you—you're different. I tried to hate you, but I couldn't. There's something about you that's different. You're not like the other women I've known."

"What does all this have to do with anything?"

"Just that I want you to stop hating me. I want you to forgive and forget. I was wrong to have taken your virginity, and wrong to have frightened you into submission. I know that now and I want to make it up to you, if you'll let me. I want to love you . . . and I want you to love me."

His declaration surprised her. That he confessed to loving her gave her something she hadn't had before: power. Suddenly, she realized *she* could hurt him. "I'm afraid you want too much, Gordon. I remember something my mother once told me when she was grieving: 'Neither time nor forgiveness can erase that which is written on a woman's heart.'"

"I hope, for your sake, it isn't true," he said, leading her back toward the house. "If I recall, there's something in the wedding vows about 'until death do you part.' That's a very long time, Heller. A *very* long time."

Back in her room, Heller told Abigail what Gordon had said. "He's fallen in love with me, Aunty. I don't think it was his intention to do so, but he has."

"So it seems. But I cannot fathom him asking you to love him after all he has done. But then, as we both agreed, he is mad. People like him do not think rational thoughts or act in the normal manner. You must be very cautious that you do not anger him. There is no telling what he will do. We simply must find a way to escape, and soon.''

"Yes, Aunty, I know. I think I might know just how we can do it, but I hesitate to say until I'm sure, so be patient a little while longer until I can work things out.'' She picked up the sampler she had started out of desperation for something to occupy her time and studied the messy, uneven stitches. She regretted that she couldn't share Joaquin's plans for their escape with Abigail. The poor old dear had been valiantly trying not to let her fear show. But for safety's sake, Joaquin had demanded that she say nothing of his plans to her aunt.

Now, it occurred to her that even for Joaquin to get them away from the ranch, they would have to go on horseback. If they rode double, the horses would be slowed and the danger of Gordon and his men catching them would be greater than if they rode their own horses. Heller had been trained to ride sidesaddle, but during practice sessions, when the instructor had left her on her own, she had unsaddled her mare and ridden her bareback, and she had discovered that riding astride was much more to her liking. Consequently, she wasn't worried about herself, only about Abigail. "Can you ride a horse, Aunty?'' she asked suddenly.

"A horse? Certainly I can ride a horse. I didn't live in the city all my life, you know. I was raised on a farm. It's been a good many years, but I think I can manage it.''

Heller realized now that she really didn't know her aunt at all. Imagining the oh-so-proper Abigail Peyton, Boston's matriarch, riding a horse was indeed a humorous thought.

Now, knowing the wedding date, Heller was anxious for Joaquin to pay her another visit. Though he hadn't specifically said when or how he would manage their escape, she had decided in her own mind that it would be the day of the wedding, when most of the guards would be together in one location. Not only that, but by ending the wedding before it had begun would be yet another way for Joaquin to get revenge.

She sat up half the night, unable to sleep, wondering what danger there would be. Would Joaquin plan to surround the house? Did he have enough men to do that? Would there be shooting? Or would he come the night before, as he had in the past, and steal her and Abigail away? She could hardly wait to ask him. The anticipation would make the days speed by.

In many ways, she resented having to *wait* to be rescued, when, in fact, he could have freed them almost anytime he desired. But she had become a pawn in his game of revenge, and he was determined to make his move only when it suited him. And yet, knowing what she did about him, she understood his motives and sincerely hoped her efforts would help him achieve his goals.

A week passed without sign of Joaquin. A small gold shipment went out and the guards returned without incident. After that, Gordon sent two empty wagons into Angels Camp for much-needed supplies and had a note delivered to the local padre, requesting him to perform the ceremony. He also had his men wire Abigail's message to Alexander Rice, telling him when she would be boarding the train and on her way back to Boston.

As evening overtook the valley, Heller went into the *sala* to try to find the poetry book she had left there the previous evening, and she saw a group of guards clustered outside on the *corredor*. Gathering her skirts close to stop their rustling, she moved silently toward the open window and stood with her back against the wall. They were talking about Joaquin. One of them expressed relief that there had been no more incidents and that things seemed to have returned to normal. To that another said he thought the *bandidos* had grown tired of their game and moved on. "After all," he said, "the El Dorado gold shipments are small compared to those being shipped from the other mines along the Stanislaus and American rivers."

Heller walked back to her room feeling depressed. This was one conversation she wished she had not overheard. If what they said was true, then she and her aunt might never leave El Dorado. It can't be true, she told herself. Joaquin wouldn't abandon two helpless women. And neither would he give up the revenge he had spent years seeking.

With each passing day, Heller became more convinced that Joaquin had no intention of rescuing her and Abigail. And neither had there been any further harassments or incidents. It was as if he had disappeared.

When the morning of her wedding day dawned, and still Heller had not seen or heard from Joaquin, she had no choice but to believe that he had indeed abandoned them, which would mean that the wedding would go on as scheduled. And afterwards, Abigail would return to Boston, and she would be left alone with Gordon.

The thought of her wedding night, and the many intimate nights to follow that she would have to spend with Gordon, made her throat clog and brought a misting of tears to her eyes. Nothing could make her love him. He could be ten times the gentleman he was pretending to be now, and she wouldn't love him. Without love, there could be no lovemaking, only sex. And just thinking about Gordon's sexual perversions made her ill.

302			*Chelley Kitzmiller*

Since the afternoon when Gordon had asked her to walk with him along the river and she had discovered that he was in love with her, there had been several other *invitations* which she had not been allowed to refuse: a picnic in the meadow beyond the house, a candlelight supper under the pines, and a horseback ride to a beautiful waterall several miles upriver. He had been the epitome of gentility and had treated her with the upmost respect, almost to the point of reverence.

The padre arrived shortly before dark, as Lu began lighting the multicolored paper lanterns that hung from the overhang of the *corredor* roof and from the trees. From her bedroom window, Heller and Abigail watched the tall, broad-shouldered man ride into the courtyard on his big chestnut horse.

"He looks better suited to a parlor than a pulpit," Abigail observed dryly. She was dressed, as usual, in a black long-sleeved gown and was wearing her jet beads. When Gordon had asked her to wear something more colorful for the wedding, she had vehemently refused, telling him that as far as she was concerned, she was going to a funeral.

"He doesn't look like any priest I've ever seen," Heller commented, nodding. "He's too young and too handsome." Despite his black broadcloth garb, which gave him a look of distinction, the only thing that looked truly priestly about him was his white Roman collar. He dismounted and took a black book out of his saddlebag.

"We do not have much time to get you ready," said Abigail as she smoothed nonexistent wrinkles out of Heller's wedding gown, which wasn't a wedding gown at all but a lovely mint-green day dress with sprigs of embroidered violets edging the neck, sleeves, and hem.

Heller drew the curtains closed, her expression spiritless. "Maybe . . . if I could get the padre alone for a moment and tell him that I'm being forced— No, it wouldn't do any good. Even if he sympathized with me, Gordon would find a way to force him into performing the ceremony."

"After you are married, dear, Gordon will keep his promise and allow me to go. Rest assured, I will go straight to the authorities. They will send a posse to rescue you. Once you are away from that madman, we can have the marriage dissolved either by annulment or divorce. Either way, it will not matter. What does matter is that you will be rid of that man, and they will send him to prison where he belongs."

Heller put her finger to her lips. "You must be careful not to let him hear you say anything like that, Aunty, or he won't keep his promise."

"I know, dear. I—"

A knock at the door interrupted whatever Abigail had been about to say. "It is time, señora, señorita." It was Marta, the cook, who called them.

"We'll be right there," Heller called back. Turning, she flung herself into Abigail's open arms.

"Now, now, dear," Abigail crooned. "You have to put on a brave face. You do not want Gordon Pierce to think you are weak."

She pulled back. "No. I don't want him to think me weak. He would only find a way to use it to his advantage."

Heller opened the door leading out onto the *corredor,* and she and Abigail walked side by side to where Gordon was waiting. He was dressed in a dark brown suit with a silver brocade vest and Dickens watch chain. His blond hair had been immaculately groomed and his sideburns neatly trimmed. He looked more handsome than she had ever seen him. How was it, she wondered, that a person could be so pleasant to look upon and yet so evil?

He moved toward her, smiling. "You look lovely in that gown, Heller, but every bride needs a wedding veil and a bouquet." He signaled to a servant, who came forth with a small basket full of wildflowers. "You can carry these." After she took the proffered basket, he reached beneath his coat and pulled out a white lace *rebozo*. He unfolded it, laid it over her head, and gently draped the ends over her shoulders. "There now," he said, smiling with satisfaction, "you look like a bride."

The sun slipped behind the mountain, silently turning afternoon into evening. At Gordon's bidding, Heller followed him around the house. She stopped before passing the half-dozen food-laden tables covered with boldy colored serapes. Heller's nose took in the sweet and spicy scents. She had lost weight in the weeks she'd been held prisoner; food had all but lost its appeal, and she had eaten only what was needed to stop the insistent gnawing. Now, instead of gnawing, her stomach felt queasy and she wondered if she was going to be sick.

As they turned the corner, Heller saw the Chinese paper lanterns. In spite of herself, she thought them beautiful. Strings of red and green chili peppers hung from the support posts holding up the roof—the whipping posts, Heller reminded herself. Someone began playing a violin. The servants, dressed in their Mexican finery, were lined up, as were most of the guards, waiting for the bride and groom to enter the courtyard. The padre stood alone on the *corredor*, watching their approach.

"We're ready, Padre," said Gordon, bringing Heller around to the steps.

Heller glanced over her shoulder at Abigail, who had tears streaming down her face. Steeling herself not to show what she was feeling, and willing her stomach to behave, she took a deep breath and looked up at the padre, whose expression softened as if to say he understood.

Only he didn't. He couldn't. He had no idea what his holy words were about to do.

"Friends, we are gathered here," he began in a solemn voice. After addressing the assemblage, he said a few words on the sanctity of marriage.

Heller listened but didn't hear. Though she was Irish-Catholic by birth, her upbringing in Five Points had given her no opportunity to involve herself with the church or her religion. In fact, she knew nothing about being a Catholic, save the rosary, which Mam had taught her. Her only association with priests had been when she was nine, when she had been caught trying to pick one's pocket. He'd made her kneel in front of the altar for hours, rosary in hand, and say a penance. The second time had been the day the priest came to Cow Bay, the day Mam had died.

The padre went straight into the Nuptial Mass invocation, speaking in Latin while Heller studied his pointed-toed leather boots. What, she wondered, would Elizabeth Pennyworth have to say about a priest in riding boots? Would he fall into the *savage* category? Or were priests excluded? To date, the only savage Heller had met was the one standing next to her. Her husband-to-be.

The invocation was surprisingly short. Heller had thought she would be able to make it through the ceremony without breaking down, but suddenly there were tears filling her eyes. She used the handkerchief

Abigail had thoughtfully stuffed up her sleeve at the last minute to dry her eyes. Turning slightly, she looked at her aunt. Abigail had rescued her from Five Points, given her a home and all the love, kindness, and understanding a girl could ask for. And now it was time to repay her. Marrying Gordon was the only way Abigail would be allowed to leave El Dorado.

"Do you, Heller Peyton, take this man, Gordon Pierce, to be your lawfully wedded husband?"

She hesitated and felt Gordon nudge her arm. God, how she hated him—hated what he was forcing her to do. As for Joaquin Murieta . . . She hated him, too. He'd built up her hopes only to leave her hopeless.

"I—I do," she said at length. But they were only words. Out of the corner of her eye, she saw Gordon's disapproving look but pretended not to see it. She had kept her promise by saying, "I do." If he had expected her to be happy about it, he had another thing coming.

Then Gordon slipped a simple gold band on her finger, and the padre blessed them. "Live in peace, my children," he finished, and began the Mass.

Chapter 18

The padre was the first to offer congratulations, which Gordon accepted with coarse-mannered thanks and an ungentlemanly handshake. He turned away when Zeke and some of the other guards approached, then went off with them to toast the occasion.

Heller, on the other hand, stood staring at the padre, unsure of what to think. He had inconspicuoulsy left out one of the most significant parts of the ceremony, where the priest pronounced them man and wife.

"Padre? I wanted to ask . . ."

He smiled broadly, his even white teeth flashing. "*Sí.* What is it you wish to know?"

"Well, I was wondering—" Behind them, on the *corredor,* the three musicians struck a harmonious chord, strummed their guitars, and broke into song. Determined to ask her question in spite of the noise, she stood up on tip-toe and spoke close to his ear, but he shook his head, implying he couldn't hear her.

Heller stepped back and the padre shrugged helplessly. Nodding her understanding, she turned and moved away, bewilderment stamping her features into a frown. Across the courtyard, Marta was issuing orders to her helpers to uncover the food, and the guards were taking up plates and forming a line.

The question still heavy on her mind, she glanced over her shoulder at the padre. Was it possible that he had guessed the circumstance of her marriage? Perhaps someone, one of the servants, had told him.

The padre stepped away from the *corredor* as Abigail started across the courtyard toward Heller. He reached out his hand to stop her, then took her arm in his and led her to a quieter spot near the side of the house.

Standing alone in the middle of the courtyard, holding her basket of flowers before her, Heller knew that from now on she would stand alone no matter how many people were around her. As if to bring her comfort, a warm summer breeze caressed her face and lifted the edges of her *rebozo*. But she was beyond being comforted. She gave the end of the lacy scarf a yank, pulled it off her head, and dropped it on the ground along with the flower basket.

The musicians stopped playing and all eyes turned to Heller.

She glanced sharply at the staring faces, daring them, challenging them to say a word. The breeze, stronger than a moment ago, whipped her skirt around her legs. With a look of pure defiance, she lifted her chin and started toward Abigail and the padre.

Then, a sound, unlike anything she'd ever heard, stopped her. She turned into the breeze, facing the trees. It came again, still a long way off but louder. What was it? An eagle's cry? A wounded animal? She cocked her head to listen and heard it again.

The ground beneath her feet started to vibrate like a small earthquake. A low rumbling accompanied the vibration. Frozen in place, she saw a large black mass coming down the road. Through the trees. Toward the house.

"*Venganza! Venganza!*"

The women shrieked and huddled together.

Again the cry, "*Venganza! Venganza!*"

The guards ran to the bunkhouse to get their weapons.

"El Jefe! He comes!" shouted Marta.

El Jefe? Heller looked to Marta for the answer and saw only fear.

The rumbling grew louder and the vibrations grew stronger.

The mass took shape.

Fear and anticipation made her heart leap. "Joaquin!" Her hands flew to her face to stop herself from saying his name again.

The horse thundered through the trees at a full gallop. Riding low over his back, Joaquin cried out again and again, his voice carrying on the wind.

Joaquin! He was magnificent—a black-clad devil, riding at breakneck speed with his black cape waving behind him. Upon reaching the courtyard, his horse cleanly leaped one of the trestle tables covered with freshly baked tortillas, then charged toward Heller.

Again, his name broke from her lips. "Joaquin!"

Reining the animal to a half-halt, Joaquin leaned over the side of his saddle, grabbed her around the waist, and scooped her up against him.

She screamed as he picked her up.

"A bride for a bride, Mauger," he called over her head, then spurred his horse to a run and headed back into the trees.

Not realizing the firm hold he had on her, Heller screamed again and again. She was sure he was going to drop her. Surely his strength would give out. Fearing her struggles were only making matters worse, she forced herself to be still and clung to the arm around her waist.

By the time they reached the end of the stand of trees, Heller thought she was going to break in two. Just when she could bear it no more, he called out to his horse and drew back on the reins. Then, at last, after what seemed hours rather than minutes, they stopped and he pulled her across the front of the saddle into his arms.

"Heller, *querida,* are you all right? Did I hurt you?" She could hardly breathe, let alone speak. She had wrapped her arms around his waist and was afraid to let go. "I'm sorry I frightened you, but there was nothing else I could do with you until we got away from there."

"I—I hate you!" she managed with great effort. She tightened her grip and he responded in kind.

"*Que*? You hate me?" His chuckle rumbled against her ear, which was pressed against his cheek. "Why do you hate me, Heller? I just risked my life and the life of El Tigre to rescue you! *Dios*!"

"Speak English, damn you, so I know what you're saying!"

He clasped her arms and gently pushed her back. "You are *muy*—I mean *very* angry with me, yes?"

"Yes! I thought you had abandoned us."

"Ah, I see. But you have to understand, *niña,* it was better that you didn't know when I would be coming for you."

She was in a red rage. "*When* you would be coming? Because you didn't come back, I thought you weren't coming at all! You have no idea how horrible it was for me to think that I would remain his prisoner. I made myself sick thinking about my wedding day . . . and about my wedding night. And all because *you* thought it was better that I didn't know." Much to her mortification, she felt her anger turning to frustration, and it was all she could do to hold it inside her and not pound him with her fists.

"I know. I know. And I'm sorry for that," he said in a calming voice—the kind of voice one uses to quiet a temperamental child. Holding her arms, he helped her into a more comfortable position behind the saddle's pommel. "I thought if you knew exactly when I'd be coming, your anticipation might give you away. I couldn't risk your safety like that."

He had turned it back on her, using her safety as his motive, but she wasn't having any of it. "I think I'm old enough and wise enough to keep a secret," she snapped back, then clamped her jaws together and closed her eyes. She didn't want to argue. Didn't want to fight. The *only* thing she wanted was to be comforted and assured that she was safe and that she had seen the last of Luther Mauger.

She stiffened at a sudden, terrible thought. "Abigail!" Her face was as white as the new moon. "What about Abigail? You can't leave her there all alone. He'll hurt her. I know it."

"Your aunt is safe, Heller." He inclined his head toward the direction they had come. "She's in good hands."

Coming into the clearing was the big chestnut. The padre! And Abigail was seated behind him, riding astride, holding onto his waist.

"Hola, amigo!" shouted the black-clad padre as he pulled his horse up next to Joaquin's. Smiling, he exclaimed, "That was quite an entrance, El Jefe. I thought a herd of mustangs was coming through those trees."

"Aunty?"

Abigail peaked out from behind the padre's back. "Here I am, dear. All in one piece, I think, though I am still not sure exactly what is going on."

Joaquin and Lino laughed.

"We've been rescued, Aunty."

"Well, I gathered as much, but who are these men, Heller?"

Joaquin touched the brim of his hat. "*Buenas noches,* señora. If you will be patient only a while longer, we will explain. But first, we must get you both safely back to camp."

The camp went wild when Joaquin and Lino rode in with the two women. The men tossed their sombreros into the air and the women waved their *rebozos.* Amid the cheers and shouts, Joaquin and Lino dismounted and led the two women to the campfire, where Pepe poured steaming coffee into tin cups.

Abigail turned away Pepe's offer. "I do not want coffee. I want to know who you people are!"

Heller went to her aunt's side and put her arm around her shoulders. "Aunty," she said, then turned to Joaquin. "Take off your mask so that she may see you."

"Don Ricardo!"

"No, Abigail. Joaquin Murieta. I hope you will forgive me my little masquerade."

Abigail raised a white brow and gave him a considering look. "And who are *you,* if I may ask?" she said, turning to the padre.

He took off his hat and bowed low. "Lino Toral, señora. Joaquin's lieutenant."

"Not a padre?"

"An ex-priest. We intercepted the real padre, borrowed a few things from him, then sent him back to Angels Camp with a poke of gold—for the poor—which made him somewhat more agreeable."

Heller started, the import of his words hitting her with the force of a Boston snowstorm. "Then that means— The ceremony—?" She held her breath, her brown eyes bright with hope.

"Why do you think I didn't pronounce you man and wife?' said Lino.

She expelled the breath she'd been holding, bowed

her head, and stared at the ground. Her stomach gave a violent lurch and she rocked forward on the balls of her feet.

Both Lino and Abigail stepped forward, but it was Joaquin who caught her. He bent her forward, curved an arm behind her legs, and lifted her up, cradled in his arms.

"Heller! Oh, my poor dear," cried Abigail. "I fear this has all been too much for her. Is there someplace you can take her and lay her down?"

Joaquin had already turned toward the cave. "*Sí*, señora. Follow me."

Inside the cave, in Joaquin's personal chamber, Heller was laid on the pile of animal skins that served as his bed.

Abigail solicited Lino's help in getting to her knees beside Heller. "I need a dampened cloth, if you have one," she said, smoothing Heller's disheveled hair back from her face. "Heller, wake up, dear." She patted Heller's cheeks. Joaquin stood at Heller's feet, alarm making him look fearsome. As soon as Lino returned with the damp cloth, Abigail wiped it over Heller's face and neck.

"Come on now, Heller. Wake up."

Heller slowly regained consciousness. She lifted one eyelid and saw the blur of Abigail. Her tongue felt thick and awkward. She barely mumbled, "I think I'm going to be sick, Aunty," before she leaned onto her side and retched. Having eaten nothing since early that morning, her empty stomach produced only bile. Joaquin knelt down near her head, took the cloth from Abigail, and wiped the spittle from Heller's lips. He felt himself responsible for her illness, though he was certain it was a result of fear, anxiety, and shock. Maybe he should have told her when he planned to come for her, and maybe he shouldn't have kept his identity a secret.

When she tried to sit up, he encouraged her to lay back down. The retching had made her pale and weak. She needed rest. "I'll stay with her, señora, while you get settled in," he volunteered. "Lino, *por favor,* see that the señora is made comfortable."

Abigail's nose pinched as she leveled a look on him. Joaquin returned her stare. "She will be fine, señora."

"I am more worried about you than her. How can I trust you to take care of her after what you have done? You have disguised yourself. Lied to us. Lord only know what else!"

"I'll be fine, Aunty," Heller said in a hoarse whisper.

"Heller, dear—"

Heller reached out her hand and patted Abigail's. "I'll be fine. Really, I will."

Lino offered Abigail his hand, which she reluctantly accepted. She stood up and snorted, her gaze unwavering as she turned it back on Joaquin. "Heller is my pride and joy, Señor Murieta. She had made my life worth living. If any harm comes to her because of you . . ." Tears gathered in her eyes.

Joaquin rose up and took the old woman's hands in his. "I would never intentionally do anything to hurt her, señora. She's made my life worth living, too." He looked down at her and saw a tremulous but happy smile. "You *do* remind me of my *tia.*" He shook his head. "Only I think I gave you a bigger bouquet of parasols than I gave her. You will have to promise never to tell her."

He heard her small gasp and saw her chin snap up. She looked to be grievously offended, but he knew now that it was only a charade.

She pushed him away and quickly wiped away all traces of her sentimentality. "I know what has happened between you and Heller, and quite frankly I think you took advantage of her naivete," she stated unequivocally. "However, I believe you have discovered that you love her. I *know* she loves you, though she is much too stubborn to admit it. If only you could have seen how distraught she was after I interrupted you and you left her room. Now that you have found each other again . . . Well. Well, I an getting up in years, you see, and I would like to see Heller happily settled with several children before I pass on."

"Children?" Joaquin threw his head back and laughed. "You have many years left, Señora Peyton." He handed her over to Lino, who had been patiently standing by.

Heller was fast asleep. He bent down beside her and brushed his knuckles across her cheek. "*Mi vida. Mi corazón,*" he whispered, then took off her shoes, covered her with a serape, and lay down beside her.

It was near dawn when Heller awoke. Disoriented and frightened, she sat up and called into the darkness. "Gordon? Gordon, no please!"

Joaquin had fallen asleep next to her. He reached out and took her hand. "Shh, you're all right. Nothing is going to hurt you."

"Don Ricardo?"

"No, Heller. Joaquin."

She turned to him. "Please. Please, promise me you won't let him ever come near me again. Please, Joaquin. I hate him. He's a monster."

He pulled her into the circle of his arms and settled her head on his shoulder. "I promise, Heller," he whispered softly, nuzzling his lips against her temple.

"Go back to sleep now, *querida*." The words were hardly spoken when she sighed and closed her eyes.

Literally overnight, Heller's life had taken yet another turn. She and Abigail were no longer a madman's prisoner. There would be no dreaded wedding night. No threat of whippings. She could put her dreams and goals back into place—she could do anything she wanted to do.

She had spent the day at Joaquin's side, acquainting herself with the cave's main chambers and passages, the camp, and the men and women who made up El Jefe's band.

Through conversation, spoken mostly in English, for her benefit, she was sure, she learned the bizarre account about how the band had been formed. They were not all relatives or friends of the men Luther Mauger had enslaved, but they were all loyal to one man: Joaquin Murieta. El Jefe. And they made his cause their cause.

Having read the fictionalized story of his past, Heller felt she had a unique view of the present. He was, in many ways, repeating his own history, doing all the things he had done once before: seeking his own personal revenge against a brutal enemy—the same enemy—fighting for a cause he believed in, and commanding a band of loyal men and women.

He was truly an enigma, this man, Joaquin Murieta. An educated gentleman. A leader of men. A feared bandit. An avenger.

A man alone, she thought, like El Cid.

She was looking forward to discovering all she could about him. She was looking forward to loving him through the years to come.

Heller also met Pepe Lopez and Paco. Pepe, she remembered, was the man who'd brought Joaquin back to life. Paco, his burro, was Pepe's constant companion. The little, long-eared, jackass followed Pepe almost everywhere he went, dutifully plodding along behind him, head bent, ears back. When Pepe stopped, Paco nudged him in the back with his nose to get him going again.

Heller quickly discovered Paco's one weakness when she stroked the insides of his ears. Paco stretched his heavily muscled neck and rolled back his lips, exposing large yellowed teeth. When she left him, he brayed, and she thought she had never heard anything so mournful.

Heller and Joaquin spent the afternoon talking to each other in the lowest chamber of the cave, sitting on flat boulders beside the underground river.

Although it was no easy task, for Joaquin was as closed-mouth as a clam, she did get him to talk a little bit about Mauger. He told her what actions he and Lino has taken against him in San Francisco.

"When did you begin?" she wanted to know, although she already had a good idea.

"The night he escorted you and Abigail to the Foxhall Theater to see Elena's performance. "I tested him to see if he recognized me."

"I remember. He compared your questions to the Spanish Inquisition." She looked up expectantly. "What if he had recognized you?"

His expression was reflective. "I suppose I would have had to shoot him where he stood."

Heller imagined the scene and thought how fortunate for everyone that Mauger hadn't recognized Joaquin. He went on to tell her about breaking into Mauger's house and stealing the whip, his dealings with the Chinese merchant who supplied Mauger's goods, how he and Lino had effectively put a stop to Mauger's bank loan and alerted Wells Fargo. As he talked, she was able to match the action to the reaction, which she had seen for herself.

"Now it is your turn," he said suddenly. While he was short on words, he was long on listening, especially where Heller was concerned. He wanted to know everything there was to know about her. Reluctantly, she told him about her childhood in Five Points, Mam, Abigail's finding her and bringing her back to Boston, her schooling, and the dreary years that followed.

"I came to San Francisco to prove something to myself—that in spite of where I came from, I had learned the art of being a lady." She bowed her head. "I know how silly that must sound, but at the time it was the most important thing in the world."

"I don't think it's silly, Heller." He put his arm around her shoulders. "Are you ready to tell me what Mauger did to coerce you into agreeing to marry him and coming to El Dorado?"

Heller fell silent. Steeling herself against the horror just thinking about it evoked, she recounted the sequence of events, beginning with waking up to the sounds of a disturbance in her room, then the ether-soaked rag.

She told him of her fear that Gordon would indeed carry out his threat of dynamiting the Boston-bound train. But there was one thing she couldn't bring herself to talk about: her rape. She didn't know if she would ever be able to tell him about it.

Joaquin, sensing her disquiet, took her into his arms.

"Joaquin! Joaquin!" Lino's voice echoed through the cave.

Both Joaquin and Heller ran toward Lino's voice. They met in another smaller chamber.

"Lino, what is it?"

"I am glad I found you, El Jefe. Four of Mauger's men have ridden out of the valley and taken the road toward Mariposa. They were packing bedrolls and riding hard.''

Joaquin considered the implications of such a move. ''It's time to act.''

''*Sí, mi jefe.*''

To the men waiting around the ever-burning campfire, Joaquin said, ''Tomorrow morning, *mi amigos,* we will ride to El Dorado and free some of our *compadres,* as we have planned. Prepare your weapons and make certain you know exactly what position you will take.'' He turned on his heel and strode over to the map.

Heller grabbed a warm tortilla and stood behind them as they went over their strategy. They confirmed the positioning of the men, discussed the possible use of dynamite, taking extra horses, and how to best use the element of surprise.

''The guards overseeing the river operation are stationed here and here,'' said Joaquin, pointing to the areas with a slender, bare pine branch. ''The slave camp is here, just down from the bend in the river. Half the slaves will be chained at their camp and half will be working in the river. The sluice boxes are down here, and the slaves working them are chained all the time to their boxes. They're guarded from this point on the riverbank, and their camp is here.''

It took Heller a few minutes of studying the map to understand what markings represented what. Once she did, however, she could easily follow the conversation, but their talk of the sluice boxes confused her.

''What's a sluice box?'' she asked, moving up close behind Joaquin.

''It's a rough wooden trough used to wash the soil away from the placer gold,'' he explained with sharp impatience, not bothering to look at her.

Any other time, she would have been irked by such

callous treatment, but his description—brief as it was—
triggered a memory. The day before the wedding,
Gordon had once again insisted she walk with him
along the river. They walked much farther than usual,
and he showed her how the gold was being mined.
The workers had been shoveling up mud and dumping
it into odd-looking wooden structures. Sluice boxes.
They'd worn leg irons, similar to the ones in Gordon's
San Francisco house, and they had been chained to the
sluice boxes. Only their camp wasn't where Joaquin
had pointed.

"Joaquin," she said, tapping his shoulder.

"*Sí* ? What is it, Heller?" He didn't look around.

Heller walked around in front of him to gain his full
attention. "The slaves that work the sluice boxes—
their camp is here, not there," she said, putting the
tip of her finger on the map. She explained how she
came by her information, then stood back and ner-
vously moistened her lips.

Lino stated the obvious. "The camp must have been
moved."

Joaquin stared at the map. "Do you see anything
else that doesn't look right to you?" His dark gaze
lifted, and she felt the heavy gravity of his question.

"No, but then I haven't seen all of El Dorado, only
what Luther would allow me to see."

A muscle quivered in Joaquin's cheek, betraying his
frustration. "I'm sorry I was short with you, Heller.
Your information is of great importance. It could save
lives. We all owe you a debt of gratitude." He stood
and took a step toward her.

She knew he was going to kiss her, and she looked
forward to the moment with excitement. She drew a
sharp breath when he cupped her chin in the curve of
his hand and bent toward her and touched his lips to
hers. The kiss lasted only a moment, but it was a mo-

ment she would never forget. When he backed away and returned his attention to the map, she wondered how one small kiss could have such an overwhelming effect.

Because you love him, her subconscious reminded her; only she didn't need reminding, she knew. She went off to find Abigail.

Toward sunset, Pepe and Wong Ho started calling the camp to supper. Heller and Abigail pitched in to help pass out tin plates piled with food. At length, Heller took her plate and sat down on a log. She was studying her portion of meat, trying to determine what it was, when Lino Toral sat down beside her.

"It's quail," he informed her, then began to eat.

"Oh, I was wondering." Copying Lino, she picked it up and took a small bite. "It's good. I'm surprised. Well, not *really* surprised. Maybe relieved is a better word. I wasn't sure what to expect." She realized she was making needless conversation, when what she really wanted was to ask him about Joaquin. "Señor Toral—"

"Lino, please."

She laughed. "All right, then, Lino. Obviously you're Joaquin's friend and confidant. There's so much about him I don't know that I want to know, but I fear I'll never learn it from him. I get the impression that he dislikes talking about himself."

"He's a very private man," Lino offered, "but I may be able to tell you what you want to know without breaking a confidence."

"How long have you known each other?"

"We grew up together. Our mothers were friends and our *haciendas* were just a few miles apart."

"What about his father? Does Joaquin take after him? He must have been a very strong influence to have fashioned such a son."

"Joaquin never met his father, which is, by the way, a subject I wouldn't broach if I were you. His father was a Yankee by the name of Ross. He came from Virginia to California with his younger brother. Both were civil engineers and were employed by several of the most influential and wealthy dons. He met Joaquin's mother while she was visiting a cousin in San Diego, but he left her soon afterward, unaware that she was expecting his child."

She nodded, understanding perfectly. "I know what it's like to be raised a bastard. For a boy, I would think it would be even worse." She worked on her supper a moment as she tried to decide how to ask the next question. "Lino. I was wondering about his relationship with Elena Valdez. They seem . . . so devoted to each other."

Lino nodded. "It goes back many years, Heller. Elena grew up near us. She's loved Joaquin from the time she was old enough to know the meaning of the word."

"But he married Rosita," Heller supplied. "She must have been very upset."

Lino rolled his eyes and chuckled. "Upset? *Sí,* you could say that."

Heller frowned. "Was it you, Lino, who found him after Mauger had whipped him?"

"Elena and me. We had been coming to visit when we found him. He insisted we bury Rosita before we did anything to help him. Elena was the only one who didn't grieve—not a single tear. But she tended Joaquin night and day for weeks until he healed. She was there for him again after the ambush at the Cantua. If it hadn't been for Pepe and Elena, Joaquin would be dead."

Heller looked down at her plate. She had misjudged the sharp-tongued señorita; she wasn't a whore, after all. Simply, pitifully, a woman desperately in love. "I feel sorry for her," Heller said sadly, "because Joaquin will always love Rosita." The words had no sooner come out of her mouth than she realized the truth of them. It was like a blow to her senses. She supposed that what she needed to know now was whether he could love her as well. And if he could, could she stand knowing that she had only half his heart? She bit into a forkful of beans and chewed them slowly. Swallowing, she said, "That's why he's doing all this, isn't it?" She turned her gaze to a group of men who appeared to be engaged in serious conversation. "It's all for her."

"*Sí*," Lino agreed. "He will always love Rosita, Heller. She was but a girl when he married her and brought her to El Dorado, and a girl still when she died in his arms. We carried her body up here and buried her in a chamber at the back of the cave."

"Here? Oh, God. I didn't know." A chill chased itself down Heller's spine.

"You mustn't be like Elena and be jealous of that love, Heller. But you must respect it. Rosita will always be a part of his life—a bittersweet memory. There is no harm in memories. Thanks to you, El Jefe has learned to love again. You will be a good wife to him."

Heller laughed. "Wife?" She sobered quickly. "You *know* that he loves me, Lino?" She could barely believe she was speaking this way to a perfect stranger, but there was something about Lino Toral's easy manner that made her want to confide in him. Then she remembered. He'd been a monk.

"*Sí*, I know El Jefe loves you. And as soon as this is over, he will take you back to Mexico with him and we will have a real wedding and a fiesta."

Heller knew he was talking to her, but she couldn't hear a word he said. Instead, she studied the mass of beans on her plate and felt her stomach turn. She set the plate aside and stood. "Thank you, Lino. I feel better for having talked with you. I—" She felt light-headed and reached down to touch Lino's shoulder to steady herself. "I guess I got up too fast. I feel a little dizzy. I'm sorry if I seem abrupt, but I think I need to go in and lie down."

She had only just snuggled into the skins when Joaquin came into the chamber and lit a small oil lamp. "Lino said you didn't eat your supper, that you aren't feeling well. Maybe you need to see a doctor."

"I don't need to see a doctor," she protested, warmed by his worried look. "Wong Ho's food isn't quite what I'm used to, if you know what I mean. I've never seen such an odd combination: Mexican beans and Chinese quail." She raised her hand to her mouth to stifle a giggle, but she couldn't hold it back. And when Joaquin started to laugh, she burst out and laughed until there were tears streaming down her face. "I'm in love with you, you know," she said, surprising herself at her bold admission. She hadn't meant to tell him, but it just came out.

He knelt down next to her and touched a lock of her hair. "I love you too, *mia cara*. I never thought I would say that to anyone again."

"Joaquin, there's so much we need to talk about. I want you to tell me about Rosita. I want to know what she was like." *Am I as pretty as she was?* she wondered. *Do I satisfy you as much as she did?* It was ridiculous to wonder if she was a good as a dead woman, but she couldn't help herself. Rosita, it seemed, had no equal. How could she ever hope to measure up? "And there're so many misunderstand-ings—"

He put his finger to her lips. "No, Heller. Rosita is dead, and any misunderstandings we had are all in the past now. We have only our future to think about, all the new tomorrows.'' He unbuttoned his shirt and tossed it aside.

In the glow of the oil lamp, his hard-muscled shoulders shone like burnished gold. She longed to reach out and touch the springy hair that covered his heavily muscled chest, longed to trace the dark trail that led beneath the waist of his pants.

He turned his back on her and pulled off his boots and stripped off his pants. Her eyes widened when she saw the dozen or more whip marks that crisscrossed his back. Deep scars. Terrible scars. She wondered how anyone could have survived such a whipping. She raised up and ran her fingertips over the white ridges. ''Oh, Joaquin.''

She flattened her palms and splayed her fingers against his broad back and began a slow massage. She rubbed his shoulders, kneaded the muscles beneath his shoulder blades, then pressed her thumbs into various places along his spine. ''Feel good?'' His nod emboldened her to move up behind him and pull him back against her while she massaged his arms. The thick veins below the surface of his skin bulged even though his muscles weren't flexed. Closing her eyes, she braved another move and reached her arms around his waist and began massaging his stomach, which went rigid at her touch. It was doubtful she would been so daring if she were facing him.

''Heller.'' He swung around and took her into his embrace. ''You're a constant surprise.'' He started working the buttons of her dress—her wedding dress. ''One of these days, I'm going to buy you some new dresses, without buttons.''

She giggled and leaned into him. ''I don't think they make dresses without buttons.''

''Then we'll have a dressmaker design some. I don't

want to have to go through a battlement of buttons every time I want to make love to you.'' His impatience at an end, he didn't wait until she had wriggled out of the dress before he kissed her.

''Do you think that will be often?'' she asked, her voice already husky with desire.

He growled against her mouth. ''Just every day for the rest of our lives.'' His mouth was fiercely insistent, twisting across hers, demanding she open to him. And when she did, his hot probing tongue elicited a series of moans from her that seemed to increase his desire.

Joaquin reacted to Heller's moans with a passion that surprised even him. Never had he lost control where women were concerned. He had always prided himself on being the kind of man who could keep his head even while indulging himself in sexual pleasures. But now all that was changing—changing so rapidly he hardly had time to realize what was happening.

Ever since that night in Heller's hotel room, he had dreamed about the moment when he would again be able to hold her, touch her, make love to her. He had spent many a sleepless night thinking about her, remembering both her boldness and her shyness. Then, he had wondered what she was about. Now he knew. And because he knew, his need for her was fierce, and though he willed himself to go slowly, mindful that lovemaking was still new to her, he found that his body was giving the orders, not his head.

He laid her back against the thick pile of furry skins. She snuggled down and held out her arms to him, inviting him to join her, an invitation he couldn't resist. He finished undressing her and quickly covered her lush body with his and breathed a sigh of relief.

This was where he belonged and this is where he would stay, he told himself. Heller was everything a man could want, the El Dorado of his heart, his golden reward. He could search the world over and not find another woman such as she: both fire and ice, he thought, not for the first time.

He pulled her on top of him and kissed her, then he raised her and suckled her breast. She tasted as sweet as honey. He pulled her taut nipples into his mouth and teased the tight buds with his tongue. He heard her draw a ragged breath and felt her body come alive atop his. Her legs straddled his hips, and she moved against him with increasing urgency. She seemed to literally vibrate with her need—a need not unlike his own. With his hands spanning her waist, he gently coaxed her to move lower and lower still, until the tip of his manhood was firmly pressed against the core of her femininity. Her wet heat made his senses reel.

"Joaquin—I don't think this is how—"

"Trust me, *querida,* there are many ways to make love." He lifted her hips above his, then brought her down on top of him. He groaned in ecstasy as her femininity slid down and surrounded him. "*Dios,* you make me forget myself. You make me . . ." His words died on his lips as he pushed himself up inside her as far as he could go. "You feel so . . . good," he said, grasping her hips and showing her the rhythm. He felt her muscles simultaneously tense and relax and knew she was unaware of the extraordinary pleasure her involuntary responses were giving him.

Lost in a world of heady physical sensation, he stopped playing the teacher and let her do what came naturally to her. She held herself above him, her spine arched, her head thrown back so that her glorious unbound hair fell behind her and tickled the tops of his thighs.

As his thrusts became more frantic, she leaned forward, putting her hands on his chest to keep her balance. Her hair fell forward and made a curtain that enclosed them.

"Joaquin—I—"

He heard the desperation in her voice and knew what it was she wanted. "I know, Heller. I know. Soon. Very soon," he assured her. Holding her, he turned her onto her back and reversed their positions, driving himself into her with all the power he possessed. Almost immediately, he felt her body spasm and heard her cry of pleasure. He gave her a moment to savor the feeling before he took his own pleasure with a last powerful thrust that sent his seed deep into her womb.

Long minutes later, still wrapped in each other's arms, still intimately joined, they talked quietly.

"I don't think I'll ever understand you, Joaquin Murieta." Her voice sounded rusty, unused, and a little breathless.

He eased himself out of her and groaned at the sudden chill. "Is that so important to you?" Lying on his side, he covered her breast with his hand and squeezed gently.

"Yes. I don't know why. I only know that it is."

Lifting up, he ran his tongue over her nipple. "What is there to understand? I told you before. I am a man— no different than any other."

She turned on her side and stared at him knowingly. "No, Joaquin. That's not true. You aren't the same as other men. I know that now. That guard was right, and though I don't agree with the word *peculiar*, I'm convinced there *is* something very different about you—something that can't be explained. It's as if you possess some sort of magic. And the wind—I want to know, to understand."

How could he explain what he himself didn't understand? "There is no magic, Heller, only the inability of men to see what is right before their eyes.'' Lovingly, his hand traced over the softness of her stomach.

She nestled her head into his shoulder. ''Who are you, Joaquin? A man? A myth? A devil? Or an angel? Tell me so that I may know.''

''Only a man, Heller. A man who loves you, who will always love you.''

How much more clear could he make it? Rosita was his past, his youth, just as Mam was her past and her youth. For Joaquin, that past was now behind him and he was free to open his heart to the future, their future. Long into the night, she thought about the twists and turns her life had taken and about her feelings for her mam.

Swallowing back a sob, she freed the emotions that had been pent up inside her ever since her intimate conversation with Abigail. ''I forgive you, Mam. Please forgive me,'' she whispered into the stillness of the cave.

Joaquin mumbled sleepily and reached out for her. She nestled closer in his arms, savored the warmth of his hard, muscular body, and thought she had never felt better, or felt more loved, than she did right now.

At last, she slept.

Chapter 19

It seemed to Heller that she had just fallen asleep when she heard echoing footsteps, followed by Lino's voice.

"Joaquin. Joaquin, wake up."

Joaquin sat up abruptly. "What is it?" He looked around, then saw Lino.

"Sorry to wake you, but Levi just rode in. He saw Mauger's guards return."

Joaquin shook himself awake. "Then they couldn't have gone to Mariposa."

"No. He has no idea where they went, but they came back with some old friends of ours. Sam Murdock and his coyote pack. Ten of them all together. They brought a packhorse loaded down with rifles and ammunition."

"*Sangre de Christo*!" Joaquin jumped to his feet. "Sounds like we've got trouble."

"What do you want to do?" asked Lino.

"I think we need to talk to the men." Joaquin dressed quickly, buckled on his gun belt, tied the leather thongs around his thighs, then left the chamber with Lino.

Though pretending to be asleep, Heller had heard every word. Yesterday, the chances of Joaquin and the band taking El Dorado and freeing the slaves would have been good, but today things were different. Now, if she'd interpreted Lino's information correctly, ten professional gunmen, loaded down with weapons and ammunition, had been brought in to help Mauger in his fight against Joaquin.

As soon as Joaquin left the chamber with Lino, Heller sat up. In her excitement over having been rescued from El Dorado, she hadn't considered the ramifications of her leaving. By rescuing her, Joaquin had forfeited the information she had been passing on to him during his visits. He still had his spies, of course, who kept him well-advised of the majority of the activities, but as in the case of Alvarado's whipping, this was something the spies hadn't been able to anticipate. Had she been more aware at that time, she could have easily discovered Gordon's plans and might possibly have been able to prevent it from happening.

Just as she might have been privy to Gordon's plans to hire the gunmen.

Without conscious invitation, a plan to help Joaquin began to take form in her head. She would have to return to El Dorado, to Gordon Pierce. She would be taking a huge risk, because it would only work if she could make him believe that Joaquin had taken her against her will. But it was a risk worth taking if, by paying very careful attention to everything that was going on around her, she could provide Joaquin with information that would help him achieve his goals.

Twice, as she was buttoning her dress and finger-combing her hair, she considered abandoning her plan. The last week had worn her down to where she was constantly fatigued. No amount of sleep seemed to help. But then she thought about Mauger's Cantonese slave girls, about Alvarado and the other slaves held at El Dorado, and about Rosita Murieta. She wondered what kind of future there would be for her and Joaquin if he didn't carry out his revenge. But she knew the answer. None.

Heller took a deep breath, resolutely filled herself with purpose, and started poking through Joaquin's personal items until she found what she needed: a piece of paper and a pencil. Thinking quickly, she wrote:

Joaquin, I overheard you and Lino talking. You're out-numbered and out-weaponed. I knew if I went back to El Dorado, I could help your cause by continuing to spy for you. I'll tell Mauger that I escaped you. He'll believe me. In spite of himself, I believe he has fallen in love with me and wants me to love him. Day after tomorrow, I'll leave you a message in the tree where the guard left his gold.

I love you.
Heller

She left Joaquin's sleeping chamber and entered the main chamber. It was empty. The men were beginning to gather outside around the larger campfire. Figuring whoever saw her leave the cave would think she was going to attend to personal needs, she hurried along the path that led behind the cave, where the horses were corralled. She looked around for a saddle, and finding none, decided it wouldn't do any good anyway. Her long-ago training didn't include saddling a horse. She would have to ride bareback. She hoped she still remembered how.

Singling Lino's chestnut out of the herd, she led him to the corral gate and tied a rope to the rings on either side of his halter. "Now, listen, horse. It's been a long time since I've ridden, so behave yourself." Without a bit, she wasn't going to have a great deal of control, but she'd heard Lino brag on how well-behaved the gelding was, and she hoped he was right.

Grabbing a hunk of the chestnut's mane, Heller used the bottom rung of the corral gate to vault herself onto the horse's back. The horse nickered as she settled herself and adjusted her skirts. Then she nudged him into a slow walk and tested her rope-reins by guiding him around in a wide circle. Finally, she felt confident enough to leave the corral and start down the mountain.

The way out of the camp was hidden from where the men gathered at front of the cave. She knew no one would see her leave, but she also knew it was only a matter of time before her absence was discovered and Lino found out his horse had been stolen.

Halfway down the mountain, when the narrow road became less steep, Heller urged the gelding into a trot, then at the base of the mountain, she dared a slow canter.

Sometime later, as she neared the stand of trees and the entrance of El Dorado, a warning shot rang out. Heller pulled on the rope reins, bringing the horse to a stop. A trio of Gordon's men came galloping out of the trees, their rifles at the ready. Heller prayed they would recognize her.

"Jesus H. Christ. It's her," Hank shouted to his friends. He broke into a gallop, came up beside her, and grabbed the rope out of her hands.

Heller pretended to look utterly relieved. "Oh, thank goodness. I wasn't sure I'd be able to find my way back. I've been riding for hours and hours. I thought I was lost."

"Back from where?" asked another man.

"From Murieta's camp. Where do you think? I escaped him late last night, stole one of the bandit's horses, and rode as fast as I was able."

Hank looked at her in disbelief. "You escaped Murieta?"

To avoid having to give an answer, Heller pretended to feel faint. She touched her hand to her brow. "Why, yes, I—Oh—Please, just take me back to the ranch and I'll explain.''

Hank reached out a hand to steady her. "Hold on there, we'll get you back. Hold on." Taking charge of her reins, he pulled the chestnut behind him while the others rode close beside her.

Gordon's reception was not at all what Heller expected. He seemed overjoyed to see her. He pulled her off her horse and hugged her. "Heller! I can't believe you escaped. Are you all right? Where's Abigail?"

"She wasn't where I could get to her," Heller lied. "So I had to leave her." She pulled out of his embrace and tried to look wretchedly desperate. "We have to get her back, Gordon. She's in grave danger." She burst into tears, which wasn't hard to do when she thought about what was at stake. "You don't know him. He's evil. He'll kill her. I know he will. He'll do anything to get to you. He hates you!"

At this point, all she could do was hope her act had been convincing, because if it wasn't, if he suspected she was lying, she would face more than the dreaded wedding night.

"Yes, I know," was all he said. Putting his arm around her, he helped her to the house. "You must be exhausted. I'll have Lu bring you a bath and lots of hot water."

Installed in her old room, Heller sat down on the edge of the bed and massaged her forehead. She hoped she hadn't done something she'd regret. She'd counted on Gordon's professed love for her to gain his confidence. Once she had that, she would have the freedom she needed to pass along important information. She was also counting on him sympathizing with her plight and not demanding what he thought were his husbandly rights for a few days. Hopefully, it wouldn't take any longer than that for Joaquin to accomplish what he needed to do.

Later that morning, having had her bath and a hot meal, Gordon came to her room and asked her if she would join him in the *sala*.

"Heller, I want you to meet Sam Murdock. I hired him and his men to find you and to capture Murieta. Sit down and tell him everything you know about Murieta's hideout."

Heller had barely taken her seat when Murdock began questioning her. "Just exactly how *did* you escape, Mrs. Pierce? Murieta isn't the kind of man to lower his guard and allow a prisoner to get away."

Murdock was a bear of a man. He towered over her, trying to intimidate her with his size and his bulk. He was as ugly as he was big, with wild brown hair and gold eyes—cat eyes. His face was deeply lined and his skin looked as tough as old saddle leather.

"It was after everyone had fallen asleep. I got up and sneaked out of the cave and stole a horse. As I told your guards, Gordon," she said, emphasizing her preference to talk to him rather than Murdock, "I rode all night. I wasn't certain how to get back here. If Hank and his men hadn't found me, I'm not sure I would have ever found El Dorado."

Murdock jumped on her answer. "You said you sneaked out of the *cave*. "Where is this cave? Can you take me to it?"

Heller pretended to give the matter some thought, but in truth she was damning herself for mentioning it. She would have to be very careful of her answers from now on. She would never forgive herself if she gave anything away. "It was dark when we reached the cave and dark when I escaped. I have no idea where it's located. All I know is that it took me a lot longer to get back here than it took Murieta to get us there."

Murdock paced the floor. Every so often he would turn, ask another question, and glare at her with those cat-gold eyes. Sensing that he was astute enough to mentally log her answers and then analyze them later for content and continuity, she endeavored to keep them brief and indefinite.

After more than an hour of unrelenting questions, Heller rose from her chair and exclaimed in irritation, "Gordon, I'm tried of being interrogated by this man. I've told him everything I know. I escaped Murieta and came back here—to you, in spite of *everything*," she said pointedly, "because I thought there might be a chance for us. But if this is your way of showing me how much you care for me, then I would have been better off with Murieta. With him, at least we would have been ransomed!"

Gordon inclined his head. "That's enough, Murdock. I think she's answered your questions as best she can. Leave her alone for now."

Triumphant, Heller stood up. "If you don't mind, I think I'll lie down for a while. It's been an exhausting few days." Gordon walked her down the hallway to her bedroom. At her closed door she turned around, trying not to show her nervousness. "Thank you for coming to my rescue. He made me feel like I was on trial. Who is he, anyway? And why is he here? He's an extremely unpleasant man."

"He's a bounty hunter. The best bounty hunter west of the Mississippi. Murieta still has a price on his head and Murdock intends to collect it." He took her hand in his and twisted the wedding ring around her finger. "I'm sorry he upset you, but his questions were necessary. I'll see you at supper."

But at supper time, when Gordon came to collect her, he found her still sleeping, and when, after supper, he checked again and still found her sleeping, he went into the *sala*—to his pipe.

Heller woke up just as fatigued as when she'd lain down yesterday afternoon, over eighteen hours ago! She'd never slept that long in one stretch in her whole life. Now that she thought about it, she hadn't been herself since the end of June. She'd experienced a gamut of symptoms: nausea, light-headedness, fatigue, even swollen ankles.

She threw back the bedclothes and leaped out of bed, only to become so dizzy she had to sit back down.

"What on earth—Oh, no. I can't be—Oh, God." The answer was all too clear. She was pregnant! Grabbing one of her pillows and hugging it against her, she tried to think when she'd had her last menses. Two weeks before boarding the train in San Francisco— around the middle of May. And this was . . . Good Lord, this was the eleventh of July. Still holding the pillow, she sat back and wondered what Joaquin would say when he found out. Would he be pleased? What if he wasn't—No, she wouldn't even think such a thing. Of course he would be pleased, and he would want to marry her immediately. Wouldn't he? If he didn't marry her, she would be left to return to Boston and raise her child herself—a bastard, just like Mam had, just like Joaquin's mother had.

Reaching her hand beneath her nightgown, she touched her stomach and tried to imagine the child that was growing within her. Her child. Joaquin's child. Created that night in her hotel room.

Suddenly, her mind reeled with a thought so devastating that she felt like she'd been kicked in the stomach. She had casually assumed that she was carrying Joaquin's child, when, in fact, it could just as easily be Luther Mauger's!

* * *

Joaquin couldn't remember ever having been so angry. An hour after he'd left her sleeping, he stormed out of his chamber, note in hand, and presented it to Abigail, who stood near the campfire sipping her morning coffee and talking to Pepe.

Abigail read the hastily scribbled message and cried out in disbelief, "Oh, dear Lord! Whatever was she thinking?"

"You tell me," Joaquin rejoined. "She's your niece."

"I have no idea. I haven't seen her since supper last night."

"And she didn't say anything then about her plans?"

"No. Nothing. She was talking to your lieutenant, Señor Toral."

Turning on his heel and walking away, Joaquin found Lino returning from the corral, looking, for all the world, as though he was about to shoot the first person who crossed his path. "Somebody stole my horse!" he shouted when he saw Joaquin.

"That damn fool woman," Joaquin spat out contemptuously. He handed Lino the message. "She's going to get herself killed, that's what she's going to do."

"Calm down. It won't do any good to—"

"I'm not going to calm down, dammit! That female just may have cost me my revenge, not to mention the lives of those slaves." Clenching his hands into fists, he continued, "When I get my hands on her, I'm going to wring her pretty little neck. And if you try to stop me, I'll wring yours, too!"

"*Sí, mi jefe. Sí.* Let's go talk to the men again and tell them what's happened. Then we can make a decision about what to do. Maybe things aren't as bad as they seem. Maybe Heller has a point. If she succeeds in making Mauger think she escaped you, he'll trust her more and she'll be able to help in getting past Murdock's bounty hunters.''

The men voted to do whatever El Jefe thought best. And best, Joaquin decided, was to watch El Dorado and wait to see what kind of information Heller provided over the next few days.

All that day and the next, Joaquin and his men watched the comings and going at El Dorado. During the day, Mauger's guards diligently patrolled the valley floor like desert troopers, while at night, Murdock, along with four of his men, scouted the outer reaches of El Dorado. They'd followed the river south several miles, then turned around and rode north.

They were looking for the hideout.

In the hour before the dawn of the third day, Joaquin and Lino rode down the mountain. Skirting their usual route, they rode through the river to hide their tracks. Leaving Lino to wait for him behind an outcropping of boulders, Joaquin cautiously made his way on foot up close to the house, to the tree Heller had mentioned in her message. True to her word, she had left him a note stuck deep inside the hole.

With the rumpled piece of paper tucked inside his shirt, he then headed toward the corral. His low-pitched whistle brought Lino's big chestnut to the gate. ''Come on boy, there's somebody real anxious to get you back,'' he said, blowing against the animal's muzzle. He threw his leg over the gelding's bare back, bent low over his neck, and rode him out of the corral, using only the pressure of his knees and the animal's halter to guide him. A patrol of four guards came around the south side of the house, heading toward the corral. Joaquin kneed the chestnut around and carefully walked him into the trees where they stood unmoving, until the guards started to dismount. Their loud conversation while they unsaddled their horses gave Joaquin the cover he needed to continue his escape.

Not until Joaquin and Lino returned to the cave did Joaquin read Heller's note.

> *I hope you've forgiven me by now and understand that I had to do this, to help the slaves, you, and me. Mauger seems to have believed my story. He's been a perfect gentleman and has kept his distance. In all truth, he seems different somehow. Preoccupied.*
>
> *Now that Murdock is running things, Mauger spends much of his time sitting in the* sala *smoking his pipe and staring at the wall. Marta, the cook, told me he was smoking opium. She also told me he was haunted by his old memories and that the opium helped him to forget. I think I know what's haunting him, Joaquin. Rosita.*
>
> *As I mentioned, Murdock has taken over things here. Overnight, he's organized Gordon's men and has been sending them out on patrols to find your cave. That's my one mistake. I accidentally mentioned the cave to Murdock when he was questioning me, but no one seems to have any idea where it is. If they continue searching the way they have been, they're bound to eventually find it.*
>
> *You need to know that Murdock and his men sleep during the day so they can be on guard at night, which is when they anticipate a visit from you. Murdock's bedroom is next to mine, where Abigail was. He has nine men, and they sleep all over the house. I'll leave a new note the day after tomorrow, when I know more.*
>
> *Love,*
> *Heller*

Joaquin was relieved to know that Mauger accepted her story, and that he'd been keeping his distance, though he questioned such uncharacteristic behavior. Mauger had always been one to take what he wanted when he wanted it, and Joaquin knew full well that he wanted Heller.

The information she'd passed along would prove particularly useful, and he was grudgingly proud of her in spite of the fact that he was still so angry he could hardly see straight.

Later that night, inside the main chamber, which was lit by torches, Joaquin and Lino discussed Heller's information with the band.

Santos was the first to speak. "We've wasted enough time. If we wait any longer, they will find our camp. I vote we ride to El Dorado tomorrow!"

His suggestion was accompanied by a chorus of agreeing murmurs.

Joaquin looked at Lino. "And what does my lieutenant say?"

"I agree with Santos. The longer we wait, the more we risk: the band, the slaves, and Heller."

"It will take more than one raid," Joaquin pointed out. "And whoever is left behind will be at great risk." In his heart, Joaquin knew Heller would be one of those left behind. But there was no help for it. There were many slaves—fifty or more. Even if everything went perfectly, they could only hope to rescue a small number of them at once.

Abigail looked around anxiously. "Do you think you should wait for Heller's next note? She may have gained even more valuable information. She— Oh, my. I will never forgive her for this foolishness. She is such a headstrong girl. I suppose it is the Irish in her."

Joaquin gave a thin smile, then turned back to face his men. "*Amigos,* we'll begin with the upriver operation and capture the slaves there. Santos, tell Ocho and Pepe that it will be up to them to ride in with those extra horses after we've rounded up the guards. They're to get the slaves mounted and back to camp as quickly as possible. Most of them will have to ride double." He moved over to the map. "Now, let's go over everyone's position one more time."

It wasn't yet midnight when the lookout screeched

like an owl to signal the camp. The men jumped to
their feet, their weapons drawn and ready. Joaquin positioned himself near the mountain road, hiding himself behind a tree. Nothing could have surprised him
more than when a familiar figure came galloping toward him, her horse sweating and winded.

"Elena!" Joaquin stepped out in front of her horse,
grabbed for the bridle, and pulled the animal to a halt.
"What the hell are you doing here?"

Wearing a fawn-colored split skirt and fancy leather
riding boots, Elena Valdez put her weight in a stirrup,
threw her leg around behind her, and jumped down
into Joaquin's arms.

"I knew you would be here." She sounded breathless. "I knew it."

"Answer my question, Elena. What are you doing
here?"

The men reholstered their weapons and went about
their business.

Elena made a moue. "I have come back to you,
querido. I knew you didn't really want to say good-
bye, so I swallowed my pride, and as the French say,
voila!" She twisted away from him and gazed around
at the camp. "Ah, Joaquin. It is just like the old days,
yes?"

"No. It is not at all like the old days," he said,
holding himself back from taking her by the shoulders
and shaking her senseless. "You don't belong here. I
want you to get up on that horse and go back to San
Francisco."

"I did not come from San Francisco. I was in Sacramento, playing the new theater there, when I heard
the rumor that Joaquin Murieta, *El Bandido Notorio,*
had returned to El Dorado. And so it is true. you have
returned. Why, Joaquin? What is it that you do here?

Tell me and I will consider going back—that is, if I am satisfied with your answer.''

''You're a bitch, Elena, but then you always were.'' He walked away from her, his hands tight at his sides. He had to get away from her before he did something he would regret.

From the shadows, Joaquin watched as Elena unsaddled her horse and removed her saddlebags. She strolled into the firelight and introduced herself to the men. Levi Ortega and Pepe she hugged and kissed like the long-lost friends that they were. Lino she ignored as if he didn't exist. Then, turning toward the cave entrance, she espied Abigail Peyton.

''You!''

Warned by her tone, Joaquin left the shadows. ''Elena.''

She turned wrathful eyes on him. ''What is this *gringa* doing here? And where is the other one—the paper-skinned one?''

Abigail stiffened her spine and drew herself up. ''The *other one*, my niece, has put herself in grave danger as a spy in Mr. Mauger's home.''

''A spy?'' Elena whirled around to confront Joaquin.

Joaquin ignored her questioning look. ''If you want answers, ask someone else.'' He waved the woman named Lupe over and told her in Spanish to find Señorita Valdez a place to bed down.

''No,'' Elena protested vehemently, holding her saddlebags close to her. ''I will sleep in El Jefe's chamber.''

Abigail cocked an eyebrow.

Joaquin grabbed the saddlebags and bedroll from Elena and handed them to Lupe. ''You'll sleep where Lupe puts you or you go. *Comprende?*''

* * *

The sun was high in the sky when Joaquin and his band galloped their horses across the Stanislaus River and captured the half-dozen guards who had been watching over their charges from the bank while they ate their noon meal. Joaquin counted almost twenty slaves. They had been working knee-deep in icy mountain water, shoveling river sand into flour sacks.

The guards had given up without a shot being fired. Brandishing their Colts, Joaquin and Lino covered Santos, Levi, and the others while they blindfolded and tied the guards, then put them onto their own horses.

Meantime, Pepe and Ocho were busy helping the weakened slaves get mounted onto the string of spare horses they'd brought.

Galloping hooves announced the approach of more of Mauger's men. Joaquin turned to see four riders, coming from the direction of the house.

Joaquin called out behind him. "Santos, take those men back to the cave. Lino and I will take care of things here." Over his shoulder, Joaquin saw that Pepe and Ocho had the slave rescue under control and were heading out. "Lino, you take right, I'll take left." They wheeled their horses around and took up their positions.

Lino yanked his Winchester out of its scabbard and rested the butt against his shoulder, looked through the sight, and fired.

His knees tight against El Tigre's sides, Joaquin readied his Colts. He waited a moment longer than Lino, until the riders were within pistol range, then he fired, first one, then the other, causing a continuous barrage of bullets.

Two of the men were blown out of their saddles, the third jumped off his horse and hid behind a tree, but Lino, riding around, then behind him, called him out of his hiding place into the open, where he forced the man to throw down his weapons.

The fourth man yelled a challenge to Joaquin. "Just you and me, Murieta. One on one. They say you're the fastest there ever was and now's your chance to prove it, because I say I'm the fastest."

"As you wish, señor." With Lino providing cover, Joaquin dismounted. He took his time reloading, then he spun the cylinder and reholstered the Colt. "Ready when you are, *amigo.*"

"On the count of five."

Joaquin started the count. "One." He took a step forward. He didn't bother to watch the man's gun-hand, which hovered over his holster; he could find out everything he needed to know by watching his eyes. "Two. Three. Four."

Joaquin saw his opponent's eyes narrow. He drew and fired.

The other man barely had a chance to clear leather before he realized he'd been killed.

Back at camp, Santos was put in charge of incarcerating the captured guards. He took them to one of the lower chambers and posted his own guards. Elena made herself useful by supervising the care and treatment of the slaves. She directed the women as to how to tend their wounds. Those men who were well enough were given a poke of gold, a horse, and sent home to their families.

Using Heller's information about Murdock's schedule, Joaquin made a second trip down the mountain later that night. He and eight men circled El Dorado until they encountered Murdock's midnight patrol. As the five riders entered the clearing beyond the trees, the bandits opened fire. Like an army general, Murdock ordered his men into the trees. While only one

of Murdock's men was killed, Joaquin managed to
wing Murdock himself.

The next night, as Joaquin stole up to the tree to
collect Heller's note, Lino, Levi, and Santos set the
bunkhouse on fire, causing a diversion that took everyone's attention.

Back at camp, he read the note.

> *Murdock's wound proved to be much more serious than
> it first appeared. He lost a lot of blood. Without him, his
> men are unwilling to act on their own in spite of Gor-
> don's insistence. And as for Gordon's guards, many of
> them have lost their will to fight you. Zeke, the mine
> operations foreman, is leaving Saturday morning with six
> men for Angels Camp. They're taking a small shipment
> of gold.*
>
>   *Heller*

There were no more tears left to cry. Murdock stood
in front of Heller, his great bulk so close she could
smell his sweat. He slapped her hard across the face.
"I'm tired of your lies, Mrs. Pierce. I've had my men
watching you. You've been leaving him notes, telling
him what's going on here, and he's acted on what
you've told him. He'll believe anything you say."

Heller's head reeled. She would have to curb her
tongue if she was going to survive this. She not only
had Joaquin and his band to think about, but the rest
of the slaves . . . and the baby.

In spite of being proved a spy, Heller sensed that
Gordon was sympathetic. When Murdock leaned over
her and started threatening her with various tortures,
Gordon stopped him as before.

"Leave her alone, Murdock. I was a fool to trust
her, but she's my wife and I'll handle her in my own
way, in my own time."

Murdock left the *sala,* slamming the door behind

him. Heller's mouth tasted of the dust that the door had stirred up. "Gordon, please—"

"Please?" he interjected. He leveled a look on her that made her draw into herself. "You bitch! You're like every other woman! A goddamn liar. You weren't Murieta's prisoner. You were his whore!"

Heller's whole body shook uncontrollably. "No, Gordon. You're wrong. How can you even think such a thing?"

"Because I remember how you looked at him when he danced with you at the ball. And I remember the look on your face when he left you standing there in the middle of the ballroom. You're in love with him, goddammit! You're in love with my enemy!"

Heller didn't try to deny it; she knew nothing she could say would make him believe her. She'd been caught putting the message in the tree. The only thing she could do now was to try to scare him. "You can't win, you know. He's spent almost two decades hating you for what you did to him and his wife. He's dedicated his life to hunting you down to get his revenge. You couldn't kill him with your whip. Captain Harry Love and the California Rangers couldn't kill him. What makes you think you and Murdock can kill him? He's Joaquin Murieta. He's invincible! If he'd had a mind, he could have killed you a dozen times—that night at the theater, at the ball, at the museum . . ."

Gordon looked thunderstruck. "What are you saying? What do you mean he could have killed me at the theater and the museum? Murieta wasn't there, it was some Spanish—"

"Don Ricardo," she supplied, mockery curving her lips. "Don Ricardo *is* Joaquin Murieta, your enemy." She gave him a moment to ponder what she'd said. "He's watched your every move since he came to San Francisco. He bribed your Chinese broker into increasing the cost of goods and demanding immediate payment. He went to your bank and saw to it your loan was denied. He broke into your house and stole the bullwhip that you had used on him years ago. And he told Wells Fargo that you'd bribed a certain warden into letting you go.

"And you think you and Murdock can stop him from getting his revenge?" She shook her head. "No, Gordon, you'd better think again. There's nothing you can do. You can't even use me. I mean nothing to him. It's Elena Valdez that he loves and cares about. Think about that night at the theater and Elena's performance to the man in the box opposite ours. Don Ricardo. Joaquin Murieta." The last, of course, was a lie, but she wasn't above saying anything she thought would get to him. And she had. The blood had all but drained from his face, but he recuperated quickly.

He stomped across the room, grabbed her by the arm, and dragged her into his own personal suite of rooms.

Heller shrieked. "No, Gordon. Stop it. Let me go."

"Shut up, bitch or I'll make it even worse for you." He threw her down on the bed, then straddled her backside as he quickly bound her arms and legs and tied them to the bedposts. Grabbing the back of her dress, he gave it a savage jerk and ripped it down to her waist, then pulled it off her shoulders.

Heller was mindless with fear. She couldn't begin to control her sobbing or her shaking body. She turned her head to the side and saw him open a cupboard. A cupboard full of whips. He seemed to study them closely. At length, he took one out and held it in front of her.

"Now this one is a little beauty. Only four feet long. And look how thin the lash is."

"I'm pregnant, Gordon," she called out in desperation. "I'm pregnant with *your* child!"

He stood staring at her, his features twitching perculiarly. Then he laughed. It was a hollow, humorless laugh that echoed in her ears.

"My child?" He could hardly get out the words. Then, he sobered suddenly and glared at her. "No, Heller. You're not pregnant with my child because, you see, we've never made love. You only thought we did. That was chicken's blood you saw on the bedclothes." He nodded his head and laughed again. "Yes, Heller. Chicken's blood. Put there so you'd think I had compromised you and you'd agree to marry me. Chicken's blood, Heller, not virgin's blood!"

Tears of astonishment leaped into her eyes. She couldn't believe it and yet she knew it was true. "Y—you monster!"

The first strike took her breath away, effectively stopping her admonishment. With a flick of his wrist, the narrow lash bit into her shoulders and cut downward across the middle of her back. She pushed her face into the bed. She had barely caught her breath when the whip came again, striking her from the opposite direction. Biting down on her lip, she willed herself not to scream, fearing that it would only thrill him. After the fifth strike, she sensed by his comments that he was softening, and that if she whimpered like a wounded animal and begged, pleaded, for him to stop, he would. But her pride pushed her on, strengthening her will, and in the end, after the tenth lash, he threw down the whip and stalked out of the room.

She had won. The enemy had been vanquished.

Chapter 20

It was Marta, crooning encouraging and comforting words, who half-dragged, half-carried Heller back to her own room after Mauger had finished whipping her and gone to the *sala* to smoke his pipe. It was Marta who eased her onto the bed which had been thoughtfully stripped of pillows and coverings so that nothing but cool sheets would touch her skin.

Heller was grateful for Marta's help. With her knees weak and trembling, she could not have made it to the room on her own. The burning pain surpassed any she'd ever experienced. It was a hundred times worse than that of the previous whipping, and yet she inherently knew that it was nothing compared to what Alvarado or Joaquin had suffered.

"It is not so bad as the boy, Alvarado," said the old Mexican cook, her English broken and difficult to understand. Her observation gave Heller little comfort. "I think maybe you heal, but I worry for the little one." Heller's eyelids flew up and Marta confirmed her mute question. "*Sí*. I know about the little one. I have eyes, ears. I take good care of El Jefe's woman and pray for his child."

Heller wanted to trust her instincts but was afraid to. Marta worked for Gordon. A few kind words and a few smiles were all that had been exchanged between her and the cook since the day she'd arrived.

"Why? Why do you want to help me?" It was an effort to move her lips to speak.

Marta's expression turned somber. "Many years ago, El Jefe save Marta's life. I no forget."

A spark of hope ignited. If Marta was to be believed, then she felt she owed Joaquin a debt. "Marta, I need you to help me," she ventured, deciding there was nothing left to lose.

"*Sí*, I say I help you."

Heller closed her eyes and prayed she could make the woman understand. "No! Not me—I mean—" she cried out in frustration. She licked her lips and began again, slowly, distinctly. "I have to get a message to El Jefe. Have to warn him." She swallowed back a sob. "The message—in the tree. It's a lie, Marta. They made me write it!" She started to lift herself up, but Marta held her down.

"No, señorita. You need much rest. For the little one."

She wasn't strong enough to fight either the pain or Marta, so she gave up and settled back down. "Then, you must do it, Marta. You must get word to El Jefe that the message is a lie. Do you understand? If you don't—Gordon and Murdock, they'll kill him!"

"*Sí, sí*, I *comprende*, but how do I do this?"

With the last of her strength, Heller tried to tell Marta how to get to the cave. "You'll have to get a horse and—Get me a piece of paper and a pen. I'll draw you a map."

Marta shook her head. "Oh, no, señorita. Marta no ride horse."

Heller released a long sigh and the spark of hope died within her breast. Defeated, she wept.

Throughout the night, Marta stayed by Heller's bedside, laying cool wet cloths across her back and checking her for fever.

Two days later, Saturday, while Marta was in the kitchen cleaning up after the morning meal, the door to Heller's room burst open. She didn't have to guess who it was; the opium smoke that clung to Gordon's clothes had become familiar to her. She hadn't seen him since the night of the whipping.

"Get up, Heller."

She lay on her stomach, her face turned toward the window where a light breeze moved the curtains. She was naked, except for a muslin sheet that Marta kept draped over her bottom and legs. Gordon snatched the sheet away, then grabbed her arms and pulled her off the bed.

She gave an uncontrollable cry of pain. Her back had just begun to heal; the skin was stretched tight across her shoulder blades. "Gordon," she panted his name. "If you ever cared anything about me . . . Please, please don't hurt me anymore."

"*Cared* about you?" His voice lashed at her now as his whip had done two days ago. "Hell, yes, I cared about you. As a matter of fact, you're the first woman I've ever cared anything about. Goddammit, Heller, I even fancied myself in love with you. But that was before you betrayed me, with my enemy." He shook with fury and his hazel eyes darkened to the color of a smoke-filled sky. "Do you have any idea what your lover has put me through for the last twenty years?" he grated. "Not a day has gone by that I haven't regretted taking that job to run Murieta off his claim."

Heller's head snapped up. "Someone hired you? Who?" She was momentarily oblivious to her nakedness and her pain.

"I don't know who. Never did. I just took the money, rounded up three men, and did what I was paid to do. No questions asked." He looked down his nose at her. "Now get dressed. Murdock has a nice little rendezvous all set up." He flung her away from him.

Rendezvous? Biting down on her lip to stop herself from crying out, she walked over to the bureau. Bending ever so cautiously, slowly, she pulled her nightgown out of the drawer then dropped it over her head. It was the only garment she owned that wouldn't bind or cling. Bending over to put on her shoes, however, was impossible, and Gordon wasn't about to help, so she went without.

"Somehow I don't think your aunt would approve your attire, Heller," he commented sarcastically, then pointed her to the door leading outside to the *corredor*.

Girding herself with pride, Heller raised her head and walked out outside. Two horses had been brought up and were tethered to the tree where she had left Joaquin's messages. Assuming one of the horses was meant for her, she mustered her courage, put her left hand on the pommel, her foot in the stirrup, and pulled herself up onto the saddle. Pain ripped like eagle's talons across her back, from neck to waist, side to side, inside out. She clenched her jaw to stop herself from screaming.

Once Gordon mounted his horse, he snatched the reins out of her hand. "I'll take these just so you aren't tempted."

He led out at a fast trot to the north end of the valley, then up to a pine-covered hill, where he reined to a halt. The entire valley lay before her and off in the distance, she could see the rocky ledge that led to the cave. Below, from out of the stand of trees surrounding the house, came the freight wagon, headed north, toward the valley's exit.

She knew now what was meant by the rendezvous. Gordon had brought her here to this hilltop to watch an ambush. The freight wagon and the guards men-

tioned in the message she'd been forced to write would
be the bait that would bring Joaquin and the band out
of their hiding place into the open, into a trap.

Still holding Heller's reins, Gordon brought the two
horses side by side. From his pocket, he took a length
of rope and bound her hands together, then tied them
to her pommel. "If it hadn't been for you, Heller,
Murieta might have gotten his revenge." He leaned
farther across his saddle and stuffed a bandanna into
her mouth. While reaching for the second bandanna,
she spit out the first one.

"He'll still get his revenge," she railed, not bothering to hold back her hostility. She smiled at him with
cold triumph. "Because, you see, no matter what you
do to him, he'll come back." She lowered her voice
an octave. "You can't kill him, Gordon. *Nobody* can
kill Joaquin Murieta."

Gordon guffawed. "What are you saying, Heller?
That Murieta's immortal?"

She lifted her chin and boldly met his gaze. "You
already know the answer to that question. You tell
me," she said, maintaining the same chilling smile.
It was a bluff, of course. She wouldn't have even considered such a ploy if she hadn't caught him staring at
the *sala* wall and surmised the significance of his odd
behavior.

"Shut up, goddammit." Before she could utter another word, he stuffed the bandanna in her mouth again
and wrapped the second gag around her head, tying it
in back. "No one's immortal. Murieta's just a man—
a damn lucky man, until today."

She may have failed at everything else, but at least
her seed had been deeply planted. If Joaquin was
killed, Gordon would always wonder if the day would
come when Joaquin's ghost would pay him a visit.

Gordon rose up in his saddle. "Any second now,

we should be seeing *El Bandido Notorio.*" He laughed, a low, contrived laugh. "There," he said, pointing to a swirl of dust rising off the valley floor. "What did I tell you?"

She couldn't just sit there and do nothing. Breathing through her nose, she filled her lungs, then screamed against the gag.

Again, Gordon laughed. "Scream all you want, Miss High and Mighty, because from up here it won't do one damn bit of good. He can't hear you."

She knew what he was saying was true, but it didn't stop her from trying again and again, until she was gasping for air and had to stop. She slumped forward over the front of the saddle and endeavored to catch her breath. From beneath her lashes, she saw that Murdock and his gunmen were hidden behind a large outcropping of boulders, and Gordon's guards waited around the bend in the road. She looked back and forth between the three groups. Tears gathered in her eyes, ran unchecked down her cheeks, and were absorbed by her gag. Her body shook with violent sobs.

Joaquin, Lino, and the entire band would die this day because of her. Her plan had seemed so simple, so foolproof. If only she hadn't been so impulsive. If only she'd thoroughly thought things out!

The seconds passed.

Gordon reached across between horses to check her wrist bindings. When she glared at him, he said, "Just making certain, my love. I wouldn't want you to get any foolish notions."

Heller whimpered against the gag when she saw Joaquin and his men close in on the freight wagon.

No. God. No. Please see them, Joaquin. But she knew he didn't, and he wouldn't until it was too late.

When the wagon driver turned and saw the band in pursuit, he whipped his horse into a lather, but when the shooting started, he braked to a stop. Both the driver and the shotgun threw down their weapons and raised their arms in feigned surrender.

Murdock made his move. He whooped like an Indian as he waved his men to attack. At the same time, Gordon's men, led by Hank, came around the bend.

Joaquin wheeled his horse around and called out to the band, but just as Heller had predicted, it was too late. They were surrounded.

Dust and gun smoke rose into the sky, muddying the air. The report of pistols, rifles, and carbines mingled to sound like one continuous explosion. Throwing her weight on the saddlehorn, Heller stood up in her stirrups. She saw first one man then another fall from his horse, then a horse screamed and fell, tossing his rider onto the ground. Another horse bolted and reared.

Above the din of shouts and guns, came Joaquin's command to retreat. Ocho and Santos shot four of the guards, which created a gap big enough for others of the band to escape through. The retreating band spurred their horses and quickly disappeared into the trees while Joaquin stood his ground, his twin Colts belching fire, providing cover for his men.

Then Heller espied Murdock coming up on Joaquin's backside.

"No!" she screamed against the gag. It was all she could do, and it wasn't good enough.

Murdock pulled his rifle from its scabbard, took aim, and fired directly at Joaquin's back.

Heller's heart stopped and the breath went out of her body.

The single bullet unseated Joaquin and sent him flying off his horse into the tall brown grasses that edged the boulders.

Rifle in hand, Murdock raised his arm high over his

head. "I got him. Murieta's dead!" He dismounted and strode toward where Joaquin had fallen, shouting, "The great Joaquin! California's celebrated bandit! *El Bandido Notorio*!"

A patch of black moved within the grass. Heller's eyes widened and her heart swelled with hope. She blinked, not trusting her blurry vision.

She saw it again and gasped. She glanced at Gordon and saw that he was staring at the same spot. He started to raise up in his saddle to get a better look.

Thinking quickly, she wrapped her hands around the pommel and kicked her horse's sides. He started and reared, causing Gordon to break visual contact and concentrate on getting the animal back under control.

Down below, Murdock started into the grass to retrieve his quarry. Suddenly, Joaquin jumped out from behind a boulder, fanning his Colt. Murdock staggered backwards, a look of utter disbelief on his face, then crumpled and fell. Even before he hit the ground, Joaquin was on his horse, riding for the trees.

Gordon gave an enraged roar, then tossed Heller's reins in the air and galloped down the hill. He never looked back to see what had become of the woman he had left behind.

The reins fell slack over the horse's neck in front of the saddle. Heller raised her knee and caught them over her bare foot, then pulled them back toward the pommel, where she was able to gather the leather strip between her fingers and work up the slack. She would have to use her legs and feet to guide the horse, but she could do it. She had to do it.

Turning the horse around, she rode north, down the hill to the bend in the road, where Gordon's guards had waited for Joaquin. Then, undetected, she crossed to the other side. She headed for the rocky ledge that led up the mountain to the cave. Once she was high above the tree line, she stopped and looked behind her.

At least a dozen bodies lay on the valley floor. From this distance they looked like doll-sized figures, and she couldn't tell whose they were. Near the outcropping of boulders, Gordon and his men crowded closely together. Suddenly, they turned, kicked their mounts and headed for the mountain ledge.

Heller's heart sank. They knew how to get to the camp. She kicked her horse into a gallop. Remembering her long-ago training, she leaned forward in the saddle to ease the horse's uphill climb. Though uncertain, she didn't think she had too much farther to go. Nevertheless, the minutes seemed like hours, and she prayed her strength would last long enough to reach her destination and warn the band.

Upon reaching the top of the mountain, her horse shied when six armed Mexicans jumped out from the trees and barred her path. All she could do was scream against the gag until one of them recognized her and stepped forward, removed the gag, and cut the rope binding her wrists.

"Mauger! He's coming," she cried. Then, looking over her shoulder, "They're just minutes behind me."

"Lieutenant Lino," a man she remembered as Manny called out, "the *gringa*, she come."

Lino Toral hurried out from the cave's main chamber. His face was smeared with dirt and blood, his expression belligerent. "You've got a lot of nerve coming here after what you've done. Aren't you satisfied? Or did you come to watch El Jefe die?"

"Lino, for God's sake. Mauger's men are right behind me. Please, order the men to safeguard the camp."

Lino nodded to his men. "Take your positions,"

was all he said. Then he took Heller's horse and led him to the other side of the camp, near the corral.

When Heller started to get down, he stopped her. "You're not staying. You're not wanted here."

She gazed at him in despair. "Lino, you have to listen to me. I love Joaquin. I never meant to hurt him. I never meant to hurt anyone. I thought Mauger and Murdock believed my story. They gave every indication they did. I didn't know they were watching my every move. My God, Lino, if I had known . . ."

"You set El Jefe up with your last message," he intoned bitterly. "You set us all up. We lost five men down there. Five men, Heller. Good men, with wives, children, people who care about them and depend on them. Whether you knew you were being watched or not, this wouldn't have happened if you hadn't been so foolhardy and taken it upon yourself to spy on El Dorado."

His words cut deeply, because of course, he was right. There was no denying it. She hung her head. In a quiet voice, she pleaded, "Please let me see him, Lino. Just once. Then I'll go. I swear it. Just once."

An explosion on the mountain ledge spooked her horse. She slid off the left side of the saddle and fell against Lino, who managed to grab her before she hit the ground. An unbidden cry escaped her as searing pain streaked across her back. .

He stood her before him. "You damn well better hope that dynamite did the trick and none of them got through or—"

"I didn't lead them here, Lino."

Seconds after the explosion, Abigail came to the mouth of the cave. "Heller. Oh, my God. Heller!"

Heller threw her arms around her aunt. "Oh, Aunty. I saw Murdock shoot Joaquin in the back, but then he rode away. . . . How badly is he wounded?"

Tears welled in Abigail's eyes. "Very badly, dear. Very badly, indeed. Pepe says the bullet is lodged next to his spine. He is preparing to remove it now, but he simply is not sure of the outcome."

Heller released her aunt and swung around to face Lino. "Let me go to him, Lino. He needs me to be with him, to help him through this."

Lino's eyes were cold, unsympathetic. "No, he doesn't need you with him. Elena is with him. She's what he needs. Go back to El Dorado. Take your aunt with you."

"I can't go back," she screamed. "Gordon, I mean Luther, will kill me!"

"You're his trusted confidante, Heller. Why would he want to kill you?"

"Because! Because I—" Her voice gave out, as did her ability to defend herself. Her hands flew to her face and she tried to hold back the wave of hysteria that was threatening to overtake her. She couldn't blame Lino for denying her permission to see Joaquin; he thought he was protecting him, but even though she understood his reasoning, it didn't lessen her hurt. Looking over the top of her hands at Lino, she made one more appeal. "At least let me stay until I know whether or not he's going to live or die. I won't go near him. I swear it. Once I know, I'll go, but don't make me leave not knowing, Lino. I couldn't bear that. Please, in spite of what you think of me, grant me that."

He gave a nod. "You can stay until Pepe says one way or another, but under no circumstance are you to try to see El Jefe. *Comprende*?" Before she could answer, he turned on his heel and strode away.

Once Abigail had Heller in her chamber, she sat her niece down on the pallet and gently bathed her face and brushed the tangles from her hair. "Do you want to tell me what happened?'' Abigail asked timidly. ''Did Gordon hurt you? Did he. . . ?'' She turned away, evidently unable to speak the words.

Heller shook her head. ''No, he didn't molest me.''

Abigail placed gentle hands on either side of Heller's face. ''What did he do, Heller? How did he hurt you?''

Pulling back, Heller worked her filthy nightgown up over her hips, then over her head. ''He whipped me again, Aunty, only this time he really hurt me,'' she said, turning at the waist.

Abigail gasped, then tentatively reached out a hand and touched her fingertips to Heller's skin. ''Dear God.''

Clutching her nightgown to her breast, Heller turned back to her aunt. Abigail's face had paled and her eyes looked stricken. ''Please, Aunty, I beg you not to say anything about this to anyone.''

''But Heller—''

''No! You mustn't. I have my reasons,'' she insisted, and Abigail reluctantly agreed, then went off in search of an extra blanket. While her aunt was gone, Heller worried over her impromptu decision. She didn't doubt that showing Lino her whip lashes would convince him that she hadn't betrayed Joaquin or the band. He would, of course, apologize and take back all the hurtful things he'd said. But there was no taking back the truth of what he'd said, and there was no taking back what she had done. She'd been naive and foolish to think she could outwit Sam Murdock, a man who made his living hunting down and killing other men. If only she had listened—really listened—to Joaquin and Lino's discussion about Murdock, maybe she wouldn't have been so anxious to prove what a help she could be.

Help. She had helped Joaquin all right. Helped him ride right into an ambush.

A chill ran the length of her spine and a lump of regret congealed in her chest. There were some things that couldn't be excused away, some things that couldn't be rectified, some things that couldn't be forgiven.

She thought, too, of what Lino had said about Elena being what Joaquin needed. Lino knew Joaquin best of all. A person would have to be blind not to see how much Elena loved Joaquin. The exotic señorita had loved him for more than two decades. Every word she'd spoken, every gesture she'd made, was testimony to that emotion. She'd stayed by him through the best and worst of times. She'd been there for him when he was wounded, when he wanted someone to talk to, and when he was lonely.

She was there for him how.

The irony was the Elena Valdez loved Joaquin as he had loved his wife, Rosita.

Heller put her nightgown back on and covered herself in the warmth of Abigail's blanket. So much had happened since she'd arrived in San Francisco and stepped off the train platform into the anxious crowd. She had come with the goal of proving herself, proving that she had risen abouve her ignoble birth and had, in spite of the odds against her, become a lady.

What she would give to turn back the clock. Knowing what she knew now, she would challenge Elizabeth Pennyworth and tell her that there was nothing shameful about her being born out of wedlock. She would tell her she had been conceived in love, and had not a series of unfortunate circumstances intervened, Mam and Gerald Peyton would have married and she, their daugher, would have been born and raised in Boston.

Unfortunate circumstances. How well she had come

to understand those words. Like Mam, she had barely experienced passion and love when her world had turned upside down. And now, like Mam, she found herself separated from the man she loved and motherhood looming on the horizon.

Her heart lightened when she thought about the child she carried. There hadn't been time to sort it all out: the significance of Gordon's confession, Marta's innate knowledge. Until now.

It was Joaquin to whom she had given what Abigail called that precious gift—her virginity. Her child was Joaquin's child, not Gordon Pierce's. But her joy was tempered with sadness. Like her own father, Gerald Peyton, Joaquin would never know about the child he had helped create.

Exhaused, she fell into a deep, troubled sleep.

Heller awoke mid-afternoon of the next day. Pepe was sitting cross-legged beside her, singing a slow, mournful chant. He stopped when she opened her eyes. Misinterpreting his presence, she panicked. "Joaquin, is he . . . dead?"

"No. He lives still. But the bullet, it was very deep. He has lost much blood." Pepe shook his head.

Tears filled her eyes and cascaded down her cheeks.

The next four days were sheer torture. Pepe had not been back, and no one would talk to her or Abigail about Joaquin's condition. She assumed the worst. He was dying.

On her way back from the privy, she passed Elena. They didn't speak or in any other way acknowledge each other. Acting on impulse, Heller raced back to camp and made her way to Joaquin's inner chamber, breaking her promise to Lino. But she had to see him one last time. She had to say good-bye.

He lay on the pile of skins, his head slightly elevated, his muscled arms still at his sides. A wide strip

of bandage had been wrapped around his waist. Above
the bandage, his chest was bare. A red-and-gray
striped blanket covered his lower body. Silently, she
knelt behind his head, and though she longed to reach
out and caress him, she didn't dare, fearing he might
awaken and be disturbed by her presence.

"I love you, Joaquin Murieta," she said so faintly
that her voice hardly made a sound. "I never meant
to hurt you. I'd do anything I could to make it up to
you, to prove my loyalty, my love."

Joaquin's eyes opened slowly. "Hell—er?" His
baritone voice was weak, raw.

She clamped her teeth together and dared not move.
After a moment, his eyes closed and he went back to
sleep. Stricken with grief, Heller rose and left the
chamber, certain she had seen Joaquin for the last time.

Until this morning, Joaquin had been convinced he
was indeed dying. Even Pepe had not given him much
hope, but as before, his salves and tonics, combined
with his healing hands and chantings, had worked their
magic on his body. Today, five days after he'd been
back-shot, he was sitting up. He hurt all over and felt
like hell, but he didn't begrudge one ache of pain; it
reminded him that he was alive. He'd slept enough in
the past five days to last him for the other six lives
Elena said he still had left.

This was the third time he'd narrowly escaped death.
On one level, he wished he hadn't survived, as death
would have released him from the damnable vow and
spared him from his own unimpeachable integrity.

He knew that Heller was in camp; Lino had told him
about her arrival following the ambush. He'd spent half
the morning vacillating between being hurt that she
hadn't come to see him or inquiring as to how he was,
and being angry that she'd betrayed him. What had he

done that had made her hate him so? He knew she'd been furious with him that he hadn't rescued her sooner. He should have had enough confidence in her to tell her his plan. Obviously, she'd suffered more than the fear of abandonment. He'd told her his reasoning and thought she'd understood and forgiven him. He'd thought wrong.

In spite of his bitterness, he realized he had no one to blame but himself for everything that had happened. It was his fault that Heller had come to El Dorado in the first place. She'd accidentally blundered into his path of revenge. Rather than be patient and wait until she'd gone home, and rather than alter his plans so that she wouldn't be affected, he'd used her like a chess pawn to play his game with Mauger.

Tomorrow, when he was stronger yet, he would ask Lino to bring her to him. They would talk. He would find out what was on her mind. Then he would tell her how much he loved her.

As if the pain of Joaquin's certain death wasn't bad enough, Heller was plagued with guilt over the fact that because of her Joaquin's vow to Rosita would go unfulfilled. Throughout the afternoon and night, she sat in her chamber, thinking about all the people who had been hurt or killed directly or indirectly by Luther Mauger. But for her interference, Joaquin would have succeeded in his well-devised plan of revenge. If only there was *something* she could do.

Moonlight showed her the way down the mountain. She saw where the dynamite explosion had blown away a whole section of the ledge and was careful to keep her horse close to the opposite side. She knew from whisperings around camp that two of Murdock's men had died in the explosion, so she didn't wonder that Mauger hadn't come back and tried to take the camp.

Lino's horse nickered softly and she patted his neck. Besides the horse, she'd stolen a gun and holster, one of the extras that were kept in the main chamber. If the situation wasn't so serious, she would congratulate herself for her daring. She absently wondered what Elizabeth Pennyworth woul think if she could see her student now—dressed in a striped Mexican shirt and white *camisa,* riding astride, with a holster belted around her waist. If ever she got the chance, she would like nothing better than to tell the venerable Miss Pennyworth that some things were simply more important than propriety and circumspection. Love, for instance. Honor. Revenge.

When she saw the lights of the house, she shivered, but she wasn't about to let a little thing like fear get in the way of what she had to do.

She reined to a stop yards from the side of the house. Leaving Lino's horse tied to a tree, she cautiously walked past the corral and the privy. There were no guards in sight, yet she knew enough to be wary, just in case. She waited and watched. And she waited some more. It seemed an interminable amount of time. Then, feeling confident she would not be observed, she ran from her hiding place up onto the *corredor,* opened the door, and entered her own darkened bedroom.

The room had been destroyed, the bed coverings and curtains sliced into strips. It looked as if Gordon had . . . Oh, God. The reality of what he'd done couldn't have frightened her more. It nearly made her turn around and run for safety. Her former bedroom had been subjected to Gordon's wrath—his whip.

She took a deep breath, striving to regain her courage, then she reopened the bedroom door and stole down the hall. At first, she thought the house empty,

but then she smelled the smoke. Opium. If she lived
to be a hundred, she would never get that sickly sweet
odor out of her nostrils.

Like a cat she stalked her prey, inch by inch until
she reached the *sala*. He was sitting in a deep-
cushioned chair, staring at the wall. The opium lamp
on the table next to him sputtered and black smoke
rose into a cloud above it.

"I've come for Joaquin," she said in a voice she
hardly recognized as her own. "I've come to avenge
Rosita Murieta and all the other women you've hurt
and killed. I've come to kill you."

Chapter 21

The note Heller left behind explained everything that had happened since she had gone to El Dorado on her own. It asked that Abigail, Lino, and the band try to find it in their hearts to forgive her for her foolishness. "This time I will not fail," she wrote, ending the note.

In spite of the late night hour, Abigail didn't stop to contemplate what to do; she went straight to the main chamber, where she found Lino.

"Joaquin needs to see this," said Lino, after scanning the note.

Abigail appeared confused. "No, Lino. Please, do not trouble him. A man's last hours should not be filled with worry."

Lino's look was patronizing. "I think he'll want to know."

Joaquin had spent an anxious evening with Lino and some of the other men going over a final plan to take El Dorado. They'd decided on a date two days hence. Joaquin felt certain he would have most of his strength back by then. And even if he didn't, he couldn't afford to wait. With all that had happened, he was concerned that Mauger would take revenge on the remaining slaves.

"El Jefe," said Lino, entering the inner chamber. Joaquin had been sitting at the table, absently carving notches into the wood tabletop. "Heller's gone back down to El Dorado."

He stood up, wincing at the stiffness in his legs. "Why?" Abigail stood next to Lino; her expression prepared him for the worst.

"I cannot be certain. . . ." Abigail twisted her handkerchief. "We—she thought you were dying. She felt responsible."

"She's gone to kill Mauger," Joaquin stated in a flat voice, which rose angrily as he asked, "You allowed her to do this?"

Abigail's eyes were filled with tears. "No," she cried. "I went to the privy, and when I came back she was gone. If you hurry, you can catch up with her."

Seething, Joaquin snatched the piece of paper out of her hand and read it quickly. "*Madre de Dios!*" He threw the paper aside and grabbed his bowie knife off the table and sheathed it beneath the red sash binding his waist. Then he strapped his gun belt over his hips and tied the leather thongs around his upper thighs. "Lino, tell the men there's been a change of plans. We take El Dorado tonight. Now!"

Abigail took a tentative step toward him and touched his arm. "Be gentle with her, Joaquin. She has been terribly distraught. I have never seen her in such a state, blaming herself for the ambush, shouldering the full responsibility of the men who died, fretting over you, thinking you were dying. And then, on top of everything, that horrible man whipped her. Why, the poor child, her back was a mass of welts."

Joaquin stopped in the middle of checking his guns' cylinders. "Mauger whipped her?"

Abigail rubbed her hands together. "Oh, dear me. She made me promise not to tell anyone."

Joaquin started to leave, then he turned back and

pulled Abigail against him, hugging her. "It will be all
right. I'll find her and bring her back."

Mauger's gaze circumvented the sala as if he expected to find himself surrounded.

"It's just you, me, and Rosita's ghost," said Heller,
without so much as a flinch to betray her innate fear
of the gun she held out in front of her like a scepter.
All she had to do was squeeze the trigger and shoot,
and it would all be over. But like Joaquin, she felt a
need to prolong the agony, if only for a few more
minutes while she taunted him with his own fears. "I
understand that this room was the original house."
She waved the gun toward the wall. "Was Joaquin and
Rosita's bed over there against that far wall? Is that
where you and your men raped her? Did you whip her
afterwards?"

Luther squinted his eyes. His hands balled into tight
fists, but Heller wasn't about to let up. "Yes, of course
you did. Whipping is something that gives you immense pleasure. How many of those Cantonese slave
girls that you bought did you murder with your whip?
Do you cut notches in your whip handle like gunfighters do their guns?" The taunts rolled off her tongue.

He stood up. His eyes were cold, hard.

Ignoring his look, she tilted her head and slid him
a disdainful glance. "But of all of those you killed,
Rosita is the only one to come back to haunt you, isn't
she?" Two months ago, she wouldn't have been capable of speaking to *anyone,* even someone she detested, in such a jeering manner. Neither would she
have been capable of holding a gun on a man with the
intention of killing him. But things had changed. *She*
had changed.

Luther Mauger stepped forward, his hand reaching
out for her gun. He stopped abruptly when the sound

of gunfire fractured the air. "Something must have happened down at the slave camp," he said, then turned toward the doors.

"Stay where you are or I'll shoot." She cocked the gun's hammer and had the satisfaction of seeing his face go white.

Joaquin and his band left their horses downriver from the slave camp. At his signal, the men circled the camp. Each had an assigned task to perform, and though they were now fewer in numbers than the guards, they had the element of surprise in their favor.

Quiet as a cat, Joaquin stole up behind one of the lookouts. He lunged forward, grabbed the man around the neck, and squeezed until the breath left his body and he went slack.

The guards were sitting around the campfire talking quietly among themselves. Without Murdock to lead them, they had reverted back to their lackadaisical ways.

Joaquin smiled. It would be easier than he had thought. He gave his men a moment longer to close in on the camp, then, confident that all was ready, he shot a tin cup out of one of the guard's hand.

Suddenly, the night was ablaze with gunfire. The guards unholstered their weapons and shot into the darkness beyond the campfire. The *bandidos* shot back, their targets clearly defined against the firelight.

Within minutes after the first shot, Joaquin stood in front of the fire and shouted, "It's over, *amigos*!"

Leaving Lino behind to follow up his orders, Joaquin ran back to where he had ground-tied El Tigre. He was beginning to tire and weaken, but he couldn't let it stop him. He had to rescue Heller from Mauger.

He wasn't certain how many men still guarded the house itself, but he was certain they would be prepared

for an attack, as they would have heard the gunshots
down by the river.

As predicted, one pair of guards was positioned by
the barn, another by the corral, and still another near
the road. If there were others, Joaquin couldn't see
them, yet he had to assume they were there, armed
and waiting. Weaving between the trees for cover, he
slowly made his way around the house, looking
through the windows, hoping to see something that
would tell him where Heller was. He saw her and
Mauger in the *sala*. Seeing no guards near the kitchen,
he made a dash for the door.

The kitchen smelled of spicy pork and warm tortillas. Ignoring the mouth-watering aromas, he drew his
guns and crept down the hall. At the *sala's* arched
opening, he stopped. In the mirror above the mantel
he saw Heller's and Mauger's reflections. He pulled
back, stunned, then he looked again. Heller was holding a gun on Mauger.

"You can't shoot me, Heller," said Mauger in a
confident tone. "You don't have it in you to take a
life."

"A few weeks ago, I would have agreed with you,"
she affirmed, "but things have changed. I've changed,
in case you haven't noticed," she said, repeating her
thoughts of a moment ago. "You're partly responsible
for the change, you know. First, by convincing me that
you had compromised me, then threatening to murder
the entire Boston Board of Trade, then making it look
like I had betrayed Joaquin, and finally forcing me to
watch the ambush. Oh, and I almost forgot the whipping. Do you really think I don't have it in me to take
a life—specifically your life? Think again."

She raised her arm and held the gun level to her
shoulder, her thumb heavy on the hammer.

Luther backed up and tripped over a footstool.

"Don't be foolish, Heller. Think about what you're doing. If you kill me, you'll have to live with guilt for the rest of your life. And what about your baby? What if people discover you murdered an unarmed man. They'll—"

Baby? Joaquin turned his gaze toward the ceiling. Heller was pregnant? *Dios!* Why hadn't she told him?

From outside came the sound of thundering hooves and gunshots. Then an explosion near the house. Dynamite.

Heller glanced toward the window.

Luther Mauger seized the moment and leaped across the distance that separated them. He pushed Heller against the wall and knocked the gun out of her hand. It flew across the room and landed on a cushioned chair.

Like a cat, Joaquin sprang from his hiding place and fired two shots close to Mauger's head.

Mauger struggled backwards, regained his balance, and stood facing his enemy. Breathing hard he said, "So we meet at last, face-to-face without disguise."

Joaquin reholstered his guns. "How do you want to die, Mauger? Guns? Knives? Fists? It's your choice. I've been waiting a long time for this moment. Ending your life will be my final revenge."

Heller leaned against the wall for support. "Joaquin!" Her voice was raw with emotion. She started toward him, but he waved her back. "I thought you were dying. That's why I left camp—to avenge you and Rosita."

He threw her a glance over his shoulder. "I know, Heller, and I'm sorry. I didn't realize. I should have come to you right away and told you. I wasn't thinking."

From the hallway came another voice. "A woman will do much for the man she loves," announced

Elena. "I should know, eh, El Jefe?" She moved out
from behind the wall into full view. In her hand she
held a long-barreled gun, pointed directly at Joaquin.

"Elena! What are you doing here?"

Elena laughed. "I came for you, Joaquin. I followed
you, just as I always have, but I will follow you no
more. Once again, you have betrayed my love, Joaquin."

"Dammit, Elena—" He started toward her.

"No no," she said, then fired a warning shot at his
boot. "Do not come near me, or you force me to kill
you before I am ready." He stopped. "*Gracias*. Now,
take your guns out of your holster and lay them down
on the floor and very gently push them over to me."
When he started to balk, she shot over his head. "Your
guns, *por favor*."

Unwillingly, he complied, then stepped back in front
of Heller, shielding her.

"Such a noble gesture, Joaquin, but then you always
were a noble man. You have spent your whole life
fighting noble causes. You have become what *los gringos* call a legend. Years from now—long after you are
dead—people will speak of the things you have done.
'*Viva* Joaquin!' they will shout."

The *sala* doors flew open, admitting a whirlwind of
dust and dirt. Elena was forced to raise her arm to
protect her eyes as the wind swept past her.

Mauger bolted for the chair and retrieved Heller's
gun.

"Joaquin!" Heller shouted a warning.

Joaquin's hand dove beneath his sash. He pulled
back and flung the bowie across the room. The weapon
unerringly found its target and embedded itself in
Mauger's chest.

Mauger stiffened. He clenched his fingers and the
gun fired, the shot going wild. He started to fall for-

ward but caught himself on the back of a chair. "You still don't have your revenge, Murieta," he said, gasping for air.

"How's that, Mauger?"

"Someone hired me to run you off your claim and kill your wife. And as long as that person lives . . ."

A shadow of disbelief crossed Joaquin's face. "I don't believe you."

"It's true," Heller shouted behind him.

Mauger started to open his mouth, but all that came out was a gurgle of blood.

Joaquin shook Mauger's lifeless body. "Who? Goddamn you, who was it?"

Heller ran across the room and threw her arms round Joaquin. "Stop. Joaquin. Stop. He never knew who hired him. Whoever it was didn't want him to know."

"Then it isn't over." He turned away. "It will never be over," he murmured.

On the other side of the room, Elena said, "*Sí,* it is over, *querido.*" Her gun dropped from her hand and fell to the floor with a thud.

"Joaquin! Elena's been shot." Heller bolted across the room and rushed to Elena's side.

Then Joaquin was there, picking Elena up in his arms and carrying her to the sofa. He tore at her clothing and found the wound. "She's been gut shot." He applied pressure with one hand while he unwound his waist sash with the other. "Heller, see if Pepe is outside."

Heller started for the doors, but saw Lino and Pepe already headed toward the *sala*. Their triumphant smiles turned to frowns when they saw Joaquin bending over Elena.

Lino took Heller's arm and led her across the room, out of the way. Pepe hurried over to Joaquin.

"You have to help her, Pepe," said Joaquin. "You're

the only one who can. Use whatever magic you've used on me to save her.'' Pepe nodded and Joaquin moved aside and knelt down near Elena's head. "Damn you, Elena. What's gotten into you, anyway? Why did you do this?''

Elena smiled weakly. "You of all people should understand why, Joaquin. Only you have loved as deeply as I have loved you. I am a jealous woman. I would rather lose you to death than lose you to another woman.'' She gritted her teeth and looked up at the ceiling. "Only now can I tell you—I had my *padre* hire Luther Mauger. I thought killing Rosita would bring you back to me, but I was wrong. Forgive me, Joaquin. Forgive me.''

Joaquin drew back sharply. His face was the color of parchment. "You—You and your *padre* hired Mauger to kill—'' He choked on the words. Behind him, he heard Heller's weeping, but couldn't make himself turn around.

Pepe stepped back. "There is no magic, *amigo*. She does not wish to live.''

"*Te amo*, I love you, Joaquin,'' Elena cried. "I have always loved you. Forgive me?'' She reached out her hand. "*Por favor, querido mio.*''

Joaquin didn't move. A muscle worked along the side his mouth.

After a long moment, he dropped down next to her, then smoothed a dark strand of hair back from Elena's cheek. He knew he had to let go. "I forgive you, Elena,'' he whispered. He bent forward and placed a kiss on her slightly parted lips.

"*Gracias,* my brave *vaquero. Vaya con Dios.*'' Her hand brushed his, then fell to her side.

"Elena? Elena!''

"Come, Heller,'' Lino gently urged. "He needs time to sort things out.'' Lino led her outside and helped her mount a horse. Before reining around, she looked back through the doors: Joaquin was still kneeling beside Elena's body, still holding her hand.

With the exception of Pepe, Joaquin, and one or two others left behind at El Dorado, the band headed back up the mountain. It was well after midnight. The band's whoops of joy mingled with those of the slaves who rode double on the horses taken from El Dorado's barn and corral.

"What will become of them?" asked Heller. She was referring to the nine surviving guards who rode ahead of her and Lino.

"They'll be taken to Mariposa for trial. I expect they'll hang, if I have my way."

"And me?" she asked.

"That's up to you, Heller. Joaquin loves you."

"I thought so, too, for a while, but now . . . I'm not so sure."

"I think we should collect our things from El Dorado and go as quickly as possible," Heller told Abigail moments after her arrival. "The sooner we leave here, the sooner we can board a train and get back to Boston where we belong. Everything that's happened—it's all happened because of me. Even if Joaquin loved me and wanted me to stay with him, I don't think I could adjust to this kind of life. It's too . . . primitive, too hard. Elizabeth Pennyworth was right about one thing, Aunty. These Westerners are savages. I—" She dissolved into a fit of weeping and hid her face in her hands.

"Heller, dear, you must not blame yourself. You are not responsible." Abigail reached out her arms and wrapped them around her niece. "And as to leaving—you can make that decision once you have rested and recuperated."

Heller wore a dazed look. "Yes, Aunty, you're right," she said woodenly. "I don't want to make another hasty decision. I think I'll just lie down awhile and rest. I'm really awfully tired."

It was near dawn when the sound of loud singing broke into Heller's dreams. She stretched and yawned, then turned over to see that the other side of the make-shift bed was empty. Worried over Abigail's absence, she got up and started toward the chamber exit. The closer she got to the outside, the louder the voices became, and now she heard a guitar as well.

A roaring bonfire lit up the entire camp, whose population had increased dramatically with the addition of the slaves and a number of women, some of whom Heller recognized as servants from El Dorado. Pepe and two others walked by where she stood, singing and swinging tin cups back and forth to the rhythm of the guitar.

A fiesta! A frown turned down the corners of her mouth. How could they celebrate at a time like this? People had just died! Their bodies hadn't even been buried yet!

Lino left the pretty señorita he had been dancing with and walked over to Heller. "You do not approve of our celebration?"

Heller shot him a disdainful look. "Approve? No, I do not approve. I think its barbaric to sing and dance when—" She stopped, a sob preventing her from continuing.

Lino shrugged. "Perhaps it is by Boston standards. But this is not Boston, Heller. Look at those men." He pointed to a group. "They came to El Dorado for one reason and one reason only. They had heard that Joaquin Murieta needed their help to free the slaves of El Dorado. Yes, some of them had friends or family members among the slaves, but not all. Some came

simply for the honor and privilege of riding with El
Jefe and serving whatever cause he was fighting for.
Yes, people have died. Unfortunately, it was inevitable, but they knew that—all of them. And now they
have won and they are glad to be alive. That's what
they're celebrating, Heller. Life. Not death. I think
maybe you misjudge them just as I misjudged you after
the ambush.'' She looked up and met his steady gaze.
''I should never have accused you of betraying Joaquin. I hope you will forgive me.''

Struggling not to break down, she replied, ''There's
nothing to forgive, Lino. I knew you were protecting
Joaquin. I would have done the same.'' She reached
out and squeezed his arm. ''Now, if you'll excuse me,
I'm still awfully tired. I think I'll go back and try to
get some more—''

Suddenly, a voice called out from among the sing-
ers. ''*Viva* Joaquin!'' Immediately the guitar silenced
and all conversation ceased. At the place where the
road led down to El Dorado, Joaquin and El Tigre
appeared. The magnificent horse danced impatiently
as Joaquin held him in position. Then a group of men,
led by Juan Alvarado, ran across camp and pulled Joaquin down off his horse. Laughing and shouting they
half-walked, half-carried their leader over to the fire.

Levi Ortega struck a loud note, then strummed his
guitar to begin a new dance.

Heller stood back from the gaiety in the shadows,
her need for rest no longer uppermost in her mind.
Without warning, Lino grabbed her hand and pulled
her along with him toward the dancers.

''Lino, please. No. I don't want to dance,'' she protested.

''In celebration of life, Heller. Remember?''

She sighed and nodded her head in agreement, then

took Lino's hand. He proceeded to show her the basic steps, but she refused to even attempt them.

In spite of herself, the dance, the music, and the beautiful moonlit night were having an effect on her. She closed her eyes. Her thoughts turned elsewhere, to a San Francisco hotel room where Joaquin had stood before the window and moonlight had gilded his body. Her lips parted ever so slightly as she smiled at the memory, and began to dance.

"Is that smile for anyone in particular, señorita?"

Joaquin watched her slowly open her eyes. He lifted his arm and held out his hand, but she jumped back out of his reach, teasingly. There was something very intriguing about her smile, not a laughing smile but a smile of promise, of things yet to come.

She raised her arms above her head and snapped her fingers to the beat of Levi's guitar. The other dancers fell away one by one, as they, like Joaquin, became enchanted with Heller's dance. Except for the strumming of Levi's guitar, there wasn't a sound—not a nickering horse, not even the crackling of the fire behind her.

He stood gazing at her, mesmerized by the golden corona of light that circled her body like a halo, illuminating her hair, which had long since fallen into soft disarray about her shoulders. In all his life, he had never seen a more beautiful, more seductive woman.

He was bewitched.

He was in love.

Unable to stop himself, he moved toward her. Hands on hips he circled her, then she him. They seemed to uncannily anticipate the other's moves, so that they appeared to have rehearsed the steps. Then they met on mutual ground, their bodies coming so close together they almost touched.

Then the music stopped, and they stood facing each other in a frozen tableau of breathless passion.

Heller couldn't take her eyes off him. His darkly handsome features and awesome virility were melting her resolve. It sent her into an emotional panic, for she knew that if she didn't turn away and flee to her chamber, if she allowed him to talk to her, touch her, she would never be able to go home. With an effort, she turned away.

He caught her by the arm and turned her back to him. "You're not leaving me, Heller. Not now, not ever."

She didn't trust herself to speak but she had to say something. "I can't stay with you, Joaquin. There's too much between us: Rosita, Elena. I am not like either of them. I can't take their place."

"I wouldn't want you to, *querida*."

"But you loved them so."

"I loved Rosita long ago, Heller. In my youth. And Elena—I *cared* deeply for Elena, but I never loved her. She knew that. She had always known that. I suppose that's why she tried to kill me." He drew her into his arms and nuzzled his chin into her shining hair.

Before she knew what was happening, Joaquin's arms surrounded her, lifted her, and carried her away from the fiesta to the far edge of the camp, overlooking the rushing river.

He set her down and they stood side by side gazing at the sky which changed colors as they watched, from blue-gray to soft pink to gold—El Dorado gold. Levi continued to play his guitar, softly now. A love song.

"I love you, Joaquin, but I'm afraid. So much has happened. How will we ever be able to get past it all?"

"By believing in each other, and trusting in each other. I love you, Heller Peyton. I love you more than

I can possbily tell you. Together, we can put our pasts behind us and start anew.''

"Oh, Joaquin,'' she sighed, then rested her cheek against his chest and watched the sun creep up over the mountaintop. "I want so much to believe you . . .'' she whispered. She placed her hand against her stomach and thought about her child, their child.

"Look Heller. The sun. A new day. A new beginning. What do you say?''

"I say, yes. I think where you are concerned, I will always say yes.''

"Good, because I hate the word *no*.''

She leaned back and looked up. "Who are you, Joaquin? Who are you really? A man, a myth, a devil, or an angel?''

He looked down at her upturned face and smiled. From out of nowhere, a warm night wind wrapped them in its embrace. . . .

Epilogue

As the darkening shadows stole over the Sierra Nevada, so did a robber wind steal into the mouth of the cave to snatch away the scarlet sash and midnight cape. Filled with air, the cape billowed, a vivid reminder of its legendary owner. Fueled by the wind, the cook fire burned brighter, casting its yellow light upon the old man huddled beneath his serape.

"Grandfather," said the small boy crouched beside him, "let us go from this place. I am afraid. There are ghosts here."

The old man laughed. "There are no ghosts here, only the memories, and the wind. . . ."

Outside the cave, a night bird screeched an ominous warning.

With a thin hand, Grandfather poked a stick into the fire to stir the embers into flame. "There is a legend I wish to tell you, *muchacho*," he said, his fathomless black eyes reflecting the fire's golden glow. "It is of Joaquin Murieta, *El Bandido Magnifico*. You have not already heard it, have you?"

The boy shook his head. "No, Grandfather."

The old man grinned. "Good. Well, it was many years ago," he began, exactly as he had so many times before. . . .

Above the valley of El Dorado, silhouetted against

a golden moon, a horsemen called out into the night.
"I am Joaquin. You will remember my name!"
The night wind whispered, "*Viva* Joaquin!"